HardBall City
Vol. 1
Katrina's Baby

A Novel Trilogy
And Mixtape Soundtrack
By
Troy Joyner

©2012 by Troy Joyner

Black Minx Publishing

B-Mega Media Group, Inc

This book is dedicated to my late Grandfather

Floyd Joyner,

one of the greatest men I have known.

It's also dedicated to the victims and children of

Katrina and other natural disasters.

A portion of the proceeds from this Trilogy will be

donated to the Emergency Supply and Education

fund for Gulf Coast disaster victims at

Urban Light Community Development, Inc.

Houston, Texas

I HOPE YOU ENJOY THIS 1ST VOLUME...

WELCOME TO HARDBALL CITY

A middle-aged man was residing in a Houston motel as a Hurricane Katrina evacuee.

A FEMA support rep was making his rounds to check on his clients. He knocked on the motel door in good spirits, hoping to spread some joy today. He knew his clients had been through hell.

The middle aged man answered the door with a careless nod and a half smile. He let the FEMA support rep into the 60 degree motel room and flopped back down on the bed with his TV remote control in one hand and big bag of cheese puffs in another. "Whats happenin?" the client asked in his N'awlins drawl as he flickered through channels aimlessly.

The Rep tried to ignore the recent marijuana residue in the air as he scanned the junky unkept room quickly, then asked, "Why aren't you out looking for work? Your FEMA support is not going to last forever.."

"I'm handicapped." The client answered bluntly, still flipping through channels.

"You're handicapped?" the rep asked, confused. "Well, whats wrong with you?"

"I have anal glaucoma." The client answered as if he had just received his official diagnosis from his regular physician, which didn't exist.

"Anal glaucoma??" the rep was really stumped now. He was almost afraid to ask, "Whats that?"

The client looked the rep right in his eyes and answered, "I can't SEE my ASS working!"

TABLE OF CONTENTS

Introduction: KATRINA

$26.5 billion dollars; U.S. currency, cold, hard cash. Compute that in your digital matrix, fortress, add it to the deficit, whateva. For what, you ask? Why, to repair the damage I'm about to inflict on yo ass. Mmmhmm. Get your checkbook out, America, but leave the dollar amount blank. This might take a while.

Oh, no, no, don't get it twisted; I'm not gonna stay with you very long. Nah. I'm a come-and-go kind of girl, if that's what you people wanna call me. You all like to use names and big, fancy words like you know what's going on. Hmph. You don't know shit! And I'm about to prove that to you without even trying. But yeah, I'll come and see how you livin', you know, make certain you feel my presence in the most profound way and then I'm gone, just like that. That's how I do. That's how I'm cut. My whole family is that way.

Personally, though, between you and I, I consider myself like none other, a true anomaly of nature. Because when I come, I'm comin' hard. I'll have you runnin' and hidin' for your life, packin' up your lil' belongings and breaking camp. Scared straight. I'll give you nightmares and flashbacks; you'll be waking up in cold sweats, screaming my name. I'll rip your world up from its foundation and leave it so dismantled; you'll wish I'd have just taken you with me.

Cry then; cry out to the skies, cry out to the rain. Cry all you want, but I'm comin' hard. I'll make you change your religion, or find one. Yeah, I have that kind of power over people. My last name should be Truth because I bring the truth out of people from all colors, classes, shapes and sizes. It don't matter to me, you're all the same. I rain on the just and unjust; Destruction should be my middle name. You all really should have evacuated, but now it's too late. I'm approaching land now; it won't be long.

Since we're getting a little face time, you and I, I want you to understand some things about me. You people named me Katrina; that's fine, I accept that, but that's not my name. You see, I have no use for names or titles. My power and force are such that they speak for themselves. I am what I am, I do what I do, *and I do it well*. I'm a performer; I dance and sing my way across the face of the earth every chance I get. When the elements align themselves, I'll arrive. When the *i*'s are dotted and the *t*'s are crossed, I'll be there.

What? What's *this*, some sort of barrier, an attempt to stop my show? Ha! Foolishness. Don't worry; I will allow you to remove yourself before I do it for you. But you'd better hurry because I have a schedule to keep and a job to do and that's exactly what I'm *going* to do, with or without your authorization, security measures or whateva. Oh, you think I'm playin'? Since we seem to be experiencing a breakdown in communication, here's a little pressure to help you see things my way...ahhh, that's what I thought. You're pretty quick on your toes...I like that. Look, just try to work with me here. This has to be done either way so we'd might as well accommodate each other, right?

You see, if I had a choice in the matter, it would be the ocean every time. I love the ocean. The water and I, we have beautiful chemistry. I'm truly an all-natural species, no meat, and trash annoys the hell out of me. But when the ocean and I are together, which is most of the time, it's always exciting. And the morning after, you gotta see it. Pure serenity, like a new world has been born.

But God said let there be land, and that's not good! Not for me, at least. Every time I'm forced to get my hands dirty with land by swinging through these lil' towns and cities, it's always a big fucking mess! That's why I don't stay long. I can't even breathe around you people or with all that dirt and debris flying everywhere. It's disgusting! Land and I have zero chemistry. That is why I cause so much destruction, and that is always the beginning of my outro song. It's really too bad. Please understand, however, that this is not my intention. I *have* no intentions. I simply am, and I come hard. That's how I'm cut.

People call me the wrath of God, but that's just mankind's religious conscience speaking jibber-jabber, always trying to label every damn thing, right or wrong, good or evil. It's irrelevant, and who are they to judge, anyway? I just *am*. I'm part of the package just like you are, except I have no choice in the matter. I have no control over the elements, when or where I'm going to perform, or why. Therefore I have no mercy, no pity, no emotional attachment to the death and destruction I leave in my path, dissipate from and never look back. There is no pride in my legend.

And yet, I am an event, and I come hard. So cry, pour your soul out to the sky. Hate me if you want, but understand that I am a force and an inspiration with the power to trigger a chain of events, stories, conspiracies and legends like the one you're about to experience. Keep in mind that there is no good or bad, there are only events, actions and reactions and how they affect you. One's pain is another's pleasure, and vice-versa. If you believe that, you'll always be able to accept that. It won't hurt long. You'll be all right as long as you do one thing...Stay Hard.

Welcome to

HardBall City

Vol. 1

Katrina's Baby

Novel and Mixtape Soundtrack

Chapter One: JEWEL

The rain. The rain was the song of fury that I will never forget. It was the chant of aggravation, the desperation and hunger of ten thousand pairs of black fists beating against the walls of poverty, trying to get out for dear life. Strictly survival. But on this day, August 27, 2005, *mis amis*—my friend—it was Hell. Hell trying to get in and terrorize that very same survival instinct that has carried Black people all this way. Oh, yes be' be, I'm here to tell you that Hell is very real, and it must be a woman because Hell bears children. This abomination jumped straight up from the bowels of the underworld, and this bitch ain't playin'. She ain't nice, she has no mercy, and her name is Katrina.

Yeah, I heard you out there, mama, beatin' on my damn lil' bitty ass house like you lost your damn mind. I knew you were coming long before the news reported it. I have to admit, your ancestral reputation carried a little weight for a long while; you're kind of a legend around these parts. But I still wasn't scared. No, not I, not Sandra Landau, also known as Jewel. I am the descendant of the *voudou*-practicing Haitians. You send Hell, I send it back: fried, sautéed, or still kickin', however you want it. The goddess of war Ouisikanzo is my witness.

But...damn, Katrina...I...I wasn't...ready for that song you sang. It was too deep, too painful. There was too much animosity involved, as if you were finally taking revenge on an old enemy for whom you were waiting and waiting and saving your energy. The thunder.

What did we ever do to you but respect you? What? What was that? Speak up. Don't get quiet now. Ohh...*we didn't believe in you.* You don't think we believed in your capability to wreak that much havoc, to cause that much confusion and separation? Hmm. Nah, you took this shit way too personal. You destroyed my home, my city; you pillaged everything that made this place what it was. You left it abstracted beyond recognition. Like a thief in the night, you stole. That was low. That was dirty. That was fucking trifling, Katrina. And for that, I will be demanding a refund for my ticket to *that* concert. Ha, ha, ha. I guess I can laugh now, or at least I *should* laugh, just to keep from crying. I mean, what's done is done, right? They *will* try to fix it, though; they'll redevelop and restructure the whole geography; they'll label it as bigger, better, and safer, but we all know it will never be the same.

Shit, you did them White folks a favor. They was happy to get rid of the poor Black community. They got rid of all those projects they were too scared to even come near. Them niggas woulda liked to kill some crackers comin' into the projects talkin' 'bout some redevelopment. But now, thanks to your song and dance, I bet every single one of those project developments is top priority on the demolition list. All the White folks sing along, now. And then they wonder why and how the Black community could *possibly* believe the higher-ups would blow up their own levees to guarantee a certain level of destruction, to constitute an absolute rebirth. They will show up to their neighborhood and district council meetings and scream, "This is ludicrous!" Even their coffee-in-milk mayor will scream, "This is ludicrous!" All of them will get on television and scream, "This is ludicrous!" so much until even *they* actually believe it is. Shut your lyin', crooked-ass face!

Tell me, was it ludicrous when you were building all those project developments to trap all the underprivileged in one central location? Was it ludicrous when Blacks were openly and publicly discriminated against? Was it ludicrous when we finally *did* achieve something, that you racist White folks would go out dressed in white hooded cloaks to hide your identities and burn wooden crosses in our front yards and throw Molotov cocktails in our windows because you could not stand the thought of us living and working where you did, then disappear into the night? Oh, and what about raping and killing one of our innocent, virginal little girls then planting the murder weapon on a Black man and turning him in to the sheriff yourself 'cause he was your fucking uncle? Isn't *that* ludicrous?

We haven't forgotten your character, how scary you are, how sick you are and low you'll stoop to accomplish your agenda. That Kanye or Kaine West—whatever his name is—was absolutely right: *they don't care about us.* They never did. It's all an act, a game they play to get along. These "uppity Negroes" and so-called gangsters and rappers have come up out of the projects and become rich and they won't say shit. The war for equality still goes on. White folks say "That's in the past, get over it, move on." Why, because *they've* moved on? Yeah, with bigger houses, businesses, bank accounts, college educations and trust funds.

The majority of White people have all of that while the majority of Black people...we still here: in poverty, in the ghetto, trapped physically and mentally. We have not forgotten. Why *wouldn't* we believe you helped this bitch Katrina? From my perspective it's a sacrifice of war. Give up a lil' bit of what you got and eliminate everything you don't want to gain everything you *do* want: *money and power.* That's what it's all about in any city in America and across the globe. It's all about money and power.

9th Ward, New Orleans, Louisiana used to be my home, but I had to get out of there. My life hasn't been the same since and the sad part is that I don't know if it's for the better or for the worse. One thing I do know and can't help but feel deeply in my heart and soul full of fire; every time I add it up, I realize that whatever I've willed into creation, whatever has happened as a result, it's because of you, Katrina, you red-faced calamitous harlot from Hell, and I hate you for it.

******

I don't know why this woman is so stubborn, Gerald Madsen thought to himself as he sloshed through the mid-shin-high water, which saturated the ground of his 9th Ward neighborhood. There was no question that this was the worst rainstorm he'd ever experienced in his six years in New Orleans. He was here by way of Cleveland, and by way of some heavy influence from a fine-ass light-skinned female with the body and smile of a goddess and twice as much ass. He'd met Raquel at the '99 Bayou Classic and fell in love with her southern drawl and her I-know-how-to-please-my-man hospitality, not to mention her mind-blowing doggy-style. Now here he was, about to drown in the name of love. He was drenched, soaking wet from head to toe, and his feet felt like they were swimming in his shoes. Ms. Landau's house was only about a country block down the street on the opposite side, but with the rain pouring down the way it was and hardly being able to see beyond three feet in front of him, that country block felt more like a country mile. Every drudging step in this potentially dangerous situation reminded him that they did have somewhere to escape to.

Less than forty-eight hours earlier, Gerald said to Raquel, "Let's just drive up to Cleveland for a couple of days. We can stay with my mom or one of my friends."

Of course, Gerald knew that Raquel was aware of his mother's disapproval of his decision to move so far away to be with some strange woman he barely knew. She ridiculously blamed Raquel, who, unbeknownst to the hateful mother, had quit escorting when the man of her dreams moved all the way to New Orleans and took a construction job in order to take care of her and her small seven-year-old son.

Gerald was a good man who loved her for the person she truly was, and did not hold against her the fact that she used to hustle by having sex with strange men. She loved Gerald and her son more than anything in the world. There was only one other person in this cutthroat city that she loved as much, if not more, than her own mother, and that person was Sandra "Jewel" Landau. Raquel had known Jewel for over half of her twenty-eight years and she was the only person with whom she could be one hundred percent honest about *anything*. She really had no choice. Jewel was some sort of psychic gangster priestess who could read a person like a book.

"Baby, I am *not* going to Ohio. For what?" she asked indignantly. "It's just gonna be a lil' rainstorm. You know the news always exaggerating. Besides, Jewel said our futures are full of life. We'll be all right. Let's just sit it out."

Gerald shook his head and said mockingly, "There you go with that 'Jewel said' shit."

"Uh, uh, don't even play," Raquel retorted. "You know she's not gonna tell me nothin' wrong."

Gerald couldn't deny it; Jewel's predictions and advice had proved themselves invaluable in financial and life-threatening situations. Raquel actually believed that Jewel was responsible for saving her life and her and Gerald's relationship. Therefore, it was no surprise to Gerald that when the electricity started trippin', surging on and off like it was fighting for a life of its own, Raquel was adamant that he should get Jewel and bring her back to their house. The previous owner must have had some kind of foresight to have had it built on an elevated platform. He also had the three-bedroom house built on a reinforced pier and beams as it stood several feet higher than most of the other houses in the neighborhood. What had been an annoying architectural quirk had become a source of confidence to Raquel.

******

Knock, knock, knock. *Who is that? Is someone knocking on my door?* Jewel frantically thought to herself as she watched the news reporter in his custom-fitted suit warn the city for at least the twentieth time that a mandatory evacuation was in effect for all within city limits. She visualized herself leaving her home, but in reality, despite the warnings, she had no plans to leave, and had no idea *how* she would leave in these horrid weather conditions anyway. She instinctively snapped out of her vision, set down on the smoked glass coffee table the remote control she had been fumbling with these last forty-five minutes next to which sat her black carry-on sized travel bag.

She padded across the already soaked tan shag carpeting that had already begun to emit the foul, nauseating odor of mildew, and she knew that the disgusting odor would only get worse. Sandra walked around the living room until she spotted another one of her most cherished possessions, a framed picture of herself, her mother, father and younger sister Sariyah in the French Quarter.

******

In 1969, Sandra and Sariyah were eleven and nine years old; beautiful chocolate kisses in barrette-fastened pigtails and wearing pretty pink lace Sunday dresses. The dresses looked white in the black and white photo, but Sandra distinctly remembered the dresses being pink. The two girls stood in front, holding hands. Sandra wore a bright smile, while the younger and slightly smaller Sariyah just looked into the camera with a curious gaze, unafraid, but at the same time unfamiliar with the object being pointed at her and her family.

Their mother, Francine Landau, stood closely, protectively, behind her precious girls. She was fairly tall at five feet, eight inches; while wearing short heels she towered at five feet, ten inches. Francine's mother was Black American Indian and her father was Haitian like her husband. She was beautiful with milk chocolate brown skin and long, silky black hair that flowed down to the small of her back that she wore wrapped up in a long French ponytail. She was adorned in a pretty burgundy dress that appeared to be black in the photo and fell almost to her ankles. Her smile was proud and confident; it belied her petite, innocent face and eyes and made her look as if she'd had some sort of victory.

Papa Jacques Landau, a full-blooded Haitian who'd emigrated from Haiti some thirteen years prior, towered over his wife at six feet, three inches.

He was clad in a trim suit and tie, and although Jewel remembered him wearing his hair longer back when she was a child, in the photo it was cut low to his head, a style that complimented his smooth dark brown skin which was pulled tightly over high cheekbones, a perfectly proportioned African nose, full lips, slightly dimpled chin, and the darkest, most intensely penetrating set of brown eyes Sandra had ever seen in her entire forty-seven years of existence. Even to this day when she would pick up this picture and hold it close to her face, it felt like Papa's stare was slicing straight into her conscience and examining her thoughts. According to their beliefs, there was truth in that. The smirk on his face confirmed it, as if to say, *"I know what you don't know and what you think you do know."*

Jewel repeated a short chant in remembrance of those who had passed from this life far too early and admired the picture briefly before stuffing it into the bag. She missed Papa and her younger sister whom she'd loved dearly, but could not save from the ruthless, drug-infested streets of New Orleans. The father of the two boys Sariyah birthed introduced her to heroin, supposedly to help her deal with the post-partum depression she'd suffered after her youngest, Purnell, was born. This was the beginning of a downward spiral that ended in a doubly-fatal shootout brought about by unpaid debts. Papa's death soon followed.

In tears, he had passionately vowed to avenge the death of his youngest daughter; he cursed with a *gris-gris* of death the four he believed to have been responsible. Papa thought he was invincible because he was protected by that *gris-gris*. He marched into the Calliope projects with a machete and a snub-nosed .38, bringing sudden and painful death upon the four cursed murderers before he himself was gunned down. This was an extremely stressful experience for Sandra and her mother, and they were left to raise Sariyah's two young boys, four-year-old Dwayne and two-year-old Purnell.

The loss of Sariyah's young life was just too much; consequently, Sandra turned to Mondo, a young Hatian spiritual advisor who had reached out to the family in their time of need. He gave Sandra much needed consolation, spiritual healing, and guidance in the knowledge and practice of *voudou*. Shortly after, he also bestowed upon her a moniker, *Jewel*, which meant "she of the ruby with many facets". Jewel became totally fascinated and infatuated with Mondo and *voudou*, and the power that both carried. Her mother, on the other hand, was appalled by Sandra's new religious preference and obvious change in demeanor.

Francine fought tears as she begged her now grown and only remaining daughter to help her understand the changes she'd undergone.

"Sandy baby, why? After losing your sister and then your father under those circumstances…what are you thinking?"

"If you can't figure it out, Mama, then I can't explain it," Sandra replied evenly.

"Help me to understand."

Sandra knew that even though her mother was very sensitive at that moment, she also had the kind of split personality that could go from caring and compassionate to *get your ass out of my face before I cut you!* in a heartbeat.

"Mama, this is what helps me understand life, the world and things in it; it helps me relate to daddy and deal with the loss of him and Sariyah."

Unsuccessfully attempting to suppress her emotions, Sandra continued to speak around the lump in her throat. "This is how *I* am able to cope, Mama...this is how I'm able to make the best of my situation. This is what empowers me!"

While considering what she knew of the *voudou* religion, Francine listened to what her daughter was telling her but she knew that with that last statement, there was no changing Sandra's mind. There was only one other option to discuss. Sandra was not surprised when Francine's usually soft demeanor hardened right before her eyes.

Francine rubbed her hands together and shook them once for emphasis before placing them on her thighs and straightening her back.

"Actually, I *do* understand," she stated firmly while looking Sandra squarely in the eyes, "I'm done with New Orleans. I'm washing my hands completely of it and anything that has to do with it." She paused. "I'm leaving...giving myself and the boys a fresh start...in Houston."

Jewel instantly thought of her two beloved nephews Dwayne and Purnell, whom she and Sariyah had nicknamed Fatso and Prince. Dwayne was nicknamed Fatso for his fat, kissable baby cheeks and Purnell was called Prince for his striking good looks as well as the fact that he was the youngest. Her heart sank into the pit of her stomach at the thought of them growing up away from her.

Sandra knew the tables had turned. "Whyyyyy?" she wailed.

Francine turned to her daughter and said in a tone that implied she was the only one thinking rationally in this conversation."Because I want my grandsons to have a fair shot at life, education, and success without this madness from their pasts following them around."

Even though she knew Francine's mind was made up, Sandra was not done.

"But Mama, they *can*," she implored.

Francine refused to give up her advantage. "Sandy, my mind is made up, and my plan is already in motion. Now, I want you to get your affairs in order so you can come with me to help me raise the boys."

There it is, Sandra thought, *she's trying to manipulate me.* She stood up. "I'm *not* leaving New Orleans, Mama. My whole life is here. *Our* whole life is here!"

Francine rose to her feet and faced her daughter. "There is no longer a life here for me or for my grandsons. I lost my daughter and my husband here, and I will not lose anymore!"

Sandra looked into her mother's eyes and said weakly, "But Mama, *I'm* still here..." Francine impatiently waved her hands and cut short her daughter's plea.

"Now you listen to me, Sandy. You can either pack your things and come with me, or you can just stay away from us altogether."

Sandra was hurt and angry that her mother had put forth such an ultimatum. She was not interested in going to Houston, nor was she interested in leaving Mondo, all of her friends, or, most importantly, her father and sister's place of rest. Their spirits were strongest here, and she was not about to leave them. No, she *was not* leaving. Instead of debating with her mother, she simply walked towards the door. She was tempted to say goodbye to her nephews but she knew that would just make her give in to the pressure her mother had put on her. She left.

******

That was in 1991, and Sandra hadn't spoken with her mother since. This was Francine's decision, not hers. She picked up the photographs of Mondo and of her with her nephews from the mahogany picture table that stood against her living room wall and placed them inside her bag. She walked to her bedroom and pulled open the middle nightstand drawer and collected her most precious possession, a gift from Mondo given to her on the day of her new birth, the day he gave her a new name. It represented everything he had ever taught her and then some.

The box was made of some sort of imported wood; Jewel guessed it to be walnut, but was not quite sure. Its handmade construction was impeccable. It was like a jewelry box in appearance but larger; its dimensions were 14 x 12 x 5, with a cherry-stained surface that was engraved with a large stone that resembled a ruby. The box's lid lifted like that of a coffin with hinges made of fine strips of leather. The interior was of red velvet and every time Jewel opened this special box, it was almost as if the box had just been constructed the day before; the scent of fresh wood permeated the air, and the aroma of age-old vellum paper stained with the knowledge, wisdom, practices and beliefs of Voudou welcomed her and whispered to her senses that she was a special human being who had been granted powers that could only be exercised by the gifted.

She gently placed the box inside her bag before stuffing it with several hygiene items and some underclothes. She returned to the living room and sat down to watch the news. Each time the electricity surged on and off, she sat repeatedly pushing the power button on the remote. Then, expectedly unexpected, someone knocked on her door. She pushed the power button one more time and the television came to life as she went to open the door.

Gerald stalked inside looking like a wet Raggedy Andy doll, his eyes showing concern.

"Ms. Landau," he began without greeting, "you need to come with me."

Sandra was only mildly disturbed by the circumstances; she'd already known she'd be leaving with him. "And where are we going?"

Gerald looked at her. "We are going to my house. It's elevated, and that is the best place for us because the water is rising fast. Pretty soon it'll be too late to move around out there, so we need to go now."

Jewel nodded in agreement. "Okay, let me just grab my bag." She was glad she'd already been prepared to leave.

He paced the floor while she retrieved her belongings.

"Let's go," he said impatiently, and they headed for the door. When he opened it, a huge explosion reverberated through the night, momentarily silencing the rain. Gerald and Jewel looked at each other. *What the fuck?*

As if on cue, the news reporter stated, "The levee has broken...I repeat—" The television went blank; the neighborhood's power had been extinguished. Their journey fueled by fear and the instinct of survival, Gerald and Jewel toiled off into the darkness.

******

KATRINA

Miles away, the man-made reinforced walls that were erected many years ago on the edge of the city that faced the ocean to protect modern civilization from the very force of nature with which it was now coming face-to-face began to yield. This expansive structure was waving the proverbial white flag to the sky as if to say, *"No more. This is not what I signed up for."* It started with a hairline crack in the dense concrete, which began to buckle under the pressure of the billions of gallons of water.

The ocean and the sky, now using that hairline crack as an ally in their mission of mass destruction, tag-teamed and became a formidable enemy. The crack began to grow. The ocean edged forward again, constantly recruiting millions of gallons of more water as if this battle had just begun. More pressure. It ebbed and flowed back and forth with massive movement, like the breathing pattern of a colossal living creature about to awaken from a long slumber.

Exhale. More pressure—the crack grew even bigger. *Inhale.* The sky poured intensely with no intention of letting up. The ocean gathered its troops. *Exhale.*

With one last burst of energy, the beast prevailed. The man-made structure screamed out like a woman whose womb had been ripped from the inside out, penetration, forced entry. Who and whatever inhabited this path of mayhem was now doomed.

******

WINNIE

Winston "Winnie" Marshon was a free man, or at least he was as far as *he* was concerned. He thanked every god he knew by name for the miracle called Katrina, which forced the city to release prisoners from flooded jails.

"Shut up, bitch!" he grunted in the ear of the young Black girl as he forcefully covered her mouth and pushed himself inside of her. "Funky cock hoe, shut up if you want your son to live!"

Sheena's three-year-old son Shon lay sleeping, mercifully oblivious to the fact that less than three feet away, his beautiful mother was being violently raped by a dread-headed, red-eyed man who had threatened to take the little boy's life had his mother not cooperated. *And this man would do it.* He'd done it before. But pleasant was the boy's dream and safe was his life as his mother, too exhausted and afraid to defend herself, surrendered to Winston's carnal aggression.

Wishing someone, anyone, could read her mind, inside her head she screamed, *Oh, my God, why is this happening? Someone please help me! This man is raping me!* He continued to pound inside of her; it was so painful. The only lubrication was the blood seeping from the rips and tears in her wounded vagina. It hurt. It hurt so bad. But all Sheena could think of was her son; she'd do anything to protect him.

Tired, exhausted and dirty, Sheena and Shon had arrived at the New Orleans Superdome, which had become a refuge for anyone who could make it there in one piece. Sheena, in an attempt to get a little rest amongst the chaos of people running around looking for their loved ones or whatever missions they were on, found a vacant corner and laid down the two blankets she'd packed. Thinking she and her son were safe, Sheena was relieved. Unfortunately, however, her relief was short-lived. She was soon rudely awakened by someone on top of her.

"What the fuck?!" she'd instinctively cried out before being punched in the side of her head. As her vision and thoughts became clear again, she realized several things: one, her sweatpants and panties were down around her ankles. Two, there was a crazed lunatic on top of her and in between her legs. Three, when she tried to scream for help, she could not because he had her neck in such a grip that she could not get air in or her voice out. The adrenaline started pumping inside Sheena as the most intense explosion of pain shot from between her legs and through her entire body— pain unlike any she'd ever felt in her twenty-one years of life.

Just as she was about to pass out, he released her throat to allow her brain and lungs to absorb a little oxygen before he covered her mouth and continued to whisper threats in her ear. Now that she was able to breathe through her nose, she could smell the intensely foul body odor emanating from this monster on top of her, poisoning her world. She didn't know who he was, but she hated him, hated what he was doing to her. Even more, she hated all these people running back and forth...they had to have seen, they had to know what was being done to her, but they would not help her. They either thought he was her man or they were too consumed with their own circumstances to be concerned about her. It would be over soon, though, and she would take this secret to her grave. *Most importantly, my son will be safe,* she thought as Winston released himself with a violent orgasm inside her unwilling womb. He lifted himself off Sheena and wiped his piece off with her blanket before throwing it back down at her.

Winnie pointed a long, skinny finger at her. "And you better *stay quiet!*"

She quickly pulled up her pants and reached for her son. Winston looked around to see who had been paying attention to what had been going on, and he locked eyes with an older lady who lay about thirty feet away. He recognized something familiar in her eyes, and even though he'd contemplated confronting her, he refrained from doing so when she closed her eyes and turned away. Fuck it. At this point, his hunger for some real food was the next primal necessity to deal with. *I'ma let that old bitch make it,* he thought to himself as he moved along and surveyed the premises for his next take. He was a dog out of its cage, on the hunt for fresh meat.

Winnie had been locked up for the past eight months while awaiting trial for a variety of charges ranging from rape to manslaughter to animal cruelty. He had no remorse for the things he'd done and he'd told his court-appointed lawyer as much. He would have been spending the rest of his life—or a good majority of it—in Angola if it weren't for God showing him favor with the immaculate conception called Katrina. He looked around at all the broken souls in the room and breathed in the stench of mildew and sadness that reminded him that all of this was real. A mother fought back tears as she attempted to feed her kids and encourage them by letting them know that everything would be all right. *Damn, that canned ravioli looks good right about now,* Winston thought.

A husband and father, a strong-looking man with a square face and angry eyes, embraced his wife, speechless. As they sat on the concrete floor she leaned her head into her husband's neck and cried uncontrollably.

"Why, Terrance...why?" she moaned. "Where is our baby? *Where is my son?!*"

The tears flowed from her red, puffy eyes. She looked like she'd once been a beautiful woman, but life had defeated her unexpectedly, snuck up on her with power and vengeance in the last round and now her son was missing. This was the straw that broke the camel's back. All she had left was her husband, who looked as if he'd fought all his life for what he had, a lil' piece of the American dream. In a city filled with destitution, he'd fought and risen above that free cheese line, that false pity line, that nigger-stay-in-your-place line. He was a hard-working man and his wife and only son depended on him to lead the way. But this situation...these catastrophic circumstances have knocked all the fight out of him, and he hated losing, hated hopelessness. So he sat there, still embracing his tearful wife because he knew she needed him. He was angry as hell, though. Frustrated. In his eyes, the world was on fire with no plan of attack. He had lost everything and this is what all his years of struggle had come to.

Winnie saw and understood all of this but he was just unable to feel what these people felt. The course of his life had changed as well, but, unlike these people, his turn of events was undoubtedly for the better. He was thrilled. He was free, along with three hundred other criminals who, just a short while ago, had faced a fate similar to his. They had been told warrants would be issued and they would be apprehended after everything had settled down, but right now this was their only option. The hardened criminals couldn't believe their ears; it was a pure-dee muthafuckin' miracle.

Winnie was now walking around the Superdome with a kool-aid smile on his face and no one could understand why. He tried to change it to a straight face or at least a smirk, but it wasn't working. He was feeling good. He figured that whoever saw him would think that anyone this happy in these circumstances must be able to help them somehow, but they would be so wrong in that assumption. Winnie was only out to help one person in this world, and that was himself.

This whole analogy was amusing to him. His smile brightened even more when he locked eyes on a small group of White people handing out sandwiches. A man and woman passed them out while three other men attempted to prevent a literal stampede. A large crowd had already started to form as one of the volunteers made an effort to get them in a single file line. Winnie knew there were only so many sandwiches in the large plastic trash bag from which they were being pulled. *I need to knock that muhfucka upside his head and take that bag,* he thought to himself, but he knew that would cause a riot. "Very well then," he quietly said to himself with his French-Haitian accent, "time to eat." He began to maneuver his way to the front of the ever-growing line, ignoring the angry, violated stares from men, women, and children who were just as hungry as he, if not more so.

Jewel had locked eyes with him, and instantly she'd sensed the evil that radiated from his being. Disgusted, she'd looked away, uncomfortable with what her senses relayed to her. She knew this man had just raped that young girl by the way she'd cringed under his penetrating gaze, and by the way he'd thrown her blanket down at her as if she were nothing more than trash. Jewel was reminded of her past, the violent and merciless history associated with her environment: her dead sister and father, and her mother, who had left all this behind in the hopes of a better life.

Intense feelings of hatred, which were now focused on this man, this demon, quickly manifested themselves within her. He was the epitome of everything that haunted her past and the city she grew up in and loved. She cursed him under her breath in French, "*Pouvez vous mourir les mille décès comme le diable vous sont. Vous ne méritez pas la vie, ainsi il sera saisi de toi. Les éléments de ce monde sont maintenant pour toujours contre toi. Il est fait.* (May you die a thousand deaths like the devil you are. You don't deserve life, so it shall be snatched from you. The elements of this world are now forever against you. It is done.)" She visualized Winnie in complete agony, strapped to a chair while experiencing such excruciating pain that only death would relieve him. Winnie would cry for the Grim Reaper to be his savior, to remove him from his misery: "Take me..."

"*Ms. Landau.*" Jewel snapped out of her reverie and looked up to see Gerald standing over her.

"Are you all right?" he asked, genuinely concerned after catching her last mumbled words about something being done.

"Huh?..Uh...*ahem.*" Jewel cleared her throat in order to resume her normal speaking voice. "Excuse me, sweetheart. Yes, I'm fine. Don't worry about me. You've done more than enough by saving my life."

"Are you sure, Jewel?" Raquel chimed in. "I know it's been rough, but without your vision we might not have made it this far. You knew we was gonna be all right, and here we are. We're all right," she said while smiling at Jewel, Gerald and then down at her son Damon who lay asleep in her lap.

"Girl, please, I'da drowned in that house if it hadn't been for you two," Jewel mused while trying to take her mind off any negative energy. She glanced back in the direction that Winnie took and pulled her duffle bag closer to her.

"So, Raquel, how's my baby doing?" Jewel asked, referring to Raquel's seven-year-old son Damon, with whom she had an almost maternal bond.

"Sleeping like he's back in my belly," Raquel answered quickly, matching Jewel's tone and wit. She affectionately rubs Damon's small, recently faded head. "He's been so strong through all of this. He hasn't even cried."

"That's my little soldier," Gerald said proudly. Even though Damon wasn't his biological son, he loved him just the same. It was as if Damon could read the situation perfectly, but without fear.

Damon's child instincts told him that his parents would protect him from anything, and it was he who'd first voiced the idea to use the motorized canoe they used for fishing to ride far enough into the shallow waters and then walk the rest of the short distance to the Superdome. Gerald then turned his boat over to the Red Cross personnel so they could hopefully utilize it to save others who were stranded in high, otherwise impassable storm waters. Gerald had refused to leave his family, and now they were safe.

"Yeah, we're all right," Jewel agreed.

Chapter Two: FATSO & PRINCE

Dwayne "Fatso" Landau and his younger brother Purnell—better known as "Prince", now seventeen and sixteen years of age, respectively, were outside in front of the two-story four-bedroom brick home on Scarlett Street in the Houston, Texas neighborhood of South Acres. In the driveway sat a light blue 1983 four-door Chevrolet Impala. The original paint job was horribly faded as a result of years spent in the merciless Texas sun. Fatso was under the hood with some reddish-orange concoction he himself had blended along with a combination of chemicals he'd picked up from Auto Zone. The smile on his face said that whatever it was he was pouring into the carburetor of the old Chevy was going to work.

"All right, try it now!" Fatso yelled, poking his head from under the hood and making eye contact with Prince, who was sitting in the driver's seat with one foot resting on the accelerator and the other planted firmly on the cracked concrete of their driveway. With his favorite Astros hat turned to the back of his short, curly mop of hair, Prince nodded and reached to turn the key in the ignition. The starter attempted to bring the eight cylinders to life, winding itself over two intervals at a time, sounding like a drunk, oversized alley cat doing his best to gain a pity meal.

"It's not working," Prince stated as if he were an expert on these matters.

Fatso threw the empty pint-sized bottle down to the ground.

"Damn!" he swore. "Did you even give it any gas like I told you?"

Prince paused for a moment, then shrugged. *You got me.* He reached for the ignition.

"Okay, let me try again."

"Nah, nah, nah!" exclaimed Fatso, gesturing for his little brother to get out of the car, "No. I'll do it myself."

Prince's feelings were hurt, but he climbed out of the driver's seat and moped, "You act like I don't know how to start a car or something."

Fatso didn't bother to respond to his younger brother's pouting. He knew Prince was smart; smart as hell and devious, too. Prince surprised his older brother at some of the things he did and said, and Fatso admired his street smarts. At sixteen, he naturally understood the ghetto politics that governed the hood. He could watch a John Singleton film or a Martin Scorcese flick, or just watch a couple cats from around the way get into a fight at the park. But whenever the drama popped off, he could tell you what was gonna happen next, or what *should* happen. Fatso would just sit back and spectate, mainly to see if Prince's confident forecast would be correct or not. Ninety-eight percent of the time, he was dead on. This made it hard for Fatso to doubt his brother.

Prince, still pouting, continued: "*I'm* the one who told you old man Charles was selling the car for two hundred dollars anyway, shit, and..."

Fatso shook his head and thought to himself, *No matter how sharp he is, he's still my spoiled lil' brother.* He pushed down on the gas pedal two quick times and started the ignition. After two or three growls from the drunken alley cat, the three hundred and fifty dead horses came to life. Prince pumped his right fist up and down as he excitedly jumped into the air.

"Yeah! Yeah!" he yelled. "It worked, Fatso, we rollin'...we rollin!" Fatso just smiled. *Of course it worked.*

Unlike his little brother, who was admittedly more instinctive and street smart, Fatso was extremely book smart. A natural chemist with a photographic memory, he could cook anything after only one time of watching someone prepare it. Fatso loved chemistry so much that he'd read and break down the ingredients in most common cleaning agents for fun. He'd even cooked dope for some of the cats in the 'hood who moved weight. His homeboy showed him how to do it once, and the next time, Fatso was showing his homeboy how to do it better. Before he knew it, some of the dope-boys in the 'hood had heard the word about a youngsta who cooked dope like he himself had invented the whip game, then they was comin' to scoop him and take him to their spots so they could witness the magic of two kilos of crack being made out of one kilo of cocaine.

Now, most of the dope dealers who commissioned Fatso's services knew how to cook, but there were two reasons why they'd rather have *him* cook. For one, the majority of mid-level crack slingers are lazy. They would much rather keep their occupational hustle simple: pick it up, break it up, drop it off, collect money. So, if they can employ one or a few cats they can trust enough to handle those first two steps, they'd do it in a heartbeat, skipping straight past go and collecting their paper. *Oh, but wait:* this shit has to be cooked, and cooking is a tedious process. Most importantly, you gotta know what you're doing, because it's not as easy as it looks in *New Jack City*.

When this 2-for-1 whip game hit the streets in the late 80's, that was a hard coupon to keep secret. Who wouldn't take that look? Shit, everybody else was. The Mexicans invented the game with that 50/50 recon shit, distributing mass random shipments of kilos that were fifty percent cocaine and fifty percent horse tranquilizer to make up for lost shipments. The 'hood just worked that same principle: when you get your hands on some good dope, at least eighty percent, stretch that shit as far as you can without fucking over your clientele. And when you had a young chemist like Fatso to pro-chef your shit to a scientific perfection while having a sportsman's conversation about the Astros, the Texans and his high-school football team for five hundred a brick—as if you're not even getting over when the going price for less quality was fifteen hundred—well, that's a real luxury in this game. The other reason is a much simpler one: *the boy is good, real good.* Big timers just liked to watch him work. It was like being in the presence of a star chef while he prepared a gourmet meal for the President, and the finished product was just as pleasing. The dope fiends loved it. Even the veteran fiends the d-boys would use to test the product were fooled, and they usually *always* knew the difference.

As far as Fatso was concerned, the money was good. He made a couple thousand a month just from cooking for the d-boys in South Acres. He saved a few dollars here and there, kept himself and his little brother in the latest gear, and had just copped his first hooptie with neither he nor his brother having to sling crack. He was all right with that. They could always be there for their grandmother, who had raised them from babyhood, and she didn't have to worry about them being in no mess, *but damn;* all that money Fatso and Prince knew them boys were making out there sure was tempting. They used to walk home from the bus stop and fantasize about what they would buy. Before they went to sleep at night they would discuss and debate what they would do with specific large amounts of money starting at one hundred thousand, then one million, then ten million. They'd compete over who'd do what for Mama, who'd have the most profitable business, the flyest whip, the bombest crib, and over which celebrity chick they'd have on their arm. As they would talk, they'd ultimately be teaching each other about the world, business, and themselves, then fall asleep with smiles on their faces and dollar signs in their heads. But for now, it was all a dream.

******

Fatso revved the engine again, but instead of hearing them ponies roar, this time, they coughed and gagged. The engine sputtered and died.

"What happened?" a confused Prince asked.

Fatso reached for the ignition and tapped the gas pedal again. "I don't know," he replied, "but it *must* be something else. I know the mix worked."

He turned the ignition over and there went that alley cat again, but he had eaten whatever Fatso had fed him and went on about his business, never to return. Not today, at least.

From the front door, Mama yelled, "Boys!" They had been so caught up in their temporary triumph that they hadn't even heard her open the screen door.

In unison, they replied, "Ma'am?"

"Come inside. I need to talk to you two," Mama said calmly, then disappeared back inside the house.

Prince, slightly worried, looked at Fatso, who replied for the both of them: "Yes, ma'am."

Prince was the devious one, always into some shit. It was never anything too serious, but if something was broken or out of place, or if a neighbor complained about some miscellaneous occurrence, nine times out of ten, Prince was the culprit. What made it so bad was that he'd committed so many mischievous acts that he had no idea what would catch up with him or when. He couldn't keep up, so he stopped trying; he decided long ago to just enjoy his practical-joking self, at least until times like these. This could be trouble.

Fatso glared back at Prince. Mama's tone was calm, but that could be deceiving. Fatso hated the fact that every time Prince jumped out of line, *he'd* get the second degree too, as if Mama somehow assumed that every time Prince decided to be a misfit, Fatso would be ever-present to prevent trouble and save the world. That thoroughly annoyed him, but the truth of the matter was that Fatso usually *was* there, and even though he would rarely assist Prince in his Dennis the Menace routines, rarely was he able to prevent them.

Actually, Fatso found most of Prince's antics to be hilarious. He'd be cracking up laughing before Prince would even do anything, which usually motivated Prince to up the ante on whatever scheme he was cooking up in that brain of his. His big brother was his favorite audience, but Fatso knew that there was a good chance he'd pay later for that sidesplitting laugh. Today seemed to be one of those times.

Fatso took his grandfather's penetrating gaze off Prince and headed towards the door. Prince fell in behind him like any other time he found himself in a situation like this. Fatso's nickname belied his tall, slim frame. With cocoa-brown skin and cornrows to the back, Prince found it easy to hide his shorter, slightly stockier and darker physique behind his big brother, whom he knew would speak first anyway. The first thing the boys noticed upon walking into the living room was that the TV was blaring the news.

They knew there was a big storm rolling through New Orleans because Mama had been staying tuned to the frequent updates for the past two days, grumbling in her old southern woman's voice,

"Them people need to just get out of there!" Then, talking to herself as if she weren't a native of New Orleans, "But they won't. I know they won't. Them people can be some of the most stubborn people in the world because they just don't believe that Hell is real."

Fatso turned to Mama, who was now pretending the TV didn't exist as she poured herself a glass of lemonade. Prince zoomed in on the cold, sweet liquid that filled Mama's glass and his mouth began to water. He made a mental note to pour himself a glass once this business with his grandmother was handled.

"Is everything all right, Mama?" Fatso asked.

"I just got off the phone with the Red Cross," she began, her solemn tone suggesting she was both relieved and worried. Prince and Fatso were also relieved, but they were now anxious to hear the rest of the story.

Mama continued, "Your Auntie Sandra was rescued from the storm."

The boys' faces brightened. Even though she hadn't mentioned it, they knew Mama had been worried about her only surviving daughter. She would hardly discuss Auntie Sandra with them, but they knew that she and their aunt had this strange love/hate relationship between them. What the boys didn't know was whether or not it was related to the death of their mother and grandfather. They had no idea and Mama wouldn't talk about it, so they had stopped guessing and had long ago quit asking.

"She...she's coming to stay with us for a while," Mama said reluctantly, as if her mind hadn't quite grasped the words that were coming out of her mouth. She glanced down at her glass of lemonade, then looked back up at the boys with a slightly encouraging grin. The boys weren't fooled; they knew that grin was more for her than for them, but they were still delighted, nonetheless.

Prince spoke for the first time since he'd entered the house. "For real?!" he yelped. "Aw man, I can't wait!"

"So she's okay and everything, right, Mama?" Fatso asked, making sure he hadn't missed anything. She nodded.

"They said she was fine," she answered, deep in thought.

"That's good. That's real good, Mama." Fatso nodded, preoccupied with his own amazement. He couldn't believe it. This was an incredible opportunity for him and Prince to learn more about their past, their family, and even more, why Mama never talked about any of it. This could answer so many questions. Fatso could tell that his grandmother was concerned; worried, even. But why? Before he and Prince had been conditioned not to bark up that tree, he had asked that question so many times, but to no avail. And today was no different. Besides, he was too excited about the impending arrival of his auntie.

Prince's brain was moving a mile a minute as he placed a glass on the countertop and began pouring himself some homemade lemonade.

"When is she coming? She can have my room if she wants," he offered, as if his typical sixteen-year-old boys' socks-and-tennis-shoe-smelling locker room was the ideal spot for a grown woman.

Amused at his enthusiasm and generosity, Mama snapped out of her zone and laughed. "No, baby, no."

She laughed again and shook her head at the thought of her oldest daughter, whom she hadn't seen in fourteen years, staying in her grandson's room. Wouldn't *that* be something. But she knew that it was a big deal for him to offer his personal space. She stayed on him about keeping his room neat, and it was most of the time, but *that smell.* It wasn't horrid; it was more like an old funky pair of socks that had been hidden and had refused to be found for so long that the odor had immersed itself into every other object in the room. After trying all the store-bought cleaning agents along with Fatso's concoctions and deodorizers, she decided that the only way to get rid of that smell was to change the carpet and replace all the stuff in his room.

Unfortunately, that was not about to happen on her tight budget, which was only bolstered by social security payments and monies from her husband's life insurance policy. It was Princey's room, and *he* was the one who had to deal with it. She just stayed out of there, which worked to his and Fatso's advantage because they didn't want to have to explain all the new clothes and shoes Fatso had purchased over the past few months. Fatso thought it was funny, but Mama knew that his room wasn't too far behind Prince's on the odor-meter. Mama was much more comfortable with the idea of Sandra staying in the guest room, and she voiced this to the boys.

"I will prepare the guest room for her tonight," she stated with finality.

Still awaiting an answer, Prince pressed on. "So, when is she going to be here, Mama?"

Fatso chimed in, "Yeah, when is she comin'?"

Francine looked both boys in the eyes. "She will be here tomorrow." The boys looked at each other and smiled.

The news continued to blare in the otherwise silent room, catching their attention,

"Damage predictions suggest that close to seventy-five percent of New Orleans' population will be forced to relocate until repairs can be made in what is now known as the most devastating natural tragedy in America's history. We're now going to Kimberly Strauss, live at the Superdome."

The screen flashes over to another chaotic scenario inside the Superdome as Kimberly Strauss attempts to report over the bedlam.

"It is near pandemonium here, John. Many are desperately searching for family members, food, or both. There have been reports of attacks and rapes inside the Superdome. The city jail has also flooded, forcing the jailers to release more than three hundred dangerous criminals onto the streets. It is just a mess, John. There are still no updates on emergency response vehicles' time of arrival. If anyone is listening and you think you can help, please call—"

Suddenly, the television flickered off. Mama set down the remote and began to walk away.

"That's enough tragedy for one day," she said. "that city was doomed from conception." Prince and Fatso exchanged confused glances. Mama seemed to be so bitter. As if she'd read their minds, she turned back to the boys and said wearily,

"Boys…you have no idea. Just be grateful."

******

All kinds of thoughts were running rampant through Jewel's mind as she arrived in Houston. Her body was exhausted and she couldn't wait to take a hot bath. The ride from New Orleans had taken three times longer than the usual six hours it usually took pre-Katrina. She'd thought she'd never make it here with all the flooding, accidents and detours.

The twelve-passenger van smelled of bad breath, body odor and mildewed clothes as it made several stops along Interstate 10 and beyond to drop off other passengers who had been fortunate enough to contact family members and catch this free ride with the Red Cross.

After what seemed like forever, it was her turn to be dropped off. *Houston looks nice and big,* she thought while wondering why she'd never visited in all this time. She felt a little ashamed and nervous; ashamed because these circumstances were the only thing that was able to reunite her with her mother and nephews, and nervous because they had separated on bad terms. And...it had been so long. Jewel sighed. According to the directions, they were getting close to her destination. The white van pulled into a residential area that appeared to have been really nice twenty years ago.

It had decent-sized one- and two-story homes, some looking better than others. She knew it was a Black neighborhood just by looking at some of the kids outside, and also by the teenagers on bikes conversing with a few scattered adults with that hungry expression on their faces. They appeared to be up to no good, but Jewel didn't want to judge. *Looks like Mama is doing all right,* she thought. She took a deep breath and forced a smile. This was another chance at life with her family in a new city, and she wouldn't waste it. She promised herself that she would do everything she could to make it work with her mother and pick up where she left off with her nephews.

"Here we are," the driver announced, matching the address on his list with the numbers stenciled above the door of the house's attached garage, "Fifty-five-twenty-two Scarlett Street."

"It looks like you'll be just fine," the other Red Cross volunteer complimented upon his assessment of the area. Based on the other neighborhoods they'd passed through on their journey, this definitely seemed like a more comfortable situation. Reaching for the door handle, Sandra again looked at the house and agreed.

"I certainly will be just fine. Thank you all so much," she said sincerely, and exited the van.

With her duffle bag on her arm, she reached up and rung the doorbell. A curly haired, dark-skinned teenager whom she immediately recognized as her youngest nephew Purnell quickly answered the door.

"Auntie?" he asked excitedly, knowing it was her.

"Princey?" Jewel squealed in response, already holding out her arms for a hug.

"Yeah, it's me," he answered, and Jewel grabbed him and hugged him. Energy renewed, she forgot all about being hungry, about needing a bath, all of that. She couldn't believe how handsome he'd become.

"I can't believe it! Look at you!" Sandra exclaimed while Prince just smiled, overwhelmed. Fatso came skipping down the stairs with a big smile on his face.

"How you doin', Auntie?" Fatso said, grinning like a Cheshire cat.

"Fat-Fat!" Jewel squealed. "Oh, my precious, look at how tall you are!" she said, reaching up to give him a hug. Fatso grinned even harder because he was so happy that his auntie was safe and that they'd finally reunited, but he was also blushing at the new nickname his auntie had bestowed upon him. It soon dawned on him that it must have been what he had been called as a baby. Mama had never called him that but she did call his little brother "Princey."

Fatso looked her over. "Are you okay? Do you have any bags?"

"This is it, baby," Sandra said, clutching the one bag that represented all that she had left. "Just me. The storm wiped out everything else." Embarrassed, she turned and looked behind her.

"Hold on, baby, I'd almost forgotten about these people." She turned again and waved at the Red Cross drivers to let them know she was all right and that they could leave.

Prince, smiling, turned to his brother and teased, "Fat-Fat."

"Shut-up," Fatso shot back, still grinning.

Mama had decided she'd let the boys greet their aunt when she arrived. She sat there in the living room in her big sitting chair with a big smile on her face, listening to all the happy chatter being shared between the boys and their aunt. She'd waited long enough. Just as Jewel inquired as to her mother's whereabouts, Francine rounded the corner leading to the entryway. Mother and daughter locked eyes, and so many memories, both good and bad, came flooding back through each of their minds. But at that moment, they realized that none of the bad memories mattered.

"Welcome home, baby," Mama said, smiling.

"Hi, Mama," Jewel said, filled with emotion like she was a little girl again. She walked over and hugged her mother tightly for the first time in a long time. Tears rolled down her face as she realized she was finally home, with her family.

"We got a room all set up for you, Auntie." Prince said while jogging up the stairs. "Come on in, I'll show you."

Jewel watched Prince ascend the stairs, wanting to follow him but finding it hard to remove herself from her mother's presence. Francine tenderly observed her daughter and examined the lines in her face that told her the story of the last fourteen years.

"Go on, sweetie," Francine says. "You've got everything you need up there. Go take a hot bath and clean yourself up. Take as much time as you need, and when you're ready, we'll serve dinner, okay?" Jewel nods absently.

"Okay, Mama," Jewel answers, inhaling deeply. "Mmm-hmmm…smells like music to my soul," she says with a smile. Francine smiles back, amused at Jewel's humor.

"*Merci beaucoup, Mama,*" Jewel says to her mother as she rises, shoulders her small bag and heads upstairs. Fatso follows closely behind her.

"Auntie, you think you can teach me French?" he asks.

"Of course. I can teach you a lot of things." Jewel answers with a tired smile. Fatso smiles; he is looking forward to this.

Jewel stops on the landing and turns to look at Fatso and admires his tight cornrows and familiar facial features. "You know, you look a lot like your grandpapa," she says, smiling and remembering how Fatso looked as a little boy, not so far removed from the near-man he is now.

"That's what Mama says," Fatso stated, blushing shyly and looking down at the floor.

"Does she?" Jewel asked. Fatso nods.

"He was a very handsome man," Jewel reminisces, looking him over again and squeezing his cheek. "And so are you."

As she turns around to find her room, Prince pops into the hallway.

"Right here, Auntie, come on in."

The guest room is impersonal and reminds her of a hotel room. It smelled as if it had just been disinfected with Lysol and deodorized with potpourri. The sun shone through the window and onto the beige-and-cream colored paisley comforter, upon which rested a small pile of folded clothes, towels and various hygiene items.

"You like it?" Prince inquires.

"It looks comfortable," Jewel replies as a wave of exhaustion suddenly invades her happiness. She gently placed her bag on the floor by the small nightstand near the bed.

"You boys let your auntie get comfortable!" Mama yelled from downstairs. Fatso stands in the doorway and gestures to his brother.

"C'mon, P, you heard Mama." Prince's welcoming tour guide smile fades away, and he pouts slightly.

"Man!" he exclaims, turning to walk out. Jewel grabs Prince by the shoulder to turn him back to her and kisses him on the cheek and tells him that they will talk later, that she is not going anywhere.

Prince's smile returns and he nods. "Ok Auntie..Yes Ma'am."

Jewel sighed and smiled as she was too tired to dispute her nephew making mer feel her age.

******

Jewel steps into the bath, which is steaming hot just like she likes it. As she slowly eases herself into a relaxed position, she reminds herself that a hot bath is a spiritual experience. The bubble bath soothes her and washes away the pain, the loss, and the anguish of a thousand souls wishing upon a star. The burning candle on top of the toilet tank fills the steamy bathroom with a tropical coconut scent. Jewel lay back in the tub and soon she feels like she is floating away. She then thinks of Raquel, Gerald and their son, hoping they make it safely to Cleveland. She smiles to herself, thankful to be secure and relaxed in this tragic time.

******

While Jewel relaxes in the tub, Francine steps into the guest room. The long-dormant room finally has the feeling of being occupied. The first thing Mama notices is the duffle bag sitting on the floor next to the bed. She knows that this is all her daughter brought with her, so she assumed that whatever was in the bag must be of importance to her. She knows it is rude to snoop, but she is extremely curious about what is in the bag, *And besides,* she reminds herself, *this is my house, after all. I have the right to know what is being brought here.*

She steps over to the bag and picks it up and sits it on the bed. Unzipping it, the first thing she notices is the picture of herself, her husband and their two girls, taken over thirty years ago. It immediately brings a smile to her face. As she surreptitiously glances toward the bathroom, the other thing that captures Francine's attention is the wooden box with the big red

jewel embedded in the lid. She already knows what it is, and begins to shake

her head from side-to-side. *Oh, no, not in my house.*

She pulls the box out of the bag and opens it to reveal the book of

gris-gris and the *voudou* bible. Nodding her head, she closes the box,

knowing exactly what it is she has to do. Holding the box in both hands, she

heads out the bedroom door, closing it lightly. She says a prayer to herself as

she stops at the door leading upstairs to the attic. From the chain around her

neck, she pulls out the key to the attic door and walks the box up the short

flight of stairs. Once inside, Francine sets the box down in a dark, obscure

corner. As she steps back down the stairs into the hallway and snaps the

Master U-lock back into the locked position, she thinks to herself, *I cannot*

allow my boys to be exposed to that madness. Francine then determinedly

walks back down the hall to the bathroom door and knocks on it gently.

"Sandra, it's me," Francine warns as she enters. Jewel is submerged

in bubbles, so she has nothing to hide. As she comes back to reality, she looks

up to see her mother standing there.

"Hey, Mama," she says in a relaxed tone. Francine chuckles a little.

"It looks like you're enjoying your bath."

"Oh, you have no idea, Mama; I was so exhausted."

"Well, bless your heart. The news made it sound horrible."

Sandra nods. "It was. It really was."

"Well, I just wanted to talk to you for a minute," Francine says as

she sits down on the toilet lid.

Now fully snapped out of her reverie, Jewel nods. "Okay, Mama,

I'm listening."

"I know it was a terrible thing that brought you here, but I was hoping, for your sake, that we could look at it as a good thing; an opportunity for you to start fresh and leave all that nonsense behind you."

Jewel processed all the possibilities of what her mother could be talking about and nods apprehensively. Francine continues,

"I've come too far, raising the boys, giving them a new life and..." she pauses. "I can't afford for all that mess from New Orleans to be messin' with they heads. Baby, you understand, right?"

Jewel stared into the bubbles, thinking of Prince and Fatso and all the things she'd wanted to share with her beloved nephews.

"What do you want me to do, Mama? I love my nephews, and I want the best for them, too."

Francine looks her daughter square in the eyes to prepare her for the seriousness of her next request. "God has given you a chance at a new life. I want you to start new and leave all that *voudou* stuff in New Orleans."

Jewel had known this was coming, but she hadn't expected it so soon. She knew that her mother's decision was non-negotiable. Jewel had already made up her mind to do what she needed to make this situation work, but she knew in her heart that giving up her beliefs was something she just couldn't do. She despised the fact that her mother was making such a request, but she agreed.

"Mama, on the way out here I had a lot of time to think, and I promised myself that I would do whatever it took for this to work for all of us," she began, while Francine nodded and brightened up at the direction of her daughter's logic. Jewel continued,

"And that hasn't changed. We'll make it work, Mama. I just need some time to adjust."

Francine did not like the sound of that, and communicated this to her daughter. "The time is *now*, Sandra. You've had fourteen years to adjust."

Sandra was frustrated, but she remained quiet for a moment. Her mother was still impossible, but she knew the only way out of this conversation was to agree with her.

"Whatever it is you want me to do, Mama, I'll do it, okay?"

Francine smiled. She'd won. Her actions were now justified. Rising from the toilet seat, she said to Sandra, "I'll leave you to your bath now. Take your time."

Jewel spent another twenty minutes relaxing in the tub until the hot water became lukewarm, telling her she was done. Finally starting to feel fresh again, she brushed her teeth and deodorized. When she stepped back into the guest room, the cool air that hit her lungs mixed with the aroma of Mama's soul food reminded her how hungry she was. She thought of how sweet it was for Mama to have had everything prepared for her, while at the same time upset because she was taking another shot at trying to run her life. *What am I going to do with her?* Jewel thought as she put a gown on over the bra and panties she'd removed from her bag earlier, which was still sitting right where she'd left it. She put her long, silky brown hair into a combed-out ponytail, threw on a robe and headed downstairs to enjoy her family and her Mama's cooking. She was long overdue for a full-blown southern meal prepared by the woman who had taught *her* how to cook, and Francine could definitely burn in that kitchen. Sandra "Jewel" Landau could think of nothing else.

******

"Oooh, Mama," Jewel teased, "you done pulled out *all* the stops. Candied yams, collard greens, hush puppies, macaroni and cheese, stuffed Cornish hen *and* chicken boudin!"

"I know you love that chicken boudin," Francine replied matter-of-factly with a big smile.

"Me, too, Auntie, that's my favorite!," Prince added. "My favorite is stuffed Cornish hen, huh, mama?"

"That's riiiighhht," Mama sang.

They all made their plates and sat down for a family reunion dinner. They laughed and joked, and the boys told Jewel about Houston from their perspective, with Mama jumping in here and there with adult clarification. She also told Jewel about Houston's job market.

"It's not like New Orleans, Sandra. They're always saying on the news how this city is growing. They say it will be bigger than Chicago in about five years."

Jewel was surprised. "Oh, really?"

Mama nodded. "Mmm-hmm. Black folks doing real good for themselves here. That medical industry is booming."

"I'd heard something about that," Jewel said. She had heard from Raquel that home health care was really on the rise and some of the highest probability of success for new businesses was in and around that field.

"Well, maybe you can get a job doing something like that," Mama hinted.

"Maybe," Jewel said evasively, even though she was actually considering a job in palm reading. She'd heard that was doing pretty good down here, too, but she knew not to buck her mother.

Prince jumped in and changed the subject. "So, what was New Orleans like?"

Jewel looked at her mother, and Francine smiled slightly and nodded, giving Jewel the okay to talk to them about the city in which they'd been born, the city that would never be the same.

"Well, New Orleans was a fun city, a party town with the casinos and the French Quarter," she said, smiling. "But…it was also a dark place with lots of housing projects and poverty."

"I've heard that it's very rough down there," said Fatso. "They say it's the murder capital."

"Violence had become a big part of the environment," Sandra said vaguely, hoping the boys wouldn't want her to go into more detail about this last statement.

"You're not going back, are you, Auntie?" Fatso asked.

"Yeah, Auntie, we want you to stay," Prince chimed in with a smile.

"Baby, there ain't nothin' for me to go back to."

"It was *that* bad, sweetie?" Francine inquired. Jewel nodded solemnly.

"So what happened?" Prince asked enthusiastically, prepared to hear a story, but Mama nipped that in the bud real quick.

"She doesn't want to think about that right now, Princey," she snapped.

"It's okay, Mama, I don't mind," Jewel interjected. "I'm safe now."

She went on to tell them about her experiences with the nightmare that was Katrina. They talked for a good while over the rest of their dinner and dessert of bread pudding until Jewel was so tired she could almost hear that rain again, beating down inside her head. *Yeah, it's time to lie down,* Jewel said to herself, then excused herself from the dinner table.

"Well, this was so good, Mama, but I need to lie down. Is there anything you need me to do? I can wash the dishes later...." Hearing this, Fatso and Prince both crossed their fingers, hoping that Mama would take Jewel up on her offer and let them off the hook of carrying out one of their most tedious, hated chores. Mama, however, would hear nothing of it.

"No, baby, you go on and lay down. Me and the boys got this," she replied, really meaning that since *she* had cooked, *the boys* had it.

******

Within minutes of laying down, Jewel was on the brink of a deep sleep. She fell into that abyss of REM hibernation where your dreams seem real. The colors are so vivid and that one primal human nature from which all negative feelings derive, *fear*, is as real in your dreams as it is in your waking moments. Jewel fell into a dream in which she had a child. Being a woman without any children in reality, this filled her with happiness. But somehow, this child was taken from her, stolen. She became very sad and angry, and no matter what she did to try and find her child, nothing worked.

Years later, her child, now strong and powerful, returned to take care of her and fulfill her dreams. She realized it was all a part of the plan; it was for the best. It was all in the book. She saw her box, and then it vanished. Fear filled her, and she suddenly awoke with a gasp.

Jewel looked around the darkened room and tried to get her bearings. Nighttime had fallen on the city and filled the room as she remembered where she was. She reached over the side of the bed for her duffle bag, and she immediately noticed that it was much lighter. She unzipped the bag and all she saw were the pictures she'd brought with her. *"Mama!"* she hissed to herself as anger filled her entire body. For the first time, she realized the room had no clock, and she had no idea what time it was. She didn't care. She was determined to get to the bottom of this right now. As she stomped across the floor, the reason behind her and mama's conversation earlier that evening dawned on her. She hesitantly knocked on her mother's door and, realizing that this *was* her aging mother she was about to wake out of her sleep and confront in the middle of the night, no longer felt as much anger as she'd felt before. But the sound of her knuckles rapping on the thin wooden door brought her back to her dream.

In the next room, the boys, who weren't quite in a deep sleep yet, looked at each other. The digital alarm clock in their room displayed the not-quite-late hour of 11:30 pm.

"What's that?" Prince asked.

He sat in front of the muted TV with the Playstation controller in his hand playing *Grand Theft Auto: San Andreas*. He hit the pause button and looked back at Fatso, who'd already begun to doze off in the same twin-sized bed he'd had since elementary school.

"I don't know, lea' me 'lone…" Fatso said grumpily and rolled over. Prince shrugged his broad shoulders and got up to check it out.

******

In her bedroom, Mama wakes up to find her daughter standing over her, tapping on the bedpost.

"Mama, mama, wake up. We need to talk."

"What, Sandra, it is the middle of the night. Talk to me tomorrow," Mama said indignantly, laying back down on her pillow.

"You know what I want. I didn't wanna talk in front of the boys."

"They go to school tomorrow! We can talk then!" Mama snapped.

"Oh," Jewel paused. "Well, you're up now. Where is my box? I want it back *now*, Mama," she demanded.

"First of all, I don't know who you think you're talking to like that," Mama snapped with venom, propping herself up on one elbow. "Second of all, you brought that nonsense into my house when you knew I'd have nothing of it."

"But it's *mine*, Mama," Jewel insisted in a loud whisper. "*It's mine!* If I don't use it, it still belongs to me. You can't just take stuff that don't belong to you just because you don't agree with what it stands for. That's very un-Christian of you."

Francine was losing her patience. "May I remind you that I can do whatever the hell I want to do in *my* house?" *Here she goes again with the power trip,* Jewel thought. "Besides," continued Francine, "if you're not gonna use it, then what you need it for, huh? What's the point of having it around? I don't want the boys runnin' into nothing like that. That's why I told you that you need to start fresh."

"And I told you I would," Jewel stated with attitude, but then she softened her tone. "Mama, that was a gift from my friend. It can never be—"

Francine interrupted her. "I'm *not* givin' it back." This was a bottom line statement that told Jewel that her mother's decision was non-negotiable. Fury bubbled up inside Jewel's gut and she felt like she was gonna burst, blackout, and attack the woman who'd given birth to her. But almost instantly, she became calm again. She thought of her dream and locked eyes with her mother in the dim light from the lamp on mama's bedside table. She knew this woman was an uncompromisable enigma. Pleading with her was useless.

Jewel forced a smile. Her eyes softened and she shrugged her shoulders.

"You're right, Mama," she said. *What* do *I need it for?* Jewel thought. *I have committed to memory every verse and every recipe for every gris-gris, so if she wants to play me like that, fine. Let her have her way.*

"I want to start a new life with you and the boys. I really don't have a choice, and I don't want anything to hinder that. So you can keep the box, but I want you to remember something, Mama. We are still who we were before we got here. Before Houston and even before New Orleans, we *were* Landaus. Nothing will change that. I love you, Mama, and I hope you feel good about all of this. I'm sorry for waking you."

Jewel felt as if she'd taken control of the situation, and she liked that. As she strolled out of the room she said a short prayer, that all truth and power be revealed to her nephews. She closed her mother's door and as she turned to walk back down the short hallway to her room, she saw through the small opening of the door to Fatso's room that Prince was hiding. She wouldn't have noticed him at all if it hadn't been for the light from the television. Jewel smiled and walked back into her room, knowing he'd heard their entire conversation.

Chapter Three: SOMETHING WICKED THIS WAY

COMES....WINNIE

A turquoise-colored long-bed pickup pulls into the parking lot of Houston's Astrodome. When the truck came to a stop, Winston "Winnie" Marshon hopped out the back along with the other three who'd hitched a ride from New Orleans with him.

"Thank you very much for everything. Be blessed now." Winnie says to the driver, but at the same time he is thinking, *Man, I shoulda robbed that muthafucka!* The driver, a middle-aged Hispanic guy, had picked him up on the outskirts of town while bringing the other three hitchhikers to the Dome, which was being used as a Katrina refugee point of contact for assistance. His good deed for the day accomplished, the man drove away with his *compadre* riding shotgun. It was time for tacos and beer.

Winnie and his three companions, whom he could really give less of a fuck about, begin walking towards the entrance to the massive building which is accompanied by another huge building to the right, called the Astro Center, and the Reliant Center, larger than both afore-mentioned structures put together, stood in the near distance behind them.

One of the guys, a short, dark-skinned brotha with one gold tooth says while rubbing his midsection, "I'm hungry than a muthafucka, whodie...I *know* they got some food in this bitch!" He'd been saying the same thing for the last thirty minutes. Even though Winnie's stomach was playing kiss-and-tell with his backbone, too, he said nothing. This lil' dude was really getting on his nerves.

"Oh, hell yeah," another guy added, "they said Houston layin' it out for a nigga. Food, a place to stay, *and* they gon' kick us some bread to cop that first pack. We sign up for that FEMA shit right chea'," he finished with a country, ghetto accent and flashing a gap-toothed smile.

"We sign up for that shit in here?" Shorty asked, pointing at the building they were walking towards and speeding up his pace a little bit.

"I wonder how much they gon' give us?" mused the oldest of the group. Winnie acted like he wasn't paying attention, but he was listening closely.

"I don't know all that, but it's better than nuthin'. It's free! And as cheap as dope is out chea', a nigga can't do nuthin' but come up."

Shorty was damn near running to get inside that Astrodome. "Hell, yeah! New Orleans 'bout to run dis bitch!"

Winnie laughed to himself. Even though he knew he was unable to take advantage of any kind of government assistance due to the fact that he would have to fly under their radar, the conversation was interesting. This government assistance gave people hope. It felt good to know there was money being passed out behind this shit, but Winnie knew them White folks wasn't about to give *him* nuthin' so he had to take whatever he had coming. He also knew it was little dumb niggas like this cat here who were always talkin' 'bout runnin' somethin' when they ain't runnin' shit but they mouths and they asses into a wreck when this shit gets real.

Winnie had made it to Houston, but as far as he was concerned, he could have ended up anywhere as long as it was away from Louisiana. But, this seemed to be where everybody was going or was trying to get to, so he worked his influence and here he was, feeling like an old dollar bill, wrinkled and stankin', but still money, nonetheless.

Once he was inside the Dome, Winnie shook his temporary crew who broke out looking for the FEMA assistance line where you coulda swore them White folks was passin' out free hundred-dollar bills on the spot. Guess crack and heroin fantasies had outweighed their hunger for now. Winnie wandered on over to where some lunch packs were being handed out. He needed food. Since he'd kicked that boy habit to the curb while he was in jail, it seemed like he was always hungry. But he knew that FEMA ain't have shit for him except an eventual warrant for his arrest. Thirty minutes later, he was meandering through the Astrodome, trying to come up with a plan, a plan to come up. Chewing on a baloney sandwich, he peeped out how much cleaner and more organized this situation was compared to the debacle at the Superdome.

"Winnie!" exclaimed a voice from behind him. Winnie turned around, thinkin 'Who da Fuck?...'

"Wha's happenin' brah?" said an excited light-skinned brother of medium height and build, pock-marked face, short afro and four golds in his mouth, top and bottom. He was covered in tattoos, a big dollar sign on his neck, two teardrops near his left eye and a small outline of the state of Louisiana by his right eye. These were all that Winnie could see, but he knew there were more. Unlike most of the other people in the building, he was well-dressed and smelled clean. Winnie, trying to remember where he knew the dude from, paused briefly. Then it hit him.

"Money Mo," he said slowly, a smile spreading across his face. "Wha's poppin', brah?"

Mo and Winnie had been locked up together just a few months back. Mo had been a suspect in a murder, but he'd been released when they found the real killer.

"What the fuck you doing here?" Mo asked. He looked around, then lowered his voice."They let you out?" Mo could not believe his eyes. He knew Winnie had been facing life the last time he seen him.

"They let a whole bunch of us out, ya heard me? They had to when that nasty ass jail flooded." Winnie stated matter-of-factly.

"What?! Nigga you got lucky than a muthafucka!" Mo said, shocked. He shook his head, all the while thinking that this nigga must have pulled that *voudou* shit to get that damn lucky. Mo had always liked Winnie, though. They'd chop it up day in and day out, and Mo found that Winnie was smarter than a lot of niggas, wise beyond his years. He'd trip Mo out, sayin' some fly shit that made a lot of sense, his Haitian accent revealing itself like there was another person inside of him or something. The shit made Mo laugh, and he thought Winnie was cool as hell.

"It was fate, youngin', ya heard me? Even jail bars can't stop that." Winnie said with a devious smile. "When you get here?"

"Shit, been here since last week, when they first start talkin' 'bout floodin' 'n shit. Came up here with my girl and got a room. We waitin' to get this money back plus some from FEMA," he explains, then adds, "You better get on that shit!"

Winnie shook his head, "Nah, brah, them people let us go because they had to. It ain't over. "

"Aw, yeah, I feel you," Mo replies, thinking about Winnie's situation. "Well fuck it. You free now, brah, and there's money out here. All you gotta do is stay low."

Winnie agreed. "Like a ghost. But I need to find some ID."

"Yeah, yeah, that's what you need." Mo says absently, looking around at the different lines of people scattered here and there.

"Who you lookin' for?"

"My mama, whodie," Mo answered solemnly. "Been comin' up here hopin' I see her or somebody who seen her."

"What she look like?" Winnie asks, tryin' to help his boy out. Mo describes her but Winnie can't recall anything that would help him.

"Don't worry 'bout it man, I'ma find her eventually. She probably aw'right, just goin' through the struggle like everybody else," Mo said dismissively. "Check it out, brah. Why don't you come back to the room with me and get cleaned up? I got somebody I want you to meet."

Winnie nods in assent. "I'm 'bout that," he says, as if he has any other choice.

******

Winnie hops out of the shower, thinking about the possibilities of this situation and this girl he's 'bout to meet once she comes back from runnin' errands with Mo's girl. Her man was supposedly killed in the storm. She has her own room, FEMA was 'bout to kick in, and she has a hooptie. Shit, that's all he needed to know; the rest was irrelevant. Mo hooks Winnie up with all new fresh whites, some jean shorts, and a rag to clean his boots up with.

"Yo' feet bigger than mine, whodie, so you gon' have to clean them bad boys up. That is unless you wanna squeeze into a pair of them Reeboks over there," Mo says, smiling and pointing at four pairs of Reeboks lined up against the wall.

"Nah, brah, you done more than enough," Winnie says, wiping his leather boots down inside and out before sprinkling some orange peelings from his lunch pack inside them. He slides on a pair of brand new white socks and stares at his feet for a second while Mo fires up the blunt he'd been rolling.

"Money Mo," Winnie says, smiling and feeling very grateful. Mo looks up while he takes his first good drag of the blunt and exhales. When Winnie knew he had Mo's undivided, he continued, "Good lookin' out, brah. I won't forget this."

Winnie's former cellmate and new partner doesn't say anything; he just smiles and offers Winnie the swisher sweet. Winnie grabs it and takes two good puffs, first inhaling, then exhaling, enjoying the familiar flavor.

"Ahhh," he sighs. "Now, what's up with this girl?"

"Misty, I want you to meet my potna Winnie. Winnie, this is Misty," Mo said casually as they all stood in front of Denny's.

"How ya doin', sweetheart?" Winnie asked in a deeply Haitian-accented and debonair tone while extending his hand.

"Hi," said Misty, a 5'5", brown-sugar hued heavy-set sister with a radiant smile. She dug his accent, and she had a thing for brothers with dreads, too, and Winnie's were long, hanging down to the middle of his upper back, and thick. Winnie could see that she was blushing.

"You 'ave a beautiful smile," Winnie said, laying his accent-heavy mack game on thick. He knew he had her. The blushing gave him the green light. It had been a while, but it was still all good. She wasn't as fine as Mo's girl, but Winnie did find her cute in her high-heeled Sketcher tennis shoes, black capris and red spaghetti strap top. She was definitely more than what he'd expected.

"Thank you," Misty said, continuing to blush furiously.

"Well, let's eat!" Mo impatiently exclaimed.

Mo's girl Taisha made a playfully disgusted gesture and said, "Y'all make me sick, ugh!" Actually, she was happy that her girl was getting some attention. Since her dude passed, Misty had been complaining about how hard it was for a big girl to find a good man. They went inside and talked and ate well into the wee hours of the morning. The more Misty talked, the more Winnie liked her.

Later on that same day, Winnie sweet-talked his way into Misty's heart. He told her that she was precious and beautiful, something to be cherished and that she deserved a knight in shining armor. The sentiments he laid on her had tears rolling down her face as they sat by the swimming pool of the Extended Stay America hotel they were staying in. Once Winnie had said he wanted to be her man, she offered up everything she had to help him. She told him about her upcoming financial situation and explained to him how the FEMA thing worked. She also told him she still had all her deceased boyfriend's info, his birth certificate, social security card and driver's license.

"His name is good, and you can use those until you get that other stuff straightened out, or..." Misty paused, "...or until his death certificate is issued. "

She was still having a hard time dealing with her loss and couldn't believe that she had even suggested such a thing. Winnie, sensing her hesitation, grabbed her hand quickly. Misty and everything she had to offer was exactly what he needed, and he wasn't about to blow it.

"Baby," he said compassionately as he looked her in the eyes, "I'm here for you now." She nodded, and he was elated. *Got her*, he thought. *This shit isn't gonna be so bad.*

******

Knock, knock, knock. *What the fuck?* Winnie thought to himself as alarms went off in his head. He quickly but silently arose from beside Misty's warm sleeping body. He'd been restless for the past couple of days, trying to decide on a plan of action, the right thing or the wrong thing. In his situation, he felt there weren't many choices, so in his mind, the wrong things were the right things.

That's what was running through his mind when someone came knocking on the door like they had a pistol in one hand and an arrest warrant in the other. Winnie calmed down and told himself that it was probably just Mo, which was confirmed when he crept over to the door and looked through the peephole. He swung the door open with his finger to his lips, signaling for Mo to be quiet. He wanted to preserve his morning silence for as long as possible. Mo had a big-ass kool-aid smile on his face, and with a death grip, held in his hand a white envelope. He held it out in front of him and grinned.

"I got the check, whodie," he whispered loudly.

"What?" Winnie asked, stepping out into the outside walkway that encircled the building. "FEMA came through?"

"Yep." Mo was still working that smile but Winnie was confused.

"Why didn't Misty get hers?" he asked.

"Probably because me and Taisha filed before she did, but hers should be comin' right behind ours," Mo explained to his potna.

Winnie looked at the check in Mo's hand. One part of him was happy for his road dog, but another part of him wanted to go with him to cash it and rob his ass right then and there, and rob the check-cashing place, too, while he was at it.

"So what you gonna do?"

"Nigga! The same thing I been tellin' you. I'ma put this with the other lil' change and cop me a one twenty five soft, whip me about six zones of some good and get this money, ya heard me?" Mo answered, a little too enthusiastic for Winnie's mood.

"Yeah, sho 'nuff," Winnie said, looking out into the morning sunshine. He was irritated. Houston is a big, pretty city, but this bitch gonna have to pay.

"Wazzup Bruh, don't even trip," Mo said, recognizing the stress in Winnie's face. "Misty said she gon' let you flip that check when it come. I already got the connect. We good. You my roll dog, bruh, and we gon' come up. We gon' do this shit together." Mo knew Winnie was a killer for real and wanted to stay on his good side.

"Yeah, yeah, it's all good. Do ya thug thang, baby. I know we gon' get it. Like I say, I don't know where I'd be right now if we ain't hooked up," Winnie replied with a smile that masked his real feelings.

"A'ight, then. Well, I'ma get all this shit taken care of."

"A'ight."

"I'ma holla at you later," Mo said, and they shook hands. Mo trotted off like new money floating in the air, leaving a jaded Winnie standing there in his boxers, leaning on his elbows against the motel railing. *Fuck this. It's time to get money.*

Once Winnie was dressed, the first thing he did was wake Misty up and tell her to get on top of that FEMA situation, check the mail, make calls, whatever. He told her that he was going to walk to the store right quick to get some fresh air and a pack of cigarettes, and by the time he strolled into the parking lot of the Exxon gas station and convenience store on Westheimer and Beltway 8, he had his plan in order. He briefly laughed to himself because behind the gas station was a Chase Bank and on the other side was a Whataburger. In his temporary insanity and hunger for money he'd considered robbing all three places, which was lunacy and a guaranteed way to get caught up, but it was in actuality only a few times more daring than the stunt he was about to pull off.

Winnie walked inside the store and quickly made a mental note that the middle-aged white guy behind the counter was busy with a line of customers who were buying gas, cigarettes, etc.; you know, all the bullshit people buy while they're on their lunch break so they won't have to deal with it during after-work drive time. They can be caught up with their vices while sitting in Houston traffic and feel as if they'd planned their day right. A pretty yellow-bone sister in a hunter green skirt suit and matching pumps was yakking away on her Blackberry about rescheduling a meeting and drawing attention to herself, and she had a large cappuccino in the hand she was gesturing wildly with. Winnie again noted that the guy behind the register didn't even see him enter.

He cut right over to the automotive supplies and picked up a roll of duct tape and a pair of brownies, which are brown mechanical gloves usually worn while working on cars. Today, however, the gloves would serve a different purpose. Winnie quickly pocketed them while making his way over to the small, overpriced toys that were placed near the front of the store so kids would see them as soon as they came into the store and bug the shit out of their parents to buy for them, then only play with either until they got home or lost it in the car.

Winnie found what he was looking for. *Bingo,* he thought. He grabbed it and headed back towards the coolers in back. He'd been in this store before so he knew they had his accomplice in their inventory, a black plastic water gun that looked like a nine-millimeter. He ripped the package open silently while pretending to look for something to drink. He stuffed it down into his pants, and his job was done. He thought about buying something but quickly changed his mind. No eye contact. He headed out the door before the talkative professional sister could pay for her coffee.

Once outside, he walked over to the Whataburger to use their bathroom. After a nervous piss, he was in the mirror wrapping his dreads into a stocking cap and inspecting his get-up. He wrapped a bandanna over the water gun, went outside to fire up his last cigarette, then walked back over to the gas station. *Fuck it!* He was a vulture on the prowl. Shortly thereafter, a gray Denali on 23's pulled into the station. Winnie watched as a medium-height brother hopped out to feed his fly-ass gas guzzler, then he noticed the dude had left the truck runnin'; he could see the keys in the ignition from where he stood. *Stupid muthafucka deserve to get got,* Winnie thought with a smile.

He quickly snuck over to the passenger side and quietly opened the rear door and hid on the floor of the backseat. Homeboy came back from paying for his gas and he was ready to go. He put in a Young Jeezy CD and started jammin' to Jeezy and Akon's "Soul Survivors". He left the gas station's parking lot and hit the Beltway 8 feeder road, and as soon as Jeezy grunted out an exaggerated "Yeaahhhh," Winnie pops up out of the back like a jack-in-the-box.

"Park this muthafuckin' truck if you wanna live, nigga!" Winnie said menacingly, pointing the gun at the dude's head so he could see it in the rearview. Dude was so startled that the scream that tried to jump from his lungs got caught in his throat and he started coughing.

"Pull this bitch over and turn that shit down!" Winnie demanded.

"Where?" The dude asked nervously while trying to think of some way to save himself.

"Here, nigga, right here!" Winnie yelled, pointing to the side of the road. The scared driver pulls to the shoulder.

"Now, if you cooperate, you live. If you do something stupid, you might make the news. Now, take off everything you have on and set it right here," Winnie said, pointing to the passenger seat.

"Man, you can have *all* this shit. I ain't doin' no trippin'," the dude said, trying to sound cool and calm, all the while knowing he was about to shit on himself from the fear that had taken over. He was thinking about snatching the door open and jumping out of the car, but Winnie sensed his hesitation and punched him in the back of the neck, literally knocking that idea right out of his head.

"Hurry up, stupid, don't play with yo' life!" Winnie yelled.

After dude stripped, Winnie duct-taped his mouth, hands and eyes, then he drug him back to the cargo space of the truck, where he taped his ankles together.

"Let me see what you workin' with," Winnie said, searching the clothes and finding $950, a diamond piece-and-chain, a diamond bezel Aqua Master and a nice pinky ring. On top of all of that, he had some new Timbs and an outfit. Plus, Winnie figured the rims on this truck could net him at least fifteen hundred if he could find someone to buy them quickly enough. Winnie knew he had to move fast.

"Take a ride with me, young boy."

Winnie drove back to the gas station and pulled to the rear of the building. He put on dude's blue button-up, pulled the stocking cap down over his face and put on dude's Astros ball cap.

"Stay here, I'll be right back," Winnie said facetiously, knowing good and damn well dude couldn't go anywhere.

When he walked in the door of the convenience store, he reached down and pulled the corner of the rug just so to keep the door open.

"Hey, what are you...?" The middle-aged white service attendant's question was answered when he saw that Winnie's face was covered with a stocking, and that a gun was pointed at him.

"Put all the money in a bag, and don't do nothin' stupid!" Winnie yelled, running up to the counter and pointing the fake gun with a bandanna tied over it at the other customers, who were frozen in fear.

"Everybody put they wallets and purses on the counter!"

They obeyed. Fear gave them no choice. The store attendant knew the routine: cooperate. He put all the cash from the register in the bag. Winnie gestured for him to put the wallets and purses in the bag, too. He laughed to himself, thinking, *Shit, I could do this every weekend.* He got away, $2,657.00 richer.

******

Winnie's robbing spree went on for a couple of weeks, and at the same time, Mo struggled to move his work. He found several spots to hustle, but every time he started getting money and hitting a few licks back-to-back, it was always the same thing: Houston niggas ran him off.

"What's up, lil' daddy? Where you from?" they'd ask, looking at the tattooed map of the state of Louisiana under Mo's eye.

"N'awlins," Mo would reply.

"And you tryin' to get paper right here? Naw, homie, niggas got mouths to feed out here. You gotta move around with that shit."

Mo didn't have a choice. He knew what the consequences would be if he didn't, and he wasn't strong enough to go to war. This shit was getting annoying. Mo discussed his problems with Winnie, and Winnie agreed.

"These Houston niggas think they too fuckin' fly," Winnie told Mo one day after he'd been run off for the umpteenth time, "They think they can't be touched."

"Hell, yeah," Mo agreed, exhaling a thick plume of weed smoke. Thinking in terms of murder, death and killing, Winnie said, "I'll give these niggas what they looking for."

"All I'm saying is, goddamn, it's enough money out here for everybody to eat. Fuck it, whodie, we oughta just get our own crew together and take over one of these spots that be boomin'."

"That's what I'm talkin' 'bout. Fuck these Houston-ass niggas. I don't like these niggas. They don't wanna let us in. We'll tear the door off the muthafuckin' hinges, burn this bitch down if we have to. We ain't got shit to lose..."

"...but everything to gain," Mo adds, feeling much less irritated and more confident. It's cold but it's fair, and the streets is hard.

Chapter Four: ...FINDERS SCORE

"Hold the wheel steady, man, damn!" Fatso yells at Prince.

"I'm tryin'!" Prince yells back irritably. "I got this, man, just chill."

Fatso sighs heavily. "Maybe I *could* chill if you'd stop drivin' like we in a fuckin' bumper car," he said, trying to calm down and work with his lil' brother.

He had to admit that Prince was getting a little better at driving, this being only his second time whippin' the hoop around the 'hood. Since Prince had told Fatso about the car old man Willie was selling, Fatso agreed to let Prince drive sometimes, even though he would actually have to teach him.

"Just relax, man, and try to focus on the road 'cause if you crash my car *I'ma* focus on kickin' yo' ass." Fatso's tone was playful, but he was serious.

"Don't worry, Fats, I'm chillin'. Let's go by the park," Prince says, finally expressing what's been on his mind ever since he'd climbed behind the wheel.

"A'ight, pull over. I'll drive." Fatso answers.

"Nah, lemme drive. I got it," Prince says quickly.

Fatso looks at Prince like he'd left his mind at home. Prince turns on the turn signal, pulls up to a stop sign, looks both ways and whips a left turn with one finger inside the steering wheel. Fatso busts out laughing.

"Ha-ha. Oh, I see now. You wanna pull up at the park, because you hope Tamara is there to see you rollin'," Fatso says as if he'd solved a crime.

"Wrong," Prince retorts.

"Oh, I'm wrong, huh?"

"Yeah, you're wrong. I *know* Tamara's gonna be there so she can see me rollin', yeah, and when I take her for a ride I'ma tell you what it's like to get some coochie," Prince answers, smiling. Fatso thinks about it. The park is not *that* far.

"A'ight, let's go! But uh, you late, Peachfuzz. You can't tell me nothin' about no coochie. And who still calls it coochie, anyway?"

When Prince pulled the old Impala into the Orleans apartment complex, the basketball court was jumpin'. There were all kinds of people hanging out; girls in their late teens and even girls in their early twenties were out there flirting with the homies, young and old, just tryin' to get that attention. But if you were dressed to impress, smellin' good, talkin' fly, piece-and-chained up, whippin' somethin' with either some candy paint or some swangas on it, then those same girls were tryin' to get way more than just some attention. This is the land of a/c, where brothas is cool than a muthafucka and the sistas is just as fly, slick talkin' and on top of their game; where the youngstas learn too early and the old school cats don't know when to quit; where runnin' game is a way of life and it was a shame if you had none; where material possessions determined if you was about anything and trumped all else, so that was what all the young guys and girls were truly concerned about.

Prince, excited and nervous all at once, drove slowly, hunched over the steering wheel. He realized he had never driven with this many people so close to the car, and he didn't wanna hit nobody because that would be a mess and he'd never hear the end of it. He couldn't even take his eyes from the wheel long enough to look for Tamara, so this whole experience was already proving to be the total opposite of what he'd imagined. He knew his cool points were being depleted fast when he heard this twenty-something sista who wore tight jeans, a spandex tube top and some door-knocker earrings and leaning up against a brotha on a burgundy Fleetwood say, "Look at that lil' boy tryin' to learn how to drive."

Damn, Prince thought to himself, *is it that obvious?*

"Man, you see her?" Prince asks Fatso, trying to ignore what he'd just heard.

Fatso smirked. He'd heard what the girl had said, but he decided to leave it alone.

"Nah, man, just pull over here and park so we can see what's up. It looks like they got a good game going," Fatso says while looking towards the court. A bunch of people were crowded around the full court watching an urban street battle take place. These games of four-on-four basketball were more than just fun.

Some of these cats had money on these games, side bets and all, so when you step on that court, you better be working with something and playing like your ghetto pass depends on it.

Prince gets nervous again when he thinks about parking.

"Shit!"

"What?" Fatso asks.

"Man, I'ma just pull over right here on the grass."

"That's what I just said, Prince. What the hell is wrong with you?"

Prince ignores Fatso and pulls into a spot on the grass between a Buick and a Cadillac. When Prince hops out with the keys in his hand, he immediately sees a group of his friends from school walking his way. He also sees Tamara, the whole reason he was there. He steps back and taps the horn real quick to get her attention, but everyone but the ballplayers look over to see what was going on. Oops.

Tamara and her best friend, Kesha, turn to see Prince waving them over, and Prince's boys run up on him when they see him on the driver's side.

"What's the deal, P? Who load this is?" Lil' Mac asks, sizing up Fatso's Impala like he's about to drop cash for it right then and there.

Prince looks at Fatso nervously, and Fatso can read his brother's mind.

"Mine," Prince says casually, dangling the keys in his hand like a proud owner.

"Lemme drive around the parking lot!" Ronnie quickly demands. He's the youngest of the bunch and the most irresponsible.

"Hell, naw!" Prince barks. "When yo' lil' ass crash, who gon' pay for it?"

Aw, nigga, you actin' funny," Ronnie pouts, walking away. "Don't nobody wanna drive that raggedy piece of shit no way."

"Why you ask, then, fool?" Prince yells, and his crew laughs. He sees Tamara and Kesha coming his way.

"Say, I'ma get wit' y'all fools in a minute. Lemme holla at Tamara right quick," he says, trying to rush them away.

"Ah, this nigga wanna try to get his lil' rusty ass mack on," Boo-bo teases with a smile, then he becomes serious. "Nah, nigga, we ain't leavin'."

"Oh yeah we is, nigga," Big Baby says, turning to eyeball Boo-bo.

"You finna give me my twenty dollars back or it's gonna be a chunk fest out this hoe!" Big Baby is the fat boy of the clique; he's smart, stays on top of his hustle and cool than a muthafucka, but he don't take no shit, either.

"Nigga, I told you I was gon' give you that. You ain't gotta keep sweatin' me about it," Boo-bo spits back.

"Well, let's get to it, 'den. Stop bullshittin' nigga, I'm hungry. I told y'all niggas I'ma buy some pizzas for us wit' 'dat."

Boo-bo looks at Big Baby and then at Prince.

"Prince, we gonna holla at you, dog," he says while giving daps to Prince and then to the rest of the crew.

Two fly ass young girls, Tamara and Kesha, walk up. They are fast as hell from hanging around and learning from the older chicks. Tamara is developed like a grown woman with her full lips, breasts, hips, and a big, round booty that had a lot of brothas trippin and forgetting about them statutory rape laws. She wears her natural silky brown hair in a layered perm down past her shoulders, and she has that pretty light brown sugar colored skin and an around-the-way-girl attitude that wouldn't stop. Prince was infatuated with this girl.

"Hey, Prince," Kesha said flirtatiously, then, looking at Fatso, "What's up, *Duh*-wayne?" Kesha was being messy; she knew Tamara had a crush on Prince. It was all in good fun, though; Kesha wasn't interested in either Prince or Fatso. She liked older dudes.

Prince was equally uninterested. "What's up, Kesha?" Fatso nods, already annoyed. He'd always had mixed feelings about Kesha. They all went to school together, and yeah, he thought she was cute, but she was just annoying. Tamara shot a look at Kesha that said, *"Bitch"*.

"What's up, T? What's going on with you? I thought you'd be up here," Prince enthusiastically said to Tamara.

Tamara smiled. "Let me find out you checkin' for me," she quipped, then, noticing Fatso's car, "Who's hoodoo you drivin'?"

"Why it gotta be a hoodoo?" Prince asked, thinking, *There she go with that flyer-than-thou attitude.*

Fatso looks at Tamara and Kesha venomously. He knows they're about to start talking shit about his lil' ride, and he wants to walk away, but he thinks to himself, *I might have to talk bad to these lil tramps.*

Kesha replies, "Because it is. Look at that dingy paint."

"And it ain't got no rims," Tamara points out.

"No rims, no paint, and it's old. That makes it a what...?" Kesha asks as if they are contestants on a game show, and on cue, the girls look at each other and say, *"...a hoodoo!"* they scream in unison, high-fiving each other and chuckling like it's an inside joke.

Fatso is getting pissed. "Come on, Prince, let's go. Fuck 'em."

"Aw, somebody's feelings is hurt," Kesha remarks sarcastically.

Attempting to defuse the situation, Tamara says with a smile and a wink, "It's okay, y'all, damn! We just playin'. Prince, you still a cutie. You just gotta step your whip game up, boo." With that, the two girls turn and head back towards the court where some of the other older girls and guys were hanging out. Prince nods and smiles as they walk away. He hated to see her go but he loved to watch her walk away.

"Damn, that girl is *fine*!" exclaims Prince. "I gotta have her, Fatso."

"Kesha gets on my nerves!" Fatso says, irritated and in his own frame of mind. "Come on, man, let's get back and cut the yard for Mama before it gets too late."

******

"Shit!" Prince exclaims as he throws the Play Station controller down onto his bed. "I can't beat this mission for nothin'!" he explodes, referring to one of the many individual criminal objectives on *Grand Theft Auto: San Andreas.*

"I know you'd better keep your voice down, 'cause if Mama wakes up that's gonna be another mission you can't beat," Fatso says, picking up the controller and flopping down on his bed to start a new game.

"Mama in there knocked out, bro…what you talkin' 'bout?" Prince retorts as he gets up to peek out the bedroom door to make sure he's not lying to himself.

"Say, Fatso," Prince begins, closing the door and walking back into the room, "why you really think Mama keep that lock on the attic door?"

"You back on *that* shit again?"

"You *know* you wanna know what's up there."

"Man, Mama just told us again the other day to stay away from her attic. You trippin'," Fatso says dismissively.

"Why? Why she say 'dat? She ain't said nothing about that attic in I don't know how long. Plus, there's a lock on the door, so what's the point in sayin' anything about it?"

"She probably know you can pick that damn lock."

"It's somethin' up there."

"Obviously, and it ain't none of our business."

"Why you think she know I can pick that lock? Why you say that?"

"'Cause she knows you're bad, fool. She knows I wouldn't do nuthin' like that," Fatso answers, smiling.

Prince shakes his head. "That's messed up. Everything *we* do, *I* get the blame."

"And you know why. *You* be da one startin' shit. Mama ain't stupid, dog."

Prince sits quietly for about thirty seconds as Fatso plays the game.

"Let's go up there."

"Man, I'm not messin' wit' that attic."

"Mama ain't gon' know, she don't even hardly go up there."

"You trippin'."

"Plus, if she finds out, who's gonna get the blame?" Prince asks, already knowing the answer. Fatso ignores Prince and keeps playing the game. Truth be told, Fatso really does want to know what's up there and he knows Prince can pick that lock without damaging it at all, but damn! He's always pushin' the envelope; always into some shit. He cuts his eyes at Prince and Prince knows that he's thinking about it.

"Come on, man, we gonna be quiet," Prince insists in a whisper as if they're already in the attic.

"What you mean 'we'? *You* goin' up there, not me," Fatso says. He can't believe he is conceding to his little brother again. "I'll watch the door, just in case." Prince thinks about it for a second. He'd hoped Fatso would come up with him, but Fatso was right. He *should* watch the door.

"All right," Prince agrees, then goes into Fatso's closet and digs around on the floor, pulls up the rug and grabs a small set of wires. "Come on."

Within minutes, Prince has the U-shaped Master lock off the door and is quietly tiptoeing up the stairs. "Hurry up," Fatso whispers to Prince, who is fiddling around in the dark trying to find the pull-string that would turn on the light.

"Got it." *Click.* Light fills the small stairwell and the storage space above.

Prince doesn't waste any time; his curiosity level and the adrenaline pumping through his veins are on high. Fatso closes the door behind him. When Prince gets upstairs he can see where Mama has pushed rows of the insulation to the side so she can walk around. There are old clothes sticking out of trash bags, as well as a couple of trunks that resemble treasure chests with old, rusted-out locks on them. Prince wonders where they came from and considers picking those locks too, but he just takes it all in. It's like another world up there. He hardly recognizes anything, and it smells old and dusty. Prince again wonders where all this stuff comes from and why Mama was so adamant about keeping them out of there. He tiptoes over to the trunks. The floor squeaks loudly, stopping Prince in his tracks. *Silence.* Heart beating. He looks at one of the trunks; the lock is rusted-out and dusty, and they would be so easy to pick that they'd might as well not even be there. He stoops down on one knee and tries to move it, which is much easier said than done because the thing is heavy. *How'd this even get up here,* Prince muses to himself. *What's in there?* Determined to fulfill this mission, he turns and looks around.

"What is Mama hiding?" he whispers aloud. Then he spots something he hadn't noticed before: a brown wooden chest of drawers hidden in the shadows behind the half-wall with the handrail used to climb the short set of stairs. Prince gingerly walks over to it and finds a small chair nearby. In the top drawer, he finds an old photo album with pictures of people he'd never before seen. Some of the photographs reveal a young lady who looked as if she could have been a much younger version of his grandmother standing with a tall, dark-skinned man who had scary eyes. But somehow, they looked happy. *Is this what Mama was hiding?* He continues to flip through the photo album, coming to pictures of some little girls, and he instantly knew that he was looking upon pictures of his mother for the first time in his life. *The other girl must be Aunt Sandra,* he thought, *but why would Mama hide this stuff?* He begins to wonder what else she's hiding, and he feels himself start to get angry.

Chapter Five: SECRETS ALIVE

The other drawers contain strange-looking objects, antiques, and books written in French and in titles he couldn't pronounce. Then he comes to the bottom drawer, but when he opens it, there is only one thing inside: a cherry-wood box with a big red ruby set into the lid. It's about the size of a shoebox but not quite as tall. He pulls it out of the drawer and places it onto the floor, and then he opens it. Thinking he heard something, he freezes. Suddenly, fear rushes through his body again, and he is unable to move. He looks at the box and, taking two deep breaths, tells himself to calm down. Inside the box are several items, and he first pulls out a very expensive-looking book. He then discovers that there is a second, thicker book, and he debates on which one to explore first. The two books have identical leather-type covers with no titles. The smell of leather and wood rises from the box as Prince opens the thinner book. The words *Book of Gris-Gris* jump out at him from the first page.

"What the hell is *gris-gris*?" Prince wonders aloud, pronouncing the word "grizz-grizz" when the actual French pronunciation is "gree-gree."

As he thumbs through the book, he finds that it is something like a recipe book, with symbols and signs by the title of each new recipe. He again looks inside the box to see the dried chicken's foot, a rabbit's foot and yet another book. He quickly flips through that book, which resembles a Bible; it doesn't interest him at all. He gets up and steps back over to the stairwell and whispers loudly,

"Fatso...Fatso!" The door opens slightly, and Fatso pokes his head inside and nods his head slightly. *What's up?*

"Come up here, I gotta show you somethin'," Prince whispers, waving for Fatso to come up and join him. Fatso waves back for Prince to come down.

"Come on, man, you gotta see this," Prince whispers again, no longer nervous at all. Fatso disappears for a second, then reappears as he silently creeps up the stairs.

Fatso is also stunned after reviewing what Prince had to show him. He again looks at the pictures as Prince flips back through the book of *Gris-Gris*.

"What you wanna do with this?" Prince asks, very fascinated with the book.

"What you mean? We can't do *nuthin'* with it. We can't move any of this stuff. What is you thinkin'?" Fatso asked incredulously. He waited in silence for a moment, then he looks down at Prince sitting on the floor, mesmerized.

"What's that?"

"Man, look at this," Prince says, handing Fatso the book.

Fatso looks at the symbol next to the title of the *gris-gris* recipe Prince had been reading. "Rabbit's foot," he muses. "Wait...what is *that?*" Fatso asks suspiciously, pointing at another diagram on the same page.

Prince giggles. "It looks like a man and a woman freakin'."

Fatso smiles. "Hell yeah, that's exactly what it looks like." He reads the short description below the title that confirms their speculation. "This is a sex potion, an aphrodisiac," Fatso explains as he looks over the ingredients.

"Hell yeah, shit, let's make some," Prince suggests, as if it is a recipe for an omelet.

"There's shit on here I ain't never even heard of, but there is also stuff we can get at the grocery store, too," Fatso says, still looking over the ingredients. He looks at Prince with hope in his eyes, and Prince reads the look perfectly.

"Let's make it," Prince says deviously.

"I think we can."

"Should we take the book?" Prince asks. Fatso shakes his head.

"Nah, let's leave it up here until we need it, then we'll come back and copy everything down. The main stuff that's gonna be hard to get are mandrake, whatever that is, pure Jamaican rum, and—get this shit—a rabbit's heart."

"Damn."

"The rest of the ingredients we can get easily, but the hard part is making it." Suddenly, they heard a toilet flush downstairs.

"Oh, shit, Mama's up," His eyes were as wide as two half-dollars. Suddenly regretting this whole thing, Fatso quickly puts the book back inside the box and quickly places it back into the drawer. He begins to step towards the stairs, but Prince stops him by grabbing the legs of his shorts.

"Don't move, she'll hear you."

They both remain still for the next two minutes, then five minutes, listening so intently that they could have heard mice making babies, and they thought they did. *Silence.*

"Let's go."

In the next minute they are back in Fatso's room with a whole new kind of excitement on their minds. Prince is mainly thinking of Tamara along with a few other choice honeys who decorated the hallways of Worthing High School. Fatso, on the other hand, is thinking of putting together a new creation, a potion. Some sort of concoction that would give him power over people. He was so fascinated by it that he didn't know what to do with himself.

Prince and Fatso sat up all night talking about their plans, and they paid for it the next day at school—they could barely keep their eyes open, but they didn't care; they were on a mission. Fatso goes to the library and checks the internet and finds out that in this state, mandrake is known as Jimson Weed. While he is online, he also does a search to find out where in Houston he can find some. There is an exotic botanical in Midtown, which hardly surprises him because it is an uppity, yet eccentric part of town.

Fatso and Prince jet over there after school, and while there, they find out from the long-haired hippie—and obvious weed head—cashier who was passing himself off as a botanical specialist that Bacardi 151 is just about the strongest rum out there, and even though it's a Puerto Rican rum instead of Jamaican, it should definitely serve its purpose.

"The last tough ingredient, a rabbit," Prince says as they ride away from the botanical.

"I told you," Fatso replies while driving down Montrose Avenue. "I'll buy all the other ingredients but *you* gotta get the rabbit."

"I ain't trippin'. Just take me to a pet store and I'll steal one," Prince says confidently. His brother knows he doesn't have any money saved up like he does from cooking all that dope for the boys in the 'hood, but Prince is willing to do whatever it took to make it happen.

Fatso sighs. "If that's what you gotta do..."

"That's what I'ma *have* to do 'cause I don't know nobody in the 'hood with no damn rabbit!" Prince exclaimed.

Fatso thinks about what his brother is saying, and if he gets caught tryin' to steal a big-ass fancy rabbit, it would open up a whole can of worms.

"Fuck it, I'll buy it," Fatso declares. Prince tries to hide his smile.

"But you owe me big time, kid," Fatso admonishes.

Prince has conquered again. "It won't be the first time," he quips.

They go to a pet store to price a rabbit and tell them they'll be back Saturday to pick it up. Saturday comes and Prince and Fatso take off to the organic grocery store with a foreign grocery list. Their plan is to hide everything and then put it all together Sunday when Mama goes to church. They are also hoping that Auntie San is not back by then.

******

Like clockwork, Mama wakes them up bright and early on Sunday morning.

"Rise and shine, boys!" she sings. The boys know what time it is, but they ain't tryin' to hear it, so they play sleep and feign illness. Mama ain't havin' none of it.

"Fatso! Princey! Wake up, now. Y'all goin' to church with me today."

"Aw, Mama..." Fatso groans and chokes up two or three good coughs. "I don't feel good. I think it's a bug floatin' around."

On cue, Prince joins in. "Me, too, Mama," he says in the worst morning voice he can conjure up. "I think Fatso got me sick, too."

"Don't blame me," Fatso snaps.

"It's your fault!" Prince retorts.

"It ain't!"

"It is!" they exclaim as they simultaneously break out in fits of coughing as if the mere act of word swapping has taken so much out of them.

"Oh, Lord, you babies don't sound too good," Mama Francine says, thinking that she should probably stay home. "But I know this *better* not be no act to get outta Sunday service. I know y'all think y'all slick...*Princey*!" Mama says loudly, identifying her main suspect.

"No, ma'am," Prince responds.

"Come on now, Mama," Fatso pleads. "I just wanna try to sleep this off so I don't have to miss any school this week." That was all he needed to say. Mama was serious about school, even more serious than she was about church.

"Well, all right. Y'all get some rest. Fatso, you make a can of soup when you get up and I'll bring you two some church dinners, okay?" The boys nod.

"Besides, your auntie should be comin' home sometime today. I need to talk to her about these disappearing acts, so y'all tell her to stay put until we talk," Mama ordered. Fatso and Prince both nod and exchange glances. *This* could be a problem.

They give their grandmother time to get ready and pull out of the driveway before they jump into action. They've already agreed that they were doing this, regardless of the now-doubled risk of being caught due to the impending return of Auntie Sandra. Prince picks the lock to the attic and retrieves the book of *gris-gris*. Fatso immediately starts copying down the recipe for rabbit's foot word for word while he gives directions to Prince. Within twenty minutes Mama's kitchen is converted to Fatso's laboratory. Prince is happily playing Igor, the evil assistant.

"What's next, Fatster?" Prince asks, humorously turning his brother's nickname into an combo of "Fatso" and "Master." Fatso doesn't think it's funny.

"Chill out man, everything is going. We need the rabbit's heart."

Prince, continuing to impersonate Igor, rubs his hands together mischievously. He's getting a kick out of this. "Yes, yes, the rabbit."

"Who's gonna kill it?"

"I am."

"*And* get the heart out?"

Prince doesn't answer; he just giggles under his breath and walks out of the garage. This is the hardest part for Fatso, but Prince enjoys sick shit like this. Within minutes, Prince has placed his Louisville slugger against the wall and pulling the dead rabbit out of the bag to be dismembered.

"It's dead, c'mon," he says.

Fatso looks at the book. "Wait. Put it down on the floor. We gotta say this prayer over it."

Prince sets the rabbit's limp body down, Fatso hands him the book and reads from his copy. The prayer or chant is in French and English and it reads like a request from some goddess. Fatso just reads it and pronounces it the best he can, but of course Prince gets all dramatic and otherworldly with it, changing his voice and all. This is clearly fun and games for him. Soon, the short chant is finished.

"You think it worked?"

Fatso shrugs. "I don't know. We're just doing what the book says."

"Let's go. It's gonna work."

Prince grabs the rabbit and goes into the backyard with a butcher knife and his grandmother's old rubber dish gloves to handle the bloody work. Playing overseer, Fatso admonishes Prince to be careful.

"You don't want to damage the heart. It's probably real small. And keep all the blood on the plastic." They spread two trash bags on the back patio with newspaper overlaying.

Prince rolls his eyes skyward. "I am, man, damn. Stop sweatin' me. You makin' me nervous...now, where is his heart?" Prince asks, pointing the knife at the rabbit's soft underbelly. "Here?"

"Start there. Cut it open, and we'll find it."

Within ten minutes, the small heart was boiling in pure spring water and Bacardi 151, and in two hours they have the rabbit's heart, coconut, oysters, jimson weed and other ingredients chopped up in little pieces, mixed together and spread out on a cookie sheet, which will then go into the oven so it will all dry out. They clean up their mess and put the book of *gris-gris* back in the attic. Knowing Mama would be home soon, after about an hour of the grisly ingredients "baking" in the oven, Fatso pulls them out and stirs them around so they wouldn't stick to the pan and lets the mixture dry before they put it in a large plastic container.

"All we gotta do now is grind it down to a powder and make the pills with the honey," explains Fatso in a nervous whisper.

Prince smiles."We can do that when Mama takes her nap."

"I just hope Auntie San don't show up by then."

"Yeah, I know. Fatso, you think Mama used to make some of this stuff back in the day?"

Fatso shrugs again. "I don't know; I doubt it. But then again, why'd she have it?"

"Exactly. I *don't* doubt it. Mama was probably wild back in the day, getting her groove on." Prince says, convinced that his grandmother had led a totally different life when she was younger.

"Shut up, man! You nasty, dog. I can't see Mama like that, or messin' with no shit like this. Maybe Aunt Sandra, though. Now come on, let's finish cleaning up before Mama gets home."

******

"What's that smell in here?" Mama Francine demands to know as soon as she walks in the front door. Prince and Fatso are upstairs in Fatso's room playing *Madden '05 Live*. They look at each other, then hop up and go downstairs.

"Ma'am?" Fatso says as if he hadn't heard her.

"What is that smell? Is your aunt here?" Mama places the plastic bag containing two aluminum-wrapped Styrofoam plates on the kitchen counter and looks around.

"No ma'am. I was hungry so Fatso tried to make us some food..." Prince answers.

"...soup. And fried bologna sandwiches. But they burnt," Fatso quickly adds.

"See there, now I *told* y'all I was gon' brang you boys some plates from church. That's why y'all need to go to church. Y'all hardheaded."

"We still hungry, Mama," Prince says, unwrapping his semi-warm plate of yams, greens, fried chicken and cornbread.

"You better be. And that don't smell like no bologna, either. You sure your auntie ain't been here?" Mama presses.

"Yes, ma'am," answers Fatso while grabbing a fork from the silverware drawer.

"Hmmm...well, I'm going to take myself a nap, so you wake me up if she comes home, ya hear?"

"Yes, ma'am," Fatso nods before shoveling a forkful of collard greens into his mouth. The fact that they were starving was one thing they didn't lie about.

After they eat and let Mama Francine get good into her nap, they go to the backyard to retrieve the mixture that was drying in the sun and take it into the garage. With mama's salt and pepper grinders they spend the next two hours grinding the dried-up mixture into a fine powder and smashing the viscous raw honey into the powder to roll the thick, hard dough into almost seventy little balls that resembled pills. They then put the pills in Fatso's closet to dry until the next day, and Prince wraps a little of the leftover powder into a piece of paper and stuffs it into his pocket.

Later that same day as they are playing their video games, about to fall asleep from the sheer exhaustion caused by all they work they'd put in that day, Prince suddenly says,

"Fatso, I got an idea. Check it out."

Fatso was all too familiar with his brother's "ideas."

"Aw, shit!"

"Naw, man, look…let's call it 'Ball'," Prince says, smiling.

Fatso thinks for a moment. "I guess we *shouldn't* call it by its real name, huh?"

"Naw, that's just in case Mama or somebody recognizes that name, plus, they look like lil' balls. And when it jumps off, we gonna ball."

"Rabbit's foot, I don't think I'd forget that, shit, we don't even know if it works."

"Shut up, man, it's gonna work. We did everything right."

"Yeah, I hope so. We'll see. I'm tired, man, and we gotta go to school tomorrow," Fatso says, rolling over in his bed.

"One more thing."

"What?"

"We gotta go to the park tomorrow."

Fatso laughs. "First patient?"

Prince laughs, also. "Already."

"We'll see what it do."

"Bet." Prince turns on regular television and closes his eyes to try and sleep, but all he can think of is Tamara.

Chapter Six: GIRL GIMME DAT...

Later that night, Jewel returns to her mother's house. As soon as she enters, she inhales deeply, and with her sensitive nostrils she detects something different in the air, yet, something very familiar. She looks around in the dark and smiles. Jewel heads upstairs, following her senses to Fatso and Prince's room. She opens the door and steps inside, and immediately her acute senses go into the red. She smiles again. The boys seem to be sleeping but she knows better. Fatso was in his twin size bed, and Prince was on the floor in front of the TV.

"I know you guys aren't asleep," Jewel says softly. They don't move, and she continues, "I want you to know that I love the both of you. Anything you need, any questions you may have, I am here for you. I owe you that," she says. She knows that they can hear her.

Prince takes a deep breath, sighs heavily, and rolls over. Jewel watches them for a few moments then walks out, closing the door behind her.

After a few minutes, Prince opens his eyes. He crawls to the side of Fatso's bed and yanks on his blanket.

"I heard her," Fatso whispers.

"What do you think she meant?" Prince asks excitedly.

"I don't know."

"You think she knows?"

"She knows *something*."

"She ain't trippin', though."

"I know. It's like she knows something and she's cool with it."

Prince thinks for a few seconds.

"I don't think those were Mama's books."

"Me, either."

"I don't think she'll say nothin'."

"Nah, like she said, when we need her, we'll holla at her."

"A'ight."

"Now take ya ass to sleep."

******

They spend their next day at school prospecting which of their friends and girls they're gonna share their secret with. Both are anxious to test the results. In science class, during an experiment, Prince tells his friend Jason about what he'd found in Mama's attic and what he made with it. Jason wants to try it; Prince has another customer.

When they get home, Mama is in her flower bed in the front yard, spreading fertilizer and watering the yard. They run a few errands for her and pretend to knock out what little bit of homework they have, then they check out their product "Ball," which is drying out under Fatso's bed. It's ready. Fatso and Prince both wrap a couple of the hardened pills in a piece of notebook paper and stick it in their pockets.

"All right, Mama, you need anything else? We were gonna head to the park," Fatso says walking down the stairs, Prince behind him.

"That homework had better be done," Mama challenged.

"It is. I finished mines and helped Prince with his."

"Your auntie ran off again."

"She'll be back," Prince states knowingly.

"How do you know?" Mama asks quizzically.

"I just know."

"Hmm…well, all right y'all go ahead. Be careful." Mama finishes her lemonade and gets ready to take a bath.

******

When Prince and Fatso pull up to the park in the '83 Impala, there's a tournament getting started. The tournament, called the Elmore, was an annual athletic tournament that took place in Houston in tribute to Lajuan Moore, an all-star athlete who broke his neck in an accident during a Sharpstown High School football game in '99. The tournament placed emphasis on safety in sports. A few teams are posted up with their ghetto sponsors by the sidelines getting a few words of thug motivation. Quiet as it's kept, these are some of the best street ballers in the city. Most of them just couldn't stick with the strict regimen required by the college and professional teams, so here they are, doing what they do, fulfilling their need to belong.

Fatso parks the car on the grass and they hop out. There are a lot of people out there; the 'hood has been waiting for this tourney to kick off, but these are just the preliminary warm-up games, so most people are just waiting until the party really gets going. Tamara and Kesha both stay in the Orleans apartments, so it's almost guaranteed that they will be there for the tournament. True to form, Prince finds Tamara over by a picnic table, flirting with one of the guys who was getting ready to start his game. He is older and is blatantly ignoring her for two reasons. One, this is the 'hood and even though Tamara is fine, in his eyes she's still the same bad-ass lil' girl she's always been. Two, his own girl is supposed to be comin' through and he ain't tryin' to get no shit started. But of course, none of that puts a stop to Tamara's flirting.

"Say, what's up, T?" Prince calls out with a smile on his face. "What's goin' down wit' you? What up Keesh?"

"Hey, Prince, ain't nothin', jus' tryin' to eat somethin' before I starve and before this game starts!" Tamara answers, raising her voice so Jimmy, the older cat barbecuing the burgers and hot links, can catch the hint that he needs to come on with the come on.

Kesha teasingly calls out, "What's up with you, Fatso, you not gonna speak to me today?"

Fatso smiles. "What's up with it, girl?"

Kesha flirtatiously responds, "See, now that wasn't so hard. Tamara, he has a cute smile! You should try that more often, Dwayne."

Dismissively, Tamara says, "Mmm-hmm." Then, yelling over to the man on the grill, "Jimmy, could you *please* let me know when the food is ready?"

Jimmy snaps back, "I told you I'ma holla at you ole' crazy ass girl!"

"Hmmph. Yeah. Whatever," Tamara mutters smartly under her breath. She looks toward the court and the new game has started. The dude she likes is already on the court.

"A'ight y'all...I'ma holla at you, Prince. We 'bout to go watch this game. C'mon, Kesha," Tamara walks off.

"A'ight, girl, I'm comin'," Kesha says. "What y'all finna do? 'Cause y'all sure come up here wit' your fly shit on," she states matter-of-factly as she gives Fatso and Prince the once-over.

"We came up here to chill and check the game like everybody else," Fatso replies.

"Yeah, and you can get off that bullshit baby 'cause you know I dress fly *everyday*." Prince retorts, dusting his shoulder off.

Kesha laughs. "Oh, boy, puh-lease...I got you...I was finna say something, but forget it," she says, walking off with a smile. Prince and Fatso check out her ass as she leaves.

"Kesha *is* kinda fine," Fatso observes as if he'd never noticed.

"What you mean 'kind of,' fool? She *is* fine. Just not fine as T." Fatso nods. "So how we gonna do this?"

Prince looks down at his fresh white K-Swiss on his feet and the denim blue Rocawear short set he's rockin, then he checks out his brother's black velour Sean John short set with the black GBX driving shoes and thinks, *Kesha was definitely flirting with my brother.*

"Let me show you how to do this, son. You thirsty?" Prince asks deviously.

"Hell yeah, I'm thirsty," Fatso replies.

"C'mon." They start walking toward the soda machine near the complex's leasing office.

"And you can't show me shit, nigga, you a sixteen-year-old virgin, remember?" Fatso says with a laugh.

"How you know that?! Just 'cause I ain't neva *told* you about it don't mean I ain't neva *had* no pussy. I ain't gotta tell you everything," Prince says, putting quarters into the machine.

"But you do. Just make this shit happen so you can join the players' club and stop actin' like you a member."

"Aw, that's cold! Damn! I ain't got no more quarters. Buy Kesha a soda, Fatso," Prince says while he opens the can of coke and dumps the powder from the ground up pill inside. He uses his finger to wipe off any sprinkles that were left on the can.

"Man, I ain't tryin' to fuck with Kesha like 'dat. She already get on my nerves."

"Well, I can't bring Tamara a soda and not bring her friend one. Then she might not want it."

"Sheeit, they better learn to share," Fatso argues.

"C'mon, man."

Fatso thinks about it. Prince *does* have a point. "A'ight," he says with a heavy sigh while digging in his pocket for change. "But don't put none of that shit in this one."

Prince chuckles mischievously. "Why not? This way we get to test two at once."

"Because if this shit works, then…"

"…then you might get some of that ass." Prince finishes with a huge grin and grabs the other soda out of the machine.

"Nah, man, just do Tamara's and we'll get to see the difference between a person who's on it and one who's not," Fatso says knowingly.

Prince sucks his teeth, and he *wants* to tell his brother that he acts like a scary-ass dude sometimes, but instead he says, "A'ight."

******

"What's up, y'all thirsty?" Prince asks as he walks up behind the girls, who were sitting courtside and watching a brutal game of four-on-four. People are yelling and starting to get rowdy as if there is some real NBA action goin' on. The one person Tamara is cheering for is really wishing she would just get lost. As Prince approaches them, Kesha turns to see him first, then Tamara.

"We brought y'all a coupla sodas."

"Oh, that's so sweet, thank you," Kesha says, taking the soda from Fatso's outstretched hand.

"Thank you," Tamara says, smiling, "how'd you know I was thirsty?"

"You're welcome," Prince and Fatso say. Prince moves in to sit next to Tamara and responds to her question. "I'm psychic."

"Believe it or not, we *do* know how to be gentlemen," Fatso says smartly, moving in next to Kesha.

"Oh, really?" Kesha semi-sarcastically asks, smiling up into Fatso's face and sipping her soda.

She's cute as hell when she's not tryin' to get on my nerves, Fatso thinks to himself. In response to Kesha's attempt at subtle sarcasm, he only smirks and says, "Yeah."

Tamara's favorite player hits a mean alley-oop dunk and people go crazy, including Tamara, who starts screaming and waving her hands, therefore spilling some of the "special" Coca-Cola, which irritates the hell out of Prince 'cause he wants her to drink every drop of that shit. The other team calls time-out and some other teams rush out onto the court to shoot around and warm up.

A tall, chubby brother tries to squeeze between the two girls and bumps Kesha's elbow, knocking her soda onto the ground. The dude apologizes to Kesha and Fatso.

"Aw, shit, my bad, baby girl. My fault, homie. You want me to buy you another one? I think I got some change in my car."

Kesha shakes her head and snaps, "Nah, nigga, but damn, you ain't no little bitty dude; you need to watch where you're going!"

"That's what *I'm* saying," Tamara adds, backing her girl up.

"Say, sweetheart, I *said* I was sorry," dude replies, getting slightly irritated.

"I heard you!" Tamara snaps. "And you heard me!"

Fatso steps in between them. "Say, homie, don't worry 'bout it. I'll get her another soda. Just go ahead and play ya game."

Dude looks at Kesha and then at Fatso. He knows this ain't his 'hood and he don't want to cause problems here.

"Say mayne, my bad about 'dat 'dere. I don't want no plex."

"Already, don't even worry 'bout it. Good luck with your game." Fatso shakes his hand and dude hits the court.

"Here, Kesha, you can have some of mine," Tamara hands the can to her friend after she herself takes a big gulp. Prince smiles and glances at Fatso whose still mad about the wasted soda.

"Fat ass ain't got no business tryin' to hoop anyway," Kesha caps, taking the can and drinking a few swallows.

Tamara laughs, "He probably can't even play a full game. Probably ain't nuthin' but a backup player with his moon-pie lookin' ass."

"Yeah, a backup for the backup," Kesha adds. They all laugh as the game resumes.

Twenty-five minutes later the game is over, and they all head back to Kesha's mom's apartment to get out of the sun for a minute. Tamara's favorite team had won, but for some reason, she wasn't all that excited about that anymore. At least not with Prince's cute ass next to her, brushin' up against her butt and touchin' her hands, actin' like it was an accident but she knew better. She couldn't explain what she was feeling. Tamara had always thought Prince was cute, but right now him being with her felt like he had turned something on inside of her she'd never felt before. Her insides were warm and tingly, her breasts felt fuller and more sensitive, and her ass felt like it was the star of its own show, about to make its big debut. She was fully aware of her vagina in a new kind of way, and she felt like busting out singing that song that Tweet wrote about touching herself.

As Kesha climbed the two flights of stairs to her second-floor apartment, Fatso is starin' at her butt with a smirk on his face. *I don't know what's about to go down or if the Ball is working but it sure seems like this shit is going in the right direction,* Fatso thought.

"Are you looking at my ass, Dwayne?" Kesha coyly asks.

"Mmm hmm."

"Good."

"How'd you know?" Fatso asks, smiling.

"Because it's hot," Kesha replies. When she gets to the top of the stairs, she stops, hikes her ass up and makes it vibrate, shakin' it every which way so fast it's as if her entire body is about to wiggle away. She then starts making her left cheek and then her right cheek bounce up and down as she walks to her door and pulls her keys out of her purse. Her skirt had risen more than halfway up her thighs, but she doesn't even bother to pull it down. She's feelin' real wild and crazy right now, like she wants to put on a real live freak show, and she's just getting started. Kesha, with her rich mahogany-brown skin, is the most sexually experienced in the group and she knows it. She doesn't know what has come over her but she likes it and she's ready to express herself. Tamara busts out laughing.

"That was impressive," Fatso says shyly.

"You like that?" Kesha asks, putting the key in the lock.

"Don't be showin' them *all* our secrets, Keesh," Tamara remarks playfully.

"You can do that?" Prince asks, standing close behind Tamara.

Tamara ignores his question. "Kesha's got a nice ass, huh?"

"I like yours better," Prince whispers in her ear.

"Oooh, say it again," Tamara moans, pushing her round softness up against Prince's crotch. He feels the pulsing sensation of that familiar hard-on. He rubs his hands on her butt, grabs her hips and pulls her into him so she can feel his hardness up against her.

"I like yours better," he repeats softly.

By the time they get inside the air-conditioned two-bedroom apartment, both girls' hot bodies have totally taken control. Before Tamara can turn around from locking the front door behind her, Kesha has already disappeared inside her bedroom with Fatso's hand in hers, dragging him onto her merry-go-round whether he wants to ride or not. After Fatso saw her do that trick with her booty, his mind is made up; he definitely wants to ride. The door closes behind them.

"They didn't waste any time, huh? I guess it's just me and you now," Tamara says with a devious smile.

"What you wanna do now?" Prince asks, already knowing what's up.

"I can show you better than I can tell you," Tamara says sexily, slowly walking over to Prince and wrapping her arms around his neck. He reaches around to palm and squeeze all that extra cushion. He'd finally reached his green light and he was ready to go; he was rock hard. They start kissing and tonguing each other down. Prince *has* had experience in this department. Tamara's tongue is hot and her hands are busy rubbing on Prince's neck and then his back. It was as if electricity was surging through her most intimate body parts and she is feeling so sexual and freaky. She grinds her pelvis up against Prince and feels that stiffness, and her pussy begins to react by becoming extra wet and tingly.

"Ooh, Prince, I want you to do it to me," Tamara whispers. "Take my panties off."

Prince already has her cheerleader skirt pulled up and his hands were on her bare ass. He grabs the top of the black cotton T-back and pulls the material out from between those cheeks. They get stuck.

"Damn you got some ass, girl," he says, twisting her hips to turn her around.

"You like it?" Tamara asks, knowing damn well he does.

"I love it," he replies. He reaches up around her hips and pulls down her panties, rubbing his hands over her smooth legs while doing so. She steps out of them and walks away, disappearing into the hallway.

"I'll be right back," she says.

Prince takes a moment to check out the apartment and figure out how they're going to do this. The crib is nice. There was a big, fluffy burgundy leather couch and love seat, brass and glass-top table and end tables with matching burgundy candy dishes and lamps with the plastic still over the shades. There's a small entertainment center below the windows on the back wall of the living room. The white mini-blinds were closed, and Prince noticed the clock on the VCR still blinking 12:00 because it hadn't been set. There's a receiver and a CD player, too, which was hooked up to some decent-looking speakers. On the plain white walls there were a few music-related pictures in brass frames. It smelled good, too, like strawberry candles. He figured the only place they could do it in there would be either on the floor in front of the TV or on the couch. Tamara resolved this issue when she came back into the living room and spread a blanket on the carpet in front of the TV like she did this shit every weekend.

"I thought I was gonna have to come find you," Prince says. Tamara smiles.

"Come here," she says, beckoning him closer to her with her finger. Prince walks over to her while he scans her body and her bare feet.

"Damn, you look sexy."

"I *feel* sexy," she replies, undoing the buttons on his shirt. "Take your clothes off."

Prince kicks his shoes off. "I can do that."

As Prince strips down to his boxers, Tamara takes off her skirt and tight shirt. No bra. Her breasts were full and perky with pert nipples. She stood there naked for a second so Prince could admire her body. He is in awe at finally seeing Tamara naked...that small waist and those thick thighs and hips; her small, slender patch of pubic hair was trimmed and neat, like a woman's should be. She lay down on the blanket and threw part of it over her legs. Her breasts exposed, she closes her eyes and rolls her head around, tweaking her nipples. Just as Prince lay down, psyching himself up by looking at her body, he hears a loud knocking against the wall. *Knock, knock, knock.* He looks at Tamara, paranoid.

"What's that?"

Tamara laughs. "That's Kesha and your brother."

"Aw, damn, that's what *I'm* talking about," Prince says, mentally giving his brother a high-five. Prince pulls his boxers off and climbs on top of Tamara. Opening her legs, he bends down and kisses her. He's nervous now, rushing. She's anxious, too.

"Mmm, I'm *so* hot," she moans. "I want you to do it to me, Prince." Prince reaches down and grabs his piece to introduce it to a heaven it's never known. He starts up at her pubic hairs, rubbing, poking around. Naw, that ain't it. Must be lower.

"Put it in me, baby," Tamara begs, rolling her hips and trying to quench this overwhelming sensation she's experiencing. Her whole body is tingling. Her wetness is literally dripping out of her. Prince takes it lower, much lower. Tamara, lays back on her full, round booty and throws her flexible legs back, her juices moisturizing her backdoor. Prince, thinking he's hit his target, pushes.

"No, baby, that's not it!" Tamara exclaims, eyes wide open in shock. Then it hits her: *this is his first time.*

"Let me do it," she says, then reaches down and grabs him in her hand. "This is nice." She playfully smiles up at him like she's test-driving a new car.

She guides him inside of her. "Right here."

Prince pushes himself inside her.

"Ahh, ssss, that's it, baby," she moans. Catching his rhythm, he goes in and out, in and out, thinking to himself, *Damn, this shit feels good. So this is what niggas be talkin' 'bout. Hell, yeah!*

Not knowing his cover is blown, he whispers to Tamara, "It's kinda tight."

Tamara lets him have his moment. "You like it?"

"Hell, yeah."

"Well, do it to me, baby. Do it hard. I want you...I want you to be my man," she whispers, and even though she is surprised at what she said, she meant every word. She wraps her arms and legs up around his back and squeezes him. He pushes inside her three times as hard as he can before that heat explodes from his piece like fireworks. He stiffens up.

"Wait," he grunts. He doesn't want to cum inside of her but it feels too good to stop.

"No, no, no, don't stop." She continues to squeeze him and grinds her hips into him. She is this close to walking into the light herself. She screams, "Don't stop, don't stop, ohhhh, ohhhh!!!" Prince feels her pussy contracting around him, and he's shrinking, but he ain't moving. This is so hard to believe. It's like a dream. After a long pause, Prince, not knowing what to say, bursts out with,

"So…you my girl now?" Prince asks.

"Is that what you want? You want me to be your girl?"

"Yeah, that's what I want." He wants to explain more, to tell her that's what he'd always wanted since he'd first laid eyes on her, but he was recovering, trying to come to terms with all of this.

"Then I'm yours," she says passionately, hugging his body with hers.

Prince comes back to reality for a moment. "I hope you don't get pregnant."

"Can't. Birth control," she states matter-of-factly.

Prince is shocked and relieved. "So we can do it like this all the time?" he asks, getting excited.

"We can do it *better* than this. We can do it any way you want."

Knock, knock, knock. "Ahhhh! Ahhhh!" This time the knocking was accompanied by screams of pleasure from Kesha.

"Damn! Fatso in there tearin' Kesha's ass up!" Prince says. "I wanna do it like that."

Tamara laughs. "Well, what you waitin' for?" She shifts her hips a little bit, and he feels himself getting hard again. *Round 2.*

Prince thinks to himself, *This shit really works. I got the girl. With this Ball, me and my brother 'bout to get this money. Then we gonna have the power.* That made his dick even harder, and this time he fucked his new girlfriend like she wanted, like a G.

******

Within two weeks, Fatso and Prince had a system together, and Worthing High School and South Acres were buzzing with the word of a new high, a pill that gives you a mellow high and makes you feel freaky as hell; called Ball. It didn't take long before almost everybody was Ballin', feeling the effects and lovin' it. Fatso and Prince had the exclusive product line and the cash began rollin' in.

Chapter Seven: D-BOY REPPIN

A money-green CL500 with matching-colored Giovanni rims with the chrome deep-dish lip pulls up next to a black conversion van. The Mercedes driver signals for the van to follow him. After a short drive, they pull into a gated mechanic shop. The Mercedes parks behind the shop and the driver walks up to the van and hops in the captain's seat to the rear of the front passenger. He's greeted by four of his loyal soldiers, all of them 5th Ward hustlers, two of them specializing in enforcing D-Boy policy.

"What's up, Scat, you all right?" Big Don, an enforcer, says with a smile.

"What up, what up?" Scat says, exchanging pounds with his soldiers. "Yeah, let's ride. The shop gon' watch my car while we go check these niggas."

"Already," the driver says, pulling into the traffic on Lockwood Street.

Scat is ¼ of the young, notorious Houston dope syndicate called the D-Boys. A couple weeks prior, a worker out of Kashmere Gardens was killed. Right after that, one of Scat's sergeants reported to him that a small crew out of New Orleans was runnin' shop out of his worker's old spot. Speculation in the 'hood was that New Orleans niggas had killed the youngster and took over his spot 'cause youngsta's spot was booming, moving a lot of dope.

Now, whether they knew it or not, those New Orleans boys violated street policy in a major way. Scat was a diplomat with a military mind; all the D-Boys were. That's why they were in the position they were in, and growing. They had fairly small, but well-controlled territories right now. Scat commissioned the 5th Ward, Nore was over Midtown, Duce ran a good part of the Southwest, and Warren Lee, who had organized the D-Boy crew, ran South Acres and a good part of the Southside. Warren Lee was the governor. They were all young and aggressive, and in time, this crew would monopolize the entire city.

Within minutes, the black van slowly rolls past the infiltrated spot.

Big Don nods his head towards the small house. "That's it right there."

Scat looks, and he notices a youngster outside riding his bike up and down the street. The lookout. Scat remembered those days; it had been his first job.

"That's the lookout right there," the driver, Mack, says. Mack is a sergeant, and it was his worker that had been killed.

"Yeah, pull over right up here. Lon, go up to the door. Tell 'em you come in peace and prosperity. Ask to speak to the boss and relay this message from Scat..." Scat goes on to dictate a message filled with key words that let whoever is listening or relaying it know two things. One: this is not coming from the police, and two: the sender is dead serious. As Scat dictates his message, the lookout on the bike is now around the corner and has pulled out a two-way radio. He's doing his job.

******

Inside the house, Mo has just finished cutting and bagging four ounces and putting out his freshly-lit swisher, so the smell of dope and weed was still in the air. He turns the safety off on his Ruger P-90 and peers through the shades, expecting some dude to walk up. His lookout told him that this wasn't no dopefiend, and there he is. Black t-shirt. Baseball cap. Chain tucked in. Tattoos. Looks relaxed.

"He don't look like the alphabet boys," Mo says, just loud enough for his two guys to hear. Mo waves them over to the door to answer it, and he hears three quick knocks. Mo's worker looks through the peephole and uses his customary greeting.

"What you need?" Mo is standing against the wall near the door and the window, listening to everything.

"I come in peace, homie," Lon says, holding up his hands. "I'm here to relay a message from Scat, but I need to talk to your boss." Mo and his worker frown at each other. Mo is familiar with the name Scat, though, so he listens intently.

"Just say what ya gotta say," the worker says. Lon relays his boss' treaty.

"You got all that?" Lon asks.

"Yeah, man, I got that. I'll let him know."

"All right," Lon says, and walks back to the van. Mo starts pacing back and forth, and his blunt is lit and smoking again. He dials Winnie's number from his cell.

Within one hour, Winnie, Mo and four other guys from their growing New Orleans alliance meet up with Scat and his entourage. Mo is nervous; Winnie is fearless. Everybody there is strapped up and ready for whatever, especially Scat's boy Mack. But he's taking orders right now, not giving them, and he can respect that. He knows that more deaths are only going to slow up the cash flow and weaken this ghetto economy that they're tryin' to stimulate. It's about growth right now. Scat and the rest of the D-Boy clique have been clear on this.

In a Wendy's parking lot over double-meat and spicy chicken sandwiches with extra cheese, Scat laced the boys from the Boot on D-Boy policy and ghetto politics. He made an offer to Winnie, Mo and their crew that they would have been fools to refuse. Dead fools.

"With what I'm offering," Scat explains, "you keep your spot and any other spots in this territory that you've gained peacefully. I'll supply you all the work you need at exclusively fair prices, and I'll help your crew grow and maintain order." He let his words sink in as he confidently waited for a response. He wouldn't wait long.

Winnie didn't like the sound of the words "peacefully" or "exclusively", but from what Mo had explained earlier and what he already understood was that these were the main dudes in Houston to be down with, not opposed to, and if his crew was gonna grow and be a factor in any type of longevity, this was the very alliance they needed. They didn't really have a whole lot of options.

"What about spots outside this territory?" Winnie asked, playing the game.

"Just let me know so I can let whoever runs that territory know that some of my guys is runnin' a spot over there so we can negotiate and keep the peace. But no killing, no hostility. That would be a violation." Winnie and Mo nod in assent.

At the end of the meeting, the two crews shake hands and welcome peace. Scat knew he'd mixed a lil' bullshit into the negotiations, but hey, it is what it is. The New Orleans crew would grow; the D-Boys' crew was growing

faster. Winnie and Mo negotiated terms that they could live with.

For now.

Chapter Eight: BIG BOY STATUS

Trump International Hotel & Casino, New Orleans, 2010.

"Seven dice! We've got a winner!" the craps table attendant announces in a monotone as if he says this all day every day.

"Heyyyy!" "Yes!" "There it is!" Everyone who bet with the winner begins to celebrate as the attendant uses the black L-shaped stick he controls the table with to push the big red numbered cubes back in front of Fatso. The chip handler stacks twenty silver chips then replaces two stacks of chips with two gold chips, expecting the tall, slim gambler with the long cornrows to pick up his winnings. He doesn't. Instead, he picks up the dice and his whole entourage starts putting down black and silver chip bets like it ain't shit. Play money.

"SA fools in the buildin' and we ain't doin' nuthin' but winnin'." Fatso blows on the dice and throws them across the long table that is lined with mini stacks of assorted rainbow-colored chips. The dice land. Men and women start yelping and cheering; they're experiencing something better than an orgasm, winning money.

"Eleven dice. He's on fire," says the dice man.

"Oh, my God," Tamara slowly mutters under her breath while looking at all her winnings plus those of Prince and Fatso. She taps Prince, who is standing next to her.

"Baby, I've never won this much money in my life,"

Prince examines his chips and does a quick calculation of his winnings. "I already know," he says distractedly.

He's over fifty G's to the good, and Fatso has to be over one hundred 'cause he's betting most of his winnings. Prince laughs to himself, *We make that shit in a week,* but still.

"Say, look out bro. Fuck this shit! We up, bro. Everybody's up. Let's get out on top."

Fatso thinks about it; dice in hand, forty G's on the table, all eyes on him. He wants to keep shooting, but then he realizes that this shit is an addiction, and he despises addictions. Fatso picks up thirty thousand in silver and gold chips and leaves two gold chips down and throws the dice. His outro song.

"Snake eyes!" announces the dice man. The chip handler starts collecting chips. A moan of loss reverberates over the small audience.

"Told you," Prince says curtly, holding his chips in his hands. Fatso looks at his brother with a smile and announces his leave-taking to the crowd,

"Ladies and gentlemen, Tupac has left the building." He gathers his chips and a few people laugh. Not everyone gets it.

"Let's go to the club and buy that bitch out!" he tells his crew; Big Baby, Young Bread, Pimpin' Ron, and Tamaras' crew all gather up their chips so they can cash out.

The whole crew climbs into a super-stretch Mercedes-Benz GL SUV limousine that has just pulled up in VIP valet, turning the heads of all who were out there to see. All black, big chrome rims. You can see neon lights and a forty-two inch plasma screen glowing behind the tint. People are looking hard, eyeballin' each and every face of those who climbed inside, hopin' they recognize a superstar when they see one. They don't. Prince, Fatso and their crew prefer it that way.

"Say, y'all, lookout!" Prince begins to announce as the limo pulls away from the casino and the passengers get comfortable in their seats. "Today has been a beautiful day. Non-stop. For two reasons;...one!" holding up a finger, "My brother graduated from college!" The whole crew applauds Fatso on a rare accomplishment where they come from. "Can you believe this ghetto-ass nigga is a chemist?" Prince asks jokingly, pointing to Fatso who sat a couple seats away. Everyone starts laughing.

Tamara, adding to the impromptu roast of Fatso, quips, "Wait, wait, wait. Yes, he finally got his degree and we're all proud of him. But let's keep it real. Fatso has always been a chemist, whippin' up some ole' crazy shit."

"Hell yeah," Prince agrees, clutching his stomach and doubled-over in laughter just thinking of all the concoctions Fatso has put together over the years. The others laugh, but they also know that Fatso and Prince have made them rich, and while *that* is no laughing matter, it's definitely worth celebrating.

"Hold on, Prince, what's the second reason?" Big Baby asks. He and his boy Sike are bodyguarding for the night. Work and pleasure.

"Ah, nigga you ain't know, we just walked up outta there with about a quarter-million of Donald Trump's money," Prince answers unapologetically.

"Oh, yes, my pimpin' pal," Pimpin' Ron says, sounding like Kokane from the old NWA and holding a fat knot of hundred-dollar bills worth about twenty G's. "And it shall be done."

"Preach, nigga, preach!" Bread says, laughing and fingering through his own twenty-five G stack, thinking, *This is free money right here.*

"Say, Fatso," Bread calls out, neon lights reflecting off the waves in his head and the diamonds in his ears and on his chain, his money now in a neat stack in one fisted hand and a hundred-dollar blunt in between the fingers of the other hand. Feeling sentimental, he finishes, "Congratulations, big homie...you my nigga fa life, man!" Fatso nods. "I got so much respect for you and Prince, man, straight up. I always liked you niggas' style, fam. That loyalty. Y'all always looked out for me, man, even though I was the youngest."

"You always had heart," Fatso remarks.

"That's why I'll do anything for this family, man, anything. Straight up!" Bread exclaims, looking around at everybody to make sure he was heard.

Everyone believes him: Tamara, his cousin who is more like a sister, is touched by his declaration because she knows his loyalty. He brings his attention back to Fatso and smiles.

"But yo, this shit..." he begins, holding up the stack of c-notes, "...this shit tonight. Yo! Let me find out you had them dice set, cause you one lucky muthafucka!"

Fatso holds his hands up like he's trying to stop traffic. "Say, say, check it out. You win some, you lose some. And when it comes to that, Prince, what do I always say?" he quizzes his street-savvy lil' brother, the brawn to his brain.

"Life is about numbers and percentages." He knows it's true; he's just havin' fun.

"And when you're hot you're hot!" Fatso continues.

"And right now, we burnin' up!" Prince finishes. "Now somebody pass me a cold bottle."

A couple of bottles of Rose' champagne appear from nowhere, and the sound of corks popping fill the passenger area of the limousine: *pop-pop!* Pimpin' Ron and his two girls, both beautiful high-dollar escorts, his main girl, a tall yellow bone who had Jada Pinkett's eyes and similar facial features, a beauty mark on her cheek and long, reddish hair like Eva Mendes. The White girl was a medium-light brunette who could pass for Brazilian with all that ass to match her bangin' tan. Pimpin' Ron is getting' money with his young stable, but his only problem is that he can't stop fuckin' his girls, especially since he's been poppin' these Ball tabs on the regular. He *stays* up in some pussy. But that's his thang and Prince, Fatso and the crew liked to keep him around to amuse them with his pimp theatrics and vernacular.

"Yeah, we ballin' tonight, baby, back to back like the Rockets," Pimpin' Ron says, pullin' out a lil' Altoids tin, poppin' a Ball tab and passin' it around. Both his girls pop, Bread and Tamara's girls, Kesha and Serene, pop too. Prince, Fatso and Tamara pass.

"Daddy feelin' good tonight, you know. We might just encounter a tender lil' flesh wound. Dr. Feelgood gonna heal her pain, give her a new name, aim and reason to live for this game, huh? You know this pimpin' is nonstop, on-call twenty-four seven like 911 'n' 'em. Hoe in distress, out da' nest and in need of a new address. Ya peekin'?" he concludes, and his girls nod. He looks at Fatso and says loudly, "Now, tell me what is it, Fatso?!" Tamara and her girls Kesha and Serene, along with Fatso and Prince all laugh at Pimpin' Ron because even though he's funny, they know he's dead serious.

Prince grabs a bottle and opens the sunroof to stand out in the night air as the limo floats through the still freshly remodeled "New" New Orleans.

In '07 the President must have grown a brain and decided to hire some engineers from the Netherlands to rebuild the levees. It cost ten-billion, but evidently their homeland is below sea level *and* hurricane-prone, too, but they've never had a problem. Their claim is that with this new levee system it would take a Katrina that was one hundred times stronger to be a threat. Since then, the government and investors on every level have been spending billions on prime real estate that comes dirt cheap. Now you can see it, here it is: high-rise condominium developments, new clubs, schools, restaurants, shopping centers and better casinos. Oh, and of course, the projects that New Orleans was once notorious for were bulldozed. They were all replaced by townhouse developments and jazzy apartment complexes where people who used to occupy this space can no longer get near to without the new-and-improved police department being dispatched.

As the warm breeze rushed past Prince's brown face and the old Victorian world city lights raced past seemingly slower, Prince whispers into the night, "This shit is beautiful and clean. Damn, I wish we would have invested some money in this shit over here." He braces himself against the frame of the sunroof as the limo takes a long wide turn in approach to the club Nu-Yu, an ultra-modern three-story joint with neon lights and a South Miami Beach feel, complete with upper echelon crowd, red carpet and all.

"Yeah, the Prince is heah!" Prince yells, letting the people in line, the bouncers and the valet people know that not only did they have a sick Benz truck limo pullin' up, which would get much airplay on the rumor mill circuit, but that there were also some live-ass brothas inside it comin' to show these folks what it do, H-Town style.

Club Nu-Yu is thick. Local ballers, male and female, are all in their best look. Groupies are on the prowl, and out-of-towners are in full effect, as well. When the crew enters twelve-deep, it's all eyes on them. Prince, Fatso and Young Bread look like real live rap stars with platinum and diamonds glistening, suit-cut Evisu denim units, custom Gucci and Mauri tennis shoes. Big Baby and Sike dressed the parts of professional bouncers in tailored, casual-cut suits and tight-neck designer T's. Pimpin' Ron was a mix-up in a baggy black Michael Westley suit with turquoise pinstripes, turquoise Louboutin tennis shoes, loose collar, lots of jewelry and Rod Keenan brim. Ron was feelin' loose. That Ball had kicked in and he was ready to share this feeling with the whole club. He had about thirty tabs with him and he planned to give them all away tonight. His girls were feelin' it, too; they were flanking Pimpin' Ron like a couple of Vegas showgirls, wearing J-Lo dresses that looked like they were painted on.

Tamara was setting the standard far outta reach for any broad that sized her up, and she knew it. That was always her objective when she jumped fly. She and both her homegirls had their hair, nails and make-up professionally done. Her milk-chocolate skin was glowing, and she was rockin' a purple silk Escada jersey dress that was knee-length with a plunging neckline down to her belly-button, flossing her cleavage and necklace full of purple and yellow diamonds. Purple and crushed gold Lorraine Schwartz bangles adorned her wrist, and purple suede Sergio Rossi platforms with gold heels and accents gilded her feet; this was all topped off by an Adrienne Landau purple mink stole draped across her shoulders and a look on her face that said, *Bitch, you better recognize!*, and if you saw her, you did. Tamara was more than just eye candy or a trophy on Prince's arm. This was his princess, a real-live stomp-down chick in the flesh. She would kill for this nigga she loved and she was treated with the utmost respect.

They didn't wait in line, so within minutes, to add to the visual impact, Big Baby and Sike were breakin' up the crowd and making a way to VIP so everybody could relax and get their groove on. By the time they crossed that roped-off perimeter there was a cluster of groupies in line. Ron made it his duty to select the best to join them.

"A'ight, check it out!" Ron announced, hands in the air. "Houston Ball Club is in the building! We don't party wit' no squares! We lookin' for new talent!"

Bread, admiring Ron's strategy, stood there and smiled. Everyone else was getting acquainted with the VIP. A bunch of girls began wavin' their hands saying, "Me, me, me!" when they heard Ron say "new talent."

Ron continued, "I need five young ladies that want to be stars." The selection was plentiful. These girls wanted in on that high life: lights, camera, action. Within minutes, five of the best-looking and most eager were crossing that threshold with a big-ass smile on each of their faces, leaving their girls and everything else behind. They were just livin' in the moment, happy to be joining the elite. Several girls got dissed with, "Nah, baby your forehead too big," or "Your weave too lumpy," or "Who da fuck did your make-up? Your son?" or "What is that in your mouth, tin foil? Nah, get back!" So the girls who *did* get in felt privileged, for real.

They all popped a Ball tab with little resistance and the party began. Bread, Big Baby and Sike had new friends and Fatso was introduced to a Naomi Campbell look-a-like who immediately made herself comfortable.

Kesha curled up her lip and frowned at the girl, but really, she had no right to trip. Kesha had a man and a son with her man, Warren Lee, the governor of the D-Boy clique. She still had a secret crush on Fatso though, all the way from back in the day when he rocked her lil' world that one and only time. She hadn't forgotten, even though he acted as if he had.

Within twenty minutes and a few glasses of Krug Rose', Pimpin' Ron was gettin' head from his new prospect right there in the VIP booth. His two girls were slappin' her on the ass and rubbin' her titties, tellin' her, "Suck that dick, freak! Yeah, you like it, don't you? Yeah, you comin' home with us." Straight up porno shit. Everyone there was aware of the effects of Ball, especially on a first-timer. Neither Tamara nor Kesha needed to be reminded. Luckily there were three VIP booths, so Tamara, Prince, Fatso and his girl were able to ignore what was poppin' off in the next booth over, but they were fully aware and Tamara was embarrassed. Kesha and Serene got up and walked over to the bar and were being approached by some big-time New Orleans gangsters.

"Prince, someone needs to tell him something. This ain't the time or the place for that bullshit!" Tamara snaps, whispering in Prince's ear.

"Come on, T, you know how that nigga is," Prince says dismissively, hoping she don't spoil his good mood. He glances over at the other table. "Bread seems to be havin' a good time."

Bread is in Ron's booth smiling and whispering in his new friend's ear, and his hand was under the table in between her legs. She rolls her head back and bites her lip. Tamara peeks over real quick, and, disgusted with her cousin, whispers, "This is so fuckin' embarrassing."

"C'mon, let's go to the bar," Prince says to T and Fatso, whose girl is not trippin' off the scene in the next booth; in fact, she's kind of interested in it. However, she tears herself away.

Across the room at the bar, two old school New Orleans gangsters, Duro and Chubbs, are flirting with Kesha and Serene, but secretly, they're offended by the audacity of these Houston cats comin' up in Nu-Yu like they're runnin' somethin'.

"Young niggas," Duro had said to Chubbs, "back in the day they'da got they hat knocked off actin' like dat in another man's house." Now here *they* were, choppin' it up with the girls they'd seen with them, tryin' to find out who these dudes are, or who they think they are.

The VIP area is a second-floor balcony that overlooks the dance floor and the DJ booth. A new song by Lil' Wayne comes on and the crowd below gets crunk, and the dance floor instantly fills to beyond its capacity. Fatso and Prince are bobbin' their heads to the beat when they walk up to the bar and Kesha takes the liberty of making introductions.

"What's up, T, Prince and Fatso? This is Duro and..." Kesha looks at Chubbs questionably.

"Chubbs," he answers.

"Chubbs," Kesha repeats. "They're from here."

"What it do?" Prince says in greeting. Fatso nods.

"Mimi, what's happenin', sweetheart? How you been? You need to call me so we can get together again," Chubbs breaks out, greeting Fatso's lil' friend and ignoring Kesha's introduction.

"Umm..." Mimi is caught off guard. She looks at Chubbs and then at Fatso. "Okay, I guess."

Fatso laughs under his breath. Tamara and her girls look at Chubbs like *what the fuck?!*

"You know, you Houston boys should be a lil' mo' respectful when you step foot in another man's house, don't you think?" Duro asks with a slow drawl. Both men were suited and booted. Fatso makes eye contact with Big Baby from across the room, and he is there within seconds.

"Say, patna, we just here celebratin' my brother's graduation, ya dig? Doin' what we do everyday. Ballin'. Enjoyin' this thang. Now, we don't mean to step on no toes, but uh, if you feel that way, it sounds like a personal problem to me," Prince says with much attitude.

"Muthafucka…" Chubbs spits. The girls step back.

"Hey, hey, hey," Fatso defuses, stepping in between them and taking control. He is the tallest man in the group. "Listen, Chubbs…Duro. It's no plex, a'ight? Now, if there is anything that my people have done here tonight to offend you gentlemen, I apologize," Fatso says calmly, trying to keep his temper and maintain control of the situation. He continues, "I'm Fatso, and this is my party. Now, there is no reason for us brothas to be plexin'. Y'all gettin' money. We respect that. We gettin' money. Our family is originally from N'Awlins… We could all get money together."

Slowly but surely, people start nodding in agreement. In a matter of minutes, Fatso had defused the situation and made alliance with some real gangstas. Chubbs and Duro respected the fact that these boys were ready for whatever but was also willing to right what may have been wrong. On top of that, they were willing to break bread. In the world they all existed in, that was the primary motivating force, and in some cases, it was the only one that mattered.

By the end of the night they were all drinking and partying together. The Landau boys, who now called themselves HBC, Houston Ball Club, just picked up two new clients in New Orleans.

Chapter Nine: MILE HIGH

Prince was ten-thousand feet above the Gulf of Mexico, headed to Rio in a Gulfstream G5 and getting a lap dance from three Latin chicks with ass like Tamara's when the emergency signal started screaming. *Oh, shit!*

In actuality, it was his alarm clock waking him up. 12:00 noon, Monday. He popped up out of his bed. "Damn!" he said, hittin' the clock to turn off the alarm. As he walked to the bathroom, adjusting his rock hard piece, he was mad for two reasons: one, for being taken from his Brazilian dream, and two, because he wished he'd have brought Tamara home with him to take care of this damn thang. But they had been together freakin' all weekend, so he'd had the limo take her and her friends to her condo at the Houstonian. He had appointments all day.

After he relieved himself, he stepped out onto the balcony off his bedroom. The bright sunshine shocked his eyes and he was reminded of a helluva weekend. His townhouse, which sat smack-dab between 3rd Ward and the Museum District, overlooked State Highway 288 with a bomb-ass view of Downtown Houston. It was a four-story construction, ultra contemporary in a burnt orange stucco with white tube rail trim. On the Museum District side, about six blocks over, the only project more progressive within a two-mile radius was a mint-green bungalow townhouse set-up that was owned by a doctor. Prince had to admit, it was *sick.* Some Hollywood shit for real. And although he had never been inside, Prince convinced Fatso that "ain't no way they interior is sicker than ours!"

Prince looked down upon 3rd Ward to his right. He was always amazed at how the landscape was constantly changing; there were new buildings and construction projects for miles. He could see a couple of their empty lots and projects from his vantage point, but he would have to drive to the others in order to see them. 3rd Ward had come a long way to being retro and a much safer, attractive place to live. The newer residents were proud of it, but the old residents were disgruntled because taxes had risen so high that many were forced to sell out to the investors and real estate sharks. Prince and Fatso were considered to be in that group, but actually they would allow residents to stay in the properties that other investors were trying to buy and evict the tenants. A win/win.

From his balcony, Prince yelled for his brother. "Fatso!" Fatso's balcony was just on the other side of the dividing wall that separated the two townhouses. Yes, the two brothers were neighbors.

"Wake yo' ass up, fool, we got bidness to handle!"

Within forty-five minutes Prince's bowling-ball black marble Maserati Quatro Port had backed out of the four-car garage, stopped at two of their construction sites and was now pulling into a parking spot at Magic Gardens Botanical and Nursery, which was one of three locations. They were immediately greeted by a pretty middle-aged Hispanic woman named Lita who speaks almost perfect English.

"Both Mr. Landaus at once. It must be my lucky day," Lita said cheerfully.

Fatso smiled back and looked around. "*Every day* is your lucky day, Lita, you know that."

"Yeah, to be working for the greatest, most handsome brothers in the city. Come on, now," Prince added. He was having a little too much fun for it being a Monday.

"Oh, you're flattering yourself? That's cute." Lita turned to Fatso, "Congratulations on your graduation, sir. I'm sure you all had a great time at the party. Now, don't bore me with the details, I might flash back and try to stuff myself into one of my daughter's dresses," Lita said, chuckling. "Now, how can I help you two today?"

Prince and Fatso laughed with her. Lita was funny, still good-looking, detail-oriented, responsible, and, best of all, loyal and trustworthy. She managed the two Southside locations. A brotha named Ray, who spoke fluent Spanish, along with his wife Mary, managed the Northside location. They'd all been working for the Landaus' for the past two years.

"We just came to check things out...pick up some samples. Any issues?"

"Things are good. We picked up nine referrals over this past weekend for landscaping."

Each nursery had a landscaping division which had become an extremely profitable machine, as well.

"Beautiful!" Fatso exclaimed.

"Long term contracts?" Prince asked.

"One year, all of 'em," she replied excitedly. "Come on, I will get those samples for you," she says, and gestures for them to follow her to the back.

"Our landscaping divisions are growing like crazy! And I already know what you're thinking," she says, strolling casually with her apron on, curly ponytail down her back, closely observing all the plants, trees, supplies and workers as if this were her own personal garden.

Fatso states the obvious: "We're going to need more people."

"I've got a ton of hard-working Mexicans on standby."

"Good. Keep 'em comin'. We're gonna need 'em for these new stores," Fatso replies. Prince nods.

Lita calls over a worker in Spanish. She sternly instructs him to put several assorted plants inside a box, and the small Mexican gets right to it. As far as he knows, Lita is the boss and the source of his payday, and she runs the operation with an iron fist. She turns and winks at the two brothers, and they smile in return. They liked to hire Mexicans because they worked hard, long hours for low wages and preferred cash. They didn't ask a lot of questions, they just did their jobs so they could feed their families.

All Magic Garden employees were screened for two levels. Level one was for hard work, reliability, a family to feed, a place to stay and two references to confirm that all information given is true and accurate, and since they hired many illegal aliens, sometimes even to confirm their identities. Level one employees worked strictly at ground level: the nursery, landscaping, and construction or maintenance. Level two is a different thing altogether. Every aspect of your life and character is on display and observed for a certain period of time before you can become a level two employee, which paid much better. But, once you became a level two, you couldn't do anything else. You couldn't have another job. You couldn't quit. You were sworn to secrecy, an oath made in blood. Lita, Ray and his wife Mary were level twos, as well as all the workers at the cookshop. And although Fatso and Prince liked their managers and level twos at the cookshop, a violation of the oath was final. Their childhood cohorts who were now on payroll would execute judgment.

The cookhouse, professionally known as the preservatory, is a large, high-security warehouse located in the industrial 2nd Ward right outside of downtown. Once a week, a shipment is delivered from each Magic Garden location: rabbits, *lots of them*. This shipment comes from a private contract with a rabbit farm. At the preservatory, all the ingredients to make Ball are received, prepared and cooked in huge high-tech kitchen equipment. The rabbits are all killed at one time in a large pressure tank where they immediately receive the blessing from the Queen, who runs the preservatory. Jewel.

Once the powder is prepared and weighed, it is shipped off in large containers to be pressed into pills and packaged by a local pharmacist, also a level two, and who now works exclusively for Fatso and Prince. With his one assistant, the pharmacist presses and packages fifteen thousand pills per week in vacuum-sealed packages of five hundred pills each, which are then distributed throughout the crew by Prince and Fatso. Wholesale priced at ten dollars a pill to be turned around and sold retail at twenty to thirty dollars a pill. With constant demand from the streets and the club scene, everybody in the Houston Ball Club family was making a ridiculous amount of paper. And the best thing about it...Ball is still below the radar of the FDA and the DEA, making it 100% legal. $150,000 a week with low overhead and expenses, and no jailtime. Now *this* is the *real* American dream.

But these two young entrepreneurs had bigger goals. They wanted to take this thing nationwide, starting with the two biggest markets in the country, Los Angeles and New York. According to their analyst, they would have to open up four to five more Magic Gardens twice the size of the ones they currently owned, but it could be done. It *would* be done; it was just a matter of time, persistence and aggression. And aggressive they were. The taste for big money was so comfortable in their mouths, and soon, came the hunger for more…*more* money and *more* power. Because Ball is an exclusive market, it shouldn't be hard to come into. Prince and Fatso are the only known distributors; there is no competition. Therefore, they stand in a much envied position to become extremely rich. It's only just begun.

Once the samples they'd come for were loaded neatly in the trunk, Prince's and Fatso's business here was done. The Mexican worker walks back in the store.

"All right, Lita, everything looks good here," Fatso says, walking around to the passenger side. There's a nice, semi-cool September breeze temporarily disguising the ferocity of the sun. Lita stands looking at the two brothers as if she has something to say.

"What's up, Lita, everything all right?" Prince asks, concerned. Lita decides against it. She understands. No questions. The less she knows, the safer she is. She also knows Fatso is taking samples of his favorite plants, which she has come to know so well, for a reason.

"Oh, everything's good, just…let me know if there's anything I can do to help, okay?" Lita says, giving the both a look that says, *I understand, I know but I don't know, and yes, I'm down with you,* all at once. Lita is very sharp.

Fatso looks her in the eye and nods. "I'll call you." And with that, the brothers disappeared into the distance, in a hundred-thousand dollar car, on the way to a meeting with a local pharmacist.

They pull up to a single-level grey stucco strip center which housed half a dozen independent retail operations and a few vacancies. The black glass window on the front door simply reads "Baker Pharmaceuticals" in white letters. Once buzzed inside, the front room is simply a desk, chair and a picture on the wall and industrial carpet on the floor. Across from the entry is a huge security door. Once you make it past this point, the real business begins. You saw huge technical machines, digital read-outs, scales of all sizes, laboratory and packaging equipment. The security was impressive with an embankment of monitors that displayed and digitally recorded all movement inside and outside. All this was inside a small, well-lit, modestly furnished office with comfortable chairs.

"Fellas, how you doing?" Dr. Baker greets them, hand out, in a white button-up, loose, wrinkled blue jeans and loafers. No need for formalities. Baker is a light-skinned brother who used to be a pharmacist for CVS. Trying to earn a real doctors' salary, he would sell gallons of codeine under the counter to a few guys from South Acres. That's how Fatso and Prince met him. Now he *did* earn a real doctors' salary, and he was happy. "Let me get you something to drink. Bottled water, coffee, soda?" he eagerly offered as they all shook hands.

"What's up, doc?" both brothers greet in unison.

"Bottled water is cool," Fatso replies in response to the doctor's offer.

"Comin' right up," Dr. Baker says as he goes to a mini-fridge that is situated close by. Through a large picture window between the office and the lab, a lab assistant can be seen trying to appear busy around the equipment. He nods and smiles at his boss. To the rear is a set of steel double doors that lead to a small rear dock where shipments are received and sent out.

"Here you go, fellas. Let's step into the office."

The brothers sit down in the office with their payrolled pharmacist and hammer out a deal to dramatically increase production within the next few months. Prince explains that it's all just tentative right now and that it's not guaranteed, but if and when production spikes they want a better rate on pills and packaging.

Dr. Baker considers this briefly, yet thoroughly. He knows he's really in no position to object. These guys are his one and only exclusive client and they also assisted greatly in the financing of the equipment outside his office which furnishes his income and lifestyle. He went to school eating peanut butter sandwiches with no jelly and trying to fit in with the White folks all those years to acquire. He also knew that right now, he pills and packages fifteen thousand pills a week at fifty cents a pill, which grossed him thirty grand a month. If the Landaus, say, *doubled* production, and that would be sixty thousand a month. *Oh, shit,* he thought, *I could easily buy that seven-bedroom villa in Cancun then! Oh yeah!*

"All right, fellas, here's what I'm thinkin'," begins Dr. Baker. You know that I'm grateful for the relationship we've been able to develop. You also know our relationship is exclusive, which limits me in many ways." He pauses for emphasis, and the brothers nod.

"Here's what I propose. In the future, if you double your production, I'll cut your P and P by...thirty percent. That's thirty-five cents a pill," Dr. Baker states with a tone of finality and open negotiation. He knows who's really in control, and it's not him.

Prince quickly does the math in his mind, as does Fatso. Prince looks at Fatso as if to say, *Should I grill 'im some more?* Fatso nods in agreement. Turning to Dr. Baker, Prince says, "Done."

The gentlemen smile and shake hands. They review a few more details and possibilities. The nationwide launch is definitely in the works. When Prince and Fatso leave, Ron Baker sits back and visualizes himself floatin' up to his villa on a nice fifty-foot yacht. Hell yeah.

Chapter Ten: THE PRIDE OF MEN

"What the fuck is this?" Winnie yells, glaring at Mo like he wants to chop him with his machete.

"What? Three bricks," Mo answers quickly, surprised and a little nervous at how Winnie's looking down at him as he sits at a small table at the safe spot, a small house on the outskirts, breaking up a kilo and getting ready to weigh and cook it.

"What the fuck you mean 'what', nigga? Where the fuck is the other two?" Winnie asked, looking around like two kilos are playing hide and seek.

"This all they dropped off. Three books, like always," Mo replied calmly.

"I *told* that nigga we needed *five* this week!" Winnie explained, holding up his hand with all his fingers spread.

"Well, this what they brought, whodie," Mo responded with a hint of disregard. He doesn't agree with Winnie's motives to try and push Scat for more work. With the three kilos they get every week, their whole crew, which has grown considerably, by the way, is eating. That's a lil' over one hundred and eight ounces, and when they whip it, it ends up being close to a good five bricks. And sometimes, they'll have leftovers when the new pack arrives. *So what the fuck, we getting cake!* Mo said to himself. Money is flowin' like the Mississippi. But this nigga Winnie wanna try and prove a point, make an issue out of nothing. *This nigga gettin' on my muthafuckin' nerves,* Mo thought as he went back to breakin' up the dope.

"See! What the fuck I tell you? They ain't tryin' to see us come up." Winnie starts pacing the small living room. He peeks out the window at his new Tahoe in the driveway. "They wanna keep us right here where they can control us. They scared, Mo."

Mo didn't respond. Winnie continued, "I'm tired of fuckin' wit' Scat. Them boys wanna keep us up under their thumb 'cause they scared we'll get as big as them, and we said we wasn't gonna do this. We said we was gonna do our own thang. N'Awlins!"

"We eatin', whodie," Mo responds. "Look how many mah'fuckas is eatin' with us now. We almost thirty deep. Thirty families, Win. I just don't see the point in fuckin' up a good thing."

"Fuckin' what up? Fuck dem niggas! Don't you see, *we work for them*. These Houston niggas got us right where they want us, allowin' us what the fuck they think we should have, tellin' us where we can and can't hustle. I ain't wit' that shit!"

"Well, what you wanna do, man? It's more than just us. We got people dependin' on us. I ain't scared, my nigga, but straight up on the real for real, we ain't strong enough yet to go to war wit' the D-Boys. They got the whole city locked down. That's suicide. So what you wanna do?" Mo says, dumping the broken-up chunky powder into a large Pyrex baking pan.

Winnie nods and contemplates his partner's perspective. Mo's right. Winnie knows Mo is really just in this to sell a bunch of dope, stack a lot of paper, and lay up with the finest strippers Houston had to offer. Mo was a pretty boy, single again and havin' fun. He is not really interested in a street war, although he does like the idea of power. Either way he would follow Winnie in his plan.

"You remember Prince and his brother Fatso?" Winnie asks calmly, leaning back on the one and only black leather couch in the house. Mo nodded. Of course he remembered them. HBC. Rich niggas. Runnin' the "Ball" game. Pretty much stayed out of the real dope dealers' way. Winnie had secretly been tracking them for months.

"Yeah, what about 'em?"

"I got the business on dem dudes. That Ball shit. We 'bout to take that over."

"Oh, yeah? How?" Mo asked curiously. He'd heard it was a lot of money circulating in that Ball game. Not as much as the coke game but even Mo and most of his crew popped Ball tablets and freak with the honeys. Women loved 'em.

Winnie smirks deviously. "I got a plan, Mo. I'm still fillin' in some of the blanks, but what I *do* know is...they're the only ones distributing that shit. So all we gotta do is infiltrate they network. It's just a matter of time then."

"Start pickin' them apart," Mo said thoughtfully. Winnie was actually starting to make some sense. Plus anything sounded better than an attempt at biting the hand they were eating off of right now. "And what about Scat?" he asked, recognizing problems before they began.

"We keep everything going like it is. We got our people in place. Everybody's working. We can't disrupt that. We ain't gonna say nothin' to Scat right now, but we gon' start buyin' some Ball packs so our people can start pumpin' this shit. Then, when we take over, it won't be no big surprise."

By now Mo has almost forgotten about what he was doing. He's caught up in the profit potential of what Winnie is proposing. Winnie lights a blunt.

"We need to figure out how deep they are, who's behind 'em and all dat shit, I mean. We're still lookin' at a war. I don't want this shit to blow up in our faces," Mo says, ever the cautious one. Winnie explodes.

"Man, don't worry 'bout that ho-ass shit! The only thing you need to worry 'bout right now is getting' close to one of them bitches," he asserts. "Now, I heard Prince's bitch is movin' a lot of this shit."

"Yeah, ole' girl who be throwin' the parties and shit," Mo recalls.

"And...her and Warren Lee's girl supposed to be pretty tight."

There it is, Mo thinks to himself. To Winnie,"D-Boy affiliated. I knew they was behind this shit some kind of way!"

Winnie shakes his head. "Uh-uh, these niggas is independent. I already checked it out. Anyway, them broads, that's your target. Get one of them hoes to open up...*pimpin'*." Winnie says the last part with a smile, hits the blunt and passes it to Mo. Mo nods, deep in thought. He takes a long, deep puff, inhales. Exhales. He's so immune to the potent smoke he doesn't even cough, nor does he even feel the urge to cough. The thick smoke turns a silvery color when he exhales into the light fixture hanging above the table.

Mo didn't know all of what Winnie was thinking, but he knew he wasn't telling him everything. It definitely was interesting. Broads love Ball. One thing for sure though, he *was not* fuckin' wit' Warren Lee's gal. Fuck that. Now Prince's chick...she's sexy than a muthafucka. Hell yeah. And if not her, he knows she's got some other homegirls. She's connected. Every one of them is bad, too; fine as hell according to what he'd glimpsed the few times he'd seen them at the clubs where they threw parties. Yeah. There were definitely a lot of perks with this lil' operation.

"Yeah, I'ma get on top of that, whodie. I think this shit could work." Mo makes eye contact with Winnie, and Winnie smiles. He knows way more than what he's tellin'. His plan is much more savage than what he's revealing, but he knows that as the leader, it's important to only give up enough information to push forward to his next objective. He knew Maurice was smart, just not as aggressive as himself. He also knew he'd bite at the idea of targeting a female. Hopefully Mo wouldn't fuck this up. There were millions to be made if they could pull this off.

Chapter Eleven: EXPANSION

Club M Bar is undoubtedly one of the livest clubs in Downtown Houston. It's located on the seven hundred block of Main Street, in the heart of trendy Downtown amongst dozens of other clubs, restaurants and bars that cater to lovers of all flavors of music and food; all ages and ethnic groups. The rich Downtown investors and club owners spent a ton of money on interior designers and club specialists for the latest and flyest technology and trends to compete for those nighttime dollars. Almost all these clubs are established on the first floor or the basement of huge office buildings with easy access to the street. Since Houston has such a vibrant and profitable club scene, one of the most competitive legal hustles around was the promotions game. It's also a good way to wash dirty money. As far as the sophisticated urban hip-hop scene downtown, the M Bar is *it, the* place to be if you were twenty-one and older; if not, you had to have backup at the door or the bread to slide the bouncer a fifty and *faggedaboutit.* Everybody's hustlin'. The hottest night of the week for the M Bar is Thursday, the first day of Houston's weekend.

Thursday is also the first day of the work-week for Tamara and her promotions company, T-Top Promotions, which threw some of the livest parties with the hottest DJs three times a week: Thursdays at M Bar, Fridays at Visions and Saturdays at the Skybar. Tamara's crew and company had a huge following, the primary reason being that the Ball stayed flowing. It was passed out by girls in bunny rabbit outfits serving jello shots and cigars; they also handed out free samples of Ball to familiar female faces. All the wannabe models, actresses and socialites were determined to be in this group, so naturally, the ballers were always present. A perfect mix for the perfect party which stimulated peak profits and T-Top Promotions intended to keep it that way.

It was still early when Tamara arrived with Kesha and Serene. The caterers were just getting set up upstairs in the VIP, and the crowd was minimal at best, consisting mainly of staff and some friends they may have brought with them so they wouldn't have to pay a twenty-dollar cover or haggle with a ridiculous line or plead with a muscle-head bouncer who acts like he doesn't recognize their faces, only the faces of a select few dead presidents, even though they may have all just partied together the night before at a private freakfest. Either way, they were there with smiles on their faces, happy to arrive comfortably before the crowd and socialize with the people who could really pull some strings.

"Hey, Tamara!" some girl in a candy apple red evening dress bedecked with rhinestones gleefully yells to Tamara so everyone can see and hear her.

Tamara nods. "What's up, girl?" she replies, all the while thinking, *Do I know you? Anyways....*It was the same ole' thing every night. But tonight was special. *No time for chit-chat,* she thought. She, Kesha and Serene headed to the D.J. booth, commanding all the attention in the room, looking like a trio of House of Dereon's hip-hop line gangstress models.

DJ Mike City rises up from behind the DJ booth. "What's up, T?" He was sorting through his selection of twelve-inch vinyl, making some last minute changes to his playlist. Mike City is an old school DJ and producer who still preferred wax over digital.

"What's the deal, City?" Tamara replies with a big smile. Her girls speak, too.

"Damn, you lookin' ghetto fabulous, Ma, as usual."

"Thank you...I think. Did you get those records I told you about?"

"What? C'mon now, Mami, don't even play me. You *know* I went and got 'em first thing this moorrnniiinnnggg!" he answers comically, pulling out several records he'd earmarked diagonally.

"A'ight, cool," Tamara laughed.

"Now, when Fatso and your man gon' be here? Tell me around what time so I can be lookin' for 'em."

Tamara shrugged. "I don't even know. You know how that goes. I'm gonna call them in a few minutes so we can have some kind of idea."

"Bet. I can't believe this nigga graduated from college, man. That's a major accomplishment for a brotha from the streets. Make me wanna take my black ass back to school." Tamara, Kesha and Serene all agree with him.

"Oh, and before I forget...it's fucked up y'all didn't invite me to celebrate in New Orleans last weekend!"

Tamara had been dealing with this same complaint all week from people who'd considered themselves close to her and the HBC family, so she was immune. This, however, did bother her. Mike City was her boy and he really should have been there.

"I'm sorry, man," she replied sympathetically. "It was kinda last minute for me, too. Usually they have my company set all that up, but this time Big Baby and PR did everything. They just had to have that GL 450 limo, I guess, so we just rolled with it." By this time, Serene had gone to the bar and come back with a waitress who began passing out a round of Pimp Juice energy drink and vodka.

"I heard y'all busted they ass at the casino!" Mike City exclaimed with a smile.

Tamara busts out laughing while thinking of how much fun they'd had. At the same time, she was wondering who was telling him all this. Probably PR ole' big mouth ass. Kesha and Serene both chime in: "Mmm-hmm." They'd all won CLK money that night.

"We kicked it. We really had fun, City. I wish you could have been there," Tamara says.

"Damn! Well, don't forget about me next time."

Tamara nods and sips her drink. "No doubt. *You* just don't forget to have this bitch crunk tonight!" Kesha teasingly retorts.

"Oh, oh, what? I must got a clown suit on tonight 'cause both of y'all tryin' to play me. Say, Serene, you got a cell phone?"

"Yeah," Serene answers suspiciously.

"Tamara, you and Kesha got cell phones, right?" Mike asks insistently.

Tamara can sense that a joke is coming. "Yes, I have a phone."

"Well, y'all better make sure y'all are getting a signal to call 911 'cause it's gonna be an inferno in this muthafucka tonight and I'm tryin' to body somethin'!" They all laugh uproariously.

"You know what? You are really retarded," Kesha says, still laughing.

"For real, though. I got some new blends and scratch intros; I'ma fuck y'all's heads up tonight. Y'all gon' see. I'm not even gonna talk about this shit."

"All right, well, make sure you play those new joints for Fatso and shout both their names out all night. I told Fatso it's all about him tonight. He got that degree so he kinda feelin' himself." Tamara laughs and walks away.

******

The ink was barely dry on the sales contract when Prince's cell phone started singing the latest single from Drake. Prince ignored it. He continued to discuss the details of the latest real estate commitment with his realtor, Theresa. It was a large tract of land to build a Magic Garden twice the size of the others. He reminded her to get on top of the other lot they'd looked at and submit the offer immediately.

"Believe me," she begins, "I wanna close the deal just as fast as you do."

"You find it, I'll buy it, baby. As long as we can structure a cash payment plan at 60% of value, it's on!"

"I like the way you think. Buy it, own it," she says, then winks at him with a smile.

"Allll-ready," Prince drawls in reply, smiling back.

"Expect to hear from me tomorrow," she says as she walks out the door.

"A'ight," he says, watching her trot down the few stairs in a navy blue fitted pantsuit that revealed that bangin' figure she's working with. Her Cole Haan sling-backs click down the concrete steps, then Theresa hops into her BMW 325i. She was around thirty, a little older than Prince. She's fine, smart and professional with that mature grown and sexy thing goin' on that young brothas are attracted to. Yeah, Prince is definitely feelin' Theresa but there wasn't nothin' poppin' but the thrill of the hunt.

Theresa views Prince and Fatso as business associates, smart young men with too much money to burn. If she could help them wash it and invest it in real estate then she'd done her job. There is an excitement to it all, though. Playin' the game. Cleanin' up the money. Tax-free cash. She thinks it's cute the way Prince and his brother flirt, but it was the art of the deal that excited Theresa, doing her little professional dirt, getting paid thousands of dollars of cash instead of receiving a check from a title company, where she was hardly ever able to feel that cold, hard cash fan through her hands and weigh down her Chanel purse. *Ain't nothin' like cash,* she thought, heading over to meet her date in Midtown, a chocolate-brown criminal attorney who'd just made partner. *Never know, I might need him one day,* she said to herself. But for now, it's cool; residential and commercial purchase and construction deals. Cash. No split with her broker. Oh, yeah, she liked working with Purnell and Dwayne. She loved the cash she was making and the commissions were lovely. She was gonna stay on call as long as they kept dishin' it out.

Prince jumped back up the stairs just as his phone started ringing again. "What it do?"

"Hey, daddy," Tamara purred. Prince smiled.

"I'm gettin' ready to come your way," he said, picking a chrome all-purpose remote up off the black granite countertop and hitting a button that filled the whole house with music from speakers you couldn't even see, the latest in Nakamichi technology.

"What time you think y'all gon' get here?" Tamara inquired. Prince knew what she really meant was "I made all these preparations for y'all, so don't have me waiting all night," but she would never speak to him that way. Tamara loved to throw parties but tonight's getdown was for Fatso. Ain't no tellin' what she had going tonight, but it should be good. Any other night, she wouldn't call; it would only be "See you when you get here," and if not, "I see you later or tomorrow or whenever." There was no pressure.

"I'm ready!" he lied, grabbing a glazed doughnut out of the box of Krispy Kreme he'd brought home with him. They were still semi-warm. "Let me go check with Fatso, but knowing him probably about an hour, hour-and-a-half."

"So about 11:30? That's cool, boo, I guess I can live with that."

"Everything else all right, baby?"

"Yeah, we on schedule. Just waitin' on you, boo. And your big-head brother," she teased. He laughed.

"A'ight, baby, I'll see you in a minute."

"Byyyeee…" she said as if she didn't want to hang up, even though she had plenty to do. She missed him all the time; she got like that whenever they spent long weekends together. They'd had some memorable ones, too: New York, L.A., Miami, Cancun, Cairo, Paris, Sydney, Jamaica, St. Bart's. They were young, Black, rich, in love and running an operation that was damn near printing money. Fuck it. They promised each other they were gonna enjoy life and see what the world had to offer. They had fun and their sexual chemistry was off the meat rack. In every city, on every beach, in foreign restaurant bathrooms and first class plane seats. They'd done it on cruises overlooking the ocean and on jet-skis *on* the ocean. Prince was sure that if Tamara hadn't been on birth control she'd have been pregnant a few times 'cause he's been puttin' it down and fillin' her up since day one. But, that's his girl. *That's* my *muthafuckin' baby boo!* he thought to himself as he headed over to his brother's place next door.

At Fatso's stainless steel front door, Prince places his thumb on the thermal fingerprint reader and the door unlocks. When he presses the latch and enters, the security system says, "Hello, Prince," in a pleasant, computerized female voice.

"Hey, lady," he replies carelessly. His own system does the same thing, and sometimes it annoys him, while at other times he is amused by the luxuries of technology. Prince hops up the granite stairs to find Fatso sitting at his Picasso dining room table with his laptop, concentrating on typing and comparing notes on some handwritten notebook paper strewn across the table.

"We goin' to this party or you gon' work all night?" Prince sarcastically asks. Fatso, ignoring his brother's snarkiness and smiles.

"Check *this* out!" he says, hitting a button on his universal remote, then another button on his laptop. A one-hundred sixty inch projector screen rolls down from the ceiling in front of the front bay windows of the townhouse. The screen comes to life with several colorful charts and graphs.

Prince recognizes what he's looking at to some degree. "The test results?"

"Yes, sir! It's crazy, P. Lookout," Fatso says excitedly as he walks over to the wall-size screen. "These are average growth rates. The first chart is the natural cycle for all our ingredients to reach maturity for production. You wit' me?" Prince nods.

"All right. The second chart is the growth rate at which we are operating right now, with our current processes."

Prince was impressed. The numbers and the graph indicated much higher numbers than those of the natural process. He knew that, according to Fatso's instructions, Magic Gardens was implementing chemical processes to their private plants to facilitate healthy, faster growth.

Prince nodded again. "Okay," he said, waiting for the big bang.

"The last time I tried to enhance the process, well, I don't want to say it was a disaster, but it was all fucked up," Fatso explains.

Prince remembered; Fatso was irritable and moody for months, and explaining his frustrations to Prince didn't help much. Prince understood basic procedure, but scientific analysis and thesis were beyond his spectrum of interest. But he still listened, tried to understand and offer impossible suggestions and mock scenarios partly to entertain his brother, but also to comfort and support. He knew there was nobody else he could talk to about what they were doing.

"Yeah, I remember," Prince answered with a smirk.

"Well, I had fused a non-carbon based protein enzyme with the already mineral-rich steroid process we have. I just knew it could work but no matter what I did it over-accelerated the growth of the cells and killed the plant before maturity. So I been doing all this research and I found this article by this scientist in Washington who invented this new light called *Celleron*. I'm thinkin', yeah, yeah, another 'breakthrough' product, but in the article he mentioned something about this light incubating the protein enzymes, right? So, I got in contact with him, gave him an isolated hypothesis, and since he's trying to promote his lights, which I was gonna buy anyway, he offers me a tip. He says I need to decrease the enzyme fusion and add a stabilizer to the enzyme only, *before* fusion, instead of the mass, *after fusion*, because that process is already working. I'm trippin' out, like, *Damn, why didn't I think of that?* Then he tells me, 'But it won't work without the Celleron,' so I order one. It was like six grand for one light 'cause they ain't even out yet. But they ready, waitin' for approval. And just like he said, P, on everything man, the shit worked like magic. It took perfectly. Look! The third chart is the new process enhancement," Fatso says, pointing at the third chart.

Prince stares in amazement. "Am I reading this shit right?" he asks.

Fatso laughs. "Yeah, man, almost one-hundred twenty percent growth rate!"

"Wait a minute, bro. That means...we can produce twice as much product?"

"Exactly. More than twice as much product in the same amount of time, and in the same facilities," Fatso says with a devious grin, rubbing his hands together. "LA and New York, here we come."

Prince looks at his brother in awe, then breaks out in an uncontrollable fit of laughter. Fatso waits and watches while Prince wipes the happy tears from his eyes like he's at a comedy show.

"What's so funny?" Fatso asks.

"Nah, man...damn. Ah, man...finally I get to laugh at how pathetic you were acting when that shit ain't work, and now...it's...it's just a total turnaround, man. You're all animated and shit."

"Well, I'm glad I was able to entertain you. You can leave the tip on the table...P! Do you know what this means?" he asks, pointing at the screen again.

"Fats, I know what it means. I just got one question...why the fuck couldn't *I* have *your* brain?"

Fatso laughs. "Because then you wouldn't have your attitude and street smarts, and then we'd both be incomplete bro. Now come on, I'm ready to kick it!"

Chapter Twelve: CELEBRATE WELL ....N.O.

When Prince and Fatso emerge from the valet lot between the M Bar and Club Blue, the first thing they noticed besides the half-block long line is the scene on Main Street.

"This bitch is wired up!" Prince exclaims.

"Hell yeah," Fatso agrees, then quips, "Did the Rockets win the championship? Is it Super Bowl again? What did I miss?"

"Nah, everybody's here to shake *your* hand. Now, come on 'fore we get stampeded," Prince jokes, walking towards the door.

"Yeah, right. Let me find out you wanna be a comedian, P, I might put you on." Fatso knew that he and his brother were pretty low-key compared to so many other Houston ballers and celebrities. In reality, though, at least half of this crowd did want to be inside M Bar, so the unspoken consensus was, if we're not gonna party *inside* the club, let's do this damn thing right out here on the street.

And the damn thang they did. With music from four or five clubs vibrating the pavement, and a line of custom slabs and European autos traveling at two miles per hour playing the game of "Whose load the throwdest?", the entire sidewalk in front of M Bar, the sidewalk across the street in front of Live Sports Café and the Metro rail island in between had been transformed into a parking lot pimp parade. Big Baby and Shoddy, and an M Bar bouncer, met Prince and Fatso at the door. Recognized by a few people, they were quickly escorted up to the VIP through the stairs to the right of the entry and the block party outside was quickly forgotten.

Mike City was on the wheels of steel and the only breaks the crowd got was break beats. The high-energy and euphoria of the club and the DJs selections, mixed in with everybody's favorite drugs and drinks made every next song "yo' muthafuckin' song." The dance floor looked like a new-wave version of that old *Good Times* mural, with all them fly-ass Black folks rubbin' and squeezin', wavin' they hands and touchin' and feelin' like Marvin Gaye's "Sexual Healin'" record had just caught the DJ's needle. Prince laughed to himself as he peeked over the balcony.

Out loud he says, "This shit is beautiful." He looks up and around, casing the upstairs scene. Not as crazy as downstairs but definitely a baller's affair. With the big black square leather couches and frosted glass tables barely visible, the blue neon frosted glass bar and selective ultra-modern track lighting is in plain view and helping set the tone. It was definitely more of an upper-echelon situation up here. Being able to analyze and pick apart social circles and read characters was one of the things that Prince prided himself on. He finds it fun for some reason, especially in clubs and party environments, because nobody's a real person, just representatives. Dudes is comedians with that cappin' shit. Females, too. He laughed to himself, then he spotted her. Standing near the rear brick wall by the bar, staring directly at him like she was reading his mind. He locked eyes with her. She tried to hold back her smile but the feeling was too strong and the start of it cracked her composure. Prince turned to walk around the balcony to be met by all his boys: Boo-bo, Poppa, Young Bread—his right hand, Big Baby, Syke, PR, his brother and a few other underlings.

Poppa greets his boss. "P, what's going down, baby," and all the usual pounds and hugs take place. Everybody in their tight-knit family has long-ago congratulated Fatso on his graduation, so while this party is actually a celebration in afterthought, it's still a party nonetheless, one in which they would ball out and exploit their player statuses as if they had just joined the club.

"Nigga, I know you see Tamara over there eyeballin'," Bread says playfully.

"Yeah, man, reckless, huh?" Prince replies. "Come on, y'all, let's hit this bar, and get these bottles poppin'. This shit is goin' down tonight. Yep!!"

The crew follows Prince's lead to the bar in the rear of the second floor. Tamara watches their movement. The bartender sees Prince and crew coming his way. He's familiar with Prince's influence and his relationship with Tamara.

"Prince, my man, what can I do for you tonight?"

"What up, Franco, you know what tonight is, huh?" Prince asks as his crew checks out the view of the scene from this perspective.

"Yeah, it's your…brother's graduation party, right?" guessed Franco, the Italian, cool-as-a-fan bartender. Neither Prince nor his brother struck him as college material.

"Yessir! Bring us a case of Krug Rose', a case of Ace of Spaids and a case of Ciroc…. and keep the shit flowin', huh?"

"You got it, man. Yo, Fatso!" he yells to Fatso who is turned in the other direction bobbin' his head to the music, checkin' out a couple dymes who'd just entered the VIP. He turns around.

"Congratulations, man!" Franco yells. Fatso nods, smiles and raises his fist in the old "Black Power" salute. Franco gets to work.

Prince heads in Tamara's direction, and his crew follows. She anticipates his every step. Prince is looking straight at her from about ten yards away, his feet become lighter. He smiles, thinking about how she still makes him feel. He still trips out on how fine and sexy she is every time he sees her. She was fine in high school, but who she's now grown to be is an amazing woman. Tamara, standing at five feet, ten inches and with measurements of 36-24-40, is a neck-breaker, but she is much more than just that. Tamara is smart, business-wise and street-wise, she has an analytical mind, a free spirit and a loyal heart. She is the epitome of a stomp-down chick. She has Prince's back, his front. She has his mind and his heart. There was nothing he couldn't share with her that she wouldn't understand. She made his heart beat. What they shared was true ghetto love.

Watching Prince walk towards her with tall, lanky Fatso and their crew, butterflies flutter for a brief second inside Tamara's stomach, causing a huge smile to spread across her face and her cheeks to get warm. Nobody made her feel like Prince did. Nobody has given her butterflies since high school; she'd been past all that puppy love shit. She's well-respected out here. But when it came to Purnell "Prince" Landau, Tamara McArron just melted. She didn't understand what it was. She had found out that the first time they'd had sex, he had Balled her. She was mad at him for weeks.

"You could have killed me!" she'd say.

"That's impossible," Prince would reply. Or, "I'd never hurt you, boo. I'm sorry." Then he'd look at her with those puppy-dog eyes, and she'd melt. Either way, it was too late: she was already in love with him. She forgave him and she got over it. Before long, she'd realized that Ball was a goldmine and joined the team. She came to admire Prince, and she loved Fatso like he was the brother she'd never had. They all learned from each other; hustled and politicked, built a crew together, grew up together and became rich in the process. Tamara often imagined that one day she and Prince would get married, move away from the city and she'd birth him a son and herself a daughter. They'd live in a big house overlooking the ocean.

Then, she began to analyze their lifestyles and how young they were and how so many chicks run dudes off with their premature fantasies and expectations; then they just end up lying to and cheating on each other and it's not real no more. Tamara saw it happen with her best friend Kesha, and, deciding she would not allow it to happen to her and Prince, they made a pact. Tamara knows that all dudes like new pussy every once in a while. It didn't mean that they didn't love their girlfriends or whatever; it was just a fact. This one old school cat had once told her, "Bayyy-bay, variety is the spice of life...and you know niggas love it spicy!" He laughed as she absorbed what he was saying before he followed up with, "That was your lesson for today. Now, can I borrow five dollars?" and of course, she gave him what he'd earned. Tamara grew up around a lot of ballers, players and their girlfriends, so she'd seen and heard it all. She refused to shield herself or her and Prince's relationship from that reality.

The truth was, Tamara loved Prince and was not in the least bit interested in being with any other man sexually. But, in the last couple of years, she'd grown attracted to women. It started out as an experiment, just to see what it was like to be with a woman while on a Ball tab. She enjoyed it. *A lot.* Ball brought out the real freak in people, especially Tamara, and that's why she didn't do it that much. It wasn't only the fact that she thought women were sexy and beautiful, but it was the power they possessed and the power *she* had over *them*. Tamara had a bunch of beautiful girls working for her and she enjoyed dominating them and manipulating their will to fit her agenda. It was a game that she enjoyed playing for some reason. She didn't take any of them seriously and most of the time, whichever girl she selected, like her current toy-slash-worker Serene, she let them flirt with and date guys. Tamara never felt threatened by a man. It was just another opportunity to show how much power she had.

She'd shared all this with Prince, and he'd found it amusing. He didn't mind, nor did he try to manipulate her because he already saw how it was working to his advantage. He believed in Tamara, and in his egocentric mind he knew she could never be with another man. In return, she allowed him his freedom, his manhood, his "new pussy privileges" as long as she didn't and wouldn't know about it. She told him that in this way, their relationship could never be tainted, and he agreed. He held her in his arms as they lay naked on satin sheets and embraced how honest and tender she was. He admired the foresight and sacrifice it must have taken to decide on this kind of arrangement. He rubbed his hand across the small of her back, down, up and over to rest on the hilltop of that round, soft flesh.

"Well then, what's up with the ménage," he joked. She raised up a little on onwe elbow.

"I *knew* your ass was gonna ask me that. And the answer is...*hell* to the no! I love yo' ass too much to see you shovin' my dick up in one of my friends."

Prince laughed and said, "Girl, I'm just playin'. C'mere." He knew she was serious. He soothed her and they made their way into an intense round two.

That was a year and a half ago and their love and passion has grown ten times stronger since then. They both contemplate that passion and heat when Prince steps to her.

"Hey, daddy," she says playfully. Prince says nothing. His serious expression never changes. He grabs Tamara around her waist and kisses her hard, tongues her down deeply and passionately while squeezing her booty. She is surprised but she doesn't resist. His gangsta love. She wraps her hands around the back of his neck, and he kisses her like every man should kiss his woman every once in a while, just to let her know that ain't nothin' changed but the date.

Both entourages do a little nodding and flirting as they engage in conversation, but everybody knows what's up with the lovebirds.

"What's up, baby?" Prince asks casually like nothing was happening. Tamara's head is spinning as she catches her breath. She wipes the corners of her mouth with her thumb, then she wipes his, thinking to herself, *Damn, this nigga is powerful!*

"You love me?" she asks. Prince smiles.

"You know it." Tamara smiles back.

On cue, the champagne arrives to their VIP setup just as R. Kelly starts singing, telling all the girls in the club to wind for him, or whoever they with. They follow his directions.

Chapter Thirteen: WINNIE'S PLAN TO BE

A crowd of twenty-two guys enter the atrium of the already-packed club where bodies were rubbing bodies. Once everyone is in, it's obvious who the nucleus of this crew is: the four guys in the center who were wearing jewelry brighter than everybody else's. D-Boy Clique is in the building: Warren Lee the governor, Duce, Nore and Scat. They start to head towards the bar, greeting a few homies along the way, hugging a few chicks, grabbing a lil' ass and titties here and there. Ball tab poppers are scattered throughout the crowd of partygoers, and everybody is Ballin' tonight, including the D-Boys. They love to Ball when they party.

The D-Boys had now grown to controlling a large share of the drug activity in Houston, which consisted mainly of coke and heroin, otherwise known as "girl" and "boy". They left the weed, ecstasy, meth, codeine, Xanax, Ball and all the other little specialty drugs to the small-timers. D-Boy territory is well-defined and as long as other crews' operations didn't get in their way, they didn't care. The D-Boys made a little over a million dollars a month. Warren Lee and the two other families in Houston had one primary mandate as far as territory was concerned, which was that any new local operations that could bring heat to the other families, those other families must be notified. Warren Lee wanted three days' forewarning, but since the other families wouldn't agree, immediate notification was instead agreed upon. This agreement still proved to be problematic.

Warren had long ago given the Landau boys a pass to distribute their little product. It started out over five years ago when this fine ass lil' high school senior chick that Warren had been trying to get with named Kesha approached him with a proposition.

"I want you do to me a favor," Kesha said.

Aw shit, this bitch want some money, Warren thought. *Fuck it. I'll take you shoppin', lace you up a lil' bit. I been tryin' to fuck you for a minute, girl...you just don't know. A favor for a favor.* Aloud, he said, "What's up, baayyby, talk to me."

"I wanna introduce you to a couple of my friends, just some lil' dudes I go to school with. They been pushin' a few tabs around, nothin' serious. But they wanna do things the right way, so I told 'em they needed to talk to you." Kesha declared.

Warren nods, thinking, *Ok, some lil' niggas pushin' tabs, so what. I don't give a fuck about that, as long as it ain't cocaine or heroin.* Most niggas wouldn't even bother, so he had to respect the lil' niggas for respecting his authority. He was also impressed with Kesha. She might be smarter than he thought.

"Ok, and...?" Warren asks, waiting for the punch line.

"And if you meet them and give them the ok, thennn...I'll let you take me out," Kesha wheedled with a big ole' smile as if she was doing him some great service. Warren laughs, but the truth was, Kesha was about to make this nigga fall in love, and he would regret his hasty authorization for years to come.

"A'ight, bet. Tell the lil' niggas to come meet me. They from South Acres?" Kesha nods in the affirmative.

"Well, shit, I like 'em already. I don't even fuck with pills so it's automatic; they can do whatever they want. But I'll meet 'em. And *you*...I'll see you tonight at eight."

And that was that. Prince and Fatso met Warren that day, and that night, Kesha fucked him into a coma. One year later they had a little boy together, and she's been his girl ever since. It's funny how things work out. When Warren first saw a Ball tab, he laughed. Now it was his favorite party drug, and he wished he'd have taken ten or fifteen percent off the top, but it was too late; he'd given his word. Now they were making a fortune, tax-free. Secretly, Warren wanted a piece of that fortune. He knew Ball was the next big thing and it was just getting started, so he remained their friend. He kept his word, and he knew that his time would come in the future.

Across the street in front of the Live Sports Café and in the parking lot next to it, the New Orleans crew posted up. The thirty-plus deep entourage with Winnie at the helm. In their minds, everybody and anybody could get hit, robbed and left for the sidewalk crew to clean up the mess, so it seemed more convenient to party and plot outside, where they could view all subjects coming and going. Winnie leaned up against Mo's Impala SS, smoking a blunt and chopping it up with one of his young lieutenants. Mo is inside the club. Winnie deeply inhales the potent smoke and speaks without even releasing it from his lungs.

"Yeah, you just stay down, young bwah. You see what we done built?" he advised, waving his arm at all his soldiers and exhaling. "That was just the start. We 'bout to make a major move on these bitch-made niggas."

"We ready, Win, just give us the word." LuLu says, grabbing the blunt that was being passed to him. He doesn't even ask any questions about the plot, because he knows that as aggressive as he is, he is going to benefit from it.

"I got Mo inside workin' on it right now," Winnie says confidently, nodding towards the front door.

The bouncers at the front door of the M Bar, Double-D and Big G, are suspicious of the menacing-looking crowd gathered across the street, so they are keeping their eyes on them. They've seen it all before. It's like they have an instinct for trouble. Big G decides that, in a few minutes, he's gonna have one of his police buddies clear out the lot across the street. Double-D agrees.

"That Ball tab game, we about to lock that down!" Winnie claims. LuLu grins and nods his head, and Winnie continues. "It's a lotta money in that shit."

"Oh, yeah?" LuLu responds. *So that's why we start pumpin' tabs,* he says to himself.

"I got the business on them niggas, whodie. I know they weaknesses. I got they muthafuckin' card right here in my pocket. They either gonna get down or lay down. Give us the game or we gon' take it. You feel me, Lu?"

"Hell yeah!"

A street promoter walks up to hand them some flyers, but Winnie waves him away.

"This is what I want you to do, LuLu. Get three of our best kick-door artists together. I got a lil' mission for us."

"Done. When you talkin' bout?"

"Just be ready. I'll let you know." Winnie and LuLu shake hands. Two patrol cars, one behind the other, turn the corner on Main with their spotlights on the crowd in the parking lot. The lights target Winnie and LuLu, who slowly separate.

The loudspeaker blares: "Break it up over here! This is not a hang out! You either find your way into an establishment or get into your cars and leave! This is the last time I will warn you. If we come back we're making arrests!"

"Fuck you!" somebody in the crowd yells as they all disperse. Some of the New Orleans guys jump in their cars and leave, but most of them simply move around until the cops leave. The cop remains parked briefly before pulling off to patrol the rest of their beat. They plan to come back.

Winnie hops inside his Tahoe and waits for a few minutes. He considers his plan while rubbing his scruffy goatee. They'll never see it comin'. He didn't wanna reveal too much to LuLu just yet, like the fact that these Landau niggas actually *make* this shit. *Outta what?* He'd soon find out. He was sure of that. He considered going inside the club but quickly discounted it. Too many Houston niggas who think they're the shit. D-Boys was here and he was sick of them and the way they actually thought they had him in check. He knew this was an HBC party and, most importantly, if Mo was handlin' his business, he didn't wanna be seen with him. Not yet. They'd been out together before, but only rarely. Clubbing is not Winnie's thing, but he especially didn't want to be seen with Mo now.

Around the corner, three disgruntled New Orleans bangers have circled the block in an old Cutlass. During that short ride, they decided that if N'Awlins can't hang like they want to, nobody can. When they pull past the intersection crossing Main, they pull over behind the Subway sandwich store. The front seat passenger hops out with a sawed-off twelve-gauge pump, jogs to the corner and pumps two shots into the air. *Boom! Boom!* Damn near everybody on Main Street either ducks low to the concrete, takes off running or both, causing a mini-stampede and an assortment of minor physical injuries. The shooter casually jogs back to the car and they take off. The shooting mayhem takes place as Winnie sits inside his Tahoe with a big, gold-toothed smile spread across his face.

Two barely-dressed young ladies emerge from a huddle near the front door, one girl pulling the other towards her car.

"Uh-uh, let's go!"

"Come on, girl, we almost in now. Look! Them niggas was just trippin'," her friend says. She's really trying to get in this party, get her free tab and get her groove on.

"Girl, fuck that shit. I'm going home. This party is not worth getting killed over!" They leave.

At the bottom of the rear staircase to the VIP, Mo and the rest of the club are oblivious to the chaos outside. Three models wearing bunny rabbit outfits walk around discreetly passing out free samples of Ball. Damn near everybody is on it, making it very intense in there. For the past fifteen minutes, Mo has had Serene jammed up in a corner, holding her hand so she can't leave and whispering fly compliments and propositions in her ear.

"You are really tryin' to run game," Serene says, laughing and blushing.

"This ain't no game, baby. Call me superstitious, psychic or whatever, but I know what I know. I got a real special feeling about you, Serene, like you the one."

"That's just that Ball talkin'," Serene says dismissively.

"Nah, I'm bein' real with you, boo. If you wanna leave, I'll let you go, and then I'm leaving, 'cause my night is over once you leave. And every time I see your pretty face from now on, I'm comin' to get you, until you mine. Then we can conquer the world together."

Serene smiles and squeezes Mo's hand. She doesn't want to leave. At first she was offended at how he'd grabbed her hand, but he was so sweet and he seemed so sincere. He smelled good, and he was definitely sexy in a thugged-out way, with his princess-cut grills on top and bottom, and the curly, tapered-up Brooklyn. She could tell he had money, and she liked the fact that he was not from Houston. She considered all of this before she realized that she already liked him. He made her feel somethin'.

"Sometimes in life, you look back on things you wish you could have done different. Don't let me be one of those things, Shawty." Serene smiled and giggled. He was making her blush.

"You are too much...gimme your phone," she said, holding her hand out. He hands it to her and she beams her information into his phone. "Call me tomorrow."

"Soon as I wake up. You pick the place and we'll go eat."

"Brunch on the ocean, tomorrow at two."

"Classy. I like that. I'll pick you up." Serene nods.

"I'm leavin' now. My night is complete."

"Bye, Maurice," Serene says as she turns her body all sexy-cool and disappears into the crowd. Mo stares at her, mouth halfway open, analyzing her physique. *Damn! I got her...mission accomplished.* DJ Mike City throws on a new record by Lil' Keke then stops the record at the start of the first verse.

"Big H-Town shout-out to Fatso for stickin' it out at University of Houston! Get that paper, nigga! Let's go!" he announces, and the record starts over.

Upstairs, Serene gets back to the VIP just in time for a whole new round of bottles to be popped. Prince pulls out a huge stack of ones from Tamara's House of Dereon bag and hands it to Bread, then two more stacks for himself and Fatso.

"This is to my brother and HBC, to a new level of success," Prince says, winking at Fatso. "This is how we ball, y'all."

Prince, Fatso and Young Bread spread out over the balcony of the club. They fan out the huge stacks of bills, then they start throwin' em, little by little. It's raining money. The girls stop dancing and begin swiping the air, stuffing their bras. Some of the dudes try to play hard, like *Yeah, that's cool,* while some of the other broke cats down there who'd spent their last to be there are bum-rushing them singles like a stripper with five kids and past-due bills on her first day of work. That's some funny shit you just gotta see. Warren Lee and the D-Boy clique laugh. Prince, Tamara, Fatso and the whole HBC laugh, slap each others' hands and pop bottles. Mo stands at the front door and observes the whole scene. He smiles. Prepared to give a full update, he walks out the front door.

Chapter Fourteen: JEWEL & FRANCINE

It is a comfortably sunny Saturday morning in South Acres. It's late May so the summer is just beginning, and there are big, white cottonelle clouds in a pastel-blue sky. Because the Houston humidity is unusually low, people are out and about and the weekend is in full swing. A gentle breeze brings Sandra Landau to her mother's doorstep. She wasn't planning on coming here today; she'd actually been on her way to do some shopping in some of the eccentric, less-traveled Houston locations, but she was drawn by an impulse to check on her mother.

Wearing a white and rainbow-colored Louis Vuitton scarf around her neck, white-framed Fendi shades over her eyes, a white tube top, and fringed linen skirt that flowed down to her ankles, she appears to be some kind of hip-hop black magic priestess, which, in a way, she is. Her sandals, stretch belt, and Dooney & Bourke drawstring bag were all of red, and her index finger was adorned by a ring of white gold with a spherical ruby setting, which matched the large ruby red charm that hung from a chain that appeared to be made of white gold as well. The rest of her jewelry was all neo-soul. Every finger was bedecked with rings set with various stones, and silver and gold bangles lined her wrists so that her jewelry created the impression of holding a conversation every time she moved her arms. All of this excessive, eccentric styling thoroughly irritated her mother Francine, which didn't seem to bother Jewel at all.

She knocked on the door, then turned to observe recent additions to her mother's property: a new wrought-iron fence, roofing, siding and fresh burgundy and white trim. Francine had added some new flowers to her flowerbed in the front yard which was always immaculate. Jewel couldn't understand for the life of her why her mother had long-ago asked for her key back, as if Jewel didn't know where the spare was hidden. She knocked again. Her mother was still sharp as a tack and as stubborn as she's always been, but at times, it was as if she wasn't all there. Francine opened the door just as Jewel was headed around to the side of the house to retrieve the spare key.

"Mama!" Jewel called out in a cheerful tone.

Francine gave her daughter the once-over. "Sandy?"

"I just wanted to come by and see how you were doing. Are you okay?"

"I see you're still dressing like Satan's first child. Come on in, sweetie." Jewel was always amazed by her mother's ability to insult her without offending her. She entered the house and closed the door behind her. Jewel didn't see anything wrong with the way she dressed, especially compared to how some of these hoochie mamas she had seen out in public these days dressed.

Outside, less than half a block down the street, Winnie sits in a blue Hyundai watching Jewel enter Fatso and Prince's grandma's house. The colorfully dressed woman seems familiar to him in some way. *Who is she?* Winnie wonders to himself. He's pretty sure she doesn't live there. Either way, he'd found his target.

"Mama, I'm sorry I haven't been over to see you in a while," Jewel begins.

"Sandy, don't come in here trying to butter me up. I know you just saying that because you're here," Francine spat back in the sweetest old woman's voice she could muster as she pour herself and her daughter each a cup of coffee.

Her mother's sarcasm was starting to get to her, and Jewel felt the need to defend herself. "I am, too, Mama! Why do you always do that? You're the only mother I have and I promise that I'm going to come see you more often, like once a week, starting tomorrow." Jewel takes a sip of her coffee.

"Oh, so today's visit doesn't count, then?" Francine quips, casually amusing herself with her sharp wit. She sips her coffee and reaches for a cream cheese croissant. On the dining room table, she has a glass-covered bundt cake and she offers her daughter a piece. Jewel declines.

"No, thank you, and of course today counts, Mama. It's just that...well, me and the boys want to come and have a Sunday dinner with you so we can talk."

Francine chuckles to herself. "Ooohhh, so now you want to work me?"

"No, I'll cook. Tamara can help me."

"Don't be foolish, girl! I'd love to cook for my boys. You're gonna have to go grocery shopping to pick up just a few things for me that they might want. Never mind, I might order them," Francine said, remembering the phone-order service that she could use to purchase just about anything she wanted or needed. Fatso pushed her to utilize it, and even though any charges she made were billed to his credit card, she remained frugal.

"No, Mama, I'd be happy to go, as soon as I leave here. Just tell me what you need and I will make a list."

"Okay, that'll be fine. Just make sure y'all come over after I come home from church. Now...what is it you wanna talk about?" Francine hadn't missed a beat.

"Well...see, Mama, Fatso has this beautiful condo in the Medical Center reserved for you to look at, and we think it would be much better and safer for you so—"

Francine cuts her off. "I'm *not* movin' to no uppity condo in nobody's medical center. I know what you're talking about; Fatso has already mentioned it to me. It's one of those assisted living places for old people. Yes, I know. And I'll tell you like I told him, I am not *that* old, and I can still climb my stairs by-my-*self*!" she stated defiantly. "Hmph. I don't even use that contraption they spent all that money on to carry me up and down the stairs. For what? I told them my knee bothers me a little, you know, just every now and then when it rains. Next thing you know, I got all these people runnin' 'round my house with drills and machines carryin' on. Just unnecessary. Now they wanna move me somewhere around a bunch of people I don't know, outta my house...I ain't! All my friends from church are here. Those lil' Mexicans come cut my yard and help me with my flowers. And...and I got this number I call on the phone, and anything I ask them to bring me, they bring it! Haa-haa!" Francine cracks up laughing, like she is completely amused by this luxury. "Can you believe that? Anything, Sandy."

"That's nice, Mama," Sandra said nervously. She was starting to think that this was not going to work, and she also felt a little guilty. She had lived in New Orleans all those years with no contact with her mother, then Katrina brought her to Houston and her contact with her mother was still minimal. Now the boys seem to be expressing their affection exclusively with things they can buy for their grandmother.

"It sure is. I've got almost everything I want, so no, I'm not gonna go spending up all my boys' money on some fancy-schmancy condo-minium, lookin' down on the city, tryin' to find my neighborhood, my house. This is my home, Sandy, I bought it, it's paid for, it's mine and *I'm staying*," Francine stated with finality. Jewel refused to push the issue any further. She realized that her influence on her mother was minimal at best, whereas Fatso and Prince could get her to move mountains if she could. So she let it rest for now.

"Well, let me ask you this, Mama. You said you've got *almost* everything you want. Tell me what you're missing."

"Oh, just forget it now," Francine says with an angry wave of her thin hand.

"Nooo, Mama, tell me. What is it?" Sandra presses.

Francine thoughtfully looks into her half-full cup of coffee. After a brief pause, she looked up into her daughter's eyes, which were dark brown and full of compassion. The sunlight shone directly through the open drapes of the front window and onto her brown face. Sandra's skin is clear and moisturized. She looked very healthy.

"It would be nice to spend more time with my children," Francine said softly to her daughter who completely melted. Jewel's plans for the day were forgotten, and any hard feelings she may have had were obliterated. Sandra "Jewel" Landau recognized that her mother was specifically referring to her daughter, and not only to the boys as she customarily does, like she does not claim Jewel as one of her children.

"Oh, Mama," Jewel, trying to hold back her tears, covers her mouth and nose with her hands. She sniffled and then quickly regained composure. She declared, "I'll spend more time with you, Mama, starting right now."

"No, no, sweetie. Now you're all emotional. Go on and do what you have to do. I'll be here."

Reassuringly, Jewel says to her mother, "Mama, *this* is what I have to do." Francine nods in agreement.

Pulling out a pen and a piece of paper, Jewel asks, "Now, what do you need from the store?" She plans to go to the grocery store and spend the rest of the day and night with her mother and helping her prepare tomorrow's excellent Sunday dinner.

Winnie watches Jewel get in to her BMW X5 and drive off. He squints his eyes thoughtfully and rubs his tongue across his top gold teeth. He pulls away slowly.

Chapter Fifteen: SHE WILL

"She's a grown woman!" Prince protests as Fatso's platinum edition Escalade EXT floats through an underpass on Old Spanish Trail on their way to Mama's house for Sunday dinner.

"I mean that she makes her own decisions, Bro."

"I know that," Fatso argues calmly. "But that's not the point, P. What I'm sayin' is that her decision is based on limited knowledge. If she was fully aware of the depth of the circumstances, she might make a different decision."

In the backseat, Tamara is trying to remain non-vocal about the situation, but in truth, she agreed with Fatso. She didn't want Prince to think she was taking sides, but she was just itching to say *something*. Everybody knew how much rougher their South Acres neighborhood and the whole city had become since Katrina.

Many people thought that the huge increase in the crime rate would be temporary and then subside once the New Orleans community settled in, but that was all hopes and dreams. The reality was much more devastating: there had been an increase of organized and violent crime between the New Orleans and Houston factions, and while some of these opposing cliques have formed treaties to try to work together and get money together in order to keep control of the money circulation and the murder rate, it was only a temporary solution. Then there are always those isolated incidents. Those can't be controlled.

"Mama Francine's not in any danger *now*, is she?" Tamara asks, attempting to mediate as well as be sure there is nothing they're not telling her.

"Nah, she straight."

"But we all know how much rougher the hood is, and that it's only getting worse," Tamara states matter-of-factly, and both men nod in agreement.

"Man, we just gonna have to tell her!" Prince declares.

"Tell her what?"

"How serious it is. Everything."

"Nigga, you trippin'. You want this to be your last time ever talking to Mama? If she find out we got that recipe out of Auntie Jewel's book in her attic, then built a business off that shit...pssst...it's over. She'll disown our asses."

Tamara is in the backseat shaking her head. No, that's not a good idea at all.

"Bro, we've tried everything to protect her. I tried to put my pits in the yard. No go; she says they tear up her flowers. So we get that security system, she has one false alarm, and now she barely uses it. I mean...what?"

Fatso stops at a red light. "I remember that. That was funny."

"Yeah, it was. Talkin' 'bout 'God is my alarm. He gon' watch me.' Now don't get me wrong, I ain't knockin' that, but these dudes out here ain't got no principles. The only God they worry about is the one they can count and pay bills with."

"They aren't discriminating, either. These cats will bite the hand that feeds 'em, so just imagine…" Tamara adds.

"Yeah, it's fucked up," Fatso says, carefully scratching the scalp between his braids.

"She so stubborn, Fats," Prince laments. "So independent. She came to Houston all by herself. She didn't know nobody. No storm forced her out, but still, she just did it. Left her own child and took two nappy headed lil' boys."

"You was the hard-headed one."

"I was only four."

"Still."

"Anyway! She brought us here. She bought her own house, *on her own*, made sure we had a decent education…"

"*I* got a decent education," Fatso interjects, frontin' on his lil brother.

Prince held up his hand. "Lookout, playa, I got the floor right now." He was getting a little irritated with his brother's smart mouth shit. "Plus, if you got it, then I got it too nigga, so now what?"

Fatso playfully glances in his brother's direction, then shrugs one shoulder and tilts his head as if to say, *Yeah, I guess you have a point!*

"*Both* of y'all is crazy," Tamara declares through fits of laughter.

"What I'm trying to say is, she didn't just do this for *herself*, man. She did this for *us*; she raised us, she helped us become who we are. So, who are we to tell her where she should live?" There is a brief pause as the SUV gets closer to its destination.

"Baby, you were all gung-ho when we'd first started talking about this," Tamara reflects.

"I thought it was a good idea. Still do. But look how she's reacting. What? Are we gonna *make* her? It's not gonna happen. I know my grandma." More silence follows Prince's statement as the truck rides by an old apartment complex.

"Look baby, The Orleans," Tamara points out, smiling.

Prince looks and sees people still hanging out and doing the same old thang.

Prince and Tamara reminisce on the first time they'd hooked up at The Orleans.

"Aw, shit!" Fatso exclaims, knowing what they're thinking.

"Mmm-hmmm," Tamara agrees. "Kesha's old crib."

"In there punishing that lil' girl like that," Prince playfully says to his brother. They're all smiling and laughing now.

"She wasn't no lil' girl. She was *way* more experienced than I was. *Trust me,*" Fatso is looking straight ahead, but he has a sinister-looking smile on his face.

"She *was* a screamer, though." They all laugh as they pull up in front of Mama Francine's house, the nicest one on the block. Fatso offers a pact.

"All right, right now, let's agree that we are all gonna try our best to get Mama to reconsider and move to the condo, bet?" he asks, looking at Prince.

Reluctantly, Prince agrees. "All right, we'll try again."

"We gonna make this happen y'all," Tamara encourages.

"Let's go."

The aroma of Mama's Cajun-style soul food permeated the nostrils of Prince, Fatso and Tamara and their mouths instantly began to water.

"Ooh, *woo!*" Prince yelps, and Jewel laughs.

"Mmm-hmmm, it's ready, too. We just gotta set the table." Tamara jumps right on in to assist, beginning with a warm and respectful greeting to Mama Francine and then washing her hands. Tamara is family, so the only nervousness she is feeling is caused by the mystery of which direction this conversation is gonna go.

"Ms. Landau, it looks and smells like you have showed out again," Tamara says as she pulls plates down from the cabinets and Prince and Fatso both hug and kiss their grandmother.

"Well, whatever you don't like, blame it on Sandra," Mama jokes.

"Oh, I like *all* your cooking, Ms. Landau, so she's safe," Tamara replies with a smile.

"Ooh, child, I'm so glad you here so I can rest my feet. This woman been workin' me like a Hebrew slave," Jewel jokingly comments. "But we've had fun, haven't we, Mama?"

Mama answers with attitude, "I'm still havin' fun. Now turn that oven off and butter that cornbread." Prince and Fatso laugh. Mama snickers to herself and continues, "Your auntie thinks she's off the hook 'cause Tamara's here, but she's not."

"Don't worry, Auntie...Sandra. We'll get it done. I'm down wit' you," Tamara says, carrying plates to the dining room table. She'd almost called Sandra "Jewel," which annoys Mama Francine because of the connotations and history the name carries. Jewel would argue that Prince and Fatso are nicknames, but she knew it was a no-win argument, so why try? Just comply, at least in her presence; if not out of sincerity, then out of respect. Jewel felt that it was *so* much easier that way.

"You need to do that there. You know Mama don't need to be doing no work. Ain't that right, Mama?' Fatso hints.

"Yeah, that's true," Jewel quickly agrees.

"It's not so bad, but it's nice to take a break every now and then. I could have done it all myself; it just would've taken longer," Mama explains.

"Much longer," Jewel adds.

"Oh, girl, please! Get this food on the table before I find something else for you to do," Mama quips.

"Yes, ma'am."

As the food is set out and plates prepared, Prince sits and comments with mouthwatering approval of every dish: stuffed Cornish hens, boudin cakes, Cajun rice, hot water cornbread, fried cabbage, candied yams, crawfish etoufee and buttered French bread fresh from the bakery. Prince *oohed* and *ahhed* as if every dish was his favorite. He loved when Mama cooked like this because they could never finish it all and he'd always take a plate home with him, and the it always seemed like the food tasted better the next day. After everyone was full and relaxed, Mama Francine was in a good, jovial mood. She thoroughly enjoyed watching her boys fill themselves with her culinary productions. Fatso identified his moment and pulled out a color tri-fold brochure.

"What's this?" Mama inquired, peering at the brochure that had just been handed to her. "Sandra, bring me my glasses," Mama commanded, and Jewel was back on the clock.

"It's a brochure for the condo we wanna buy for you, Mama. It's beautiful...look!" Fatso exclaims as Sandra hands her mother her glasses.

Knowing she's been set up, Francine looks at Jewel and Fatso suspiciously. She takes a look at the pictures in the brochure, and Tamara squeezes Prince's hand underneath the table. They all watch her closely, anxiously anticipating some sort of reaction, vocal or facial, to confirm her approval. There was none.

"What makes you think I wanna move?" Francine asks, peering at each of them over her glasses.

Here we go. Everyone deflated except for Prince; he'd already known what her reaction would be. But the battle was not over. They all geared up with a ready strategy: Fatso started with several convincing reasons that appealed to Mama's common sense, then he passed the baton to Jewel, who then appealed to Mama's emotions by making an assortment of promises pertaining to spending more time with her mother because they're closer and in a safer environment. Then she looked towards Prince, who, basically agreeing with what Fatso and Jewel were saying, would then promise several additional luxuries, anything she wanted. Prince's position was weak since Mama already had everything she wanted besides her kids' time. His enthusiasm was half-hearted because he felt this was a useless argument, and truly, regardless of his past mischievous behaviors, he really didn't want to oppose his grandmother's wishes. He would love to get her out of the 'hood. Tamara jumped in with a few facts she had heard on the news and explained how they related to a situation that had recently taken place which involved her friend's grandmother.

"She's just as happy as can be now. She says she feels much more comfortable and secure because her environment is fit for her, that it's like a country club. Her kids come to see her all the time now because they're happy to see her happy." Francine finally smiled.

Tamara continued, "She didn't like the idea at first, either, Ms. Landau, but now, she says it's one of the best things she's ever done for herself. I know you'll feel the same way," Tamara finishes with an encouraging and subtle smile.

Prince is impressed with his girl. "See!" He adds, "You just gotta get out there and do it, Mama. It will be really good for you."

Mama Francine thought about what she'd just been told. She knew they were winning her over, and they knew it, too. *They sure are being persistent 'bout this,* she thought to herself. Then she began to backpedal.

"I don't know. What about all my friends from the church, like Mary Lou and Mrs. Dash? You know they come to visit me," she said. "And I don't even know if our church van goes to wherever this place is." She was trying to buy time to figure all of this out by worrying about trivial matters. She has a newer model Cadillac in the garage that they boys bought her two years ago, but she just didn't like to drive anymore. Her drivers' license was expired by almost a year and she saw no reason to renew it.

"We're gonna make sure you get to church every Sunday, in a car with your own driver," Fatso answered. It was actually a limo that they had arranged but he didn't want to boast. However, Prince did.

"A limo, Mama. Every Sunday you can even go pick up some of your friends if you want," Prince said, suddenly causing the dark, delicate wrinkles on Mama Francine's face to react and become more visible. Mama is conservative and knew how to stretch a dollar. She never like excessive spending or Prince's boastful attitude.

"That is just too much," Mama said, clucking her tongue. "My insurance won't pay for any of this...this...nonsense."

"Aw, Mama, you worried 'bout the wrong thing," Fatso sighed.

"I have to. Y'all obviously aren't."

"We don't need your insurance. We got this. We're all working. The money is nothing, Mama. Your comfort and security mean so much more; can't you see that?" Fatso pleads.

Prince follows his lead. "Things have changed and are still changing around here, Mama, and we worry about you." Everyone nods in agreement. "This is our gift to you, Mama. Please accept it."

Francine Landau looked into the sincere eyes of her two grandsons, the crown jewels of her life, then at her daughter, Sandra, whom she loved very much, despite their differences. Through the loss of her Husband and daughter Sariyah—Fatso and Prince's mother—years ago, Francine recognized that she was blessed to have Sandra in her life, and over the years she'd grown to love and care for Tamara, who seemed to give balance to Prince and his wild ways.

A new perspective dawned on Francine as if she hadn't considered it before, that this is what they really wanted. Not just for her but for themselves, as well. It gave them a sense of security and pride to cater to her well-being. Why deny them that? And maybe they were right. In hindsight, she herself had also been afraid when she'd set her sights to move her family from New Orleans to Houston. Her own daughter had even opposed her and stayed behind, but her mind had been made up. She was convinced that she knew what was best, and from where she stood it had turned out well. As fortunate as her own family was, Francine thought it would be a little unfair to deny her intelligent grandsons the benefit of the doubt in having that same foresight, that ability to sense troublesome situations down the road. Maybe it was time to make a change. Why not?

"All right," Francine softly conceded. "I'll try it."

"For real?" Prince was in shock.

"Aw, Mama, thank you! You don't know how much this means to us," Fatso beams, stepping over to hug and kiss Mama.

"We'll have it ready in two weeks, Mama! You can even pick your colors for paint and carpet this week," stated Prince.

"Wow, this is so good. You are gonna be so happy, Ms. Landau. I'm so proud of all of you," Tamara gushed while Jewel struggled to hold back her tears of joy.

"Well, who wants pineapple upside down cake?" Jewel offered.

"I do!" answered everyone except Mama Francine.

Chapter Sixteen: PREMONITION OF ME

After all the take-home plates were prepared and all the food put away, Tamara cleaned up the kitchen with a little help from Jewel and none from Prince or Fatso. Now, everyone has gone home and Mama Francine is tired. She has a lot on her mind. After more than twenty-four hours spent with her daughter, she was glad to have her peace and quiet again. Little did she know, Jewel was happy to be away from her, too. Francine had grown accustomed to her solitude and she needed some time to think. She giggled to herself, thinking of how funny it was that a person can get a taste of what they ask for and then begin to have second thoughts.

Francine closed and locked the door and glanced over at the security system's control panel on the wall. The rubbery-keyed numbered dial pad was backlit in green. Before they had left, Fatso and Prince had reminded her to activate the system. She'd told them she would, but what she didn't tell them was that she hardly ever used the darned thing, or half of the other things they'd bought her. It bothered her because she hated waste. Maybe moving to this condo would be a better use of the money her boys had invested in taking care of her.

"Now let's see…what's that code now?" she said out loud to herself. She reached up and punched the activate key, then entered a four-number combination. She waited. *Beep, beep, beep, beep*…nothing. "Hmm…."

She remembered changing the code because the boys had advised her that the one she'd had was too simple. It was her address: *five-five-two-two*. But, she was almost sure that this new combination she'd just input was correct. She tried again…nothing. She was sure she had written it down somewhere and thought of going to find it, but who knows how long it would take her to find *that*. *I'm too tired for this*, she thought as she headed towards the stairs. *I'll find it tomorrow. I got this stuff so I might as well use it*. She even decided to use that stair-walker contraption. She stepped onto the slightly elevated platform at the bottom of the first step. She pulled down the safety rail and held it with both hands and pushed the *up* button. On command, it slowly carried her to the top of the stairs and set her down at the second-floor landing. Francine smiled and asked herself why she didn't use the lift more often.

Within the next thirty minutes, Francine is undressed, washed up, in her night clothes and under her covers falling into a deep, deep sleep. It was a little after two o'clock in the morning when what began as a dream escalated into a nightmare. In her dream, Francine is walking through a garden, a huge maze of a garden with ten-foot-tall walls of dense shrubbery. She is barefoot and the grass is soft and cool. The summer humidity and non-stop walking is causing her to sweat and feel sticky in her summer dress. She smells smoke: *something's burning*. She becomes afraid, realizing that she needs to get out of there but does not know the way. She looks back and forth—both directions look identical. *Where am I?*

Looking up into the night sky, she bears witness to the full moon. Her heartbeat quickens and then she hears them: faint and distant at first, as if the night wind flowing above the walls of this labyrinth had carried them from far away.

Screams—voices crying into the night for help, for salvation from some atrocity, some painful death or torture from which there is no escape;

terrified voices, familiar voices, her boys' voices. Fatso and Prince were calling out for her. The voices become stronger.

"Mama! Help us, Mama, please! Save us Mama!" The smell of smoke was more distinct, and Francine begins to panic. She starts running along the wall and through the maze. She finds an opening, cuts right, runs back in the other direction about twenty yards.

"I'm comin', boys! Hold on!" Francine yells into the night air that seems more menacing now. It seems as if the entire environment is conspiring against her. *What's going on? What is this?* She finds another opening to the left, and the screams become clearer and easier to hear again, more frightening and more urgent. But this time she hears another voice as well. It was deep as the ocean, it was all-encompassing, everywhere, terrifying, inhuman. This voice vibrated inside Francine's soul as if it was speaking directly to her. She froze.

"*Yesssss. There issss noooo escape. You're alllll mine!*" it hissed. The fearful, tortured shrieks of her boys followed.

Francine becomes weak and cries out, "Oh, God, what is going on?!" She begins to pray for strength, protection and guidance for herself and her boys. Her strength returns, and she runs on, easily finding her way through the maze.

The smoke becomes thicker, more pungent, almost overwhelming. She can practically *hear* the fire. She makes two turns, and there it is. The scene before her eyes is indescribable; it could only be created in horror movies. Ten-foot-tall columns of ferocious flames, all evenly spaced apart like prison bars, formed a huge circle. She suddenly realized that the maze she was trapped in was a huge circle and she was now at the center.

Trapped like animals inside this huge, flaming topless cage, wide-eyed and afraid, are Fatso and Prince. They're able to move around, but the heat is so intense near the edges, the fear of death so real and imminent, that they've become mummified at the center, standing back to back, screaming out for their one and only obvious hope for life: "Mama!!!!"

Francine is convinced that she has to save them, somehow, some way. The columns of fire, she notices, are spaced far enough apart to walk through, but the flames are savage and hungry like sharks that smell blood. Francine steps closer, considering taking her chance at running through the passages, but the fire roars up at her as if it is alive and senses her coming near to it. She backs up and looks around for something to possibly cover herself with, but of course there is nothing. Then, something catches her eye—some human form. *Someone else is here.* It was only a glimpse, moving casually near the fire, then it was gone.

Could this be the owner of the voice?

"Who's there?" Francine yells desperately. "Please help me!"

"Mama! Ahh! It's getting closer. Please!" her boys cried out. She looked closely and noticed that the columns were closing in on them...getting closer to the center.

"*Haha-Ahaha-haha,*" laughed the evil being as if this entire scene were his own personal puppet show. The sound and vibration of the voice alone made Francine lose strength. She looked around—left, right, in front of her, behind...where was it and what was it? Then she looked up. If she were awake and this were real, what she was now looking at would have made her pass out. Hovering directly above this flaming madness is a huge cloud-like form that resembled a face; an evil, maniacal *red* face. Francine was in a trance and she froze, face-to-face with hopelessness. She whimpered and began to cry. Tears rolled down her face in her dream and in reality.

"Sweet Jesus, help me," she pleaded, then she looked at her boys. She couldn't lose hope. Not now.

Then, out of the corner of her eye, she saw it again: the other person. This time he/she moved casually out from behind the columns of fire and looked at Francine, stone-faced, emotionless.

"Oh, no, no, God, please don't do this...Sandra, my child, come to me...I love you...help me!" she cried.

Sandra's red-spirited image didn't walk, it simply floated back into the fire, which began to further close in around the boys. The menacing laugh continued.

"You're allllll miiiinnnneee! Haha-haha-haha-hah!"

"Nooooooo!" Francine pleaded. She woke up, sweating, afraid. *What happened? Was it real? What did it mean?* Her eyes come into focus, and she realizes that her room is filled with smoke, and this time, it's real. She wishes it were a dream, but it is not. She looks at her bedroom door through a silvery haze. Her door is closed. *But why?* She wondered. *I know I didn't close it last night.* She looks towards her window. The glow of fire is visible through the blinds and the drapes. She panics.

"Oh, my God, my house is on fire!" she screams and quickly jumps out of bed. She grabs a pillow and holds it to her mouth and slides on her houseshoes. She then opens the bedroom door and sees that flames have engulfed the hallway and Fatso and Prince's old bedroom. She thinks of the fire in her dream, but quickly shakes it off. With just a small space to sneak out of her door without being burned, she hugs the small pillow to her face and steps out into the hallway. The smoke is overwhelming. As she approaches the stairs, the hallway ceiling collapses behind her with a loud crash, startling Francine.

"Ahhh!" she cries out in a muffled scream. Her nerves were already fried due to that horrible dream she'd had, and now she's *living* that dream. It was too much. Inching towards the stairs, she recalled that she'd used her stairlifter last night and trips over the small platform at the landing. Francine Landau tumbled down the smoky staircase, breaking several bones and landing on the barely-smoky first floor unconscious and so near to her escape.

Chapter Seventeen: DEADLY TACTICS TEAM

One hour earlier.

"Don't waste no fuckin' time. Just get in there and find the book!" Winnie commands his soldiers. "Look in the attic first. If you don't find it there, tear the rest of that muthafucka up, but don't come outta there without that book!"

LuLu and the two guys with him, Lil' Man and 2-11, would obey and do as they were told. They knew how serious this was, and Winnie was in a very intense mood. However, this last point was not taken literally; if it came down to life or death or being caught by the police, they were coming out. Winnie also knew this.

"That house got an alarm fa sho, whodie," Lil' Man points out, peeking over the backseat of the Hyundai which was parked two houses down from the childhood home of the Landau boys. "See that lil' sign by the door?"

"That ain't shit," 2-11 scoffed. "I told you, if the alarm go off we just put that bitch on the phone when they call, put a gun in her face and make her tell 'em the password. I do this shit all the time," he finished confidently as if this were just another day at the office.

"Hopefully we don't have to go through all of that but we might as well be ready..." LuLu says. Winnie cuts him off.

"Hell, yeah. If that's what y'all gotta do, make it happen. If any cops show up, they dead, and then we burn this muthafucka down!" This last statement reminds everyone of the smell of the five-gallon gasoline jug in the trunk. "I don't give a fuck; just get-that-book, whodie!" Winnie emphasizes the urgency of the matter by banging on the steering wheel.

"Let's do this shit, whodie," LuLu says, looking over his shoulder.

"Yo' phone on vibrate, right?" Winnie asks.

"Yeah, hit me if it's a problem out here." Winnie nods.

It took no time for the three killas to penetrate the perimeter of Francine Landau's property; soon they were in the process of unlocking the rear window and tricking the alarm sensor on a rear window of the first floor with a screwdriver, a hanger and a magnet. 2-11 claims he performs this trick all the time, too, but this time, it doesn't work. The sensor breaks when they lift the window and they all freeze in shock when they hear the *beeeeeeeep* from the alarm system which lets anyone in the house who's listening that a first-floor opening is being accessed.

Tonight, no one except them heard a thing. Based on the expressions on their faces, all were apparently thinking the same thing: *the alarm is not on.* They entered quickly and quietly, much more comfortable since they didn't have a hostile alarm situation to deal with. The first thing they noticed was that the air still carried the aroma of the soul food that was prepared earlier. 2-11, the career criminal and break-in artist that he is, clicks on his flashlight and follows the lead of his watering mouth to the kitchen. LuLu and Lil' Man follow him curiously until he opens the refrigerator.

"What the fuck you doing?" LuLu whispers angrily.

"We got time; I'm hungry than a muthafucka. I know you smell that food." 2-11 answers in a whisper.

Lil' Man is eyeballin' the pineapple upside down cake on the counter, which was illuminated by the light from the refrigerator. LuLu grabs 2-11's arm and pushes him away from the fridge.

"You trippin', man; we on a mission, and we ain't got time fo' this shit." LuLu closes the double-doors of the stainless steel refrigerator, but only after peeking inside and admitting to himself that while the food *did* smell good, that was irrelevant; this little indiscretion would not be forgotten. LuLu knew this was the type of dumb shit that can get you caught up. They leave the kitchen and tiptoe upstairs to find the attic.

Outside, Winnie sits in the car waiting and watching intently, anticipating the alarm, but to no avail. After a few minutes a smile spreads across his face, exposing his gold teeth. They're in and there's no alarm. A car rolls down the street with the system bangin'. Winnie looks back and forth, all around. All is well. He sits back in his seat and assesses the situation: he'd made his mind up to seek out some information and now his clever manipulations were about to pay off. He thought to himself, *If this roach-ass car salesman lied to me, I'll bury him young.*

Winnie had met the guy through Scat. Fishing for information, he'd asked Scat about a hookup to buy a new truck, claiming that he had heard about a brother out of South Park who could hook up the financing on new shit. He had never heard any such thing, but he had nothin' to lose. Luckily, Scat bit.

"Yeah, it's this lil' nigga named Jason from South Acres who works at N-Xcess. He'll get you whatever you want," Scat told him.

"Good lookin' out," Winnie said, nodding his head. And look out, Scat did. Not knowing that he'd been manipulated, he shook Winnie's hand

and told him when he was ready to rim and kit it, take it to Fresh Rides and mention his name. Winnie secretly despised this referral, thinking, *As if I need yo' muthafuckin' approval, nigga. That's why I hate these Houston-ass niggas; they think they own the muthafuckin' South.*

When he arrived at the dealership, which was lined up with Benzes, Jags, Maybachs and Range Rovers, he once again started feeling a little salty. With the money Winnie was making now, he could easily afford the monthly payment on one nice foreign auto, but he would be damned if he let a Houston nigga make any kind of commission off him. He was here for information. If he could get what he wanted, he'd let them finance a vehicle for him, but under his alias. He wanted something nice and cheap, which after bullshittin' the car salesman he'd come to manipulate, Jason, through several viewings of high-end vehicles he'd never buy, he settled on a newer turquoise Chevy Tahoe with lots of upgrades. It was the cheapest thing on the lot.

"Oh, yeah…Scat, Warren, all them is my boys, man…if Scat sent you here, I know I can make things happen fa' sho. What's your credit like?" Jason asks, leaning back in the leather seat of the Tahoe. He was fly as can be in a navy blazer with a crisp white button-down underneath which was opened at the collar, and a razor-sharp goatee on his medium-brown skin. Since this wasn't a big sale—at least not compared to the high-priced inventory he was used to moving—Jason's mind was already working the numbers for a good markup commission. He'd always liked doing deals with the D-Boys or anybody affiliated with them because they all made a lot of money, usually used fake names and didn't mind letting him get his money because he knew what they were doing and he would make the financing go through for them. Plus, this dread-head nigga was obviously from New Orleans, so he was definitely about to work him. The lease payment on his condo was due this week, so he *had* to close this deal.

"It should be all right. You from South Acres, right?" Winnie asked evasively.

"Yessir."

"Oh, so you know Fatso and Prince."

"Yeah, man, me and Prince went to high school together. That's my boy right there. He doin' his thang now."

Winnie's pulse quickened. He was getting warm. "Yeah, they doing it. I be on that Ball shit."

"Oh, yeah? You like that shit, huh?"

"Yeah, it's all right. I like it. I just be kinda scared 'cuz I don't know what's in it." Winnie hinted.

"Oh, don't worry about it. It's all natural," Jason said reassuringly.

"How you know?"

"Believe me, I know. I was around when they first started puttin' that shit out."

"All natural...is it cocaine-based? Cocaine is natural, too."

Jason shook his head. "Nah, nah, nothin' like that. I mean, that's they thing, but they learned how to make that from they grandma."

It's gettin' hotter. "No shit?"

"I don't wanna say too much, though...like I said, that's their thing."

"Aw, man, why you actin' like that? They my boys, too," Winnie said with a little attitude, making Jason start to worry about losing his rent money right now. So he quickly tried to mend it up.

"No, no, it's just...that's not part of my world now. All I know is they learned about it from some recipe they found in they grandma attic, some kind of all-natural remedies. That's all it is, so don't worry. It's all good."

"Hmm...well, that makes me feel better," Winnie said with a friendly smile. They went on to finish the deal. Both players won, but only one got played. *Let's do the damn thang.*

Winnie liked his new truck, but later, as he was flippin' through an *Auto Trader*, he found several others just like his but better, and for far less money. Even though this was the first car Winnie had financed using his false identity, and Jason the big-mouthed car salesman had worked the deal for him, asking very few questions as if he knew this was an alias, he still felt like he'd been bamboozled and taken advantage of. Now, as Winnie sat in his little do-dirt bucket Hyundai Sonata waiting for his homies to return with a stolen treasure, those feelings of being hoodwinked returned, and he became bitter.

"Fuck these bitch-ass Houston niggas," he grumbled to himself. He climbed out of the car and grabbed the five-gallon gas can out of the trunk.

Inside the house, 2-11 had just succeeded at picking the padlock on the door of Francine's attic and was now tiptoeing his way up the stairs into the cool attic, with his flashlight leading the way.

Francine's faint voice filled the darkness. "I'm comin'...hold on..." LuLu and Lil' Man both heard it. It was a sleepy, incoherent voice. *Is this old lady havin' a wet dream?* LuLu thought, remembering how his auntie who had raised him and from whom he'd been separated since Katrina, used to talk in her sleep. Lil' Man heads towards Francine's door.

"Let's get her now," he whispers. LuLu stops him.

"She sleep, man...talkin' in her sleep. Just search the attic and find the book," he directed. Lil' Man thought about it for a second and crept back up the stairs behind 2-11. LuLu stayed back and stood in the darkness, frustrated and a lil' nervous; and also feeling like he was the only one using common sense here. He listened as his guys moved around in the small attic and the sleeping old lady made harmless noises in her sleep. *Maybe she's havin' a bad dream,* he thought.

She was lucky LuLu was here. LuLu knew Lil' Man was really into raping women, especially under these circumstances. Lil' Man is a savage and he didn't give a damn if you were young or old. LuLu, on the other hand, is not into all *that* shit. He'll rob somebody in a minute, and a shootout wasn't nothin' but a thang around his way. He'd been shot twice. LuLu's only real vice was that he liked to smoke that fry, that PCP. That's how he'd gotten the nickname "LuLu." But tonight his mind was pretty much clear, and he was glad he'd been able to save the old lady from being roughed up and worse.

After about five or maybe ten minutes, the cohorts tiptoed back down the stairs with a box in their hands.

"We got it," 2-11 said in a triumphant whisper. "Let's go." They all start to leave.

"What about her?" Lil' Man inquires, still up to no good.

"She's sleep, man. She's harmless. We got what we came for, now let's go," LuLu orders. Lil' Man resists his temptation and they all leave the same way they came in. The first thing they notice when they climb out of the window is the smell of gasoline. When they get out to the car, 2-11 hands Winnie the box with the books in it.

"No problems, man. Old lady still sleepin' like a baby," LuLu says, smiling. Winnie remains solemn as he smokes on a freshly-lit Newport.

"Good work; very good."

"I smelled gas outside. Did you do that or was I trippin'?" LuLu asks. There is no answer from Winnie this time. He pulls the car in front of the house and steps out. He takes a long glance at the burgundy and white two-story house with the manicured flower beds and wrought-iron fence. The early-morning air was cool, and power and independence were now within his reach. He'd glanced at the books in the car and quickly realized that his ticket to freedom, this mystery drug called Ball; its roots were in black magic, which only made him more furious that he hadn't realized and snapped to that prior to now. It all made sense now. Winnie had practiced some black magic back in New Orleans; Jason had told him that the Landau's were originally from there. *Everything was coming full circle,* Winnie thought to himself. *And now we begin again.* He flicked his cigarette into the gasoline-soaked grass, hopped into the car and drove away.

Chapter Eighteen: THE UNIMAGINABLE DREAM

"Yes, ma'am, this is Dwayne Landau. I'm calling about unit number 2622," Fatso says excitedly into his ear piece, pacing back and forth in his living room in his boxers, too hyped to sit down.

He hadn't realized how happy moving his grandmother into this high-rise condo would make him. Probably because, in his mind, he'd believed it was a long shot and hadn't really considered the reality of it happening. Now that it was official, he could allow himself to celebrate emotionally, and he couldn't contain his joy. He felt like a young Thundercat again, finally gaining some independence by doing something really big and special for the woman he loved more than any on this earth.

The sales associate chirped, "Yes, Mr. Landau, I was going to call you this morning. I see that you're up and at 'em early today!" It was just 8:02 a.m., and the sales office had just opened. Fatso wondered if her face was as pretty as her voice; she was not the same person who'd initially showed the condominium to him and his brother. Then he remembered that none of the women in that office were really all that attractive.

"I'm up and at 'em early *every* morning, sweetheart," he lied. "I just called to tell you that we're definitely going through with the contract for that unit, and I want it ready as soon as possible! I'll be bringing my contractors in this week for paint and carpet."

"Excellent! You got one of our best units with the best view."

"Only the best for Mama!"

"She's lucky to have you...so...shall we deposit the check?"

"Check's clear ma'am. You may proceed."

"Great! Well, I'll see you this week, and you can call me if you have any other questions."

"Thank you much, sweetheart. I'll do that."

The older lady chuckled. She knew Fatso was much younger than she and rich, but he handled himself in a very mature manner. Hearing him call her "sweetheart" made her blush a little, and she now wondered what he looked like. She said goodbye and hung up the phone with a smile.

Fatso removed his ear piece and took a deep breath. The deposit and the first six-months' lease was paid and he'd never been so happy to spend eighty-thousand dollars in his life. He went to take a shower.

******

Next door, Prince woke up to the sweet, playful giggle of his chocolate-covered diva princess Tamara. Her smiling face and eyes along with her current child-like mood belied the street-savvy, no-nonsense demeanor that she displayed to the rest of the world. With Prince, the love of her life, there were no reservations, no airs about herself. She could let her guards down and just enjoy that grown-up teenage love he made her feel. She was so close to Prince that he was on her mind all the time; she thought about her boo so much and what was best for them that sometimes she just wanted to call him and tell him with a playful aching, "I hate you for making me love you so much." Sometimes she would, but only rarely. She didn't want him to actually believe that she had any harsh feelings, but she was often overwhelmed by her feelings for him.

He would laugh at her and joke back about her being so fucking good to him; he just couldn't help it. He'd even surprise her with the same line, but worded differently. Prince would only say it when they had that rough, fuck-me-hard-like-you-hate-me sex, similar to the sex they'd had the previous night. He punished her with his doggy-style, her inflated, curvaceous ass propped up on the edge of the king size bed like a big, chocolate Valentine's Day heart with the strawberry cream filling. That heavy, sweet flesh rippled with every torturous jab, rocking along with her whole body back and forth according to his will and rhythm, not her own. Visually, Prince loved this thrill ride, so he handled her waist and ass more aggressively. The air was filled with sweet, sweaty sex; filled with moans, groans, screams of pleasure and vulgar language. Prince liked to think of these sessions as the best of Black pornography, and Tamara loved being his star. Her body would shudder with every orgasm and she was on the brink of her fourth when Prince caressed his hand from the arch of her back to her head and grabbed a handful of her hair. Still vigorously thrusting inside of her and rock hard on the verge of eruption, he pulled her head close to his lips and whispered in her ear,

"I hate your fuckin' ass for bein' so fuckin' beautiful and sexy and makin' me love you so fuckin' much!" Tamara smiled lustfully; she loved to be handled by her man, talked dirty to, loved to the near point of hate for her power. She reached her hand back and grabbed Prince behind his neck and began to contract the muscles in her vagina. Within seconds, Prince was pulsating and thrashing wildly. He fell on top of her, slamming her onto her stomach, thighs still spread, ass still propped up, pussy still contracting. They both fell over that edge to see all the colors of the rainbow, each color equally as intense.

Tamara felt herself getting moist again as she recalled last night's beautiful chain of events and closing celebration. She lightly caressed his ear as he slept, and giggled every time he twitched as if he thought something was crawling on him. Finally, he awoke. It was barely eight o'clock and it had been a long night. He was a little groggy, but once her pretty smile came into focus, it was all good.

"What's up silly girl?" he asked sleepily.

"Good morning, handsome," she purred, sexy and full of life as if she and sleep did not get along at all.

"What time is it?" he asked, knowing it was too early. He'd really wanted to sleep for another couple of hours.

"Around eight, why? You tryin' to leave me already?" Tamara asked petulantly.

Prince sat up, and the satin sheets fell from his chest as he felt the tight soreness in his abdominal and back muscles. It felt kind of good in a painful way; it reminded him of last night. "Damn, baby you got me all sore and shit."

Tamara watched the muscles in his back stretch and contract and felt her pussy begin to throb. *Damn, I love him,* she thought. *I would be with him every minute of the day if I could.* "Well, lay down so I can massage your back," she offered.

Prince liked the sound of that. Without speaking, he rolled over onto his stomach with a grin on his face, and Tamara climbed over and straddled his back. She spread her legs wide and rested her weight on his lower back and began to massage his upper back. Prince felt her hairless, wet pussy kiss his back. Damn. She knew he loved that shit. Laying there face down between her thick thighs, he felt himself getting hard again. Oh, and the massage felt good, too.

Tamara slowly kneaded her hands down the center of his back. "You like that?" she asked.

"Hell, yeah," Prince answered slowly as he felt himself begin to relax.

"Baby, I wanna ask you something," she said, leaning down to kiss him on his face.

Uh-oh. "What's up?"

"I know we been giving each other our space and everything, you know, and that's cool..." she began.

"Mmm-hmmm..." Prince knew something was coming.

"But, I wanna be here for you—to serve you and take care of you like the king that you are."

"Prince," he corrected. He couldn't help it. He definitely wasn't comfortable with the direction this conversation was taking. Tamara laughed.

"Stop playing! You know what I'm saying." She pushed him playfully on his back. "I'm trying to be serious!"

"All right, all right, what's up?"

"Well, what do you think about me staying here with you for a while?"

Oh shit! "What about your condo?" Prince asked instinctively.

"Its not goin' nowhere," Tamara replied with a dismissive wave of her hand. "I'll still meet my girls there. I just wanna be here for you, you know?"

Prince paused and thought about what she was saying. "I feel you baby," he said thoughtfully, almost in a whisper.

"So, what do you think?"

Prince was torn. He really didn't like the idea of their understanding being altered or the idea of his private space being imposed upon, even if it was by the only girl he had feelings for. On the other hand, he had to admit to himself that he loved Tamara. She was perfect in every way, at least she was as far as he was concerned. She was his dream girl.

He warmed up to the idea of having his lil' mama runnin' around his townhouse naked, cooking his dinner in just an apron and a pair of high heels. He thought of the few dimes he'd messed around with on the side; he'd fuck them and get tired of them and replace them with new side dishes, but he was never bored with Tamara; she was always exciting. She always made his heart beat. Because of her, he knew what it was for a man to love a woman. He couldn't see himself with anyone else. He wanted to say yes, but she just threw this shit at him while she had him all pinned down under her feminine power. He thought that was an unfair advantage. He didn't want to rush into this; he needed a little more time to think. Then, the phone rang. *Thank God,* he thought. AT&T just bought him a little time.

"Who the hell is that calling me this early? Bring that cordless to me, boo."

Tamara sighed heavily and got up to get the phone. She tried to hide her irritation from Prince because she didn't want to give him a reason to deny her. He rolled over and watched her breasts bounce as she rushed the still-ringing phone to him.

"Yeah, hello," Prince answered as Tamara climbed back in bed.

"Yes, is this Mr. Purnell Landau?"

Prince realized that he'd carelessly neglected to check the caller ID before answering, but the proper White voice on the other end of the line didn't bother him too much. It could have been a bank, a supplier for one of their construction projects or even just a telemarketer who'd somehow finagled their way around his security measures. It happens. But when he did finally look at the caller ID read-out on the cordless' display and saw that it said "Houston Police Department," he got nervous. His heartbeat sped up instantly. Even though his number-one commodity, Ball, was technically legal, according to their hired pharmacist, it was just a matter of time until it would be outlawed. Maybe that time had come.

Prince sat up in his bed. "Yes it is, and who's this?" he asked coolly as if he didn't have any idea.

"This is Sergeant Korbel from the Houston Police Department's Homicide Unit. There's been a fire, sir. We're going to need you to come down to the station to answer some questions."

"A fire? Where?"

When the sergeant gave Prince the address, his heart broke in two and tried to jump out of his throat. His mind instantly added up the circumstances: fire at Mama's house and the Homicide Unit calling could only equal one thing. He felt his windpipe begin to close. He didn't want to hear the rest. He was feeling dizzy. *This cannot be real.*

"My grandma?" Prince whispered.

"Sir, I'm sorry, but could you please come down to the station as soon as possible?"

Tamara stared at Prince questioningly, anticipating answers. She knew this wasn't good.

"Yeah, all right," Prince said quietly, then stiffened up. He had to be strong. He had to see this for himself.

"Meet me at my grandma's," he firmly said to the sergeant who was still holding the line.

"Sir, we'd rather—" Prince cut him off.

"Meet me at my grandma's," he repeated, then hung up the phone. To Tamara, he said, "We gotta go."

"Baby, what happened?"

"Just get dressed, T! There's been an accident, and we gotta go."

"All right," she answered, and rushed off to put on some clothes.

Prince called next door to inform his brother that they had to leave right away. Fatso was fresh out of the shower. Within minutes they were in traffic. Their thoughts were unclear and distorted. Prince was the most informed, but neither of them wanted to speculate or even discuss the possibilities. It was just too devastating.

When they arrived at the remnants of Mama Francine's residence, they were shocked to see that except for the wrought-iron fence, it was burned and destroyed beyond recognition. Their worst fears were confirmed.

It was a disaster. As they pulled into the first available spot down the street, Tamara was already sobbing. Fatso and Prince were fighting back the tears, but Fatso was losing the battle. Because all tragedies and drama attract spectators, many of the neighbors, some of whom did not know the Landaus, were crowded along the street and had to be held at bay by yellow police tape. The police department and the fire department were inspecting the wet, damaged premises as part of their official homicide investigation.

Tamara's mother, who also still lives in the neighborhood, rushes over to Tamara to hug and comfort her as well as Prince and Fatso. She gives them her condolences, which really don't help this early in the game because there's been no confirmation of anything at this point. Prince and Fatso quickly move on to figure things out with the authorities, leaving Tamara with her mother. After getting past the yellow tape area, they were instructed to stay on the sidewalk so they wouldn't destroy any potential evidence. This puzzled Prince because the entire yard was soaked from all the water the fire department had used to extinguish the fire, but this was no time to argue.

Once Prince and Fatso were identified they were given a quick explanation of what the fire department *assumed* happened, and then they were ordered to get into a police car to be taken down to the station for further questioning and an official statement.

"Say man, we drove here, and we'll drive down to the station," Prince demanded.

"We tried to get you to come to the station earlier but you refused. We would hate to arrest you for obstruction of a murder investigation, especially under these circumstances," the White officer said with an ineffective attempt at compassion.

"We ain't obstructin' shit, man. We'll follow you down there right now! We just had to see for ourselves," Prince argued. Fatso nodded, still looking at the scene, then turning towards the officer.

"And whose body is this? Is this...our grandmother or somebody else?" Fatso asked, hiding his emotions.

"We don't know. Dental records have already been requested and are being examined as we speak."

"Can't we just make the ID?"

"You wouldn't be able to," the officer said, letting them know that either their grandmother had been burned beyond recognition, or that someone had been trapped inside the house during the commission of the arson and/or possible kidnapping. They hadn't received any ransom calls, but this second and lesser of the two evil scenarios provided a glimmer of hope.

"Then it might not be her?"

"As I said, sir, we don't know yet. We will soon find out. Now please, get inside the car." The officer opened the rear driver's side door of the patrol car. Fatso and Prince didn't like this at all, and Prince thought of protesting some more but he also had hope of Mama still being alive. He'd better cooperate for now. He turned to his brother and told him that he would have Tamara follow them down to the station. Fatso nodded and Prince waved her over and handed her the keys to Fatso's Cadillac truck.

"What's going on?"

Prince sighed, frustrated. "We gotta go give our statements and answer some questions, so follow us."

"So why y'all can't drive yourselves? Why the fuck they gotta haul you off like y'all are some kinda damn criminals?" she snapped, turning to the officer. "This is their grandmother's house! What the fuck is wrong with you?" Tamara asked indignantly.

The officer raised his hands in mock surrender. He knew he was gonna have his way but he wasn't going to win this argument. "Just following orders, ma'am."

"Fuck your orders! We grew up in this neighborhood. You think our people wanna see this shit? Successful Black men being hauled off in the back of a police car after *their own grandma's house* is burned down?!" Tamara was screaming now. "Fucking assholes! And you wonder why we hate you muthafuckas!" Tamara turned around and stormed off towards the truck.

The officer was hardly embarrassed but she had spoken her mind and the minds of all who saw what had taken place. Everyone here that knew Ms. Landau's boys felt that the officers' attempt to treat them like suspects when they'd shown up of their own volition was some racist bullshit. Some of the neighbors began to loudly protest this and proclaim their shared distaste. The crowd had gone from being solemn, sad and tearful mourners of a tragic incident to an angry mob. In the experience of all the officers present, they knew that this was becoming a potentially dangerous situation and fast.

This particular officer tried to quickly and conveniently get the two young men into the squad car and down to the station before things escalated to any sort of violence, not that he feared any harm to himself or to any of his fellow officers, but he more so feared that some of these civilians could be hurt or killed if things became hostile, and the police force didn't need that kind of publicity. He got them down to the station so the sergeant could conduct his interview, and he kept it brief. Contact was made and apologies were made and accepted on both sides. Prince and Fatso both were in a sort of shell-shocked state due to their loss but they knew they didn't want to make any enemies downtown, either.

As they left the station and hopped into the truck, Prince had sunk into a deeper depression and feelings of guilt. As a courtesy to Fatso, Tamara remained behind the wheel of the Escalade, which was quiet as they pulled into traffic with no specific destination in mind. Each of their sharp minds was moving a million miles a minute, but neither of them said a word. They knew there would be plenty to discuss later. Or not.

Prince spoke first. "This was no accident."

Fatso began turning his head left to right slowly in disgust and blurted out, "Who the fuck plays by these rules?"

"I don't know, man, but I feel like this is partly my fault," Prince said dully.

"Come on, P, don't do that right now, man, you trippin'."

"I'm sayin', though. Mama shoulda *been* moved. We should have *been* got her up outta there. *I* should have been promoting that shit, Fatso."

"It's not your fault, P."

"I just feel like I was holding up the show because I didn't wanna inconvenience Mama, and that was a silly thought. We're muthafuckin' millionaires, Fatso, and we were supposed to protect her! We're all she had, and we've failed her!"

"Nothing is confirmed right now. The dental reports won't come back 'til the morning. So just calm down."

Prince pinched the bridge of his nose with this thumb and index finger. This is just too much. He was angry. He wanted to yell and cuss and kick the back of Fatso's seat and say, *"Don't tell me to calm the fuck down. I am* calm," but he just didn't quite have it in him right then. One thing he did know for sure: revenge was imminent. Tamara finally spoke clearly when she said,

"Somebody fucked up real bad, but it was neither one of you."

"And we're gonna find out who it is, no matter what. We have to, and they'd better hope the police catch they ass before we do," Prince promised.

Fatso nodded. Retaliation was certain, but he needed to stay calm. His emotions were pulling him in so many different directions right now, and he didn't want to go the wrong way. There was so much at stake. Fatso prayed silently to himself: *Mama, I'm sorry for whatever has happened. I pray that we have caused you no harm, Mama, but if we have, we will avenge you. Lord knows we will avenge you."*

"That's what we gotta do," Fatso said quietly to himself more than anybody. Prince and Tamara agreed with him just the same.

Sure enough, on the next morning, they got the dreaded call from the police department. The dental records were a match; they confirmed the identity and death of Francine Landau. The call was brief. Fatso hung up the phone and called his Auntie Jewel, who cried as if the entire world had come to an end.

Chapter Nineteen: D-BOY, DO THE RIGHT THANG

It's a cool Tuesday night in Downtown Houston. It's still early evening, so the happy hour crowds are just now getting in gear. Happy hours are cool and peaceful social gatherings where people can kick back and watch the game while discussing a little business and flirt with the other members of the working class. Houston has happy hours and reverse happy hours of all types all over the city. They rarely ever get crunked up like the true club scene but they served their purpose. People had a good time and some even preferred these mini-parties over the club scene. As for the popular ballers and drug dealers, they didn't give a damn where, when or how the party went down, as long as when it went down they had a hand in it being live.

Tonight, some of the biggest heavy-hitters in the city, the D-Boys, were gathering at the Live Sports Café as they did on just about any other Tuesday. It's football season, and tonight they'd watch the invincible Vince Young out of the Southside of Houston, Texas and the Tennessee Titans stomp the shit out of whoever wanted to step onto the field while the D-Boys dragged through the mud the Texans' administrative staff for not picking up the hometown sensation. They loved the team, and some of the players were their friends. They would also make four- and five-figure bets on the games and side bets on the trivial issues throughout the game just to keep it exciting.

Scat is on his way, floating down Main Street in his green CLS500. Although it *seemed* like a lot of fun and games, the D-Boys discussed major business at these little gatherings. They have Live Sports Café on lock so it's a comfortable environment. Scat taps a button and turns the music off. He's frustrated and needs to think in silence. He grabs the hundred-dollar blunt sitting in his ashtray and lights it before he cracks the sunroof. He usually doesn't smoke in his cars because of all the money he spent on custom interior details. The CLS is fit with tan ostrich skin with green suede piping to match the forest green candy paint on the body and the rims. He hated to have to take the car to the shop and leave it for two days just to repair a burn in his seats, but fuck it. Right now, he was ready to cancel a few muthafuckas and he needed to smoke so he could relax and maybe see this situation from another angle.

He had to pick the right tactic and then he had to present the whole problem and solution to Warren Lee and the other homies, Nore and Duce, so they could either discuss it, amend it or just flat out approve it, which is what normally happened. That's why he needed a good profitable solution. The problem was two-fold. Overall, his production was low. Just a few months ago, Scat was moving forty birds a week on average. Now, he was down to thirty. One of his workers got busted in the process of serving a major buyer. This froze that relationship for awhile because both sides are going to be suspicious of eachother. Understandable. You cant pressure these things. Then his other orders started getting a little low. He was sure the incidents were unrelated, but it put the weight on the rest of his D-Boy clique to move that work.

The D-Boys had a shipment quota of one-thousand kilos a month, and they had to move that weight—a half a ton of cocaine a month—sleet, rain, or hurricane. Warren Lee hated lowering prices but he would just so they could dump that surplus. When the D-Boys lowered their prices, the other families were forced to lower theirs so they wouldn't lose business for that month. Then everybody had to drive prices back to normal, but now the streets had surplus, extra dope that the dealers would buy while the prices were lower. It was risky, but it was a calculated risk. Lowering prices created a lot of variables and potential problems, and that's why Warren Lee hated to do it. But, he knew it was inevitable and sometimes good for the streets. It made muthafuckas pay attention to the politics of exchange regarding the dope game.

Scat knew that was a remote possibility; ten birds a week wasn't all that big a hit to their overall activity, but the second part of the problem that was bugging him right now was Winnie, the dread-head from New Orleans that he'd put on along with his whole clique, who was now copping five bricks a week and was talking about getting out soon. Scat was ready to twist this nigga's cap back. What really pissed Scat off was how Winnie acted like he didn't have to explain himself, like he was his own law or something. Scat just walked away and let the man drown in his own words, in hopes that Winnie would one day grow a brain and realize the repercussions of his decision and rewind. Scat could have had him merked on sight, but honestly, he really couldn't afford to lose that activity. Right now, five books a week was substantial enough to make Scat rethink this. Winnie said "soon" he was getting out, not right now, so Scat made a few calls to find out what was really going on inside the N.O. regime.

When Scat walks into Live Sports Café the mood is festive, as usual. Food and alcohol are in the air, music is bumpin' low out of the speakers because the game is playing out of select speakers as well. Players are dressed street casual. This is the D-Boy happy hour. It's not thick, but there's a nice crowd. Scat is glad he used the back door because he's really not in the mood for bullshit. He shakes a few hands and dips upstairs to the outside patio reserved just for his crew and invitees until further notice. Everybody is happy to see Scat. All the D-Boys smile, shake hands and hug like real blood family members. Some would argue that the ties that bind them are stronger than blood, that money and power make them real brothers to the nth degree. Scat sits down and starts snacking on a few buffalo wings and some pizza.

"Hey, Scat, we were wondering when you were gonna show up," Rhonda says in a too-friendly tone as she stands near the railing with another fine-ass chick named Reba whom Scat had freaked with two weeks prior. Scat looks at them and gives them the casual *Wassup?* nod. No smile. Rhonda gets the hint but Reba gets offended. She walks over to Scat, sexy and smiling in some black and gold Manolo Blahniks, black Applebottom capris and tube top with a Chanel scarf around her neck and Chanel stunna shades over her eyes.

"What's up, Scat? That's how you getting down, boo? You not even gonna speak to me?"

Scat looks at her face and sees that behind that glossy-lipped half-smile, she's really hurt that he didn't speak to her. But for what? She ain't his woman, she just gave up some ass. Regular shit. *She* was the one who caught feelings, but he kept himself from cussing her ass out.

"Say, lookout, I ain't in the mood, a'ight?" he barks with a stony expression on his face. He looks over at the bodyguard on the patio. He nods to him and waves his index finger around in a circle.

On Scat's cue, the bodyguard announces, "Listen up! We need everybody downstairs." The select group of girls and guys head out. They know what time it is. Scat looks at Reba as Rhonda pulls on her arm, telling her it was time to go. Reba, remembering to keep her feelings in check, looks at Scat and shakes off the attitude. This is a million-dollar brotha.

"Just call me, okay?" she says in an almost desperate tone, then turns and walks out. Scat couldn't stand a desperate broad. She probably wouldn't ever get another phone call. Rhonda, Reba and these other girls are top of the line boppers that the D-Boys allowed to hang out with them every now and then, celebrity groupies that would never admit to being groupies. But, they did have a sense of loyalty to the D-Boys and they proved themselves to be useful in bringing new girls around and finding out information from major players that the streets didn't know anything about yet.

It was now halftime; Tennessee is up by only one touchdown, so while they really would like to get this meeting over with, they knew it would go as long as necessary.

"What's on ya mind, Scat?" Warren Lee asks. Scat explains the situation to the crew in a very serious but nonchalant tone so as not to appear stressed, but just a little aggravated. Everybody was aware that Scat's numbers were down.

Warren Lee explodes. "You see? See why I never liked this fuckin' arrangement?" Somewhere along the line, it had become an unspoken rule that he was the only one allowed to raise his voice and express any emotion that they may all be feeling, but he also had the unique ability to quickly detach and calmly make a sound decision as to what needed to be done to handle the problem.

Warren Lee continued. "We welcomed these cutthroat muthafuckas to the city, give them a little piece of the cake so they can eat, feed they families and contribute to this movement, now look at 'em! They want it all! No fuckin' loyalty! I *told* you, Scat!"

Those last words stung but Scat had been prepared for such an outburst.

"Yeah, I got 'em, though. The nigga wanna be all slick and disrespectful like he don't owe this family no homage. I put my young boys on they clique a while back. They tellin' me this nigga Winnie been hangin' out with some *ese's* outta Michoacan. He still coppin' from me, but he probably about to flip their way. And, they say their crew has been movin' that Ball, and he's goin' real heavy into it."

Warren Lee looks at Nore knowingly. "Mmm-hmm, that figures…. That muthafucka!"

"What's up?" Scat asks like he's missed something. "Y'all think he's fuckin' with Prince and them?"

"Nah, man," Nore replies. "That nigga killed their grandma, man. Burned her house down the other day." Warren Lee shakes his head slowly.

"Do they know?" Scat inquires.

"They will," Nore says. "The streets is talking."

"That's fucked up, bro. What part of the game is that?" Duce asks.

"For what? To scare these niggas outta business or something?"

"Man I don't know what these dumb muthafuckas is thinkin'. It was some kind of robbery. They supposedly hit a lick. But that don't justify killin' a nigga's g-ma," Nore responds.

Scat shakes his head, regretting the day he'd met Winnie and allowed him to operate in his territory. "So, are we gonna tell Prince and Fatso or are we gonna let 'em find out on their own?" he asks.

Warren thinks for a second, then replies, "We gotta tell them what we know, what the streets is saying, if they haven't heard already. I don't want them to think we had anything to do with that. After all, Winnie *is* under *your* wing," Warren said, looking at Scat pointedly then glancing away. Again, the words stung.

"But let's look at it on the brighter side. Business and personal are two different things. Let them go to war and take care of their own problems and ours at the same time. The New Orleans crew is in complete violation and I wouldn't give a half a fuck what happens to them at this point. I'll set up a meeting. In the meantime, Scat...you better get your weight up, D-Boy." Warren Lee concluded with a penetrating glare that told Scat that there could be penalties.

"Fa' sho," was Scat's only answer. He meant it, too. They all went back to watching the game. Their entourage was allowed back onto the patio and Scat felt a little better, but he didn't understand why.

Chapter Twenty: A VOW OF VENGEANCE

"Unbelievable. Un-fucking-believable," Fatso says to himself as he sits on the curb across the street from his childhood home. This is his second day going there just to sit in the same spot and stare at his past, his memories of growing up and being raised by his beautiful, independent grandmother; the woman who refused failure, decided her own fate and the future of her beloved grandsons; who knew that opportunity was something to be created and education a necessity to be exercised. He imagined touching her soft, velvety skin and looking into her wise, compassionate eyes, and he remembered her stern attitude. Fatso knew that they all owed her so much. She deserved so much better.

"Who did this to you, Mama?" Fatso whispered. He owed her his education. She was the first person he'd thanked at his graduation. His diploma was hung on the wall in her dining room, which was now nothing more but ashes. He owed her his allegiance. She was a leader; she'd led them to a better life, a better way. He knew that there was no way he'd be where he was in life without her guidance. Without Mama. She'd been stolen by some tragedy, by some form of treachery. It had only been a couple of days, but he had decided he was tired of crying. It wasn't gonna bring her back. He wanted *revenge*. Fatso and Prince were determined to stop at nothing to fully vindicate the death of their grandmother Francine Landau, whose funeral is to be held the following day.

******

Prince stands in his full-length mirror in an all-black Yves Saint Laurent suit and shirt with the Cazabet wingtips on, making a frustrated attempt at tying his own tie. He looks at himself in the mirror and searches for answers in his own eyes. Prince is angry as hell that this day has come and at the way that it was brought about. He always knew that one day Mama would be moving on, but not like this. He understood the purpose behind the wake and the funeral procession and all, but right now, he just felt like he should be in the streets, hunting down these cowards to serve 'em Hell on the rocks.

He couldn't get his brain to remember how to tie this tie; he was too upset. He looked over at Tamara who was sitting on the bed sliding her stockinged feet into her black Marc Jacobs python heels. She was facing in the other direction and he assumed she was oblivious to his mental state. He felt himself hyperventilating and he felt tears welling up in his eyes. He wanted to yell, scream, break something or hurt somebody. He again looked at himself in the mirror, and, in a rage, clenched his hands into fists and punched the mirror where the reflection of his face once was.

Tamara turned in shock. "Baby! What happened?" She stood up and walked over to him.

"I don't wanna do this shit! Why the fuck do we gotta do this shit? I can't even tie my fuckin' tie!" Prince sobbed. He finally pulled his fists from the mirror and shards of glass fell to the floor. He'd cut his hand, not severely, but enough to draw blood that dripped down onto his black and white wing-tips.

"Ohhh, you're bleeding!" Tamara exclaimed, grabbing his hand to stop the flow of blood. She led him into the bathroom and rinsed his hand off with cold water, examined it and put two band-aids on the cuts.

"There. Now, can I tie your tie for you?" she asked tenderly, looking into his eyes. He looked away and tilted his chin up, giving her room to work on his tie. Tamara didn't try to talk Prince out of his anger. Although, she was being so sweet, that he automatically calmed down and became more rational.

"I'm so frustrated, baby...I just—"

"I know, Boo," Tamara said supportively as she tied his tie.

"I just don't know what to do," Prince said defeatedly.

"I understand. Just breathe easy, okay? We owe this day to your grandmother. Everything else will work itself out. You know that." She finished tying his tie.

"*Voila!* A magical prince in shining..." she rubs on the breast of his suit jacket. "What is that? Velvet?" she asks humorously, mocking the barber from *Coming to America,* which was one of their favorite classic comedies to watch together. This remark coerced a half-smile out of Prince, and Tamara wraps her arms around his waist and lays her head on his collar. Prince hugs his girl and realizes how thankful he is to have her. Suddenly he thinks of his brother and wonder how he manages without a stomp-down chick like Tamara in his life.

"Let's just take it one day at a time," Tamara says softly.

"Yeah," Prince concedes. "You're right."

"Okay, now." She disengages herself from his arms and looks down at his shoes.

"Take those off."

She disappears briefly and returns from Prince's vast closet with a pair of all black Mauris. "You like? Here, put these on."

Prince grabs the shoes and looks at them curiously. "Come on, baby, we're gonna be late. I gotta wipe that blood off."

"All right, all right."

Prince hurries to sit down on his chair by the bed. "Don't get to rushin' me now," he says, holding up his hand and stepping over the broken glass.

"Ok, let me do it."

After she puts his shoes on his feet and ties them for him, she watches him closely as he straightens his clothes and readies himself to walk out the door.

"At least now I don't have to shake nobody's hand. Fuck 'em. Let's go," he says coldly. Tamara is worried about him.

The wake and funeral are absolutely first class. Held at the best funeral parlor on the Southside, Prince and Fatso are surprised at how many people actually show up, as they had made no effort at trying to notify a lot of people. In the front of the newly constructed building, held up by stakes against the wall, was a banner that read *"South Acres Won't Forget You."* That was a touching sight. From the looks of it, Mama's entire church congregation had showed up for the service, along with friends and neighbors. There were far too many people to fit inside the building, so they were forced to file in and out of the closed-casket procession, dropping off flowers and saying prayers as they passed by.

Prince, Fatso, Tamara and Young Bread were seated up front. Big Baby and Sike kept the line moving along while Cesar, another childhood friend from the neighborhood and HBC family member, held people off from

Prince and Fatso, who had chosen to mourn in solitude, in the front row.

Warren Lee and Kesha made an appearance to pay their respects, as well as

Nore, Duce and Scat who unknowingly had been an instrument in the demise

of the deceased. Of course the true instigator, Jason the car salesman, was

nowhere to be found. After getting the word about what had happened, he'd

seriously considered packing up and disappearing to Dallas or even

somewhere farther away like Chicago or Vegas. He felt like shit. It had to be

Winnie. He knew there was something deceptive and heartless about that

guy, but this was too much. He couldn't believe it. The day after he'd heard

about it, he was too afraid to go to work, let alone show up at the funeral. He

didn't want anyone to see him and put two and two together, yet he felt

terrible about not being there to pay his respects, which was suspicious in

itself. But fear constantly haunted him. He knew what would happen if he

were implicated, whether it was intentional or not.

Outside, people were getting into their cars and leaving while some

were also turning the block to see if they would run into anyone they knew or

better yet, someone they knew could see them with their whip all shiny. As

ridiculous as it may sound, even a funeral in the 'hood was a chance to show

out, and some brothas just wouldn't pass up that opportunity. One such

vehicle, which passed by slowly along with the rest of the line of cars, is

tinted up and transporting a driver and a passenger who are closely observing

the wake service and the people entering, exiting and hanging out around the

entrance. The vehicle is a turquoise Chevy Tahoe, and the driver is Winnie.

Mo is riding shotgun. They spot Scat, Nore and Duce climbing inside two

Range Rovers, one maroon in color and the other champagne. They each had

a bodyguard, and Winnie found the irony of this hilarious. He sat back in his leather captain chair and laughed, a deep, hacking laughter that reeked of weed residue and bad breath.

"I like to laugh, too, whodie, but you missed me on the joke," Mo said irritably.

Winnie, however, was in no rush to let his lil' homie in on the irony. He stopped laughing.

"Oh, man…look at all these people, Mo. You really think that old witch was this popular? I know I don't. Scat, Nore and all them, what the fuck is that?" Winnie asked, still humoring himself.

Rather than state the obvious, that they came to show respect for Prince and Fatso, Mo considered what Winnie was saying.

"You think Warren Lee is here? He's from South Acres."

"Probably. But I know somebody's who's probably *not* here."

"Who?"

Winnie started to laugh again. "That fuckin' dumbass who sold me this truck and his soul in the same deal," Winnie quipped.

Mo chuckled a little bit. Winnie's guffaw was a little infectious, but at the same time, Mo found it difficult to find the humor in all of this. They were now engaged in a major takeover and they had crossed some serious moral boundaries, which seemed to have been uncalled for. Winnie didn't seem to recognize the depth of that, which, although he'd never admit it, scared Mo. *What was this nigga not willin' to do?* he thought anxiously.

"That nigga is probably somewhere shittin' on hisself, right?" Winnie asked.

"Huh. Well, Scat is here, so he probably don't suspect we had anything to do with it. That's a good thing," Mo remarked.

"Ha. Don't be a fool, young'n. You think them monkeys got where they're at 'cause they're stupid? I just told Scat we'll be getting out soon, which was probably a little premature but hey, he's got numbers to meet so if you think about it, it's good business. Honestly, we can get a better ticket on bricks now so fuck 'em. I just wanna see him sweat. As long as he knows we're getting five books a week, for however long, he's not going to fuck that up."

"And don't forget about all those spots we got in his territory. That's our shit!"

"Exactly. It ain't as easy as just cuttin' a muthafucka off. And he know that."

"But once they find out what's up, D-Boys might side with them Ball Club niggas."

"Fuck dat. I doubt it. They got they own problems. Besides, our soldiers is ready. It's whatever. It's war. All you need to do is keep pressin' that bitch. We gotta take over these niggas' whole network. Once this new shit really gets out there and people can tell the difference, all their shit is ours."

Winnie had already carefully analyzed and planned his strategy. He knew that in order to truly take over the HBC clientele, that it could not simply be by strong-arm but strictly supplying them with a more potent product. Ball gave you a high, but for the most part it made you horny and loose. Since it was all-natural, Ball was a popular alternative to ecstasy. But real pill poppers had to become excessive users to reach that optimum high.

Winnie knew he was a victim of the Ball phenomenon, and since he was already familiar with black magic and he knew that he really needed something that was gonna be extremely addictive and intense the first time it was used, he decided to play around with the ingredients.

Winnie had tried just about every drug in his troubled life and the one he found most addictive were heroin and crack-cocaine. Luckily, he had met some *ese's* from Michoacan who had both for cheap. Their coke prices were definitely better than Scat's. Winnie cooked two small samples of ball with the coke mixed in one and heroin in the other. He himself had tried both at different times, and the coke sample was good, definitely better with than without it, but the heroin sample proved to be an intense experience in drug use. It wasn't like using heroin: straight-shooting or snorting, it was like using *Ball*, but to the extreme edge...almost insane. It was perfect. The chemical mixture from the combination of the two caused an extraordinary reaction.

As soon as he started to come down, he felt an animalistic hunger to take another. He gritted his teeth and resisted because he knew where that would lead and it wasn't his purpose to go there. Yet, he felt like a dangerous animal, trapped. His mind was also filled with a delightful satisfaction of discovering something new and powerful. His dick was rock hard for that reason alone because he did not feel as sexually aroused as he thought he would. His fists were clenched. He decided to call it "Hardball."

Mo's phone rang and broke up Winnie's thoughts.

"Hello," Mo answered. "Oh, yeah...oh, yes...I was waiting for your call." Mo turned and smiled at Winnie, pointing towards the phone.

"Yes, yes, how much do you want for it? Yes, it's for personal use...yes, I'd like to see a presentation. Could you give me directions?...I mean, I'm sorry, just give me the address. I have a navigation system." Mo scribbled the address on a piece of paper. "Uh, one more thing, sir...do you accept cash?...All right, good. See you soon." Mo hung up and began typing the address into his phone, then he looks up and smiles at Winnie. "That was the pharmacist. He wants to give us a show on the pill packer before we buy it. It's going down, whodie."

Winnie also smiled. Everything was falling into place.

"You know," Winnie said thoughtfully, "I gotta admit somethin' to you and you only. I kind of have a new figment of respect for Prince and Fatso and their whole crew. They put a lot of shit on the streets on a regular basis. That takes organization. But to hell with 'em. It will all be over soon. I guess I'm lookin' at their operation a lil' closer since we're about to put 'em out of business."

"Ours is gonna be better," Mo added.

"Fuckin' right. Now, tell me about this broad," he remarked, changing the subject and shifting in his seat.

"Oh, yeah, my lil backup dancer..." Mo laughed. He went on to update Winnie on his new project as they drove towards the medical center.

******

The funeral had a much smaller crowd, mostly people who really were close to Francine and the boys. It was a beautiful day and Mama's pastor gave a tear-jerking eulogy, but Prince and Fatso seemed to miss it all. Knowing she would be watching them avenge her death from Heaven whether she liked it or not, they wished their grandmother farewell and committed her body to the earth. Their minds were made up.

When it was over, Warren Lee approached them respectfully. Everything he had on was of black silk. Versace, custom fit. His fade and edge-up were sharp. Kesha was on his arm, dressed in a female version of what her man was wearing. They all greeted each other cordially. Tamara and Kesha were best friends, so obviously there was more love between them. Prince watched Warren Lee impassively. He'd grown short of emotion.

One thing that had always bugged Prince about Warren Lee was that he had a severely chipped top right front tooth, which you couldn't help but notice when he talked. It made him look rugged and ghetto, like he had been involved in a liquor store brawl that hadn't ended too well for him, or maybe he had been hit in the mouth with a pistol. Prince didn't know and he wasn't close enough to the man to ask. It really drew from his appearance because he was not bad looking and he carried himself like a don, but what Prince always wondered was, as rich as this man is—his organization had to be pulling in something close to five million a month—why doesn't he get his teeth fixed? If he was a nickel-and-dime pushin' curb-server, it wouldn't really matter. But Warren Lee the Governor is a multi-millionaire and that fact made the disfigurement of the chipped tooth an annoying distraction while in conversation with this man. But hey, Prince had long ago reasoned, maybe that was the desired effect. Either way, on this day, Prince didn't really notice it too much. He was looking for something else...a tell-tale sign, but he found none.

"Again, you all have my condolences. Anything I can do to help in your time of need, all you have to do is say it and it's done. I want you to know that," Warren said sincerely.

"Thanks, brotha, I appreciate that," Fatso said graciously.

"We gonna make it bro," Prince said confidently.

"I know you are. Listen. I don't wanna bother you all on this day with any foolishness, ya understand, but we all need to have a sit-down. There are some things we need to discuss, all right? Whenever you all are ready, when you're comfortable, just let me know."

Prince watched and listened to Warren. Although he had shades over his eyes, he could tell that he was being sincere. Prince and Fatso both sensed that whatever Warren had to say had something to do with Mama's death.

"How about tomorrow?" Prince asked. He wouldn't disrupt today's peace, nor would he disrespect his grandmother that way. Today was hers, no matter how much he had to resist getting in them streets.

"If it's good for both of you, it's perfect for me," Warren Lee said.

It was set: they'd meet the following day. They all said their goodbyes, and Prince continued to watch Warren Lee as he and Kesha walked away with their bodyguard. Maybe he was being paranoid and overly sensitive, maybe he wasn't. Prince remembered reading somewhere that the death of someone close can overly sensitize or desensitize a person. Either way, Prince felt something was wrong. But then again, they'd just buried their grandmother. *Everything* felt wrong.

Chapter Twenty-One: TRUTH MAY COME

On the way to their scheduled meeting with Warren Lee and presumably the rest of the D-Boy clique the following day, Prince and Fatso float through Midtown in Prince's sky blue Aston Martin DB-9 with Sade's *The Color of Love: Live in Concert* in the CD player and a series of questionable scenarios running through Prince's mind. He turns down Sade's singing about an angel and presses a few buttons to change the C.D. She's a little too depressing right now. He switches discs but turns the volume all the way down and takes a deep breath of Coach leather-scented air. He's obviously a bit tense. Fatso, usually the quiet one, voices the thought in Prince's mind.

"I don't know what this meeting is about, P. We'll just have to find out when we get there."

"That's not what I'm thinking," Prince replies. It annoys him when Fatso thinks he can read his mind, especially when he's right.

"I saw the look on your face. Don't worry about it, man. The D-Boys are not our enemies."

"I know that. But check this out…you know these cats been wanting a piece of this action since we really started getting major paper. Warren never thought it would get to this point."

"That's true, but they don't step on our toes, nor do we step on theirs. We've never had problems with them, and I don't anticipate any now."

"So, now that you've had a chance to really think about it, you don't think they had anything to do with Mama's death, do you?"

"Nah, they're not that disrespectful. Besides, what would they have to gain? Nothin'. We're not makin' no deals with them 'cause of this!"

Prince thought about what his brother was saying. There was one thing that Prince had kept from his brother since high school. Back when they'd first got started, there was one day that he'd been a little too excited and he told one friend about their "invention." Jason was a square, a smart little dude that Prince had become cool with because Jason was from South Acres and would give Prince the answers to his science tests.

When they had put together their first batch and were trying to pull together some low-key clientele, Prince had explained to Jason how he'd found the all-natural recipe in his grandma's attic and the effect it'd had on Tamara. Jason bought a tab here and there for a while, then stopped. He said he'd had a bad experience, something to do with his mom finding out, but nothing to do with the product itself. Prince didn't worry about it because things had started picking up anyway. But he remembered on the day that he'd left that class, he wished he wouldn't have said what he'd said. He promised himself he wouldn't do that again, but then again, he'd figured Jason didn't matter. He was a square-ass dude who wasn't very friendly with the neighborhood thugs that Prince hung out with, anyway, and he was obviously under his mama's thumb, so Prince disregarded him. A couple of days later, Prince and Fatso vowed to tell no one the source of their product.

Now that Prince thought about it, he still wanted to believe that Jason was not an issue. He felt that he really needed to believe that. He never really kept secrets from his brother, and this one little discrepancy had been irrelevant for so long, that its now possible relevancy in relation to its consequences were just too heavy to reveal.

"No deals," Prince agreed. "We'll just listen to what he has to say."

******

"What's up, girl? Tamara asks as she opens the door of her condo for her best friend Kesha. As Kesha walks inside with a very serious look on her face, Tamara walks over and plops down on her oversized deep purple leather sofa. She'd just finished her bath; she had her hair pinned up and was wearing a fluffy lavender terry-cloth robe with matching slippers. The scent of strawberries and cream followed her into her plush living room.

"You going somewhere?" Kesha asked, sitting down in Tamara's matching leather armchair. She is dressed casually in a fitted denim House of Dereon cover-all with matching sling-backs.

"You know today is my relaxation day, and with everything that's been going on, I definitely need it." Tamara remarked, referring to the death of her man's grandmother and the funeral.

"Yeah, you do, girl. I don't see how you do it."

Tamara shrugged it off. She knew Kesha was spoiled and didn't like to work.

"At times like this, I don't see how I do it, either, but we gotta keep it movin'. You know that."

For Tamara, the first part of her week was her time off from her promotions company. She'd try and take care of her Ball clients for the week on Monday and Tuesday. lately by way of a runner, Serene, things had become much smoother. She'd get all of her money collected and on Wednesday, she'd just chill and have some down time or just kick it with her man. Tamara lifted a freshly rolled blueberry joint wrapped in licorice rizzlas rolling papers. Tamara stayed on that fly shit. She lit it with a short puff and passed it to Kesha who liked to smoke over at T's since she had her little boy at home and Warren didn't allow it. As difficult as it may sound considering the lifestyle of his parents, he wanted Lil' Warren to have a perfectly healthy, untainted childhood. Kesha agreed and she admired Warren's efforts. She took the joint in her hand and took one puff while it was still lit and set it down.

"You want a glass of wine?" Tamara asked while she was getting up and heading to the kitchen, where she pulls out two wine glasses and an unopened bottle of White Zinfandel. Tamara knew something was on Kesha's mind; she was obviously tense. She knew that Kesha was about to tell her what was going on, so she was not going to press her. She only hoped it wasn't anything that would blow her off day or damage their relationship. After all, Kesha is her best friend, and in the world they live in, that is hard to find.

Tamara hands Kesha a glass of wine. "You look like you're the one who needs some down time, mama. What's on your mind?"

Kesha sipped her wine and sat up very straight in her seat, poising herself. She began.

"Well, you know you my girl, right?"

Tamara nodded and wished she'd save all the extras.

"So I knew I had to tell you this before you heard it from anybody else," she said, obviously referring to Prince.

"What happened?" Tamara asked, getting frustrated because this was obviously more serious than the commercials Kesha was broadcasting. Kesha pauses and sips her wine nervously.

"Warren knows who killed Ms. Landau."

"What?! Who?!" Tamara yelled. A million thoughts started running through her head.

"That's why they're all meeting tonight. Warren is gonna tell them everything."

"Who? Who the fuck did it?"

"Some niggas from New Orleans," Kesha answered sadly.

Tamara went cold and began to calculate the different possibilities at once; the five W's: *who, what, where, when and why*?

Tamara is already plotting. "What's his name? Who they run with?"

"I don't know. He didn't tell me, but Prince will find out tonight. Don't say I said nothing, though; just let him bring it to you."

"Mmm-hmm. You know it's gonna be some shit, right?" Tamara asked. She knew she was gonna play her role to the fullest.

"This shit has gone too far, T. These niggas is scandalous. You gotta be careful," Kesha warns.

"I don't know *why* they did it, but they've started a war. I don't know what's gonna happen next, but they made the rules. I gotta play my role. She was like *my* grandmamma, too. But tell me this...how does Warren know?"

Kesha shrugged. She really didn't know. She only knew enough to know that she'd needed to talk to Tamara ASAP.

"Well, if you find out anything else, on the cool..."

"Girl, you already know I'm gonna tell you; I don't give a fuck what Warren says."

Tamara nodded. She made a mental note that Warren may tell Kesha things that he doesn't want her to repeat to anyone, and that could work to her benefit, but on the other hand, it raised the possibility that he had an ulterior motive. Either way, Tamara was all in.

Prince pulled into the valet-only parking lot of Michaelangelos, an expensive and quaint little restaurant on Westheimer in the heart of Montrose. The dimly lit establishment, founded by a first-generation Italian man and his wife, had been there since the 1940's. It was an old, two-story house that had been converted and expanded in several different directions, creating a variety of different dining areas, which included a large sun-porch style area in the front of the building. The floors are made of deep, dark cedar wood and the ambience was that of an old-world charm.

Michaelangelo's wasn't one of those grand opening type joints that downtown Houston had set up inside industrial and retail spaces with wide open scenery that left hardly anything to the imagination. Nah, it was obvious that this place had history and character. It's unique in that as successful as it was, there is only one, maintained for the basis of its existence, which is to provide exquisite Italian and seafood dishes to classy people in a rich environment that had earned them a four-star rating. You couldn't even get a table at Michaelangelo's without a reservation unless you were a regular. Although it does have an open bar in the front if you wanted to breeze in for a drink and hope someone would cancel or not show up, it is the kind of place you didn't just pop up at unless you belonged there.

When Prince and Fatso entered and the door closed behind them, the first thing that hit them was the obvious. The aroma in the air was something of a conversation piece, a combination of things like rich, homemade tomato sauce, lobster tails, seasoned steaks and basil chicken; wines and liquors off the highest shelf, fine leather and rich wood. There was also a possible hint of cigar smoke, and on the other side of the bar a black grand piano was being finessed by a gentleman who resembled Tony Bennett but the song he played was by Frank Sinatra. He had a nice voice, and he probably couldn't make it in Vegas but he seemed to be makin' it right here in a tuxedo with a smile on his face. The whole setting said three words: *class, class, class*. Prince made a mental note to bring Tamara here soon.

The hostess ushered them upstairs to a private dining room with one big table and a private waiter on standby. The D-Boys sat around one half of the table, leaving the other side open for the Landau brothers. Warren Lee sat in the middle, and the first thing Prince noticed was that all four D-Boys were formally dressed in tailor-made Italian suits, all in various dark colors, all very expensive. Warren was the only one who hadn't loosened his tie, but they all seemed to fit right into this scene. Prince and Fatso were dressed casually and they now wished they had been told about the dress code. They were known to jump fly, too, especially in these types of situations.

As hard as it was, Prince had to throw the feeling of being out of place out of his mind. He hated for someone to feel superior to him or even look it. As a matter of fact, he *especially* hated for someone to look better than he did. Prince spent a lot of money on clothes, cars, jewelry and houses to look his part of young, Black and successful. Now, he felt as if he were being showed up, outdone, like they purposely didn't tell him about the attire as some sort of psychological jab. He felt a wave of anger but he quickly let it go. He thought of Mama and felt regret for entertaining such thoughts. This wasn't the time. Fatso never really cared about that kind of competition; it was always Prince spurring his awareness for fashion statements.

The D-Boys stand, and as most brothers do, all the men greet each other with handshakes and hugs, bringing a little ghetto love to the solemn mood. The fake Tony Bennett is being transmitted through speakers in corners, but right about now, Prince could use some Mary J. Blige, Keyshia Cole or even Erykah Badu talkin' bout, "Danger, you're in danger." A brother's complex occupation was definitely a part of the equation tonight. What was understood didn't need to be discussed.

They all sat down and the waiter began to take their orders. Neither Fatso nor Prince had been hungry before they got there, but they'd suddenly changed their minds as soon as they'd entered the place and smelled the food. Besides, they knew that nothing would really be discussed until after they broke bread, so Prince tried to relax and enjoy himself. After all, they were just here to listen. Prince ordered the spaghetti with meatballs and the crab cakes that were recommended by the waiter. Fatso ordered the Veal Parmesan with Cesar salad and crusty Italian bread he would dip in peppered olive oil.

They talked about sports until the food arrived, then the conversation changed to local politics. They spoke on everything from the mayor to the DA on down to the local cops. It didn't need to be mentioned that some of these people were on the dime. Prince had heard that District Attorney Thomas Brody had been accepting third-party payments from the D-Boys for the past two years. He didn't know if it was true but he didn't doubt it, either. Hearing his name casually mentioned now reminded him of that rumor but now really wasn't the time to ask and, seeing that their business is a legal operation, Prince and Fatso really didn't care, either.

After a first class dinner and service, the Cuban cigars, imported Havanas, come out. The waiter scrambles to light each gentleman's stogie, and he is excused once he fills each glass of ice with Hennessy XO. Prince doesn't enjoy cigars as much as Fatso or the other guys, but tonight there's some grown man shit going on and he can't be left out.

"I'm sure you two have wondered what the meeting is all about. We all regret the loss of your grandmother, and of course, we have shown our respect. That's not what this is about. This is not a token of sympathy. I can imagine only one thing at the forefront of your minds at this point, and that is, Who did it? And, what this meeting is about?

"Our relationship has always been good. We haven't had any problems since I blessed your operation. I've been impressed with your success, and as you know," he looked around at his boys and grinned. "we've enjoyed your product. Truth be told, you boys from my 'hood, man, y'all have grown on me and we are like family now." He puffed his cigar. Warren enjoyed having people hang onto his every word.

"That's why I cannot stand by and deprive you of what's come to my attention. We may know who's responsible for the death of your grandmother," Warren said with a straight face. His eyes were sincere and perceptive, and he watched every movement of the two brothers, aware that they were observing him and his crew for any sign of deceit.

"We're listening," Prince prompted, trying to sound nonchalant, but he is more interested than his tone implies.

Warren Lee goes on to explain what he's heard and why he believes it to be true, how he could have waited until he had better evidence and what the consequences to their relationship could have been in regards to what that may have suggested. He admitted that Winnie and his crew were under the D-Boys' wing by way of Scat, but they were not willing to protect them in any way.

"I said all that to say this: we will not interfere in any way with your retaliation," Warren concludes.

"I see," Prince replied in a non-committal tone. His poker face is on; he was still trying to analyze his mock allies. This could mean too many things. It could be a serious game with the highest of wages, but Warren was also giving them their enemy on a silver platter. That could not be ignored.

"So you're not taking any sides," Fatso observed.

"Out of respect, I'm simply telling you what the streets are saying and why I believe it's true. The rest is up to you," Warren replied, spreading his hands out on the table.

Fatso instantly recognized that this was a way for the D-Boys to use this situation to their advantage, but he really didn't care. To them, it was business. To him, it was very personal.

"Say, man, I thank you for this information, and I respect your honesty and position in this situation. We gon' check it out," Fatso said sincerely, full of undertone. Warren knew that this was his way of saying, "I know that you'll benefit from our swift revenge."

"Do that. You brothas be careful, handle ya business," Warren said. All the men stood and shook hands. Somehow they all knew that they'd look at each other differently the next time they met.

Earlier, Prince had it on his mind to tell Warren before he left to let him know how to join the Brioni Club so he wouldn't be the cheapest outfit at the table the next time they had dinner, but matters had turned so serious he'd forgot all about that little informal sarcasm. Fuck the Brioni Club. Prince and Fatso were now thinking of joining the revenge, murder and mayhem organization. They'd already been initiated.

Chapter Twenty-Two: ICON KILLA CREW

"Meeting tonight at the Icon, twelve o'clock, same suite we always use…yeah, yeah, tell Big Baby and get our top soldiers down there. This is serious, so don't be late!" Tamara commanded into the burnout cell phone, which the crew kept on hand just for moments like this. Young Bread knew it was serious by her use of the word "soldiers". He dropped everything he was doing and jumped right on it.

Prince hadn't even mentioned to Tamara what the purpose of the meeting had been, or what had happened at the meeting. Besides the fact that he wouldn't discuss something like this over the phone, he really hadn't needed to. Kesha had already given Tamara the scoop; she'd get the details later. When she hung up with him, she called and booked their usual suite at the Icon, the Hollywood Trifecta. It was a three-story suite with a huge patio on the roof that overlooked downtown and being that it was equipped with a bar, big screen television and stereo system, it was the ideal spot for private parties. However, on this night, there would be no party. Anyone who thought so would be mistaken. Tamara's mind was racing; she'd thought of calling everyone herself but she knew Bread would handle it. He'd come along well, and she'd grown to depend on him quite a bit. Right now, with all this madness going on, she needed to know there was someone she could trust. Moreover, she knew business had to go on. Next, Tamara called Serene.

"What's up, T?"

"Check it out. You listening?"

"I'm listening,"

"I need you to run things for a few days, maybe longer. I need you to

hold it down. Can you do that?

"Yeah, you know I can. You need to see me? You all right?"

"I'm good. Some things just came up, that's all," Tamara said evasively. "We'll get together sometime tomorrow, so keep your schedule open. Where you at, anyway?

"At the Cheesecake Factory waiting for my food."

"Who you with?"

"Oh, you don't—" Serene began.

"Forget it. Listen, I need you to pay close attention to everything right now, all right?"

"I will. You sure you all right?" Serene pressed.

"I'm chillin'. I told you I'll call you tomorrow." Tamara hung up the phone and got dressed.

Serene hung up and smiled at her new friend that she was really feeling—Mo, the enemy underboss.

"Everything straight, bay-bay?" Mo asked curiously.

"Mmm-hmm...I, uh, yeah, it's straight," Serene replied. She had really come to like Mo. She'd become so comfortable that she almost told him everything that Tamara had just told her, but she held back. On several occasions, she found herself imagining that she and Mo were actually *together* and not just dating. He seemed as if he were really into her. She could tell, not that he held back to make her think otherwise. He'd been the perfect gentleman while they were on their first date on the short brunch cruise, and he'd surprised her when he'd told her that on that very morning, he'd called all the girls he was involved with and told them that he couldn't call them or see them anymore because he wanted to focus all his relationship energy on Serene. Thinking he was playing, Serene laughed, but when Mo looked her in the eyes with a straight face and swore on two or three graves, she knew that he was serious and she was flattered by this.

One of the girls had even called him back while they were together, and instead of him trying to excuse himself to go huddle up in a corner and talk to her or act like he didn't hear the phone or even turn it off, he politely answered the call with an honest, gold-toothed smile and explained to the girl, whose screaming and cursing Serene could hear from across the table, that he had met someone he wanted to give all of his attention to, and that if things didn't work out between the two of them he'd give her a call. She'd obviously told him to go fuck himself and not to call her ever again, and he took this like a man. He was polite; he didn't disrespect the girl, which would have turned Serene off because she knew how that felt.

Serene also noticed that he wasn't being possessive or too sure of himself; he was simply making the commitment of his full attention to try and that made Serene feel special. She blushed and thanked him for his courtesy and thought about how close Tamara and Prince are, how special and successful their relationship is. She analyzed their chemistry and what it was about them that made their relationship work out so well. She envied that. She wanted that kind of relationship with a man, a man who was about his business, a man she could hustle with and be down for, that she could plot and plan and get rich with, take trips around the world with, a man she could love with all her heart and be loyal to. Forget all this loose sex, sharing her body with whoever turned her on whether it was a man or woman. No, she wanted a good man her two kids could respect and respect her for being with. The more she thought about it and spent time with Mo, the more he fit into the mold of her ideal man.

On their second date, Serene opened up to him about her past as an exotic dancer at Onyx, which didn't seem to bother him at all. He told her that in his eyes, dancing is a respectable temporary hustle, a means to an end, as long as you didn't get trapped in it, and that he respected the fact that *she* hadn't. She went on to tell him about her kids, her son, who was the oldest, and her daughter. He told her that he didn't have any kids but he did want some of his own and he couldn't wait to meet hers one day. She saw in his eyes that he was sincere. She admitted that she hustled Ball after he admitted to hustlin' coke, but neither gave any details as far as quantity. It was obvious that both were heavy in the game.

Mo told her bits and pieces of his past, fabricating only where he saw fit and completely omitting recent matters of association. He delivered a colorful story which made her laugh and also made her cry at the loss of contact with his mother due to Hurricane Katrina. Even though Serene encouraged him by telling him that his mother was still alive and that one day they'd be reunited, in his heart he believed differently. He'd come to grips with that reality so it wasn't all that painful anymore. Honestly, Mo felt that he'd become emotionally numb as a result of things that had happened in his past, as well as Katrina and his mother, and now the person he'd become and the things he was a part of. It all left him empty and spent.

Even though he had money, nice cars and a luxury apartment, it was all material shit. None of it filled the void in his heart. Weed and alcohol couldn't fill it, lines of cocaine couldn't fill it. Ball, sex, strip clubs...none of it could make him whole. Mo was secretly longing for that *one*, that stomp-down chick, a *real* woman. He needed that feeling that some people call real love so he could feel human again. Mo didn't like the game he was playing with Serene because he was truly feeling her which made it much easier to do the whole nine yards with the whole act. Most of it was sincere, but the underlying intention wasn't, which made him miserable.

Serene was so real, so sexy and affectionate, so obviously passionate and looking for the same thing he was looking for. He knew she was the one; he could feel it. It was fate. And he hadn't been feeling much of anything lately since he'd run off his last real girlfriend five years ago, after he started getting money. It was misery every time he looked into Serene's eyes, but that misery provoked a certain realness and sincerity that he couldn't deny and neither could she. Mo dreaded the day that his scheme would be exposed to her, and he promised to do whatever he could to protect her from that deception.

On their third date, which took place on a rainy day, they rented a couple of movies, went back to Mo's apartment and Serene broke him off a piece of sunshine that blew his mind and rocked his world. They'd each popped a Ball tab, which only intensified the feelings they had for each other. They wanted each other; their attraction to each other was almost animalistic. They made love throughout the first movie and for the rest of the night and then they fell asleep in each other's arms to awake late into the next afternoon, knowing without speaking the words that they were in love.

When they woke up, Mo made Serene promise to keep him a secret from her people. He explained that he didn't want any of his associations to cause any problems with hers, claiming he understood the nature of her relationships and wanted her to continue to be successful with that because he planned to hopefully get out of the coke game and get his Ball on since it was legal. She understood completely and was comfortable with the idea because she knew how possessive Tamara could be. Serene wanted to wait until the right time to go public with their relationship, so she agreed to Mo's terms.

But now, with Tamara asking Serene to take over all her operations for a while, she might be able to seize the opportunity to analyze just about everything Tamara is doing and maybe even befriend some of her customers. Serene had her mind made up. She realized that her position as Tamara's sidekick and plaything was a limited one; once their attraction for each other faded, she'd be reduced once again to friend and customer status. With Mo on her side, she could build as big an organization of her own as she wanted. Tamara couldn't object because she'd still be making money with her. But if she did, or out of just plain spite decided she didn't wanna fuck with her at all, Serene would be ass out. She'd thought of this as a worst-case scenario, and there was really only one other way around this: a direct connect to the Ball supply, which could only mean coppin' direct from Prince or Fatso, which was basically impossible. Another option would be to get the recipe to make it herself, which, as far as she knew, was another impossibility.

At this point, she had no other choice but to go with the flow and see what she could see. More and more, Serene began to develop contempt for Tamara. She had to be honest with herself; she knew it was jealousy, a subtle hatred for T and for herself for allowing this girl who is three years younger than she to dominate the reletionship. Serene was tired of playing the role of humble sidekick. She felt that she was coming into her full bloom, and she was about to assume the role of dominatrix.

******

Prince faces the night from the roof deck of the Icon. He looks down at the bright lights of Downtown and collects his thoughts. With the information he'd been given about his enemies, he'd quickly formulated a murderous offensive strategy. Once he'd identified his opposition, it only took a few phone calls to gather the details about their operation. The most painful part of his discovery was when one of his soldiers informed him that the New Orleans crew had been getting more and more heavily involved in pushing Ball, his suspicions were confirmed: Mama's death was no accident or isolated incident; it was a malicious attack on his family and his business. Jewel's books had been stolen, and he also knew who his first victim would be. He wouldn't bother to share that one individual hit with his crew; he'd have them focus on the bigger picture while he handled this one himself.

He turned away from the railing and faced his most trusted cohorts. Everyone here was grim-faced, quiet. It was a serious mood. They'd all become independently hood rich; it was now time to pay their dues and secure their future positions in this family.

"There's no greater disrespect than to fuck with a man's family. For that, the penalties are severe, and ain't nan' muthafucka exempt," Prince stated coldly. Everyone nodded in agreement, and it felt like the temperature of the night had dropped fifty degrees.

Like a young military general, Prince began to lay out the plan of attack. The way he saw it, he knew there would be changes and new information along the way. Adjustments could be made but the overall outcome would be the same. He committed to supplying all new artillery, all throwaways. No detail would be spared.

"I want this muthafucka Winnie and whoever else was there to die a thousand deaths. We won't even give him the respect of a funeral," Prince demanded. A few questions were asked and a few ideas were thrown around. Everyone needed to be clear before they left the meeting and they would be. There would be no discussion of this afterwards on any traceable phones. Everything was going into full effect.

Chapter Twenty-Three: HARDBALL O.D.

Lavell Benson drove his white Monte Carlo out of the apartment complex on Antoine and DeSoto. He'd just picked up four Ball tabs for fifty dollars—they usually went three for fifty but they gave him one free, mainly to ensure he wouldn't cop that shit from anyone else other than LuLu, who, along with his crew, controlled this part of the complex. No one could sell any kind of dope over here except New Orleans niggas. Now that he had his little party pack for the night, it was on.

He picked up his cell and called Zakiyah, a fly little bopper he'd met at the Pink Panther one week ago. She was eighteen, two years younger than he. He'd taken her to the movies once, and they'd flirted and kissed. She let him feel on her a little bit before she got out of the car at her mom's house. They had talked about poppin' some Ball tabs together on their next date, which only meant one thing: fuck action. As a matter of fact, that was the name of the DJ Screw mixtape he'd picked up just for this occasion. The thought of tonight's upcoming festivities made him smile as Zakiyah answered the phone.

"Hello," she said sweetly.

"What's the damn deal, girl? You ready for me?"

"Hey you...I stay ready...are *you* ready for *me*?"

"I'll be there in about thirty minutes. I'm leavin' the nawf now."

"Oh. We Ballin' tonight?"

"Already!" Lavell hits the end button on the iphone and pops a pill. He's anxious to get his buzz on, and he'll hook her up as soon as she gets in the car. He'd noticed that these tabs are darker; Ball tabs are usually a tan color, but these were dark, almost black.

By the time Lavell pulls off the 610 loop at Cullen, a strong sensation had taken over his body. He became lightheaded at first, nauseous. He almost threw up, which scared him for two reasons: one, this had never happened before, and two, he was going seventy miles per hour on a four-lane freeway. After the initial effect, this new feeling took over. Lavell had been poppin' Ball for about six months and this was a new experience for him. He'd never experienced this kind of euphoria. He felt his jaws clench, and he gripped the steering wheel so tightly that his knuckles turned white and the bones poked almost through the skin of his hands. His left foot kept bobbing up and down, and he's full of nervous energy. He's definitely high but he didn't really like the way he was feeling. It was too intense and it made him aggravated.

He took a deep breath of the car's cherry-scented conditioned air, which also carried a hint of weed smoke which emanated from the seats and carpet and wouldn't go away no matter how much he cleaned and deodorized his car. He tried to relax before he scooped up Zakiyah. He cut for her, and she definitely turned him on and he was sho'nuff tryin' to cut tonight. But for some reason, he wasn't sexually stimulated as he normally was when he popped a Ball tab. It usually had him so horny that he had to jack off before he got with a chick just to take the edge off. He thought maybe he was poppin' too much, that maybe he needed to take a break so he could get that old feeling back. It should come together once that lil' sexy mama Zakiyah was on it.

He called her once he pulled up in front of her house because he damn sure was not about to go inside feeling the way he was feeling. He checked out his eyes in the lit visor mirror, not for her because she probably did more drugs than he did, but for himself. There was some strange shit going on. He noticed that his eyes looked kind of weird, which was normal when he was high, but something was different.

"What's up, lil' daddy?" Zakiyah asked as she hopped into the car and closed the passenger side door, being careful not to slam it. She had been around enough dudes to know how they were about their cars.

"Shit...chillin'," Lavell answered in a sleepy drawl. Zakiyah looked at him closely.

"Nigga, you already on it. Damn, you couldn't wait for me?"

"I should have, but I didn't," Lavell replied. "Here," he said, and handed her a pill. "These muthafuckas is potent, too," he warned.

"For real?" she asks in disbelief, smiling at the tablet in her hand. "I see. This must be that new shit," she pops the pill into her mouth and swallows.

Lavell takes a second to observe her reaction to the tab, as if it would have hit her right away. She smelled good, like she'd just gotten out of the tub, and she looked good, too. Zakiyah has that pretty, soft, dark skin that felt like it was naturally moisturized everywhere. She has good hair, too, but she still thickened it up with that long China doll black weave. She has the pretty Rhianna-shaped face, but fuller lips. She really didn't need make-up, but like most young girls, she overdid it. At 5'5", 135 pounds, her body is bangin' like pots and pans in a Rocawear workout capri set with a short denim jacket, heeled summer slides with the ankle bracelet and some light jewelry. Yeah, she's ready.

"What?" she asks, smiling at him in the dim light. "We gonna have some fun or you gonna stare at me all night?"

He was getting turned on. "Oh, we gon' have some fun, all right," he assured her.

When they arrived at the Motel 6 by the Reliant Center, Zakiyah was *Ballin'*. She didn't complain about the fact that she'd almost vomited from the stomach pains and lightheadedness because it had come and gone so quickly for her. Lavell was observing her out of the corner of his eye. She had adjusted her sitting position a couple of times as they rode along, jammin' to that *Fuck Action* screwtape, but overall, he thought she'd handled it well; better than he had, anyway. He didn't wanna tell her about his reaction because he didn't want to scare her. He was tryin' to freak tonight. However, it made him mad that she'd handled it so well; it was almost as if he'd *wanted* her to suffer like he had. *What kind of shit is that?* he thought to himself. Then he was more annoyed that she annoyed him. He was confused, and that annoyed him more.

Zakiyah, on the other hand, is charged up and ready to go. She'd gotten through the first part without losing it and now she was full of aggressive energy. As soon as they walked into the little basic room that was filled with stale air, Lavell barely had time to take his eyes off Zakiyah's ass doing the two-step and turn the air conditioning on before she attacked him. Quickly stripping off her jacket and shoes, she walked over to Lavell and shoved her hands under his shirt, rubbing and squeezing.

"Mmmmm..." she moaned. It was a semi-sensual sound but more animalistic. "I want you to fuck me...*now.*"

A small part of her was shocked at her own aggression, but she couldn't control what she was feeling. She grabbed his hands and put them on her ass, and Lavell didn't resist. He began to kiss her violently. She clutched him by the back of his neck as they lashed each other's tongues and bodies. Lavell slammed her down on the bed; Zakiyah screamed lightly.

"Nah, bitch, you not gon' handle me," he said while pulling his shirt off.

"Well, you handle *me* then," she retorted aggressively.

Lavell snatched her pants and panties off. He's anxious. He feels his temper rising. As soon as he opens his pants, she's there, eating him up, making animal sounds like a starving panther, sucking and licking him deep-throat style, only pausing for Lavell to snatch her top off, unleashing her fully-developed breasts to hang loose. He grabs a handful of her hair and shoves his dick back into her mouth and down her throat, trying to choke her but she's too willing and aggressive right now.

The three-pack of Magnums that Lavell had picked up earlier were still in his back pocket, but he was feeling reckless. His mind was clouded with some kind of new insanity that he couldn't quite explain. He thought he heard whispers in the room. He twitched, jerking his head from right to left, searching the corners of the room. His pores were wide open and he felt sweat beading up on his forehead. His heart was beating so hard, it felt like it was going to jump from his chest. The sexy, fruity smell that had previously emitted from Zakiyah's body turned into something more primal, more fierce. *Kill, kill, kill.*

Lavell pushed her shoulders back and threw her onto the bed. He kicked off his shoes and stepped out of his jeans. He slammed down on top of her, and she tried to kiss him but he turned away. He reached down and grabbed his piece; it was so hard that it felt like it was going to explode in his hand. He forcefully shoved himself inside her; he showed her no mercy. The thought occurred to him that he was raping her, even though he knew he wasn't. The whispers excited him.

Zakiyah screamed in pleasure and pain. She rolled over on top of him, dug her nails into his chest and rolled her wet pussy down on him. It hurt but it felt good. She wanted more. She wanted to hurt him with that pussy. She wanted to have him so sprung that he couldn't think straight. She wanted to fuck him into a coma and leave him dried up like an old sponge.

"Ahh! Ughhh!" she screamed and growled. "Fuccckkk meeee muthafucka! Give it to me! Yeahhhh!"

Lavell was getting more and more angry. *Why is she tryin' to run this shit?* Her aggression was pissing him off.

"I'm runnin' this shit. *I'm runnin' this shit,* you understand me?" As he said this, he felt himself swelling inside her, about to erupt like a super volcano. He gasped for air, but he couldn't place his mind on anything else to delay it. He couldn't stop himself.

"Stop, hold on," he panted, grabbing her hips, trying to force her to stop, but she was too into it. Her rhythm was strong.

"Bitch, I *said* stop!" He exploded inside her wet pussy like a torpedo.

"Ahhhh!" he grunted, rolling his head around on the pillow with a frown on his face. It felt incredible, but he was really pissed now because she wouldn't let up, and still hadn't.

When he opened his eyes he stared up into her demonic eyes. Her face was focused, her expression was devious, and he was still hard. She rocked her hips faster, her ass slapping against his hips. She was coming hard, multiple orgasms. Her body thrashed and bucked wildly like a little wild mustang. He watched her eyes roll into the back of her head, then he heard the whispers again. He hated her.

Just as she gasped for oxygen, he reached for her throat. He wrapped both his hands around her neck, squeezing with all the violence and anger built up inside him. From some hellhole he was now mentally connected to, he knew he hated her for being hardheaded and overzealous, for trying to control and hypnotize him with her pussy. Her body desperately needing air, she grabbed his wrists as she gagged. She felt the tight and hard muscles in his forearms, which scared her something terrible. She looked down into his eyes and saw death, pure hatred. The grim reaper was coming. *What happened?* Never loosening his grip on her throat, he slammed her down on the bed and rolled over on top of her. In a panic, she kicked and scratched and tried to free herself, but nothing would break the vise-like grip of his hands, the death grip. Her mouth opening and closing like a fish, she tried to suck the last little bit of air into her lungs through her closed air passageway as her body began to go limp. Her last thought was of her mother, and she wondered why Lavell would do this to her.

"Die, bitch, die!" he growled at her, leaning all his weight into her delicate neck. He watched the last bit of life, the last twinkle of her eye dwindle away. Her body went limp; Zakiyah is dead. A drop of sweat dripped off his nose onto her cheek and Lavell realized that she hadn't even shed any tears. He raised up off of her, naked, sweating, and breathing hard. His heart was beating like it was gonna explode. He looked at her lying there, dead, and began to panic.

"Wake up, girl!" he commanded.

He looked at himself in the mirror hanging above the dresser next to the television. What he saw there scared him more than anything; his face seemed contorted in some way; his eyes were raven black. The whites of his eyes were bloodshot red, and his full lips were dry and brittle. There was no saliva in his mouth. His nostrils were flared and his once medium-brown skin appeared to be three shades darker. Confused and afraid at what he saw, he continued to stare at himself while his face seemed to change shapes and become disfigured before his very eyes.

"What the...what's happening to me?" he yelled at his reflection.

He paced back and forth a few times, looking at the mirror every time he passed it. He panicked. He looked at Zakiyah's lifeless body and he ran over to the side of the bed.

"Bitch, I *told* you to wake up!" he yelled, slapping her across the face. Her head turns.

"What the fuck did you do to me? What did you do?" he yelled into her face. He grabbed her right breast and squeezed as hard as he could.

"You're tryin' to trap me, hoe!" He pushed away from her. "But I'm not gonna let you...I *can't* let you!" he said frantically, falling back into a chair.

"*Think.* Think, Vell. *What have you done?*" he whimpered to himself. He paused for a moment and looked around the room. The whispers are gone.

As if he were possessed by another side of himself, he said in a completely different voice, "Fuck it. She's dead now." He was now confident, satisfied and accepting of what he had done.

He felt himself coming down, an empty feeling building up in his gut. He shivers and shakes; he's falling fast. He rubs his arms and legs to fight off the cold and warm himself. He gets up to look for his clothes. As he picks up his pants he searches through his pockets and finds the last two pills in the little baggie. He needs another tab; his body is calling for one. He grabs one out of the bag and pops it. His mouth is too dry to swallow it, so he drinks some water from the sink. The dope hadn't even kicked in and he already felt better.

He puts his clothes on and waits, then he sits and thinks for a minute. Lavell knew he had to get rid of the body. He couldn't leave her because he'd checked into the room under his own name. Just as he began to wrap Zakiyah up in the hotel blanket with her clothes, the Hardball kicked in, more intensely than before. He almost passed out. He fell back into the chair, but he was not as nauseous this time; he was floating again. But this time, another reality dawned on him. He now knew for sure that he was hooked on what he'd thought was Ball but was actually Hardball, a much more potent version that evoked feelings of malice, hatred and violence.

"Come on, hoe, if you think you fin'ta lay up in this muthafucka looking crazy, you got me fucked up. I'm getting yo bitch ass outta here," he said, continuing to wrap her in the blanket like a big-ass blunt.

Still having enough common sense to check the outdoor walkway, he slowly cracked the door open—it was empty. It seemed quiet. He popped the trunk of the Monte Carlo open with the remote. Due to the Hardball making him feel stronger, he threw her over his shoulder with ease even though her dead weight was heavier.

"You'sa stupid muthafucka. Playin' and shit. That's what yo ass get. Uh-huhhh...I'ma fix yo ass," he said, quickly carrying her down the stairs with no one noticing. He threw her in the trunk and slammed it shut. He looked around, satisfied that he was home free. He jumped into the car, started it and turned on some music. *Fuck Action* wasn't quite what he needed to hear right then, so he switched it out with some chopped and screwed Z-Ro and let the truth be told again. It hyped him up. When he pulled out the parking lot bobbing his head, high as a kite, he figured it'd take him thirty minutes to get to the Port of Houston, and forty-five minutes to get to Galveston.

He stopped at a stoplight on the 610 feeder and turned the music up louder. Singing along with Z-Ro, when the light turned green, he smashed the gas and the Monte Carlo burned rubber. *Screech!* Lavell hadn't even noticed the Houston Police Department patrol car sitting in the Whataburger parking lot to his right. They shot out of the lot and hit their cherries.

"Oh, shit! What the fuck y'all want?" Lavell yelled, peering into the rearview mirror. There was no way he was gonna let them catch him like this.

He grabbed the .357 snub nose from under the seat and placed it in his lap, then he smashed the gas. The high-speed chase was on—the officers had called it in. Lavell knew the feeder road was coming to an end so he turned right into the next neighborhood. He turned and looked back; they were still coming, and he could now hear the blare of multiple sirens. He took a left, then a right, looking back every time. He wished he'd have just gotten onto the freeway and outrun 'em that way. Now he was thinking of stopping and dumping the body, but there was no time. The sirens were too close.

"Fuck!" He could see a police car coming towards him from two blocks up the residential street.

He raced to the end of the block and made a quick right, barely missing a car parked on the street. A young guy walking down the street with his back turned, jammin' his Walkman, doesn't even hear Lavell coming and is killed instantly when Lavell runs him over. Lavell looks back.

"Goddamn!" he exclaimed. "Niggas always in the way!" He looked back again to see the police car slow down so he wouldn't run over the boy.

"Yeah!" Lavell yelled in celebration, still speeding down the street. He thought he'd escaped, but when he made another turn he discovered another patrol car cutting him off from the left only fifteen feet away.

"Shit!" He cut right and crashed into a corner embankment of someone's yard. The airbag hit Lavell's chest and face hard; it felt like he'd been punched. He felt around in his lap for his gun, but he didn't find it. He pushed the airbag away as it deflated and reached down and grabbed his weapon. By now, four officers had the car surrounded, and the owners of the house that Lavell had crashed into were coming out into the yard.

"Please, stay inside your home!" The officer yelled with his gun drawn. He couldn't fire at Lavell for fear of endangering the lives of these civilians. Lavell immediately sensed this and jumped out of the car, firing his weapon. *Boom! Boom! Boom!* The .357 sounded like a small cannon. He took off running, but he got no more than ten feet in the wrong direction. He may have had a chance if he'd run into the house, but instead, a hail of gunfire ate up his back like a pack of angry pit bulls, and Lavell was dead within seconds.

When the bloody crime scene was investigated, Zakiyah's body was found in the trunk and a single tablet of Hardball was found in Lavell's pocket. The drug was tested and inventoried, and Ball was indicated as the main motivator behind this brutal crime. The news picked it up and ran it as the first drug-related homicide involving the new party drug called Ball.

Chapter Twenty-Four: SCRUB THE FLOOR

"Why'd you wait so long to have me come over, Dwayne?" Nancy whined to Fatso, trying not to be too serious with her bitching. "You just like to see me work extra hard for you, huh? Is that what it is, Dwayne? Let me find out," she said with a playful smile that said she didn't at all mind doing whatever Fatso needed her to do, whenever he needed her to do it.

"You know the past couple of weeks have been crazy as hell," Fatso said nonchalantly, sitting back on his forest green alligator sofa, watching the five o'clock news on the fifty-one inch plasma screen that hung above the fireplace. He smiled to himself as he listened to Nancy move around his kitchen.

She was right, and they both knew it. He *does* like to have her work hard for him, cleaning his house from top to bottom, washing his boxers and socks, picking up and dropping off his clothes at the cleaners, dusting, vacuuming, rubbing his back, whatever he needed or wanted done. She was usually there once a week, many times twice a week--she says it's less work that way, but really, she just wanted to be there for Fatso. Nancy is secretly in love with him, but it's not really a secret since Fatso is completely aware of the affection she holds for him.

Nancy is his own personal house mouse. He wouldn't even allow her to clean Prince's house, which Prince thought was pretty fucked up. Fatso didn't care; he didn't have a girlfriend or a woman like Prince did. Yeah, he had a couple of girls he'd freak with here and there, but the only female he saw consistently enough to be important to him was Nancy. He even had a special maid's outfit and apron for her to wear when she cleaned up. He thought it was sexy but professional, and she thought it was cute the way he looked at her when she wore the outfit, so one day she surprised him by wearing the apron with nothing on under it. It turned Fatso on to the point that it appeared he was carrying a nuclear warhead around in his pocket. So, Nancy cleaned and polished that up, too. Ever since then, it's been a part of her attire and her duties. "Put it on your driver's license," as Fatso would tell her after she gave him what he said was the best head in Houston.

Nancy is five feet 9 inches tall, light brown skinned and weighed 155 pounds, most of which rested in her 40-DD breasts. The rest of her frame is average but shapely, and her skin is as soft as whipped cream. Her hair was shoulder length and was shaped around her petite face that held pouty pink lips, a slender nose and big, innocent, dark-brown eyes fringed with long eyelashes. Nancy could have been a model but she'd opted for Biology, and now she was a registered nurse at a reputable hospital in the medical center. She'd met Dwayne Landau while she was in her sophomore year at Rice University, and she'd been doing this little maid routine for him for over a year. He paid her two hundred dollars for less than two hours of light work, which was a good side hustle at first, but now that she'd developed feelings for Dwayne—she didn't like calling him by his nickname—it was more of a fringe benefit. Nancy hadn't been over to clean up in two weeks, not since the day before his grandmother had passed. She was aware of how it affected him so she wanted to do whatever she could to comfort him. Nancy believed that given time, their relationship could progress, even though she also knew that men took longer to develop feelings.

"I'm almost done, sweetie. Just let me know when you're ready for your sandwich, okay?" she said while pulling dishes from the dishwasher and polishing them dry for a final time even though they were already dry. Fatso is a perfectionist and he hated to see even the smallest water spots on his dishes. Wearing only a hot pink panty and bra set under the white and black apron and matching house shoes, Nancy was obviously hoping to serve him more than just a sandwich.

"All right," Fatso answered with forced cheerfulness. Nancy did make him feel better, but he just had so much on his mind. His cell phone rang and he quickly answered it.

"Yeah."

"Hello, Dwayne, it's Marie. Are you busy?" Marie is the Southside site manager.

"Always," Fatso replied. "What's up Marie? Talk to me."

"Oh, I just had a quick question. Um…are you rushing the development of the new facility?"

"I mean, yeah, we're trying to get it up and running as fast as possible. It's still in the construction phase right now, though. Why?"

Marie was confused. "So, no extra orders have been placed?"

"Nothing out of the ordinary. What's going on?" Fatso asked, getting irritated.

"Well, I just got off the phone with one of our main suppliers, and they said they'd just filled an order for fifty rabbits, which they thought was strange because we're their biggest independent account."

It's starting, Fatso thought. *Let's play, then.*

"Did they tell you anything about the buyer?" he asked.

"No, just that they'd never dealt with them before," Marie answered innocently.

"Find out everything you can about the buyer. Anything and everything," Fatso commanded sharply.

"Ok, I'll get back with you as soon as I know something."

"I'll be waiting." Fatso disconnects the line and a sinister smile spreads across his face. When you cut the grass, the snakes will show. He'd told his managers to keep their eyes open for any strange activity without alerting them to any danger. He knew it wouldn't be long; Fatso and Prince had agreed they would weed out their enemies without endangering their people or business.

Fatso continued watching the news. He turned up the volume as a brother in a dark suit, white shirt and bow tie, outfit completed by Malcolm X-style glasses, began to make an announcement. He was obviously from the Nation of Islam or related to it in some form or fashion.

"The Black Houston and New Orleans communities must join together in a spirit of love, peace and brotherhood to end the senseless rapes, murders and other acts of violence amongst ourselves. It is up to *us* to take this leadership position, for *us* to ensure that we're a part of the solution and not the problem." He spoke very diplomatically as if he'd been listening to Malcolm, Martin, and other Black leaders speak all his life.

Fatso sucked his teeth in disdain. "You always got some five-dollar ass nigga talkin' 'bout peace while he cooped up in a church or lunching downtown wit' politicians, while me and my niggas is in the 'hood, tryin' to make ends meet and protect what we got left from these outsiders. This nigga is a fuckin' puppet! He's from my 'hood but he wanna talk all high and mighty," Fatso stated angrily.

Nancy steps into the living room. "Who is that...? Oh, that's Darnell X. I've met him. My girlfriend was dating him for a while. What he's doing is good. *Somebody* has to play that role," Nancy says defensively.

"Don't get me wrong. It's a good thing, but if you're gonna act like you're all 'for the people', you can't be lettin' these crackers tell you what to do and shit. If you following they political agenda and not ours, you doin' it for your own personal reasons, not for the Black community."

Nancy nodded and went to get Fatso's sandwich from the refrigerator. She could see that he was getting wired up and she didn't want to argue or add fuel to the fire. But she is interested; she knows politics is a complex issue. She set the sandwich down on the table in front of him and sat down next to him.

"Dwayne, you're educated, successful and you've got a story to tell. Why don't *you* take a stand for the community? I bet you'd have a lot of influence," she suggested with a smile.

"Because I'm *real*, Nancy. I ain't tryin' to save the world or the community. The world gotta save itself, and if it can't, oh, well. But I'm honest about it. I'll tell it to anybody. I'm not gonna say a whole bunch of pacifying bullshit just to make myself look good to a certain group of people. Fuck 'dem people! That's why I have so much respect for you, Nancy, because I know you really care about them people you work with at that hospital. Me, I just care about the people that's close to me. You either with me or against me. I don't really see in between no more." Fatso cast his eyes downward when he spoke the last part of his statement, and Nancy knew that it came from a painful place in his heart that not only saddened him but hardened him as well. She felt for him; she knew that he was being honest.

"I understand," she said compassionately, and she did. She walked behind the couch and began to massage Fatso's shoulders slowly. Fatso enjoyed it and began to relax. He closed his eyes for a second, and when he opened them again, Nancy's white apron was being dropped into his lap. She stepped back around the couch in her hot pink get up, barefoot and now walking on the balls of her feet. She stepped between Fatso's legs and leaned down and kissed him passionately. His tongue danced with hers hungrily as he reached up and squeezed and caressed her breasts, knowing that this was her sensitive zone. She moaned out loud, breaking their kiss. She pulled her bra down to expose her dark raspberry-shaped nipples, squeezing her breasts together and putting them in Fatso's face so he could tongue kiss them the way he liked to do. Fatso leaned forward and grabbed them, flicking his tongue from nipple to nipple.

Nancy called out, "Oh, baby, yes... you make me feel so good...."

After a minute or so of that, she dropped down to her knees and Fatso leaned back again.

"Can I suck it?" she asked. Fatso loved when she asked him that. She said it so sensually, but it sounded so innocent at the same time.

"Yeah...hell, yeah," he replied, nodding his head.

Nancy loosened his belt, unbuttoned his pants and freed his missile, and her eyes lit up like she was looking at a pot of diamonds. Her mouth was watering. She flicked her tongue around the head a few times, then licked up and down each side. She wrapped her hand around it, loving the feel of that thick muscle in her hand. She looked up into Fatso's eyes and then took him in and out of her mouth for two strokes, and then on the third, she took his whole piece down her throat without gagging. She didn't even break eye contact. After performing that trick, she went to work; her mouth, tongue and both her hands stroked his meat in complete unison. Saliva was running down the sides of his dick, and her rhythm was unmatched and unbroken. She was taking it in her cheek, sucking down the sides, then back into her mouth for the deep-throat action. She was the best, and Fatso was on his way to Heaven.

"Goddamn, baby...where you learn this shit?" Fatso asked breathlessly, trying to distract himself. He was entering those gates. Nancy didn't answer; she just looked up at him with those brown eyes and took his long shaft down her throat again. She loved sucking Fatso's dick. She'd only had a few, but Fatso's was her favorite.

Fatso's little attempt at distracting himself didn't work. He clenched his jaws, closed his eyes and enjoyed his display of Northern lights as he squirted in the back of Nancy's throat. She swallowed it all up like a true champ and still didn't want to stop. He started to go limp slightly but it was too sensitive. He couldn't take no more. He stopped her.

"Hold on, baby, shit! You keep suckin' me like 'dat, you gon' have a brotha drawed up in the corner shivering like a lil' dopefiend," he said with a half-smile, still trying to recover.

Nancy wiped the sides of her mouth with her wrists and jumped up. "I'll get you a towel," she said while walking to the bathroom.

"And bring me something to drink," he ordered. "Orange juice."

"Ok," she said cheerfully, and came back into the room with a towel in one hand and a glass of orange juice in the other. Fatso was already devouring his sandwich. He let her wipe him up, then continued eating and drinking his juice without fastening his pants.

Nancy sat down next to him. "Anything else?" Nancy asked, hoping he'd be up for a relaxing day including a round two. They'd only had actual intercourse twice and she loved how he felt inside of her. But every time she sucked it, he wouldn't let her stop. She wanted to ride that dick today.

"Naw, sweetheart, I'm straight. You've been like a dream today, but actually, I have some shit I gotta go do. A couple of things just came up," he said, standing to button his Evisu jeans and fasten his belt.

Nancy was crushed, but she hid her feelings well. "Okay, Dwayne. Well, call me. You know I'm always here for you," she said cheerfully, then hopped up to grab his plate and glass to wash them and put them away.

"No doubt," Fatso replied thoughtfully, then, "Say, Nancy,"

She stopped in her tracks. "Hmmm?" she asked, looking back at him.

"You know, you're the best. And I'm not just talking about *that*," he quipped, gesturing at the couch with a smile. "I mean I appreciate everything you do for me. I just wanted you to know that."

Nancy smiled and blushed; she had to fight the tightening in her throat. She is so in love with this man and now he was finally opening up to her in his own way. She almost blurted out how she truly felt, but instead she looked him in the eyes and said, "I'll do anything for you, Dwayne."

Fatso is no fool, and he knew exactly what was behind that statement. He nodded at Nancy and said, "I'ma call you."

When Nancy left, Fatso was not far behind her. He had an idea, and he needed to discuss this with his brother. But first, he had to make a couple of stops.

Chapter Twenty-Five: DRIVE-BY

Serene hopped out of her lavender-colored Jaguar in the underground visitors' parking at the Houstonian luxury condominiums. After signing in and being cleared by security with a phone call to the resident, she was on her way up to Tamara's to make her weekly drop. It was a hot-ass day in Houston, ninety-four degrees with the usual humidity, so she was glad to get on the air-conditioned elevator. She was already stressed out, so the heat only compounded her irritation.

On the way up to the twenty-eighth floor, she checked her reflection in the mirror. She knew she had to have her act together when she stepped into Tamara's presence. The girl is sharp. Anything out of place, any weakness or false move and she would call Serene out on it, and Serene knew it. Tamara would be watching her extra closely now that she had given her so much responsibility. It was the second week that Serene had been running Tamara's operation and it had been tense, busy and enlightening. Serene had to admit that Tamara has her shit together, and she had been taking notes daily. She only had one regret.

After an incredible night of back-breaking sex with Mo, she had broken down and told him all that was going on with her. His tongue was massaging her G-spot, and you couldn't tell her that she was not head over heels in love with everything to give. After she had popped a Ball, snorted a couple lines of coke and indulged in a spree of multiple orgasms, her mouth started runnin' like the Texas relays. She felt so close to Mo, he was perfect for her.

She loved the fact that he was a stone-cold hustler making real money on his own. No doubt he was the one. She was convinced that together, they could give Prince and Tamara a run for their money. Literally. She just didn't want to expose all her business, not yet. She enjoyed having the power of mystery to keep a man intrigued and chasing after her. She felt like things changed once they had you figured out. Even though, after she laid all the cards out on the table, Mo seemed to be just as much in love—if not more so—than she, it still was a regret because in order to reveal her hand she had to tell many things about Tamara and Prince's operation as well. She looked herself in the eye and patted down her bushy hair that was wrapped in a lavender Roberto Cavalli scarf.

"Oh, well," she said to herself. She'd accepted the fact that whenever that time came, she just had to trust herself and Mo to use everything to their advantage. She wasn't tryin' to push that time coming, either. No matter how much pressure Tamara put on her by having her under her thumb, Serene was sure that she'd rather be on Tamara's side than against her, but there was no turning back. *"It is what it is."*

She knocked on the door and Tamara yelled, "It's open!" Once inside, she suddenly felt more tense. She didn't like it, but she'd play it off the best she could.

"Hey, T," Serene said cheerfully.

Tamara paused on her way into the living room and analyzed Serene's outfit as she walked through the door.

"Damn, bitch, there you go with that lavender shit," she began with a half-serious rant, referring to Serene's scarf and strapless blouse. "Why don't you paint that damn car blue or white or something so you can get a new fucking wardrobe. That lavender shit is getting on my nerves." Tamara said as she continued walking into the living room with her open black satin robe flowing behind her, and a black satin thong and bra underneath.

She walked around her breakfast bar into her kitchen and began to pour two glasses of mango juice. Serene followed and sat down on a stool.

"What do you mean? It's not like I wear this color everyday, Tamara," Serene said defensively, digging into her oversized cream-colored Coach shoulder bag and pulling out a large Ziploc bag filled with stacks of money. She placed it on the counter.

"Bullshit. You had that damn lavender skirt on the last time I saw you," Tamara observed while placing the glass of juice in front of Serene and grabbing the bag of money.

"Oh, you know what...I sure did. That was just a coincidence, girl. But if it bothers you that much, I'll lay off the lavender," Serene conceded. Again.

"Thank you. Now, undo these rubber bands," Tamara commanded. She put the bag back in front of Serene after taking a handful of stacks herself and beginning to snatch the rubber bands off her stacks, she set the money on the counter and grabbed a small money-counting machine out of the cabinet. She turned it on, fanned out the bills and secured them in the top of the machine. She pressed a button and it began flipping through the bills faster than any human hands could count.

"Fifty-five thousand, exactly," Tamara declared after she'd let the machine run through the entire bag. "Here," she said, placing a five thousand dollar stack in front of Serene. Five G's—her pay for the last two weeks. Tamara left the other fifty in five even stacks next to the money machine.

"You're doing all right. Now, tell me what's the scoop."

Serene put the five stack in her purse. "Well," she began, "That girl Honey from Greenspoint wants to up her order by two hundred."

"Two hundred?" Tamara asked, thinking, *Who the fuck does that bitch think she is?*

"I know, I know. I told her it's either five hundred or a thousand."

"And what she say?"

"She said five hundred should be cool."

"Good. And she'd better push that shit, too. I don't wanna hear no excuses. What else?"

"Everything else is cool except Mya in Acres Homes."

Tamara sucked her teeth. "What's up with that schizophrenic hoe?"

"Well, when I came through she started actin' all funny, talkin' bout she might have to chill for a minute, and that she'll let me know when she's ready."

"Let *you* know?" Tamara scoffed, rolling her eyes.

"You know, you, me…same difference. I asked her why but she didn't really give me a straight answer. And she was actin' so strange, she spooked me out, girl, so I just left. I figured it'd be best to let you decide what to do about her." Serene explained. She didn't want to admit that she was really a little afraid of Mya. The girl is extra gutter and carries herself like a man, which usually didn't bother Serene, but it was something about Mya's vibe that screamed "ruthless." But no one could deny her hustler status. She definitely was a go-getter and Tamara never had a problem out of her.

Tamara thinks about this briefly. It's time to see what Serene is made of.

"Listen, some dudes from New Orleans is tryin' to move in on our business. They been doing some real scandalous ass shit so I wouldn't doubt if they tried to come at Mya. Shit is getting crazy, but Mya ain't stupid. I been good to her, so somebody needs to check her to remind her of that shit," Tamara said and paused in order to gauge Serene's reaction.

Serene picked up on it right away. She didn't want to, but she had to. She swallowed hard and said, "I'll take care of it."

Tamara looks Serene straight in the eyes for almost five seconds without blinking. She nods and walks over to the sink to wash her hands with antibacterial soap to wash off the germs from handling the cash. Tamara squishes the soap around in her hands and rinses, then she smells them. They smelled of apples and cinnamon.

"Come wash your hands."

"Yeah, let me do that," Serene says distractedly, then gets off the stool and does as she is told. She had so much going through her head about what Tamara had just told her, but she knew Mya was from New Orleans and she didn't want to even go there. She had to wonder if Mo was involved...if those people were the same people who had killed Prince's grandma...if she was being played. This could change everything.

"Is this thing with these New Orleans people serious?" she managed to ask.

"Yeah, but it will be taken care of real soon." Tamara said coolly, almost sarcastically. She was watching Serene over several gulps of her juice. She set her glass down.

"So, what's up with that nigga you seeing?" Tamara made it sound like casual girl talk, but this line of questioning was not at all casual. It was investigative.

"Nuthin'. It ain't shit but some dick, girl."

"Hmm. You sure about that?" Tamara said, stepping closer to Serene from behind.

"Mmm-hmm," Serene answered, drying her hands on a paper towel. She turned around to face Tamara who was right up on her. Tamara is actually two inches taller than Serene, but with Serene wearing heels, they were practically nose-to-nose. "That's all."

"Good. Let's keep it that way, all right?" Serene nodded.

"You still my bitch until I tell you otherwise. You understand?" Serene nodded again as Tamara stared her in the eyes. "Let me find out you in love. I'ma cut yo ass smooth the fuck off."

Serene looked down, then looked back up into Tamara's hard stare. "What? What's on your mind, Serene?"

"Well, I just thought that since you had been spendin' so much time with Prince that—" Serene didn't even get to finish before Tamara had her by the chin.

"Bitch, don't you ever in your life mention my man's name like you got the right to be in his category! You lost your rabbit-ass mind, hoe?" Tamara yelled into Serene's face from point-blank range. And she was right. Serene regretted those words as soon as they'd left her lips. She knew how sensitive Tamara was about Prince. Tamara pushed her away from her and walked off.

"I didn't mean it like that. I shouldn't have said that. I'm...I'm sorry," Serene stammered.

"You muthafuckin' right you shouldn't have said that. Bitch you *way* outta line!"

"I'm sorry," Serene repeated.

"You sure the fuck are. But you know what? I got you. You think you gon' handle me? Call yo'self tryin' to check me? What you *need* to do is go check that bitch Mya before I cut *both* you hoes off and feed you to the wolves! That's how you can make this up to me. Bye. Be gone!" Tamara was done talking. Serene headed for the door.

"I'll call you when I talk to her," she said as she walked through the foyer. There was no response. She left.

When Serene got into the hallway and walked to the elevator, she felt like shit on a stick with flies circling. She knew that she was not going to put up with this shit any longer. She had to make some serious moves, but she had so many new questions now that she needed answers to. And she knew just where to get them answered.

When she pulled her car out of the garage and into the street, she called Mo to find out what was really good. She had him on speed dial.

After Serene was dismissed, Tamara sits on the couch with her laptop and replies to a few emails. As she clears up a few minor concerns about this Thursday's M Bar set, she reflects on Serene's whole demeanor.

She really had some nerve bringing Prince's name up. *There had to be some kind of negative feelings behind that,* Tamara thought, *but what? I'm hookin' that bitch up. She's making twice the money she was making before. And I've always been with Prince so it couldn't truly be because of that unless she's tryin' to get too attached.* "Nah," she says, discounting that theory. *She's not around enough for that anymore.*

Tamara finishes sending her last email, or, the last one that she is responding to right now, and closes her laptop. She closes her eyes and thinks about the conversation. She places her finger on the dimple in her cheek as she cracks a smile and giggles to herself.

"Mmm-hmmm...somebody's feeling guilty. The question is, about what? I'll find out soon enough." Satisfied that she was on to her little girlfriend, she hopped up to go straighten up her bedroom. The phone rang.

"Hellllloooo," she sang into the receiver.

"Ms. McAaron?"

"Yes?"

"You have a visitor here named Prince."

"Send him up, please. Thank you."

"You're welcome."

Tamara turned off the cordless and quickly straightened up the few items she had strewn across the bathroom vanity and hung up a couple of outfits that she had thrown across her bed before she sprayed a few misty shots of Juicy Couture on the satin sheets. Prince loved that fruity fragrance; he said it turned him on. This meeting is the highlight of her day. She was already blushing and he hadn't even walked through the door yet. Prince is supposed to be coming by to talk a little business, which probably also meant he was bringing her new supply for the week. With everything that was going on, she was sure there were some things to discuss, as well. But Tamara missed her man. They hadn't made love in two weeks, and even though she understood things were hectic right now, that is just beyond abnormal.

******

Tamara is horny and excited. She takes off her robe, hangs it up on the bathroom door and admires herself in the mirror. The black satin Victoria's Secret bra is hugging her large breasts perfectly and her cleavage is screaming for attention. Her skin glistened from the coconut milk bath she'd taken earlier and the Carol's Daughter Shea Butter cream she'd rubbed all over body. Tamara knew she had a bangin' body, but she was really feeling herself right now.

Knock, knock.

Tamara checks the peephole to make sure he is alone before she treats his eyes to an early dessert.

"Damn, what's up, sexy?" Prince says when she swings the door open. He quickly steps inside. Prince is dressed casually in a dark blue linen Rocawear sleeve button-down with the matching slacks, navy blue Rocawear golf cap and blue-and-chrome YSL aviators. On his wrist was a platinum and diamond Hubloz watch, and on his feet were the classic blue-and-white Rocawear shell-toes. He is staying on top of the H-Town fashion rule that states: if you rockin' a Black clothing line then your entire outfit from head to toe must be from that line if it's available and if you got it like that. If you're not, that's a tell-tale sign that you *don't* got it like that. Just don't go clashing different items of clothing from different Black designers, even if your colors *are* matching.

"You. Just waitin' for you," she flirtatiously replies.

"Right, right. I like that. But you know you run around the crib like that all the time," he joked.

"I do not!"

Prince placed his aluminum briefcase, which looked like it should always be handcuffed to his wrist but never was, on the granite countertop.

"Oh, it looks like you have a lil' present for me, too," Tamara hinted.

"Maybe," Prince said while he matched up the numbers on the combination lock. He popped open the case and pulled out ten six-packs of Ball and set them on the counter. A hundred-thousand wholesale, two to two-hundred fifty thousand in street value.

"Surprise. Now, let's talk. C'mon, we have a lot to discuss." Prince walked into the living room and sat down, but not before he noticed the five stacks of cash sitting on the counter, which he didn't mention because he has bigger things on his mind right now. As he sits down, Tamara goes the opposite way around the coffee table to sit on the couch next to him, and the sunlight coming through the picture window glistened off her skin. He smirks as the blood rushes through his loins. *Damn, my baby is fine!* He has to remain focused, though, and he almost tells her to put a robe or something on, but he just can't get the words out. He enjoys looking at her too much.

"What's up, babe?" Tamara said with a half-smile on her face as she sat down at a safe distance from Prince. She'd caught him peeking but she knew he had some things on his mind that he needed to relay and she respected that to the fullest.

"Well, you know everything that's going on up to this point. But me and Fatso, we been talkin', tryin' to consider all the options and repercussions, you know? And...we came up with a plan, a backup plan, really."

Tamara nodded. "I'm listenin'."

"See, the thing is, baby...no matter what happens," Prince began, punching his palm twice for emphasis, "we can't let nothin' stop our push to the West Coast and to the East Coast, and eventually, worldwide." Prince made eye contact with Tamara and let that last statement sink in. Tamara nodded thoughtfully.

"Prince, we've talked about this. *Nothing* is gonna stop us. Are you worried about this New Orleans situation? Did something happen?"

"Nah...them niggas—" Prince waved his hand and looked away as if he were disgusted by the mere mention of that 'situation'.

"Look, them niggas gon' get dealt wit'. It's bigger than that. Ball is bigger than that. It's bigger than all of us. This is big business, and you're a part of this plan, Tamara." Prince looked her in the eyes and continued. "Now listen..."

For the next thirty minutes, Prince broke down a detailed plan of how they were gonna penetrate the Los Angeles market and how Tamara is going to be the main catalyst to making that happen. He gave her a couple of contacts and a list of people she needs to talk to and social circles she needs to become affiliated with.

"We don't intend for anything to go wrong with this search and destroy mission we're engaged in, but if it does, this is the protocol."

Tamara winced. She couldn't stand the thought of it, but she knows it's a reality. Prince grabbed her hand to comfort her as he walked her through it. He posed several different scenarios, told her who to contact and how to contact them, as well as how to conduct business, what to have ready, where to go and when to make each move. Tamara committed each detail to memory except for a few select phone numbers that she saved in her computer and phone as unidentified memos.

After all of that, they both felt much better about the future. Prince felt that much of the burden had been lifted from his shoulders, and Tamara was also relieved that should these emergency situations ever present themselves, she would be prepared and would know what to do according to Prince's wishes. Their preparedness made them both more secure and made their relationship stronger. Prince pulled Tamara close, hugged her to his chest and kissed her on the forehead.

"Don't worry, boo. It's gonna be all right. We gon' be straight. We just gotta be ready," Prince reassured her.

"I don't ever wanna lose you, baby. I can't ever let that happen. I love you with every breath I take," Tamara said passionately.

Damn! Prince thought. *Every breath. That's heavy.* Those words had more impact than if she'd have just said "I love you." That was some Alicia Keys' *Tears for Water*-type shit. It turned Prince on. He was really feeling her right then. Tamara is truly his heart, his one and only, his rock bottom, his stomp-down chick.

"I love you, too, baby," he said, hugging her tightly. "You make my heart beat." Prince glanced at his watch. "Oh, uh...Fatso gon' be here in less than an hour."

Tamara's head popped up in surprise. She wasn't aware that Fatso was coming by, although it wasn't unusual. But that meant that there wasn't much time to play with right now. She got the hint as they locked eyes, followed by their lips in a passionate, hungry kiss. Their tongues did a quick dance before Tamara pushed away.

"Uh-uh, come here," she said, pulling him by the hand towards her bedroom.

"Nah, that's boring," Prince said, yanking his hand from hers and stripping off his clothes and laying them neatly on the loveseat. In seconds, he's naked. His soldier, standing at full attention, draws Tamara in like waving raw meat in front of a hungry tiger. Time and place become irrelevant as she drops to her knees and begins eating him up, moaning and slurping him in and out of her mouth like a big chocolate pudding pop. Prince unsnaps her bra and palms her left breast.

"Now *you* come here," he says, pulling himself out of her mouth and standing her up. He pulls her panties down and picks her up in his arms.

"Where you takin' me?"

Prince sets her naked ass on the cool granite of the breakfast bar between the two stools.

"Ahhh! It's cold!" she exclaims, but she quickly adjusts. She's too excited to really object.

Prince places her feet on the stools on the left and right of him so her legs are open and cocked up, exposing her pretty pussy. Prince takes a quick step back to observe her.

"Now *that's* a work of pure art. Mona Lisa ain't got shit on you, baby," Prince says, stepping into her. She leans back slightly on her hands, and he leans down and licks around her pussy lips with a couple of quick flicks of her clit. He licks inside her one good time to taste her juices before sticking his tongue all the way inside her and massaging her upper wall. He knows her body well and hits all her sensitive points. He even licks around her anus before he pushes his middle finger inside and massages her G-spot from the backside while sucking on her clit.

"Ooooh, Prince, baby, that's feels so...ahhhhh! What are you doing to me? Mmmmm...*ahhhhh*!" Tamara climaxed at least three times, screaming out Prince's name each time. Her legs were shaking so violently that she almost kicked the bar stools over.

Finally Prince, cum dripping from his chin, popped up from between her legs like a deep-sea diver breaking the surface. Tamara wiped his mouth, and he picked her up and wrapped her thick, creamy thighs around his waist. He guided himself inside her hot, wet pussy. He picks her up and walks her to the bedroom and, still inside of her, falls down on top of her onto the bed.

"Oh my God, Prince, you're an animal!" Tamara screamed with delight. Prince rocked her boat for the next hour, non-stop, until all the phones started ringing non-stop. They knew it was Fatso, and they were glad he was late.

Prince opens the door for his brother. "What's up, bro?" When Fatso walks in, he sizes up his Prince in his boxers and slacks. His cut-up physique looks as if he'd just finished working out, and it was obvious what kind of work out it had been. Fatso smirks.

"I almost dipped out on yo ass, havin' me call a hundred thousand times."

"You called *three* times," Prince replies, holding up three fingers.

"Same thang."

"Have a seat, man. You want something to drink?" Prince offered.

"Whatever kind of juice you have on ice. Where's T?"

"Right here! What's up big brotha?" Tamara said enthusiastically, stepping into the living room in her robe and a huge smile spread across her face.

"Ah-ha!" Fatso said, grinning. "The other missing-in-action, literally." he said sarcastically.

"Our bad...we was..." Tamara glances over at Prince.

"Getting ya groove on. I already know. Sit down so we can talk."

Tamara sits on the loveseat, laughing and blushing. Prince walks in with two glasses of mango juice and hands one to Fatso.

"Say, man, watch how you handle my woman," he said, winking at Tamara who takes his glass of juice, takes two big gulps and gives it back as he sits down next to her. Fatso is on the couch.

"You told her everything?" Fatso asks Prince.

"Yeah," Prince replies. Tamara nods solemnly.

"You understand, right?"

"Definitely," Tamara nods, glancing at Prince.

"Good. It's of the utmost importance that you do."

"No doubt," she confirms.

"All right. Check it out, P," Fatso says, switching his attention back to his brother. "I think we got this muthafucka!"

Prince's eyes light up, and Fatso explains his plot.

Chapter Twenty-Six: THE D.A.'S FIX

It's a busy day as usual at Downtown Houston's criminal justice center at 1201 Franklin. Civilians and attorneys are out front watching the busy one-way street while they wait for family members and clients to show up, while others are being shuffled through the metal detection gateways, removing cell phones, belts and other metal objects and placing them in the small baskets provided for this purpose. Further inside this massive entryway, at the stone marble and wooden elevator banks, more attorneys and clients are glued to their cell phones trying to get the best, or most profitable, outcome from today's proceedings, depending on their position.

Most of the defense attorneys were also part actors as well, because honestly, they couldn't care less either way, unless it was their first or second appearance for a client because in that case, they really had to shine to win their client's full confidence and the other half of their retainer. Other than that, it was just another day of legal hustling; mingling with the district attorneys, judges, clerks and politicians over happy hour specials and calling in favors for the following week. But the thing is, favors were only called in for the select. If you were Black, Latino or Asian, you'd better have a clean record and a slam-dunk defense along with pockets down to your ankles. Without at least two of those three advantages on your side, see ya.

Harris County, even Texas as a whole, don't give a damn about your constitutional rights. They were trying to ship you somewhere and put you in a white uniform. *See ya.* They'll corner and coerce your grandma into a plea bargain for two or five years if they picked up charges on her, and they picked up *all* charges on *everybody*. They don't give a damn if Texas legislators and the Feds are coming down on the entire Texas Department of Criminal Justice for overcrowding and failure to follow their own parole guidelines. *Sorry, grandma. See ya, and I damn sure wouldn't wanna be ya.* No wonder the state slogan is "Don't Mess With Texas." You would think people would have learned by now.

******

Up in suite 600, District Attorney Thomas Brody's phone begins to ring as he reads over the examiner's notes on a Food and Drug Administration report.

"Tom Brody," he answers huskily.

"Tom, Chuck Yancey here. Did you get the report I emailed to you?"

"Hey, Chuck, I'm reviewing it now as we speak, and I gotta tell ya, it seems pretty consistent with our prior reports and hopefully I can get a ban on this crap. But something's fishy here."

Federal District Attorney Chuck Yancey, fifty-one years of age, is a friend and colleague of Tom Brody. They both attended University of Texas in Austin and had hustled their way into prominent positions. Chuck is a pit bull when it comes to murder and drugs. Tom shared the same passion and work ethic until he'd married his second wife who was almost fifteen years younger than his forty-nine years and an undercover big spender with expensive taste, which is what had brought them together in the first place. With alimony and child support kickin' him in the ass from his first marriage, along with a couple of vacations and shopping sprees with the new blonde bombshell, Tom decided to take up a couple of offers for an extra salary, off the books. It seemed despicable at first, but he'd grown accustomed. After all, everybody seemed to be doing it in one way or another, and besides, the money was great.

Now, with the 2010 elections right around the corner, he needed to shake things up with some big headlines. With this senseless homicide placing Ball on the center of the stage, he might be able to spearhead a huge drug investigation by introducing a new controlled substance to the administration, rack up a whole new string of indictments and convictions, therefore raising the state's revenues and his own bonuses, *and* be a hero just in time for the vote, all the while keeping his "other sources of income" undisturbed. In his mind, Tom Brody had the perfect agenda. But he needed his superior colleague, Chuck Yancey, to join the club and pull strings on the Federal side in order to get the FDA ban he needed to add it to the controlled substance list and get his investigation on the road.

"Well," Tom explained, "in a recent homicide, we pulled some of this new controlled substance off the perpetrator after he'd decided to have a shoot-out with the cops. Needless to say, he lost. The substance tested positive for traces of heroin, which made a lot more sense to me, but I don't see it here," he said, referring to the report.

"Well, Tom, maybe they're two different substances or two forms of the same, like ecstasy," Chuck replied.

Tom leaned back in his chair and laughed out loud, rubbing his pouch of a belly. "Excuse me, Chuck, but let's not go there, please. I mean, we see what happened; a frickin' international phenomenon. Now just think how the guy who could have crushed that seed feels. Pretty lousy. No, don't mind me at all when I say, whether it's one form or ten, it's all the same to me, and, on the record, it's so isolated now that it has to be coming from the same source. I'd really rather just flush them all out now before we have this ecstasy conversation again. You know what I mean?"

Chuck knew exactly what he meant. The Feds were holding up some major indictments of which there were never too many during election year. Tom also had a point about the drug craze in America. It was out of hand. This could look good for everybody.

"I do. All right, well, send those lab reports and samples over to the FDA. I'll send a memo. We'll see what we can come up with," Chuck said confidently. Tom could hear it in Chucks voice: He was in.

"I'll get 'em out today, buddy. Thanks a lot. Make sure you tell the guys at FDA to expedite the turnaround. I have a lot of pressure on me; a couple of officers almost got killed when this kid went psycho off this stuff."

"Wow. I'll make sure to mention that."

Tom hung up, feeling stronger. He picked up the report in front of him and looked it over again. Compounded effects, human reactions, yadda-yadda. 'Non-synthetic make up', 'sexual stimulant', 'natural euphoria'.

"What the hell? The FDA almost makes it sound like it's a good thing, like some sort of Spanish fly. Hell, I almost want to try it myself," he says, chuckling to himself. "Well, I'll be making sure nobody sees this report; I've got a vote to win." Tom drops the papers into the shredder, then picks up the phone and orders his secretary to send the lab reports and substance samples over to the FDA.

Chapter Twenty-Seven: BEGINNING OF THE ENDING

"Goddamn, Rock, where this muthafucka at?"

"He gon' be heah. I just talked to the nigga," Rock replied, looking down Orem Street. "Talkin 'bout dat potent shit. I'm tryin' to see what's up wit' dat."

"For real, tho. I got like eighteen-hundred dollars out there waitin' on me," said Maino, Big Rock's lil' homie. They were all hanging out by the cornerstore where they hustled. They had an arrangement with the owner, old man Black, who was an old street hustler himself. Big Rock is a popular neighborhood rapper with the Screwed Up Click who sells his own mixtape CDs out the trunk of his '97 Impala SS at the clubs, parks, 'hoods, wherever. But on most days, they'd set up shop in front of Black's cornerstore and move their products: CDs, weed, coke and Ball. Ball was becoming more and more popular. It seemed like everybody was doing it. So when Rock got the chance to get a G-pack for cheaper than he usually pays, he jumped on it.

Cap, the dude from New Orleans he'd met at Club Visions months ago, definitely didn't strike him as the grimy type. Plus, to add to his credibility, he'd mentioned that he was affiliated with Scat and the D-Boys in some kind of way. Rock didn't pry; he just let Cap buy the drinks and do exactly what his name professed, *cap*, until last week, when he'd bumped into Cap again in the Max's nightclub parking lot. Cap had told Rock that he had a big load of Ball coming, the best kind. Better than the regular kind already out on the streets. He called it Hardball, and it came at better prices. Rock told him he'd definitely call him when he was ready, and here he is. Big Rock, twenty-four, tall, heavyset, dark-skinned and cleancut; and Maino, twenty-two, medium-height, medium build. Everything medium. He made up for it with tattoos and a gold grill. Both men wore long gold chains with diamond-laced pieces. Big Rock's was a circular one that said "Screwed Up Click".

As they watch the cars, they sit on the ledge of the trunk, popped up with the neon-lit sign embedded in the top of the custom-built speaker box so that anyone who looked could see "Rock Steady" in bright neon red letters. They noticed a gray Trailblazer pull up into the small lot, the same truck they'd seen driving by just a few minutes prior.

Rock stands up. "Here he go," Rock said, noting that Cap had two other dudes with him. Cap backed the SUV into the parking spot one space over on the driver's side of Rock's Impala. He jumped out with a smile on his face.

"Whew! This muthafucka is *clean*, whodie! Candy paint, screens, rims, sound...everything. You wanna sell it?"

"Nah mane, I cant sell my load, I got too much into this hoe." Rock answered, smiling sheepishly, glancing back at hia ride. Houston boys are affectionate with their cars. Cap's two passengers, who were standing behind him, were now checking out the ride.

"Come on, Rock, I'm 'bout to get you paid, nigga. You can buy ten of these," Cap said confidently, grinning. Rock noticed a large bulge in Cap's right jean pocket.

"I'm good with this one. But I could hook you up. My nigga's got slabs for sale way mo' thowed than this," Rock said.

"Hell, yeah," Maino said in agreement.

"Oh, yeah?"

Rock nodded. "Fasho. Whenever you ready, I'll take you by the shop."

"A'ight."

"By the way, this my nigga Maino," Rock proclaimed, jerking his thumb back towards his homeboy.

Cap extended his hand and introduced himself. "What's up whodie? I'm Cap."

"All right, all right, slow boogie," Maino said, shaking Cap's hand. Cap didn't bother to introduce his cohorts.

"Let's hop inside," Cap said and nodded towards Rock's car. They all knew what that meant: *Let's do business*. Once inside the car, Cap pulled three tabs of Hardball out of his shirt pocket.

"Here it is, whodie. That new and improved shit," Cap said, dropping the three tabs into Rock's hand to examine, as he bagan rubbin his palms together.

"Damn, these hoes is dark," Rock said, peering closely at the almost-black tabs in his hand. "Ball is usually a light tan color."

"Yeah, but this is *Hardball*. It's the same thing, only better. Stronger. All them muthafuckas that was buying two or three gon' be buyin' ten, as much as they can get."

"Like that?" Rock asked incredulously.

"Just like 'dat. Try one fa ya'self. Wait, wait. You got the money, right?"

"Yeah, I got it right here." Rock reached under his seat and pulled out a stack of rubber-banded bills.

"Eight G's, right?" Cap asked.

"Alll-ready," Rock drawled, placing the money in his lap. Cap rubbed the waves in his head twice.

"Where the pack at?" Rock asked.

"Oh, right here," Cap answered, patting his pocket. Before reaching his hand inside, Cap nods his head towards the window on Rock's side in a *what's up?* motion as if he were talking to his partners standing outside.

Rock instantly became nervous. He turned to look at what Cap was so curious about, which gave Cap just enough time to pull his gun out of his pocket. What Rock saw made him tense, scared and mad at himself all at the same time. Cap's two flunkies had pulled their guns and were aiming them at Rock. When Rock looked back towards Cap, he was staring down the barrel of a .9mm. Then, *blackness.* All he saw was black. Cap pulled the trigger...*BOOM!* Cap shot Rock through the eye and he was dead almost instantly; parts of Rock's brains shout out the back of his head and onto the glass. Cap snatched the eight G stack from Rock's lap and looked around to see where Rock's boy was at.

When Maino saw the two cats pull heat, he knew it was a jack. His instincts had told him something didn't feel right at first, but he didn't get a chance to say anything. He ran around to the other side of their Trailblazer and pulled his .380 which he kept on him at all times. He'd pulled it out plenty of times but he'd only had to use it once before this. *POW!* He heard a muffled shot, and Maino knew that could mean only one thing: one of the two people in Rock's Impala had been shot.

Maino peeked through the driver's side window of the SUV, but he could only see the top of Rock's car and both vehicles were heavily tinted, he could hardly see anything inside. He didn't see the two gunmen, either. Maino hid behind the front tire so they couldn't shoot him in the legs under the car. He's scared as hell, nervous and alert, hoping they didn't just kill his homeboy. He thought of running. His mind quickly did the math: two with guns against *one* with *a* gun. He heard a car door open and close, then the whispers of imminent death. Quickly, his mind measured how frighteningly nearby gunshots can be, compared to his enemies whispering in preparation for his demise in the midst of gun battle. The whispers seemed much more ominous now. Maino figured his only way out of this was by shooting his way out.

Then, above the noise of cars going back and forth on both intersecting streets, people in their own world, Maino heard footsteps running at the rear of the SUV. He started firing in that direction. After four rapid shots and hitting nothing, he aimed at the window towards the back, firing continuously and shattering glass. But his focus was all wrong and by the time he realized he'd been tricked, it was too late. *Pop, pop*...two quick gunshots ended his rampage. One shattered the back of his skull, the other entered through his spinal cord and came out of his throat. His body dropped. They had sneak-attacked him, faked to the back while creeping around the front.

"Got that bitch!" exclaimed Cap, heading towards the driver side door. "Let's go, let's go!"

"Let's take the car!" says the youngin' who'd just killed Maino.

"Fuck that car, whodie. Get in!" Cap said, stepping over Maino's body, which laid face-down on the gravelly pavement. Youngin' takes a last look at the Impala SS.

"Damn! That bitch his hard!" He looks at Cap again.

"Get in the truck, nigga!" Cap yells. By now Black, the store owner, had heard the racket from inside the store and had called the police to report the shooting. He was now gripping his shotgun, prepared to bust down these youngstas should they decide to bring that madness into his place of business.

"Fuck that shit, Cap. I'm finna get this bitch," Young'n said. He opened the driver's side door of the Impala and pulled Rock out onto the pavement by his shirt collar.

"I'ma leave yo muthafuckin' ass. You better get in this truck!" Cap said, looking around for the police. He wasn't bluffing, either.

Youngin' ignored Cap and hopped into the driver's seat. He reached for the ignition, already formulating plans to either strip the car down or flip it with new VIN numbers. *Something is missing.*

"Fuck!" he yelled. No keys.

"Nigga fuck you!" Cap yelled and screeched out of the parking lot. He wasn't about to let this hardheaded youngster get him a murder rap. He'd gotten what he'd come for.

"Wait!" Youngsta yelled, but it was too late. Cap wasn't stopping. He was extremely desperate now. He jumped out of the car, rolled Rock's body over and patted his jean pockets. He didn't hear anything but something was there. He reached into the pockets and pulled out the keys and another small wad of cash.

"Jackpot, nigga!" Youngin' said with a smirk. "Oh, gimme this, too," he said, taking Rock's chain from around his neck. It had some blood on it, but he didn't care. He hopped into the car, started it and pulled out the parking spot in reverse, then peeled rubber out of the lot with the trunk still propped open. The motorized lift system had it locked in place. The neon lights beamed "Rock Steady", but Rock was no more.

The police arrived immediately after Rock's car had fled the scene. How convenient. After discovering that both men were definitely DOA, dead on arrival, they began taking their report, and the homicide unit showed up shortly after to investigate the crime scene. While carefully examining Rock's body for any evidence or clues that could direct the investigation, the evidence they wanted was discovered in Rock's hand: three small, dark tablets of Hardball. Within two hours, a news crew was present. They set up shop across the street and broadcasted live over a newsbreak.

Head District Attorney Thomas Brody watched the live newscast from his office. He'd specifically told the reporter to quote him: "The substance known on the streets as 'Ball' is as dangerous, if not more so, than any other controlled substance, and the city of Houston is taking steps to eliminate its presence." When he heard that, he smiled. He took a shot of Jack Daniels from the flask he kept hidden in his desk.

"Ah," he sighed as he enjoyed the burn going down. "What a day."

******

Less than five miles from Black's corner store, in a small three-bedroom, one-level secluded house in a low-income neighborhood that was completely off the radar, candlelight danced in the windows. If it weren't for the curtains hung over some windows, actual mini-blinds in others and the nearly setting sun that refused to retract its heat and brightness, the candlelight would have been much more obvious. But in this area, no one cared. The lot is huge, so the house is far removed from anything around it. Winnie knew he'd chosen well with this one.

He walked into the small breakfast area, which had been converted into an altar room since it was so close to the kitchen and had easy-to-clean linoleum floors. Winnie wore nothing except a transparent butcher's jacket over his dark brown skin. Other than that, he was completely naked. There were small, plastic animal cages with shiny metal-grilled doors all over the living room—five of them, with five rabbits in each one. The house had no furniture except for a blow-up mattress in one bedroom and pots and pans in the kitchen, a pill presser, a mock altar and lots of candles.

The carpet was old and dirty even though it had been vacuumed. The walls were dingy, and it had a musty and damp smell to it, along with the musky animal smell that emanated from the rabbit cages, and the smell of their feces and urine. It was an inhospitable, rank smell that Winnie had grown accustomed to. No one was coming here. No one was invited. The house served its purpose, which was to test produce manufacture Hardball. Winnie had become completely obsessed with the entire process. His motivation had triple purpose; its spiritual, financial and the power principle had him feeling so comfortable and in control, it was as if he was fulfilling his destiny.

He began to chant the phrases he had memorized from the book. He was already familiar with much of the language. He looked around at all of the candles.

"It's time. Life is upon us." The water in the pots and pans was coming to a boil. Winnie opened the nearest cage and pulled out a full grown brown and white rabbit. He pet the animal gently before quickly snapping its neck with a twist of both hands in opposite directions, and the rabbit goes limp except for a few twitches. Winnie cuts the rabbit open with a small and very sharp knife. He smiles as the blood pours out onto the altar, and he begins to chant again as he reaches inside the rabbit's small body with his bare hands and pulls its guts out. Chanting and laughing, he holds the entrails up in the air before he separates the heart from the rest of the rabbit's innards.

Winnie had definitely found his calling. Or so he thought.

Chapter Twenty-Eight: JEWELS VISION OF FATE

"Fatso!" Jewel yelled as she shot upright in her queen size bed. *"Oh, my, what is happening?"* she asked herself, startled and afraid. She could feel the sweat from her open pores beading up on her forehead. A drop ran down her temple. Her heart was beating like she'd just run a fifty yard dash, but she'd been having a nightmare. The only thing about Jewel's nightmares was that they were not only dreams, but premonitions.

In this dream, many people had died. Faces she didn't recognize. They were only glimpses of death, but in a final shootout, revenge was being taken. Someone survived the first round of assassinations and came back and shot and killed Fatso. Jewel was completely unnerved. She went into the kitchen of her apartment and poured herself a glass of cold water and tried to calm herself down. *I've got to call them,* she thought. *I can't hold anything back. I have to do whatever I can to help; I can't allow this to happen.* She checked the clock. It read 11:40 p.m. The boys were nocturnal creatures, anyway.

Prince answered on the second ring. "What's up, auntie, you all right?" His alertness instantly made Jewel feel better.

Should I tell him now? No, we must talk face to face. But what if the chain of events was already set in motion? she thought.

"I'm fine, sweetheart. I'm…I'm fine. I need to talk to you boys right away," she said anxiously.

"Right away…like *tonight*?" Prince asked incredulously. Then, before she could answer, "What's up, auntie? You sound a little rattled."

"Is your brother with you?" she asked.

"Yeah, he right here."

"You're not doing too much hanging out, are you?"

Something was definitely bothering her. Prince read the signals clearly without much thought or effort at all, and his aunt was not an easy person to read.

"Nah, we're just going over a few things with a couple of guys. What's wrong?"

"We...we need to talk. As soon as possible."

Prince paused. He knew it was serious. Auntie Jewel never did this, and after the circumstances that precluded the loss of Mama, which then led to this current situation, he was taking nothing for granted, especially as far as his family and loved ones were concerned.

"Say no more; we're on our way."

Jewel felt better after she hung up the phone. She decided she would not sit back while her family was in battle. She reflected on when she was living in New Orleans with her father and sister, and how she wished she could have done something to prevent their demise, but she hadn't even tried. Sure, she said what she had to say about it, she gave her opinion, but so what? She didn't offer a solution or a strategy for any kind of defense. She took no action, and both her father and younger sister ended up dead. It was a deep, sorrowful kind of guilt that she'd never really gotten over. She couldn't let that happen again. Jewel made a pot of coffee and waited for her nephews to arrive.

******

When Serene stepped into the cool air of Mo's apartment, he was sitting in the living room with his shirt off, finishing a telephone conversation.

"That's what I'm sayin'. We'll never have to shop around again. We'll have a constant supply of them lil' fuckas...all right, well, call her, check it out and let me know if you need me to do anything," Mo said into the phone excitedly before hanging up.

Serene's eyes scanned over his chiseled, tattooed body. He had his jewelry on: piece and chain, bracelet, watch and rings. He was dressed in jeans and BAPE tennis shoes; the only thing missing was his shirt and it was turning Serene on, but she revamped. There were more important things on her mind to discuss.

"Damn, why you so crunk?" she asked.

"Jus' a lil' somethin' we checkin' on that we been tryin' to make happen, that's all. Wuz happenin'?"

Serene looked into his eyes, letting him know that what she was about to say was serious.

"I've been straight up wit' you, babe. I've tried to let you in on my life and everything that's going on with me, personal and business-wise," she began.

Mo nodded. "I feel you." He was actually developing a strategy as to how he'd handle this conversation. His defenses were going up. Mo had true feelings for Serene, but he was no fool. He still realized this was still a potentially dangerous relationship because he was still unsure where her loyalties really were.

Serene went on to say, "But now it's time for you to be straight up with me. I need to know what's going on out here."

"What's going on with what?" Mo asked with a confused look on his face. However, Mo wasn't at all confused. In fact, he'd expected this conversation to come about sooner or later. But he wasn't giving up easily, if at all. There were things he needed to know first.

"What's going on with you and your people? What's up with us? Where is this going?" she asked. The three questions she'd just asked basically summarized what she was looking to get out of this discussion.

"Hold up bay-bay...you just pop up over here wit' twenty-one questions. You need to be...what happened to you?"

Serene sighed. "Let me calm down. Look, I'm sorry, but let me put it to you this way. I already told you that bitch is trippin'. I'm not real happy with my current situation—" she began, then paused. She didn't want him to think she was talking about him. "—as far as my hustle is concerned, that is. I mean, the money is good, but I'm just ready to do my own thing, ya know? Without all the extra bullshit." Serene did not feel like explaining to Mo how Tamara had humiliated her.

"And in order for me to do that, I need to evaluate everything. And with you being my man...you *are* my man, right?"

"Yeah, baby, you know it's me and you," Mo said half-heartedly.

"Well, if it's me and you, and we both tryin' to build somethin' together, I want to give this relationship all one hundred and ten percent of me. But in order for me to do that, I need to know what's up. You can talk to me, baby. You can be honest. I mean, I'm a hustler, too, and I'm down for us. I love you, Mo. But you gotta talk to me," Serene said sincerely.

Mo was stumped. *Women are always better at communicating*, he thought. But one thing he was sure of, she meant what she said. He could see the loyalty in her eyes and hear it in her voice. She would not betray him. In that moment, his feelings for her increased dramatically, and Mo realized that he had a real, live stomp-down chick on his team.

Something else dawned on him as he read between the lines of what she was saying and what she wasn't saying: *she knew*. Serene knew that his people killed Francine Landau. And if she knew, then Prince and Fatso knew. And they probably also knew that their business was in danger.

Mo looked into Serene's eyes, which had never left his as he'd drifted off in thought. She nodded at him. *Yeah, she knows,* Mo said to himself. She was just waiting for him to admit it so she could measure how much she could trust him. At this point, he needed and wanted her trust. Mo knew that he could really build something with Serene. He sighed.

"What you wanna know?" he asked in a much less defensive tone.

"Everything."

Mo was about to go for broke. He hoped he was right about what he was feeling because if he was wrong, it could cost him his life.

"Come sit down," he said. Serene sits next to Mo on his sectional sofa. He gives her all but a few select details about what has happened and what's going on. She listens intently, and as shocked as she is, she remains reserved and calculative. Mo's confession seals their bond. They were now obligated to each other with their secrets. Now, they *both* had something to lose.

******

"You all want some coffee?" Jewel asked Fatso, Prince and Tamara as they entered her upscale condominium. The floral scent of the potpourri, baby palm trees and other live plants gave the medium-sized, well-decorated condo a tropical feel.

"Nah, auntie, we're all right. We just came to check on you. What's up?" Fatso asked after they'd all greeted Jewel with a hug.

Without answering, Jewel walked away, passed through her kitchen and sat down at her glass dining room table. Hanging on the wall to her right was a large stainless steel-framed piece of artwork that bore the image of a bright, overflowing bowl of fruit, and mirrors lined the wall behind her. In front of her was a steaming cup of coffee. Her head was wrapped in a silk burgundy scarf that matched her housecoat. Her eyes were heavy with worry as she looked down into her cup. Before she looked up at her guests, she quickly fixed her face to show her strength and resilience, and with her chin held high, she began.

"We have some things to discuss. Have a seat now. And please, Prince, take that look off your face. This is hard enough, okay? Now, come on."

Fatso, Prince and Tamara sat down around the table. Prince wondered what facial expression his aunt was referring to. She *had* triggered much concern with her phone call, but this was not the first time his aunt had gotten on his ass about his facial expressions giving away his emotions. But he was relieved to see that she was okay, so he didn't sweat her comment.

"We need to be strong right now. You already know that. So I don't want you to do a bunch of talking here. Just listen," Jewel said firmly.

She went on to explain to them the history that had plagued their past, the events that were connected to the deaths of their mother and grandfather.

"He'd been a *voudou* bishop before he met Mama, and he secretly held that position throughout their marriage. He didn't want Mama to change, nor did he want her to look at him differently. But Mama read the clues, and when she asked him about some of his affiliations and some belongings of his that she had found, he told her that she wouldn't understand. I don't think he wanted her to understand. Either way, she would have nothing to do with it as he suspected. She became more and more isolated and only dealt with me, the two of you, and your mother, who Daddy had loved absolutely more than anything in this world. She was so special, your mother, my baby sister. Daddy...he adored her. Mama alienating him and being away from us was killing him. I saw it. He couldn't stand the thought of losing or hurting his family. He stepped down from his position as a bishop, denounced all of it and begged Mama to forgive him so they could be a family again. She did, but she'd grown to hate New Orleans, said it was too violent. She made Daddy get a life insurance policy, which he did, and we were all happy. At least...until your mother met your father." Jewel paused and sipped her coffee.

"She began to disappear for days at a time, then weeks. Mama and Daddy were so worried about her. They told her she couldn't see your father anymore, but she wouldn't listen. She told me she was gonna live her own life, the way she wanted."

Fatso, Prince and Tamara all listened closely, imagining every detail. This was the first time they'd heard the actual story after all the years of only being able to picture it in their minds.

"Your father, he loved your mother...but he was a ruthless drug dealer and user. He was robbed right after Prince was born; they lost everything except the habit. Heroin. He couldn't break it. He tried to get back on his feet, but he owed people money, and they wanted it. By then, they were *both* using. Eventually, the people they owed money to caught up with them." Jewel paused, assuming that they knew what happened next.

"How'd they die?" Prince asked.

"They were both shot; they died together. Daddy was devastated, and for a while, Mama just wouldn't accept it. She went back into her shell. Daddy vowed revenge, but the police had no idea who did it, so it didn't really matter to them. Daddy was a powerful man, physically and spiritually. I knew it, I could see it. I could feel it. When you looked into his eyes, you knew. We were close then, closer than we'd ever been. He told me that he went deep back into his religious practices to avenge his daughter's murder," Jewel said thoughtfully and looked away.

"I think he told me because he realized I understood. He told me that I had to understand because Mama never would." Jewel nodded and pursed her full lips. She seemed to be holding back tears.

"His spirit led him to the murderers. Daddy killed them all. But the spirit did not protect him, and Daddy was also killed in the process. I was once again heartbroken. I cried a river, but Mama didn't shed one tear. Deep down inside, I despised her for that. But Mama was strong, and she felt betrayed by everybody.

"You two were just little boys then, so innocent, she would say. She promised to leave New Orleans and give you two something better, and when the life insurance policy paid off, she did just that. I refused to leave. I guess at that point, we betrayed each other in a sense. But my father and sister's spirits were there in New Orleans, calling and nurturing me. You understand? I felt them with me, so I became powerful on my own. Some of Daddy's followers were led to me. They gave me wisdom, lessons and tools. And I grew."

Tamara and the boys listened intently. They had a million questions running through their minds, but more than anything, they were just trying to process it all.

"And you two have grown. Long ago, I came to accept that all things happen for a purpose, even tragedies. When you discovered my books, I sensed it the moment I'd walked into Mama's house and I immediately understood why she had taken them from me. I had no idea what would come of it, and by that time, it was out of my hands. You've done what I would have never imagined and overall, I want you to know that I am proud of you."

Fatso, Prince and Tamara were confused. *If it weren't for those books, we wouldn't be in this situation. Mama would still be alive. And she's proud?* Prince thought.

"But what about Mama?" he asked. Jewel quickly cut him off by holding up her hands.

"No buts. All things happen to fulfill their purposes. Now Mama is resting in peace. And I pray her spirit is watching over us, providing guidance and protection. We all need it," she stated, looking Fatso in the eyes. "We have to be careful. You understand?"

All three nodded in agreement. "Yeah, we know."

Jewel looked at Fatso. "Fatso, sweetie, listen. I need *you* to be very careful. Do *you* understand?"

"Why? Is there something I need to be on the lookout for?" he asked nervously, ready to target the enemy.

"Yes," she answered. "*Everything*. Danger is all around you, *all of you*. I tell you all of this because I want you to understand that there are powers that have been unleashed. Now, we must fight fire with fire. I need you all to tell me your strategy."

Even though he still had questions, Prince was gaining a higher level of respect for his auntie. One specific thing weighed on his mind that he'd discovered a while back that caused him to have serious doubts about all this spiritual mumbo-jumbo that she and those books went on about; He figured that now was a better time than ever to bring it up.

"Auntie, I gotta ask you something," he began, looking into Jewel's eyes to gauge her reaction. "There is a lot of emphasis in the book on the prayer over the elements. We'd stopped doing that a long time ago, but the effect is still the same, it still works. Why is that?" Prince asked, trying to mask any sarcasm or disbelief, especially after what had just been revealed to him.

Even though he knew his auntie was sort of an eccentric and doubted nothing of her beliefs, the seed of doubt had been planted long ago. After all, from his point of view, he was just a hustler out the 'hood tryin' to get everything he could get with what he was workin' with. He'd considered it a lucky break.

Jewel's answer was simple. "You only have to say it once. After you've succeeded, your power is implied. It's active because now, mentally and spiritually, you know. The connection has been made. And every time you succeed in controlling those elements, your power becomes stronger."

Prince digested this. *No shit*, he thought. *It made perfect sense, actually.* "Like confidence," he said aloud. Jewel nodded in agreement. He may not have believed all that other stuff, but he believed in what he was doing, so it worked every time. He'd been properly corrected.

"That makes a lot of sense," Fatso agreed.

"Yeah, it does," Tamara said, then thought, *I have a lot of confidence, so does that mean I have a lot of power?*

Jewel could almost read their thoughts, and as if on cue, she said, "Soon, all of you will come to understand and exercise your power."

"All right," Fatso exhaled, ready to change pace. "It's getting a little heavy in here, so let me lay this out for you, auntie."

He went on to explain where they were at with their operation, the information they had so far and what he had just learned. He also mentioned some of the biggest risks they were facing, and Jewel was proud of that. It showed that they were being realistic and not reckless in their path to revenge. Jewel thought of her dream as Fatso articulately expressed himself verbally and through his body language. He looked so much like his grandfather in that moment. *If he only knew*, she thought. She imagined how reckless her father must have been in his blind fury. One of his victims must have survived his rage long enough to exact his *own* revenge. In her dream, Fatso had been avenged upon in a similar way. The comparison struck her and provoked her to speak as Fatso summed up their plan.

"It is good that you are approaching this with humility. You only want to eliminate those who took action."

"That's why it's taken us a lil' longer to strike," Prince said.

"And we wanna make sure ain't no heat on us," Fatso added. "The police may think we're looking for revenge."

"So, let's say you get 'em. Now, it's dangerous. The heat is on, as you say. Who's next to take their place or avenge them? And who after that? And...after that?" Jewel asked. Fatso and Prince looked at each other. Tamara glanced at them for an answer to a very legitimate question.

"You plan has holes in it that concern me. You have all the information, but you have to use it to close those holes. Baby, in a war like this, with these kind of people, you have to destroy your enemy completely so that when you take your eyes off of him, it's finished, and you can go on with your lives. Now, I know it's easier said than done, but I'm gonna help you, okay? I have many things to show you. So, let's start with the head, and make him diagnose his own body."

"All right, we got him," Fatso said as they all nodded.

Both brothers now saw their auntie in a whole new light. She spoke as if she'd had military training, but actually, after she'd joined the others in her father's fellowship following his death, the wisdom and training they'd given her included advanced life and combat skills. As a gratuity to her father, they made sure that she would never feel inferior to another human being.

So many questions had been answered for the boys, and they both felt a burden had been lifted. They received answers that could never have been given by the pictures they'd seen. Now they knew that Daddy was a hustler and Mama was a rebel, Grandpa was the redeemer and Grandma was the savior; auntie is the witness. Tamara was completely intrigued and inspired by Jewel's power. Never before had she seen this side of her, and now that she had, she knew that their relationship would never be the same. She now looked up to her in more ways than one. Tamara knew that she would leave this condo tonight a stronger, more superior woman.

Chapter Twenty-Nine: REVENGE IS MINE

"It's gonna be a hot one out there today, people, so stay wet and stay cool. This is Madd Hatter, J-Mac, Jimbo and Nnete' checkin' out of the Madd Hatter morning show."

Winnie pushes the power button and turns the radio off. "Fuck that. It's already hotter than the rainforest out here," he grumbled, his Haitian accent revealing itself in his temporary agitation. He hadn't counted on traffic on Highway 59 being a complete parking lot and now he was an hour late for his appointment.

Two days ago, Mo, Winnie's right hand, had called him all excited about an opportunity for them to buy something they really needed: a rabbit farm. Winnie called the realtor right away to get a few preliminary details. As he played with the idea in his mind, he realized that although this is a great opportunity to keep a constant supply of rabbit hearts, he is not interested in running a damn rabbit farm, or any kind of farm on a daily basis. After getting the details from the realtor, he made an offer to see how flexible this deal would be.

"If I buy the bigger share in the farm, is this guy willing to stay on as managing partner?" he asked. Winnie thought this was a brilliant idea.

Shannon, the realtor who represented the deal, said politely, "Actually, he'd prefer that. He's pretty attached to it. He's offering a twelve-month management agreement."

"Perfect!" Winnie crowed. He went on to set the appointment for as soon as possible, which the realtor informed him was in two days. He thought it a little odd. *I guess rabbit farms are busy these days,* he thought. The wait actually made him want to close the deal as fast as possible as there might be some competition. Winnie decided right then and there that he wouldn't try and low ball the guy or anything; he'd give him his asking price with a large cash down payment. *This is a perfect investment!* Winnie thought excitedly.

******

When Winnie finally pulled his Tahoe into the long gravel driveway, he noticed that the whole property is actually pretty big, about five acres, upon which sat a small blue ranch house and a large barn that was situated a short distance to the rear of it. There was also a small trailer, which was new. It was similar to the ones they use at new home developments. It looked out of place. *Why would they bring a trailer out to sell a farm? Is it that fucking busy?* he wondered. Then he smiled. He had another idea. *I could build some houses out here myself. Maybe bury a safe or two full of cash in the ground.*

"Hello, Winston?" Shannon queried as she opened the door of the trailer and stepping out with her hand extended. Shannon is medium height, about five feet, seven inches, but extremely well built. Even the navy blue skirt suit she wore couldn't hide that coke-bottle shape. With glowing, light brown skin and cat-shaped eyes, reddish-brown microbraids and a smile like sunshine, Winnie was instantly attracted to her. *She could be a bonus to this deal,* he thought lustfully while surveying her frame.

"It is I. And you must be Shannon," Winnie said cheerfully, a happy man's smile on his face. He reached out to shake her hand, and when he felt her softness he felt blood rush to places that were completely out of context for this meeting.

"Yes, nice to meet you. I didn't think you were going to show up," Shannon said.

"That obviously would have been my loss," Winnie said flirtatiously. "I got stuck in traffic. I apologize."

"No problem. Come inside and fill out a visitor's card for me, if you don't mind," she said, gesturing towards the trailer.

Visitor's card? Winnie thought. *For a farm?* He could see the air conditioning units in the window and the cool air coming from the entry, and with a sexy woman telling him to come inside, instead of asking, "What the fuck for?" he simply said, "All right, no problem."

Once inside, Winnie noticed a younger version of Shannon sitting at a desk with a phone filling out paperwork.

"That's my assistant, Sherell." Sherell greeted Winnie on cue.

"You can have a seat right here," Shannon said, pointing at a chair with a piece of paper and pen sitting on a desk of in front of it. Winston sat down. He was putty in her hands.

"Just fill out that card there. It's just general information. It's how my firm keeps up with our showings. Would you like some spring water? I know it's hot out there."

"Yeah, that would be nice of you. Thanks," Winnie said, still trying to flirt. With a wave of Shannon's hand, Sherell prepared for Winnie a cup of ice cold Culligan spring water, which she then handed to Winnie.

"Thank you," Winnie said. *Sherell has to be her younger sister. They look just alike. I wonder if they've ever fucked in this trailer?* he thought as he guzzled down the first cup of water.

"Thirsty?" Sherell asked. "I'll get you another," she said with a smile and walked off. *Her ass is bigger than her sister's, though,* Winnie thought. He quickly filled out the info card with half-accurate information. It didn't matter. He was gonna buy with mostly cash, anyway. He guzzled down the second cup.

"You all set?" Shannon asked.

"Yes, ma'am," Winnie replied, handing her the card.

"Well, let me show you the place. It's not a lot to it, so it won't take long."

Shannon was right. She had changed into a pair of Nikes and she quickly walked Winnie through a barn which housed a few hundred rabbits in different sections. Some were breeding, some were feeding, but there was one thing that Winnie was sure of, and that this is exactly what he needs. The details weren't important.

All of a sudden, Shannon seemed to be in a rush. She explained away the details as she walked through the place. The house would be part of the detail with a lease to the owners for as long as they plan to stay, etc., etc. But when she returned to the trailer with Winnie, she claimed she had to go.

"I'm sorry, I didn't know you would be late, and I couldn't reschedule my next appointment. But if you like what you see..."

"I do, I do. Let's do it."

"Ok. Well I'll call you to go over some contracts later, okay?"

"Over dinner?"

Winnie had caught her off guard with that one. "Umm...well, maybe," she answered, blushing. "I'll call you at around four o'clock. Is that okay?"

"That'll work. You're gonna make a nice commission off this deal, so don't keep me waiting. I lose interest quickly," Winnie said, letting her know that he's not wet behind the ears when it comes to these kinds of things.

"I completely understand," Shannon said with a smile to mask the wave of nervous energy that had suddenly overtaken her. *This man is actually trying to pressure me. Oh, well. It doesn't matter anyway,* she thought to herself, calming down as she watched him drive away. The turquoise SUV became smaller and smaller. Shannon sighed; now she could breathe easy. Sherell walked over and sat next to her. Shannon was glad she'd brought her younger sister. She made her more comfortable.

Sherrell was also relieved that Winnie was gone. "Good riddance," she stated flatly.

"Talkin' 'bout a commission. Ha!" Shannon mocked. "Did you hear that shit, girl?"

"Mmm-hmm,"

"I already earned my check, muthafucka!" Shannon walked inside the trailer to tighten things up. Her mission here was complete. She pulled out her cell and hit a speed-dial button. The call was answered on the first ring.

"He just left. Yep...two cups...all right...no problem...yeah, I'm good." She hung up and smiled to herself. *Easy money.*

******

Winnie drove away from the property feeling like the whole setup was already his. He felt a wave of excited energy come over him.

"All this shit is about to be mine!" he yelled to no one in particular. He turned his stereo back on and put the CD changer on his theme song, Rick Ross' "Push it to the Limit." Winnie would play this whenever he was crunk. As he pulled onto Highway 288 and he prepared his mind for an hour-long ride back to Houston, which would give him time to think, a sharp pain gripped his mid-section.

"Oooh, shit!" he groaned as he waited for the pain to pass. It felt like he had gas on his stomach, or like he had to use the bathroom badly and there was no restroom in sight. But this pain was worse. Ten times worse. Soon enough, though, the pain passed.

"Thank Ja," Winnie said aloud. Then, a new feeling overtook him, one of complete and utter nausea. He knew that he would vomit any second.

"What the fuck?" he cursed as he began to veer to the right. People driving near him blew their horns at him, but he paid them no mind. He pulled over onto the shoulder of the road and immediately opened the driver's side door and leaned his head out, gagging and vomiting uncontrollably.

She must have poisoned me, Winnie thought angrily. *It must have been the water. Did she know? She had to have. I'll kill her. She'll pay.* The gagging was so violent that he didn't even notice the Magnum SRT pull up behind him.

Cesar walked up on the driver's side of Winnie's Tahoe. "Say man, you all right? You need some help?" Winnie shook his head no. Big Baby stood behind the SUV, out of sight, waiting for the signal.

"Come on, man, let me help you out. There's a hospital up the street."

Cesar reaches his hand out to help support Winnie, who was still leaning out of the truck, convulsing violently. Winnie tries to swat the samaritan's hand away, as if to say *I don't need your fuckin' help,* but it was too late. If he would have had enough energy in him to take his mind off the excruciating pain that seized his abdomen and pay attention to what was really going on, he would have seen the black fifty-thousand watt taser in the samaritan's hand.

Cesar hit him in the neck with the powerful voltage. *Tat-tat-tat-tat-tat-tat.* Winnie tried to pull his head into his shoulders to protect his neck from the shocks, which caused immediate muscle spasms and also caused his windpipe to tighten shut. It was no use. Cesar leaned into Winnie, putting his body weight behind the taser. *Tat-tat-tat-tat-tat-tat.* He trapped Winnie in his submissive position between the door and the steering wheel.

Big Baby saw that Cesar had Winnie covered on the driver's side so he rushed around to the passenger's side, hopped in and began to restrain Winnie's hands with the wire ties they'd picked up from Home Depot that morning. By this time, Winnie had passed out. The fifty-thousand volts that seared through his body along with the poison could have downed a silverback gorilla, so Winnie's 205-pound frame didn't stand a chance.

"All right, C, he ain't movin'!" Big Baby yelled. He could feel the electricity shoot through Winnie when he was trying to tie up his hands. Cesar released the taser's trigger.

"What the fuck, you tryin' to kill him already?"

"What, with *this*?" Cesar asked, holding the taser up like it was a toy.

"Man, put that shit away!" Big Baby demanded, reminding his cohort that they were in the middle of a kidnapping on a public highway in broad daylight.

"What, you don't think that shit could stop a nigga's heart?" Big Baby asked as Cesar tucked the non-lethal weapon in the pocket of his BAPE hoodie.

"Man, fuck this bitch ass nigga!" Cesar replied contemptuously.

Big Baby was getting irritated. "Hmm. Man, open the back doors." *Reckless muthafucka!* he thought as he threw Winnie into the backseat with a powerful heave.

Cesar closed the driver's door and opened the two rear doors of the truck. Big Baby walked around the back, climbed inside and snatched Winnie from the back seat into the rear cargo of his own truck. They heard something snap, like bones cracking. Big Baby instinctively checked the ties around Winnie's wrists.

"I think you just broke his arm," Cesar said with a half-smile on his face.

"Fuck 'im. Let's go," Big Baby said, slamming the door shut. Cesar jumped in the driver's seat of the Tahoe and Big Baby followed in the Magnum. As they drove away, Winnie's body was still convulsing.

******

"Wake that bitch up!" Prince commanded.

Cesar steps over and pushed Winnie's dread head. He doesn't wake up. Cesar smacks him in the forehead a few times, trying to avoid the drool and vomit in Winnie's beard.

"Wake up! Say, nigga, wake yo ass up!" Cesar demanded.

Winnie still didn't wake up. Big Baby shook his head and cursed under his breath. Cesar feared he'd tasered Winnie into a coma and indefinitely delayed or destroyed the purpose of kidnapping him in the first place.

"Mutha—" Cesar drew his fist back to punch Winnie in the side of the head. He figured that might work, but Jewel stopped him.

"Stop. Here, use this," Jewel said, reaching inside a small duffel bag she had hanging from her shoulder and handing the item to Cesar. "Break it in half, open it and wave it under his nose."

When Winnie got a whiff of whatever it was that Jewel had handed to Cesar, consciousness returned in the company of pain and agony, and neither were welcome. He woke up coughing and choking until he got his senses together. He quickly realized he was tied to a chair in a dimly-lit room in what appeared to be an abandoned house. The convulsions had subsided and he felt surprisingly calm now. He took a heavy-eyed survey of the five men and two women standing around him. He could feel that his brain was not as responsive as it should have been, but he knew it wasn't good.

"I'm glad you could join us in the land of the living," Prince said with a sinister kindness.

"Who are you?" Winnie slurred.

Prince smiled. "We're your send-off committee." Cesar, Big Baby and Young Bread laughed at Prince's humor, but neither Tamara nor Jewel found anything entertaining about this situation.

"You know, like the soldiers that go off to war; they have a lil' celebration for 'em. But, you fucked it all up for us."

"Why?" Winnie asked.

"'Cause you smell like shit!" Prince answered. The three guys laughed again, and Fatso half-smiled.

"He looks like it, too," Cesar remarked. He was standing the closest to Winnie at his near left. They laughed again.

Fatso leaned over to whisper in Jewel's ear: "Is he coherent?"

He wondered because even though Winnie was answering all of Prince's questions, he still had to ask who Prince was. Fatso had never met Winnie personally but he'd assumed that Winnie knew who they were. Jewel knew that he *was* coherent. She was still in semi-shock because she'd immediately recognized Winnie as the same man who'd raped the young girl in the Superdome five years ago. This compounded her anger and also confirmed her curse upon him. *Life comes full circle,* she thought.

"Question him and find out," she said aloud.

Fatso stepped forward. "What's your name?" he asked.

Winnie looked up at the man standing before him, and it was in his mind to say, "Fuck you!" but instead he said, "Winston Marshon." *Oh, shit!* he thought. *Why'd I say that?*

Fatso nodded. "Where you from?"

"N'Awlins," Winnie quickly replied.

Fatso figured he was on a roll, so he then asked, "Did you kill Francine Landau?"

Don't tell him, don't tell him! Winnie thought.

"Mmmphh...agghh..." Winnie grunted as pain returned to his midsection. He shook his head *no*. He looked as if he was hanging on to sanity by a mere string. Control was slipping through his fingers.

"Ahh! I don't wanna die!" Winnie groaned.

Fatso smirked. "Listen, you know that water you drank earlier? Tasted good, didn't it? Had a nice fruity flavor to it, huh? Well, that water was laced with Ricin and a truth serum called 'Judge's Word'. Ricin is a lethal poison that causes much pain, and that's what has your insides feeling like they're melting together. Luckily, my aunt here gave you a lil' shot to delay the pain. But it will return, much worse than before. And you will die. But that's the good news for you," Fatso explained.

Prince picked up where Fatso left off. "That truth serum makes you incapable of telling a lie. So, relax, muthafucka. It ain't gonna hurt long. Now, spill ya guts!" Prince said spitefully, picking up a machete that was leaning against the wall next to a gas can and a jumper cable kit. Fatso paused and watched Winnie to make sure he was getting all of this.

"Now, I'll ask you again. Did you kill my grandmother, Francine Landau?"

"Mmmph," Winnie grunted. His jaws were clenching hard. The muscles in his temples and his jaws were rippling. Not only was Winnie in pain, he was trying his best to not open his mouth and speak. He was having an extremely difficult time doing that, yet the other guys in the room silently respected his ability to resist, especially under the circumstances.

"Fuck this, y'all move back," Prince commanded. Fatso and Jewel stepped back. Prince lifted the machete and hacked into Winnie's left shin.

"Ahhh!" Winnie screamed in agony.

"Uh-huh! That shit hurt, don't it? Yeahhh, muthafucka!" Prince yelled. "Did you kill her or not? We know you did so just fuckin' admit it!"

Even though they had tried to prepare themselves for which way this was gonna go and what they were about to witness, everyone winced at the sights, sounds and smells that invaded their senses. Prince wanted it this way. He wanted to set an example of how gruesome shit can get out here. Tamara felt her leg twitching; she was beginning to feel that her presence there was a mistake, but Prince and Jewel had insisted she be there. She'd told Tamara that she needed to see a man's eyes as he begged for his life in blood and agony with no chance at redemption. Jewel told Tamara it would be liberating. Somehow that carried more weight with her than the influence of her own man, so here she is, standing in the corner, watching. Tamara kept her nervous cool, knowing that this experience would forever affect her sense of reality.

"I...I set the house on fire," Winnie stammered. His head hung low as he spoke. "She died inside."

Fuck! He'd lost it. He'd done what he'd said he'd never do no matter what, but fuck it. With what few brain cells he had left in his head that controlled his common sense, he was able to assemble the theory that if he cooperated, he could make it outta here. But that was impossible. The ricin flowing through his system is irreversible; there is no cure. It would kill him within hours.

"I'm glad you told me that," Prince said, turning to Fatso. "You made this a little bit easier for me. Right bro?" Fatso simply stared at Winnie venomously and nodded. The confession only bolstered his hatred.

"We gonna play a lil' game now, Win-ston. You gon' die anyway, so I came up with somethin' real special for you. See," Prince waved his hand at the accessories lining the wall, "I went Christmas shopping for you and everything. Except you ain't gon' be seein' Jesus no time soon, muthafucka. You ain't even getting close...yeahhh. We gon' play a lil' game called 'How Many Ways Can You Kill a Muthafucka at One Time?' You like that?"

Winnie didn't respond. Either he couldn't, or he didn't know how. The pain in his midsection had come back with a vengeance. He thought of that shot to delay the pain that was given to him by the older Gypsy-looking lady. He remembered that. He wondered how he could get another dose of that.

"So which one do you want first, Winnie? Huh?" Prince asked, not really giving a fuck either way.

"Gimme one of those delay shots," Winnie slurred, looking towards Jewel, who stood near a deteriorated wall in the doorway of a closet that had no door.

"*What?!*" Prince yelled becoming more irritated.

"Prince." Jewel said as she approached her nephew from behind. Her eyes retained fire and captured the full attention of Winnie's stare as she stepped closer. He felt mesmerized, almost forgetting his pain. Then he remembered where he'd previously felt those eyes penetrate his soul.

"Please," Winnie begged, feeling some sort of connection to this woman, as if she were his only hope for salvation.

"Shhh..." Jewel said, raising her finger to her lips, the same finger that was adorned by the large red sphere set into a silver ring. When she spoke, the words came out clear, concise and untempered.

"Listen to the voices. Do you hear them?"

Everyone, including Winnie, actually tried to tune their ears to hear what Jewel was talking about.

"No," Winnie answered calmly. Jewel's voice was soothing and hypnotic, and the whole room was under her spell.

"The souls of the innocent, the living and the dead. They cry out for your blood. They hunger for you to share their pain. Do you hear them?"

Winston Marshon, for what seemed like the first time in his entire life, actually felt a huge black hole forming in his chest and in his heart. Guilt overwhelmed him. All of his transgressions and the mayhem he'd carried out over the years, the helpless ones he'd tormented had found a representative and were now attacking him. He felt tears welling up in his eyes, and then...he heard the voices. He heard distant screams and voices in his head. He wanted to look away. He wanted to drop his head and hide his face from his enemies, but he couldn't break Jewel's gaze. He was in a trance, hypnotized. He could see flames dancing in her eyes.

"What are they saying?" Winnie choked out in a broken voice. Everyone looked at him in shock. They couldn't believe it. It was obvious that he was on the verge of tears.

"They're saying..." Jewel began with her voice full of emotion. "That it's cold. So cold. So...lonely." Then her voice became icy and menacing. "And Hell...*is hot!*"

Jewel stepped back, her final words destroyed any apprehension and provoked all the violent rage trapped inside that room, particularly that of Fatso and Prince, who, seemingly on cue, raised his machete in the image of his grandfather before him and said and in a voice not quite his own:

"Here comes the rage, muthafucka!" He hacked the machete into Winnie's other shin, deep into the bone and marrow.

"Aghhhhh!!!!"

******

Before the torture session had ended, Prince and their crew had achieved their purpose. They'd written down all the names of the New Orleans crew members who were in rank or had strong influence. There were fourteen names. They'd obtained this information by way of simply asking. They'd pretended that their variety show of torture by electrocution, machete hacks into various, non-lethal parts of his body, and soaking all these wounds and Winnie's hair and clothes in gasoline had done the trick, but all that was just gravy. No one really felt that it was fun, but they all felt some justice in their participation, especially Prince, Fatso and Jewel. It was more than just physical torture; it was psychological, too. Not as deep as Jewel had taken it but in a more twisted surface reality kind of way.

The fact was that Winnie was completely incapable of *not* telling them whatever they wanted to know when asked. Because of the effects of the Judge's Word truth serum, he'd spit it right out, whatever he knew, before he'd even had a chance to think about it. Winnie knew that this was his condition so he didn't fight it anymore. He also knew that Prince and his cohorts knew this, so it drove him to the end of his sanity.

Finally, he'd accepted his fate. He wasn't making it out of there. The convulsions from the ricin had become more violent, and he knew it would be just a matter of time. The physical pain was absolute hellfire and he wished that his sense of feeling would just shut down. He'd never imagined how excruciating it would be for gasoline to penetrate open wounds. It felt like the gas invaded and infected them, then dug deeper and deeper into the crevices of the wounds. It felt as if it would have been less painful to just cut off the entire limb. That was the worst part of the whole ordeal. His eyes burned like they were rolling around in a sizzling skillet. His hands gripped each other behind his back and his jaws stayed clenched, but there was no easing the pain. There was no escape. Winnie felt like his restless soul had died within him and was ready to depart, but before it could, he vowed that he would return from the afterlife, that he would return as mayhem and vengeance and never allow Prince, Tamara and Jewel to rest.

Before Prince and his crew left, he duct-taped Winnie's mouth shut, and before they all hopped into the waiting vehicles, Prince lit a book of matches and threw them at the base of the house by the broken-down porch. The old, dried out wood on the dilapidated structure would've burned easily, but Prince helped by having Young Bread pour gasoline around the foundation. As the cars drove off, the flames raced around to the other side of the house, and they would soon reach Winnie. When Cesar hopped in Winnie's Tahoe to drop it off at the chop shop, he saw that the display on

Winnie's cell phone read that Winnie had missed eighteen calls. Knowing it would come in handy later, Cesar turned it off and pocketed it.

******

Mo had been calling and calling Winnie to see what the deal was with the rabbit farm. They had both been so excited about it because it was a key element in their ability to manufacture Hardball. It seemed like everything was coming together perfectly; at least, it had until now. Winnie was nowhere to be found. He was always accessible through his cell phone, but now, no answer. *It just doesn't make sense,* Mo thought tensely. *He'd have called and gave me the whole gumbo by now.* Mo called the realtor.

"Yeah, yeah, he came and checked everything out and told me it was a done deal. We were supposed to get together later to sign the contract. You haven't spoken to him at all?" Shannon asked curiously.

"Naw, but uh…if you talk to him, tell him to give me a call."

"I will, and you do the same. My sellers were counting on this contract."

"Oh, we're still gonna go through with the deal regardless," Mo said confidently. He didn't want to lose this deal or damage it in any way if Winnie's disappearance meant nothing. He even quickly considered doing it on his own if he had to.

"It's probably nothin', so don't worry. We'll be in touch," he reassured Shannon.

"I hope so," she replied and hung up. She called Prince and relayed the information immediately.

"All right, that's good. I need you do me one more favor," Prince said.

"What's that?"

"I need you to tell this dude Mo to meet you at some restaurant tonight to sign the contract and put down a lil' bit of earnest money to keep the contract alive. But it has to be done tonight," Prince explained as he viewed the scenario in his head.

Shannon sighed. "How'd I know you'd say something like that?" She really didn't want to be involved any further into this thing. It was starting to sound more and more scary, especially after meeting Winnie. He looked scary. But she knew she couldn't say no to Prince, especially since she was already involved.

"This is it, Shan. This is the last thing, I promise. A'ight?"

She thought about it and sighed. "All right. Where at?"

"Call him back in thirty minutes and tell him to meet you at Razoo's in Sugarland. If anything changes, I'll hit you."

"Razoo's. Ok. I'll call you back once I talk to him."

"Already."

Shannon hung up. "Here we go again," she sighed. She called her sister.

******

Mo had just left Winnie's apartment and was now banging on the door of the new stash house where they'd been making the last few batches of Hardball. No answer.

Mo was getting frustrated. "Fuck!" he yelled, "what the fuck is going on?"

Mo sat down on the front steps with a deep frown furrowing his brow. Now he's pissed. Winnie's truck was gone so he knew he wasn't there. *So where the fuck is he?* He'd already considered the fact that Winnie could be balls-deep in some pussy, but that didn't even add up. Not with all this shit going on. He would have called back by now. Mo looked out into the clear sky. It was late afternoon. The sun was still working full time and would be for at least another few hours. Mo scanned the small field in front of the house, and he could see why Winnie had liked this place. It was situated so far back from the street that it seemed like you were in the country. A humid breeze passed through the tree and brush that occupied the property.

"Something must have happened," Mo said to himself. Once he heard himself admit it, he was sure it was true. Knowing Winnie and the things that he'd done, it was probably something really bad. Mo leaned his elbows down onto his knees and dropped his head, shaking it from side to side. *There's no other explanation,* he thought. *Even if he was in jail, he'd have still called by now.*

"Fuck it!"

Mo stood up and went around to the side of the house and peeked into the windows even though he knew they were all covered. There was another small window by the back door; Mo found a rock near the back porch and threw it through the window. They hadn't installed a security system yet. Mo was mad that Winnie hadn't given him a key, anyway. He reached inside the broken pane and unlocked the door. Once inside, he knew where everything was. He unlocked the front door and carried the pill machine out to the rear of his Aspen. He went back in and brought out a big double-layered trash bag in one hand which held fifteen thousand tabs of Hardball, and in the other hand, a small, wooden box with a big red ruby embedded in its lid. He went back and closed the door. He'd never be back. As he pulls out of the neighborhood, his cell phone rings. It's the realtor, Shannon. Mo doesn't answer. He figures whatever happened to Winnie, he was the next target. He'd taken enough chances already.

"I ain't no muthafuckin' fool," Mo declared. He was about to think for himself and do things his own way.

Chapter Thirty: AFTERMATH...THE GAME DIRTY

"I want arrests, Dan, and I want them in big numbers," DA Thomas Brody said into his office phone. On the other end of the line was Dan Nichols, the Chief of the Houston Police Department.

"Next week, we'll do a big press release letting the people know that Ball has been outlawed with a number of arrests linked to it. That will let the city know that we're not taking this thing lightly, that we're on the job!"

"I agree with you, Tom, one hundred percent. These next elections could be close. I'll get a memo out to my divisions telling them to get their informants working," he replied in a gruff tone. These two guys were on the same page. They both wanted to keep their jobs and all the perks. The public's safety came after that.

"All right. Let me know when you nail down the ringleaders. From what I understand, this is just a Houston thing, so they shouldn't be hard to find."

"Probably not. You never know, they might be well-known dealers that we're already investigating, but just breaking out some new product. Heroin arrests have been increasing recently, eighteen percent in the last six months, but hold on...seventy-eight percent over the last five years. It's coming. So it makes sense."

Tom Brody processed what the chief had just told him. He knew that the D-Boys controlled a good share of the heroin market in Houston, but they said they weren't behind this new rave. He hoped Warren Lee was telling the truth, but if not, it would be his own fault.

"Wow, we have got to work on these numbers. Let me know what big names your CIs come up with if any, all right?" Tom said, playing along with the chief and his stack of computer arrest statistics.

"Definitely. This could get interesting."

The two officials hang up, and a new attack formation was launched. Within days, a combination of raids, arrests and interrogations had swept through the highest drug trafficking areas of the city. Many of the police officers just used this as an excuse to harass young Blacks in urban areas, often times coming up with nothing. Sometimes they may get a bust for small amounts of crack, weed or maybe a pistol. If they were lucky, they'd get a runner or a parole or probation violator and charge him with evading arrest and send him back to prison, if they could catch him.

The bottom line was, which they would soon find out, was that Ball was not as widespread as crack, weed and other drugs. The police would be hard pressed to find a fifteen-year-old kid standing on a corner in the ghetto serving Ball. But, that's what they were looking for, so they really didn't know *what* they had on their hands. Ball was an exotic aphrodisiac that just happens to get you high. It was popular with the ballers and the boppers, on Black *and* White college campuses; even in high schools, strip clubs, escort services, or any dance club in Houston. The party scene was where Ball was at in heavy rotation. So, if you left it up to the cops on the streets who played by the book, this operation could have taken a while. But, there's a certain element of law enforcement that gives them an unfair advantage: *Snitches.*

******

"What's up, bitch, I know you've been getting my messages so why the fuck you actin' all brand new and shit?!" Tamara angrily yelled into the phone, holding it out in front of her face like an intercom, then returning it to her ear so she could hear Serene's response. Tamara had just dropped a stack of bills into the top of her money-counting machine. She had picked up her traps for the week and Young Bread had dropped off his and Big Baby's payload, so the clicking of the machine in the background caused her to talk louder.

"My bad, T. I've been busy tryin' to get some things in order. Everything is good, though. What's up?" Serene said nonchalantly. She was really nervous, but she was doing her best at playing it off. Serene refused to let Tamara make her feel inferior anymore. Tamara was shocked and infuriated at Serene's audacity to have such a careless attitude.

"'What's up?'" Tamara mocked, "Bitch, I need you to do a job, I ain't talked to you in three days and all you got to say is 'My bad, T, what's up?'"

"What do you want me to say, Tamara? I told you I been busy!" Serene snapped. "Besides, I still been handlin' up for you."

"Bullshit! Hoe, what you been so busy doing?"

"I been tryin' to take care of some things...with my kids," Serene said weakly.

"With your kids, huh? Like I'm supposed to believe that shit!" Tamara scoffed. "You been havin' the situation under control all this time, now all of a sudden, you missing in action behind your kids. Bitch, please!" Tamara said sarcastically, marking off another five stack on piece of scratch paper before replacing it with another stack.

"Look, Tamara, I'm tired of having to explain myself to you. I'm a grown woman!" Serene flared.

"Yeah, you so fuckin' grown and busy that you can't even make these lil' runs I'm payin' you for!"

"They said they're not ready!" Serene shot back with attitude, then caught herself. "But I'll go right now. They should be ready now, all right?"

"Ohhh, isn't *that* sweet. *Now* you wanna do your job," Tamara teased before shutting Serene down with her next statement, "But don't break your neck now, Serene...I've already taken care of it myself!"

Serene paused. She understood what that implied. "Oh, well—"

Tamara interrupted her. "Yeah, that's right. While you was so fuckin' grown and busy with your lil' stand in piece of dick, you just said fuck everything else, huh?"

"I did not..."

"You probably wasn't even handlin' ya own business, let alone mine,"

"I was..."

"Whatever. That dick must be good, huh, Serene? Tell me about it, girl. What's-his-name got that good shit? What *is* his name, anyway?" Tamara badgered.

Serene was frustrated and confused, but not enough to fall for the banana in the tailpipe. She didn't answer.

"Hello!?" Tamara yelled.

"I'm here."

"Well, act like you there and answer my question! What's your man's name again?"

"I never told you in the first place!"

Ooh, this bitch got some overnight nerve, gon' really make me stomp a mudhole in her ass, Tamara thought. Aloud, she said scathingly, "Well, tell me now, bitch!"

Serene acted as if she were finally giving in. "Reese! Ok! His name is Reese," Technically, she wasn't lying because Mo's full name is Maurice, but nobody called him Reese.

"Hmmph! So is 'Reese' dickin' you down all like that?"

"You know, what? Yes! He is puttin' it down like he's supposed to. There! You happy now?"

Tamara was the one to pause this time, but she wasn't confused. She could care less about how good Serene's sex life was, but she did want to know more about "Reese".

"Good for you. But that still wasn't a reason for you to leave my business hanging out to dry." Tamara said as she separated two bills that were stuck together so the machine could keep counting.

"I was gonna get everything together tonight, you just beat me to it, that's all."

This bitch really think she's slick! Tamara thought. "Mmm-hmm. Well, come over so we can talk about it," she said calmly as if her anger had passed.

"T, I really don't wanna talk about my sex life with you."

"Well then, just come over 'cause I wanna see you, damn!"

"All right, all right. I'll come through."

"Don't fuckin' play, Serene! When you comin'?"

"I'll be through there in a lil' while."

"All right, I'll be here."

When Serene hangs up the phone, she knows that is the last halfway civil interaction she'll have with Tamara. It's obvious to Serene that Tamara knows much more than what she's revealing and going to her territory to talk about it is walking into fire. It's over. Serene knew it was coming, but she wanted it to happen on her own terms. She had planned to go and make those pick ups and keep the money. She figured it'd be a nice bonus for herself. Once Prince's clique found out about Mo, they'd definitely come after him and probably her, too, so, why not keep the money? But now that she hadn't, she was having conflicting feelings about it. She sat back in her red terry-cloth robe on Mo's leather sectional and considered the irony. She knew it was better that she hadn't taken the money, but she wished she had. She didn't want to lose Tamara's friendship or her connect, but Serene knew that it was inevitable. She knew that she was gonna try and take over Tamara's Ball clientele and build her own empire, thus costing her Tamara's friendship and her connect, which brought her back to her first question. *So why not keep the money?* she thought to herself for the millionth time. *It doesn't even matter anymore.* Serene had close to a hundred grand saved, and a nice lil' three-to-five G a week Ball operation, so she would eat if her connect was consistent. With Tamara, it always was. Hopefully it would be the same with Mo. *The irony,* she thought. *There are advantages and consequences when a friend becomes an enemy.*

Late that night, Mo storms into his apartment. Serene is asleep on the couch. One of her favorite movies, *Rush Hour 3,* is playing on the flat screen on the wall in front of her. She wakes up when she hears Mo slam the door behind him.

"What happened?" she asked, startled.

"Get up. We gotta hurry up and pack a couple of bags. We're leaving," Mo demands.

"What? Where we going?" Serene asks. She was totally unprepared for this.

"I don't know yet. I just know that we're getting the fuck outta here. Come on!"

As they pack a couple of bags, Mo explains the events of the day and what he assumes is going on. When he left the stash house, he went to make as many pickups from the New Orleans soldiers as he could, netting a total of $17,300, which should have been $30,000. None of them had heard from Winnie, but they informed Mo that the cops and the task force had been raiding quite a few spots and were making it hard to get money unless you were making deliveries. The funny thing was, one of his trusted soldiers told him that they were raiding rock spots with "crack-cocaine" and "Ball" on the search warrant.

"What? You mean to tell me that they had Ball on the warrant?"

"Hell, yeah! Fucked me up, whodie. I didn't know they was on that shit like that!"

"I didn't know, either. Must be some new shit they just got on. Who they get?" Mo asked.

"It's fucked up, Mo, they got like eight of our guys, LuLu 'nem, Shortcut and a couple of *his* guys, too. That's why they money is so fucked up. LuLu got busted with two big-ass pill bottles, like two hundred fifty tabs. And he got like $900 in his pocket and another G in his shoe. Now he waiting to make bail and he gotta hire a lawyer," the soldier told him.

"Damn!" Mo said, thinking that was more money he could have collected.

"What's up, he got it?" he asked, referring to the bond and lawyer money. Mo knew LuLu had it. He was one of their top bread winners. But out of principle, he had to ask.

"Who, LuLu? Hell yeah. That bitch was hustlin' like a G a day, everyday. Er'body was getting money, but now thangs gon' slow up to see what's goin' down. So, we gon' lose all the way across the board. When you talk to Win, tell 'em it's gon' pick back up, that we just gotta regroup right quick." Mo nodded.

He explained all this to Serene as they ran around the apartment grabbing items to take with them.

"Damn! So it's really illegal now," she said in amazement. She paused from throwing things in the large suitcase on the floor in front of her. This changed things. Serene wished she could call Tamara and let her know what was going on, but she knew that was a dead issue. *Would the Houston Ball Club, Prince and Fatso's clique, stop? Would they change their plans? Probably not*, she decided. *So why should we?*

"So, what do we do now?" Serene asked aloud.

"I don't know, Serene," Mo replied wearily. "I'm just ready to get the fuck outta town for awhile, go to Atlanta or somethin'. It's too much shit going on right now. I don't know what's gon' happen next. What I *do* know is that I can't think while sittin' in this apartment right now, so try to hurry up!"

"Let's just get a hotel for a few days and lay low, get some things situated and see what's going on," Serene suggested. She wanted to get a better understanding of what all was going on before she made her next move. She also knew she'd have to do some high-dollar negotiating with her mom to leave her two kids with her on a long term basis.

"Yeah, I just need to get my head together so I can figure this shit out."

"We gon' figure it out, boo. It's gon' be all right, okay?" Serene said encouragingly.

"Fa'sho. You ready?"

"Yeah."

"Let's go." They went and checked into the Hyatt Hotel on I-10 and Eldridge, in the cut, where nobody but corporate executives rented rooms and where nobody would find them.

Chapter Thirty-One: HERE THEY COME

Boom! The battering ram hit Fatso's reinforced door with the force of a compact vehicle, but the door was still intact. The alarm started screaming as well as Fatso's automated host: "The police will be here in seconds. You are being videotaped. Leave now." The computerized voice repeated its ominous message over and over again.

Boom! They hit it a second time and the door frame buckled. The force-resistant hinges loosened; they were almost in. *Boom!* The door flew open.

"Houston Police! Search warrant! Come out with your hands up! We will shoot!" They weren't bluffing.

"No one's here, sir!" said a younger officer upon completing his initial inspection. The six-man crew relaxed.

"Would you *look* at this fuckin' place?!" The crew chief exclaimed in wonder and disgust. They all quickly review the interior design: the alligator-skin couches, the zebra-skin rugs, the Greek statues, the fine art on the wall; the maple wood floors, the granite, marble, the colors, the view of the downtown skyline, everything. All of this made these six officers of the law insanely jealous.

"How old is this kid?" the crew chief questioned.

"Twenty-three," the second-in-command quickly snapped.

"Two years older than my son and this fuckin' monkey lives better than all six of us combined," the chief said, walking up to an Egyptian statue of Ramses' head on a pedestal. He pushed it and it hit the floor with a loud thud. The stone head broke from the base at its neck.

"Oops," he smirked and they all chuckled a bit. "You know what we're looking for, guys, now let's find it!"

The six task force specialists began to tear Fatso's place apart, searching for that which they would not find. They cut holes in his $30,000 alligator-skin couches, broke a couple more statues and basically turned everything inside out for nothing; nothing they could find, at least.

Frustrated, they then went next door to Prince's condo with the same search warrant and repeated the destructive search to only get the same results.

"Fuck!" the second-in-command yelled, expressing his frustration.

"We gotta nail these fuckers! And nail 'em hard!" the chief stated.

After half-ass securing the entry doors in place with copies of the search warrants on the doors, the task force left. Next stop, The Houstonian. Since Tamara's building was so high-security, it was actually easier to get inside her condo. The crew chief simply went to the management office with the search warrant and they escorted the officers up with the spare key. Once inside, the most incriminating thing they could find was Tamara's money-counting machine, a registered pistol, which can both be justified in the promotions business, and a medium-sized safe that was secured to the concrete floor in a way that would not allow it to be moved. The crew chief calls in an HPD-contracted locksmith who stays on call for situations like this, and within thirty minutes, the safe is open. What the crew chief and his crew thought would be a pay-dirt moment turned out to be a bunch of neatly arranged legal papers and five thousand dollars in cash, hardly anything to get excited about.

The crew chief felt like he'd been screwed. Either his informant had given him some bad info, or somebody was tipping them off. There were two things the crew chief knew for sure: these people he was now pursuing definitely fit the profile of sophisticated drug dealers, and secondly, the lifestyle they were living made him want to arrest them even more.

******

Things were heating up fast in the Law Offices of Dick McLaren, the hottest criminal defense attorney in the city. Fatso had received a phone call from his security service provider informing him that his house had been broken into. He knew something was off since the call came in during the middle of the afternoon. They went on to tell him that the police had been dispatched. Shortly thereafter, they called back to report that it was, in fact, *the police* who had initiated the forced entry and that he needed to contact them for further information. By the time he pressed the end key on his cell phone, Prince had received the same phone call. Within minutes, Prince, Tamara and Fatso were each individually en route to Dick's office, and by the time they arrived, Dick had the information he needed for them. As the three of them sat down in front of his big mahogany desk, Dick gives it to them raw.

"All right, listen. The DA has a ban on Ball. It's now officially an illegal manufactured controlled substance with the same sentencing guidelines as methamphetamine and ecstasy."

"Son of a bitch!" Prince cursed.

"But we can fight that, right?" Fatso asked.

"Let me finish. So far, they've issued search warrants for you two guys," Dick said, pointing at Prince and Fatso. "Depending on what they find or act like they found, those will turn into arrest warrants."

"Ain't nothing to find, so whatever they say they found, they planted."

Dick nodded. "Exactly. Hopefully, we're clear. I'll tell you what, from what I'm hearing, the DA's got his panties all in a knot behind this 'Ball' phenomenon, quote-unquote. So as far as planting evidence, well let's just say that it wouldn't be the first time. But, we'll deal with that when and if it comes up. Right now, I need to know everything about Ball, what's happening on the streets with it and how things relate to you two. Tell me like this is the first time we've talked. And take your time. I need to start forming a defense in my mind."

"All right," Fatso said slowly. He takes a deep breath. He and Prince were both thinking the same thing. They'd killed a man, and they'd ordered hits on many more. Thirteen in total, all to be executed this very evening. It was too much information to divulge. They really wanted to keep things between them and Dick on a need to know basis.

Tamara sensed their dilemma and squeezed Prince's hand before she voiced her concern. "Excuse me, Dick. Has my name come up at all?"

"You know, I didn't ask, but we definitely need to stay ahead of the game as much as we can. Gimme your full name and address," Dick said, and Tamara did. He jotted down the information as it was told to him, then picked up his phone and ordered his secretary to check it out right away. Dick remembered Tamara as being Prince's girlfriend from a prior meeting.

Dick's perfectly trimmed head of brown hair tilted down and his eyebrows arched upwards. "Now, is there anything at that address that we need to be concerned about?"

"Nothing illegal, if that's what you mean. I have a promotions company, so I keep a money-counting machine and a registered handgun."

"Is your company incorporated?" Dick inquired.

"Yes," Tamara quickly replied.

"Is the handgun registered in your name?" Tamara nodded in the affirmative.

"Good, 'cause they are going to seize all of those things but I'll go get them back for you. Anything else? No drugs, no weed, excessive cash or anything?"

After Winnie, they'd cleaned up everything. The cash that Tamara had just collected went straight to a safe that was kept in a storage facility.

"Oh, well, I keep five thousand dollars in my little safe, but I doubt they'll get in there," she said dismissively.

"Oh, they'll get in with a locksmith. But don't worry, we'll get that back, too. Anything else in there?"

"That's it."

"All right, talk to me," Dick said just as his phone rang. He grabbed it swiftly.

"Yeah." He listened for a moment, then he looked at Tamara and sighed. Whatever he was hearing was not good.

"What?! That's bullshit! They're fishing! Call Mike so we can post bond right away," Dick commanded, then hung up.

"Whatever you were thinking, Tamara, you were right. They searched your place and found exactly what you said they'd find. The dumb thing is that all three of your names were on the search warrant, but now they've only issued arrest warrants for you two guys," he said, pointing at Prince and Fatso.

"For what?" Prince asked.

"Drug trade paraphernalia and a firearm. It's totally fuckin' bogus, guys."

"It's not even our place. Neither of us live there!"

"I know it. It'll never stand up. The DA's gotta be bustin' his own balls on this one," Dick said.

"So, why didn't they have an arrest warrant for me?" Tamara asked.

"Because they don't *have* shit. These guys are fuckin' idiots. They rely on two-bit criminals for information and swear they have a case. If they're charging you guys with this, I know they don't have anything. *But,*" Dick emphasized, "what they *are* trying to do is build a case against you guys. Realistically, some informant probably told them that you guys run the show, so their strategies are simple. They either start from the bottom and work their way up to the top, or start at the top and work their way down. Since your operation is isolated and you're within reach, they start at the top. They jam you guys up on whatever they can, then they go down the line and try to get your people to roll over on you."

"That's why they didn't issue a warrant for me," Tamara observed.

"Not only that, but it was your place, and you're allowed to have a registered handgun. The money machine is questionable, but they don't have enough leverage on you yet."

Fatso had been quietly adding things up in his head, figuring this new situation into the equation. It wasn't totally unexpected but the timing was strange. It was throwing his focus off the plan they'd set in motion.

"So what do you suggest, Dick?" he asked.

"I suggest you go straight over to the bondsman and post bail. They'll process you in and out in about two hours, and I'll get these charges dropped at your first court date."

"How much is bail?" Prince asked.

"$50,000 each."

Prince and Fatso both knew they could have charged five thousand on their credit cards if they chose to do so, but they needed a chance to talk things over. It was all happening too fast.

"I don't have five grand on me," Prince said.

"Neither do I," Fatso added.

Dick had a $50,000 retainer account from the Landaus' from which he could have easily debited and just had them pay back the following day, but lawyers hated to do anything of the sort. In their eyes, retainers were deposit only.

"Just put it on your credit card, no big deal," Dick suggested casually, a little *too* casually for Fatso's taste.

"Nah, I'm not puttin' that on my credit card. Check this out: why don't you give us a couple of hours and we'll go get the money and come right back?"

"You sure? I mean, you don't wanna get picked up out there and then have to go through processing. It'll be much worse. Just put it on your card and you don't have to worry about that."

Fatso felt like Dick was pressuring him. "Nah, we'll ride with Tamara. Just give us a couple of hours and we'll be back."

Once outside in the parking lot, Fatso, determined to complete his mission, declares, "Look, we're not gonna let this throw our focus off of what's already in motion. We gon' settle this shit tonight. We'll deal with this little petty shit tomorrow or Monday."

Prince nodded. He was feeling a little bit differently knowing that he was a wanted man. "Say, I was thinking," he smirked, "what better alibi than to be in jail for a day?"

Fatso shook his head. "You have a point, but fuck all that, P, we ain't spendin' *no* days in jail. Especially not voluntarily."

"For real. I can think of a hundred better alibis than that. I don't even want to think about seeing you like that. Baby, please, I think y'all should just post the bail so we don't have to worry about this," Tamara pleaded.

Fatso shook his head no again. "That's a whole 'nother ball game with a different set of rules. I don't think it's gonna be as simple as Dick's making it sound."

"Me, either," Prince stated. "There ain't no tellin' what that bitch-ass DA is gonna pull next. All this behind Winnie's bullshit," he spat.

Tamara shrugged her shoulders. It was obvious that she was trying to reason with two bull-headed men on a mission. "So, what now?" she asked.

"I say we check on the cribs and get them in order, then go set up shop at the Icon," Prince suggested.

"I don't think you guys should go home if they have arrest warrants. They're gonna be watching," Tamara remarked.

Fatso pulled out his cell phone. "I'll have Nancy go clean up. Tamara, you go on to the house and get situated, book that suite and a limo for the weekend. Prince will call you in about an hour with the address where we can be picked up."

"All right," Tamara agreed and nodded at Prince.

Prince looked Tamara in the eyes. "Babe? You remember everything I told you, right?" Tamara nodded. She'd been over and over it all a thousand times in her head and questioned Prince about certain details on several occasions.

"Everything," she answered.

"All right, I'll talk to you in a lil' bit, then," Prince said apprehensively. They kissed goodbye and embraced tightly before he jumped into his SUV and pulled it out of the lot to follow Fatso to Nancy's crib in the medical center. In that moment, you'd have never been able to convince Prince or Tamara that this would be the last kiss they'd share for quite some time.

******

Once the arrest warrants had been issued, Detectives Leopold and Polanski had been assigned to stake out the two Landau brothers' designer townhouses. Neither of them liked the idea of sitting around in a car indefinitely, waiting on a couple of drug dealers to show up, but hey, it beat sitting behind a desk, and since the DA was on pins and needles for press coverage, this case now qualified as high-profile. They liked that idea.

"What kind of bozo goes and paints his house or-*ange*? What is that, some kind of retro-hippie bullshit?" Polanski scoffed to his partner. Polanski was an old-school hard-nose from Philadelphia who'd moved south to get away from the congestion and tension of the East Coast.

"I guess. Bright-colored stucco is the new thing down here in the Museum District," Leopold answered. He was a laid-back, calculative guy from right here in Houston. He'd long ago given up arguing with his partner; he knew there was just no point. Polanski may have come from Philly to get away, but he had brought a shitty attitude with him.

"I didn't know Blacks were into that down here," Polanski said. For some reason, he thought Southern Blacks were supposed to still be picking cotton.

"Yep," Leopold said blandly, trying to resist the urge to engage in Polanski's ignorance. Instead, he took a sip of his coffee. The air conditioning from the cruiser was blowing cold. Just as he was about to school his partner, a Toyota Highlander pulled up in the Landau's driveway and caught his attention.

"We've got action."

******

When Nancy walked inside Fatso's townhouse, she was appalled.

"Oh, my God," she whispered loudly. She couldn't believe her eyes; she was on the verge of tears. Fighting back the lump in her throat, she walked through and assessed the damage. The immaculate home that she'd kept as spotless as possible week after week, the space that she'd proudly grown accustomed to, even harbored fantasies of capturing Fatso's heart and living there as his woman, was a disaster.

"Why would they do this?" she asked no one in particular as she examined the kitchen. Broken crystal and china mixed with food that had been pulled from boxes covered the floor. All containers and packages had been opened and emptied.

"What were they looking for?"

Nancy knew nothing of Fatso's activities in the street, only that he was a successful businessman with several botanical nurseries, a construction company and that he dabbled in the stock market. That all made sense, but *this* didn't.

She called Fatso to report the damages."How bad is it?" he asked.

"It's *horrible*, Dwayne. They ruined everything. Why would they do this? What were they looking for?" Nancy whined.

Fatso was glad that she knew so little. The less she knew the safer she'd be. "It's all a misunderstanding. I'll explain it to you later, just take pictures. Clean up what you can and secure the place again as much as possible."

"Dwayne, you don't understand. This stuff is ruined," she moaned, almost crying. It hurt her just to tell him. "I mean, I don't know if...maybe some of it can be repaired, but it's really bad. I just don't understand."

Fatso was getting frustrated with her hysterics. "Look, just calm down, Nancy, all right?" It was obvious she wasn't ready for the impact of all of this. "I need you to pull yourself together for me."

Nancy took a deep breath. Fatso said he needed her and she wouldn't let him down, not now, not ever. *I'm not gonna ask questions; I'm just gonna do what needs to be done,* she thought.

"Okay, Dwayne, I'm sorry. I'm fine." Her voice became stronger. "Listen, I'm gonna straighten up a lil' bit, but I'm really going to have to come back with some professionals to get some repair estimates. So don't worry, Dwayne, I'll take of it, okay? I'll take care of everything."

"That's my girl. I'll get you whatever you need, just let me know," he said with a smile. He felt better, and that made Nancy feel better.

"All right, Dwayne. I'll be there shortly. I'll come back here tomorrow with help so we can finish it up."

They ended their call and Nancy got to work. Within two hours, she'd straightened up Fatso's place and Prince's condo, which, to her dismay, was not as bad as Fatso's.

"Bastards," she cursed. As she drove away, she had no idea she had company.

******

The black Suburban that had been converted to a limo pulled in front of the duplex on the narrow street in the medical center and waited.

Within minutes, Fatso and Prince stepped down the short walkway and were making themselves comfortable in the well-appointed passenger cabin.

"To the Icon, driver. Oh, what's your name?" Prince asked.

"Henry, sir," the driver replied.

"Henry what?" Unbeknownst to Henry, Prince was establishing their alibis.

"Henry Hail, sir, at your service," the driver said with a polite chuckle. He was used to dealing with demanding clients. His record as a driver and a citizen was spotless, just as Tamara had ordered.

"Nice to meet you, Henry. I don't mean to be overbearing, but I figure you'll be our driver for the weekend, so we might as well be on a first-name basis, you know? I'm Flip, and this is my brother, T.I."

"Very nice to meet you gentlemen. Anything that I can do for you, please ask," Henry customarily stated. *'Flip and T.I".....those can't possibly be their real names. Maybe they're rappers or something,* he thought.

He generally didn't like to take these kinds of jobs. Henry was an older White gentleman who still hadn't lost his English accent, even after twenty years as a Houston chauffeur. Transplanted from the Boston area and originally from England, he was more accustomed to the White upper class oil and corporate millionaires that Houston had harvested over the years. But, a job is a job.

"Appreciate ya, Henry. I'm going to raise the divider now," Prince stated.

"Yes, sir."

Prince pushed a button and the divider separated the front of the vehicle where the driver sat and the rear passenger area, giving Fatso and

Prince some privacy. The vehicle started moving as they shared a quick laugh at Prince attempt to be anonymous.

"Man, baby girl was kinda shook up, huh?" Prince asked, referring to Nancy.

"Yeah, she ain't really cut out for this kinda shit. She's a good girl. I like that, though. She'll be a'ight," Fatso said dismissively.

"She was really trying to play it off and be strong and shit. I could tell. She cut for you brah, it's too bad she had to see that bullshit."

"Psst, they fucked our shit up. They can't stand to see a nigga livin' like that. But fuck it, when we get the charges dropped, we'll get insurance to pay for it."

"Fuck that, we still gon' sue them hoes. They gon' pay for that shit! It ain't even about the money, it's the principle. Might even get that Darnell X nigga involved to get on they ass."

Fatso laughed. "Come on, P. You know them people don't give a fuck about that pro-righteous ass bullshit."

"Why you be trippin', man? Darnell from our hood, made good, too. He makes them White folks recognize. If anything, you should be supportin' dude," Prince never understood why Fatso didn't like Darnell X. He's at least ten years older than Fatso, so it couldn't be on a peer thing. Prince suspected Darnell X of stealing Fatso's girlfriend or something back in the day and Fatso never got over it. But he and Fatso had been too close growing up for him to have missed something like that, so Prince quickly dismissed that theory.

"Dude's an actor, man. What's the first rule of survival?" Fatso asked.

"Self-preservation," Prince shot back, trying to find the significance of such an obvious question.

"Exactly. I see through that smoke screen. That nigga ain't no different from us, P. We all capitalists, we just ain't hidin' behind no picket lines and 'I have a dream' rallies. Nigga, we *are* the dream! The American dream."

Prince thought about what Fatso was saying for a moment. "I feel 'dat, but still, you never know when we gonna need a brotha like Darnell X to raise some hell for us, like right now!"

Fatso shook his head. "Nah, we got this."

Prince didn't see the point in pushing the matter, so he gave up the debate for more urgent issues.

"So what's crackin tonight?" He already knew the answer, he just wanted to redirect to a common ground.

"Tonight?" Fatso began, "Tonight we exterminate these cockroaches!"

"That's what *I'm* talkin' 'bout," Prince agreed.

"That's all the justice I need right now."

"Big Baby and everybody should be waiting. They said everything is lined up," Prince said, referring to the phone call he'd made from Nancy's crib.

"Bet."

Just as Prince's mind began to browse through the list of possibilities that could detour the mission for the night and the contingencies to reroute those detours, everything went wrong. They both saw the flashing lights through the tinted windows that faintly reflected off the peanut butter tan interior. They simultaneously turned to look back in silent panic. There was an unmarked cruiser flashing cherries, which flickered behind the windshield and the grill as well as another patrol car following with its roof cherries rotating.

"Fuck!" Prince yelled. "Son of a muthafuckin' bitch!" Prince pulled his phone off his hip as the privacy divider began to slide down.

Fatso's mind was racing. "Call Tamara and tell her to take the money to the bondsman now!" he ordered quickly.

"Gentlemen, we're being pulled over. I have to stop," Henry warned.

"Drive this muthafucka! Take us to our attorney's office in downtown on Congress Street. Don't fuckin' stop!" Prince demanded.

The driver was torn. *What to do?*

Tamara's phone rang twice before she answered, but at that moment, it seemed like ten times. She couldn't have answered fast enough.

"What's up baby?" she asked. She sounded like she'd been in the middle of doing three or four different things, but this phone call was first priority.

"They're tryin' to pull us over! Take the bond money to Dick right away! We'll meet you there. We're not stopping!" Prince yelled as he looked back.

"Sir, I have to stop. It's my civil duty," Henry pleaded. He'd begun to slow down to let the police know he was not fleeing while also following the hostile demands of his clients.

"Look, Henry, just calm down," Fatso negotiated. "Drive normally, and take us to Congress Street. We'll get there, *but don't stop*," he said calmly but firmly.

"I have to go get the money! It's not here!" Tamara cried.

It was early evening, but still dark nonetheless, so the spotlights the police cars were using to point directly into the back window shined brightly. Another cruiser had joined the trail as backup prepared for a chase.

"Pull that vehicle over now!" Polanski yelled over the unmarked cruiser's loudspeaker. Henry kept driving. He believed that there was more danger to himself inside the vehicle if he stopped, versus an evading arrest charge which was committed under duress. He was trying to keep a balanced control of the situation by either allowing the police to force him to stop or making to his destination. 222 Congress was now less than two miles away.

"Do whatever you gotta do! Just get that fuckin' money down there right now!" Prince yelled frantically.

"All right, let me get on it. You'll be out tonight, I promise."

The third patrol car began to make his move. He pulled alongside the limo, and ordered the driver to pull over. He was going to corner the vehicle off the road to a stop.

"Pull over or I'll force you off the road!" the officer blared through his loudspeaker.

"Tamara, listen. Tell Big Baby that nothing stops. Move forward with everything, you understand?"

"I understand," Tamara confirmed.

"I love you, and I'm counting on you. Now get busy!" Prince commanded.

"I love you, too, baby. I'll see you later. Don't worry, I got this!" The officers had the limo surrounded and were forcing it to pull over. Henry had no choice in the matter.

Fatso was on his cell phone, yelling at Dick. "You get us out of this bullshit right now, Dick! Call the DA, call the judge, call the fuckin' mayor, I don't give a fuck! But you get us outta this right now!...Yes, Alabama and Gray," Fatso yelled as the passenger door flew open and an officer stuck a gun in his face.

"Put the fuckin' phone down!" the officer ordered.

"My attorney Dick McLaren wants to talk to you," Fatso said and held the phone out to the officer.

"Put that fuckin' gun down, we ain't dangerous!" Prince yelled at the officer.

"I wouldn't give a fuck if it was God Himself on that phone, put it down and get your hands up!" The other passenger door opened and a bigger, more aggressive officer reached inside and snatched Prince out of the limo and threw him on the ground.

"Get your muthafuckin' hands off me, bitch!" Prince yelled.

"I got your bitch, punk!" the officer yelled back. With his knee in Prince's back, he cuffed his right wrist and struggled to get hold of his left because Prince was waving his arm around, resisting the officer's attempt to cuff him. The officer punches Prince in the back of the head then grabs his wrist and cuffs him.

"That's your muthafuckin' job, hoe. You fucked with the wrong one. Get the fuck off me!"

It was a wrap. The other officer knocked the phone out of Fatso's hand, snatched him out of the truck and arrested him. By that time, Polanski and Leopold were overseeing and were on the phone with the chief, who would in turn call the DA within minutes. They were in the back of a musty squad car, painfully sitting on tightly cuffed wrists. Shortly thereafter, they were being processed into the Harris County Jail at 701 San Jacinto. Things had just taken a drastic turn for the worst.

******

Tamara hustles into the bondsman's office, a single-level converted house with big red and blue neon lights in the picture window that read "BOND." She had a big brown and tan Dereon purse with gold emblems and studs thrown over her bare shoulder. She wore a tan chiffon scrungee dress, some blue Azzure jean capris with tan stitching and tan suede cuffs and some tan Dereon platform peep-toe shoes. The only make-up she wore was eyeliner and lip gloss. Her wavy, sandy-brown hair was in a loose ponytail. Her jewelry consisted of big hoop earrings, a thin gold chain with a diamond solitaire pendant, a diamond tennis bracelet, Tiffany watch and a gold solitaire diamond ring on her wedding ring finger. Tamara was a true fly girl diva that commanded attention anywhere she went, but right now she was about to portray the role of a drug dealer's girlfriend.

"Hi, I'm Tamara. I got here as fast as I could. Do you have the paperwork ready?" she announced to the secretary and some guy in a white button-down and a navy-blue tie that looked like he'd bought it from the dollar store who was standing over the secretary's shoulder. Then, in a voice just a little louder than a whisper, she said, "I have the money."

The guy in the white shirt extended his hand. "Hi, Tamara. I'm Jeff." He wore a fake smile that couldn't mask his anxiety. "Um...why don't you step into my office," he said, directing Tamara to the rear of the small building.

Tamara sat down in a well-used leather executive chair. She noticed how his office was colder than the rest of the place and that it smelled like old wood and cheap incense. Tamara was very perceptive, probably because she was about to pull $10,000 in cash out of her purse and hand it a White man whom she'd never before seen in her life.

Jeff's mouth began to water as Tamara began to unzip her designer bag. This was a big bond. He could just *feel* the cash in his hands. He was so disappointed. He *could* process the bond, but his friend Dick McLaren had already warned him that there would be no release, that they'd run into some problems.

"Wait...Tamara," he stammered, holding out his hand to stop her from tempting him any further. "Dick needs to speak to you. I told him I'd call him when you got here." He picked up the desk phone and dialed.

Tamara began to panic. "What's the problem?" she asked cautiously. Jeff didn't answer, but instead he handed her the phone.

"Dick McLaren."

"It's Tamara. I'm here with the money, now what's going on? Did they raise the bond or what?"

"Tamara. I wish it were that simple; I'd cover the difference myself. But I called everybody I could think of, and from the sounds of it, the DA has placed a seventy-two hour hold on Purnell and Dwayne. The DA seems to suspect their involvement in some other, more serious crimes," Dick explained.

"What *kind* of 'serious crimes'? Dammit, Dick! That's why they didn't wanna do the shit. Prince didn't trust that fuckin' asshole DA, and he was right!"

"They probably have nothing, all right? There's been so much drug-related crime that they have no idea who's who. I told the DA to raise the bond, do a house monitor, anything. These guys are no flight risk. But he wouldn't budge."

Tamara sighed. She was so incredibly pissed, frustrated, broken and sad that she could hardly contain herself. She felt as if they'd all been tricked.

"You still didn't tell me what kind of 'more serious crimes'," she said coolly. There was a pause.

"He wouldn't tell me."

"Oh, fuck you!" Tamara snapped. "Are you working with them? Did you have something to do with this? You think you're untouchable, muthafucka, but you're not."

"Tamara! Goddammit! You calm down right now! I'm on *your* side, all right? I am the best defense attorney in this city. My track record speaks for itself. I have never turned on my clients, and I never will. Now, I know you're mad. I know you're upset. But I am the best chance of Purnell and Dwayne beating this case, and we're gonna fight this together, okay? You have my word. If everything they've told me is true, we're gonna get them outta this, you hear me?"

Tamara was fighting back tears. She knew more than Dick. She'd been there, she'd seen it with her own eyes. The charges she feared were the most serious of all. Tamara was aware of Dick's defense record, and he'd beaten plenty of murder charges in trial, but he'd lost some, too. Who's to say which is which? Who picks the winners and who mourns the losers? Where is the justice in an innocent grandmother being burned alive? Where is the justice in murderers going free and innocent people getting life without parole? At that point, Tamara knew that this form of justice that Dick was proposing could not be trusted. Tamara was no model citizen, nor did she know very many, but what she *did* know and understand was that the law was not designed to protect and serve the people she loved. In the city streets, you serve and protect your own. That's the only reality that mattered now.

After a long pause, Tamara took a deep breath and pulled herself together. "Yeah, I hear you. You got paid. You have everything you need, so just do the best you can and keep me posted. I gotta go." Tamara handed the phone back to Jeff and without another word, stood up and walked out. She jumped into the driver's seat of her red GL450 Benz truck and headed for the Icon hotel. On the short drive over, she called Jewel to update her on the situation. Jewel paused and listened before selecting her words carefully.

"Do not worry yourself with things you cannot control. Instead, focus your energy and your power on what you *can* control. Do you see?" Jewel asked.

"Yes," Tamara replied, getting lost in the combination of Jewel's words and her own thoughts.

"In times of great adversity, one becomes who one truly is. This is your apex moment. You must persevere with clarity. Center your power, Tamara, and rise to the occasion, to greatness, to leadership. Prince needs you right now. We all need you right now...to become...to do what needs to be done. Do you know what that is?"

Tamara thought to herself, *Does she know? Is she reading my mind? Or is this her way of guidance? Did Prince tell Jewel what he had planned for me?* Either way, Tamara knew what needed to be done, and Jewel was telling her exactly what she needed to hear.

"Yes, I do."

"Good. Then do it as if you were born to do it," Jewel said firmly. "And Princey and Fatso won't be there long, all right? So don't worry."

"All right. Thank you, Jewel. I'm so glad I called you. I needed to hear this. It's like you're speaking directly to my soul."

Jewel chuckled. "You make sure to continue to call, honey, and I'll continue to speak to your soul. Deal?"

"Deal." Tamara said with a smile.

"The boys will be fine. You have my love and my support, sweetheart, so just pick up the slack and keep pushin' forward. Call me whenever you need me, Tamara. I'm here for you."

"Okay, Auntie Jewel, I will." Tamara said, then disconnected the call with complete understanding of how valuable her relationship is and was going to be in the future with her new mentor. Tamara believed that, being a woman with street pedigree and her position as the stomp-down queen of her HBC family, Jewel's insight and wisdom would prove to be a great asset on her short list of confidential relationships. She'd already learned a valuable lesson that drove tonight's mission: crush your enemy completely. Mercy is for the weak.

When Tamara explained what had happened when she went to bail Prince and Fatso out to Big Baby, Young Bread and the others who had gathered at the Icon suite to take action, they were pissed.

"That muthafucka said *what?*" Big Baby asked incredulously.

"He's the most powerful attorney in the city and he can't even get them a bail on a bitch-ass gun charge?" Young Bread asked.

"Hold on! He said 'more serious crimes'. What's the DA talkin' 'bout?" Big Baby queried. He thought of all the publicity and the hell the DA had been raising about the deaths and crimes related to Ball in the past few weeks. There was even an incident where a dude had taken an eighteen-year-old girl, a student at Texas Southern University, up on the roof of a high-rise apartment building and raped her, bit off two of her toes, then jumped off the roof and killed himself. Again, the news had reported that Ball was likely a motivating factor. But what they didn't know was that it was *Hardball*, Winnie's fucked-up twist on what had originally been a beautiful, natural thing.

"I just hope it ain't..." Young Bread began, but his sentence trailed off. Everyone knew what he was saying.

Big Baby quickly disregarded that theory. "Nah, that was just a few days ago."

"Well, if it's not that..."

"...then it could be a whole dirty laundry list of shit. There are too many possibilities," Big Baby finished.

The other soldiers had been listening to the two lieutenants talk, trying to stay on the same wavelength.

"This shit is fucked up." Cesar offered. He'd been the one to take Winnie's phone and set up pinpoint locations to pick off Winnie's main guys that very night. With the rest of the family's help, they had it all set up. But now, Cesar had to admit, without Fatso and Prince here, it wasn't looking too good.

Tamara had been listening, as well. She sensed the confusion and decline in morale taking place, so she quickly tried to put things back in perspective.

"Let's not get ahead of ourselves, a'ight? We still have a mission to accomplish here tonight, and it's going forward! They're gonna be all right one way or another," she said, referring to Prince and Fatso.

"Besides, it's not as bad as it seems. We can use this to our advantage," she added.

"How's that?" Cesar asked.

"Because, if they're locked down, and muthafuckas is still out here droppin' like flies, it seems like they didn't have nothin' to do with it. It's a perfect alibi," Tamara explained. "This is what they want, and it's what's best. So, let's get this shit goin'! Come mornin' time, I want them niggas to wish they'd never heard of Texas. They came down here and fucked our shit all up and we ain't finna' let that shit ride. Now, is y'all wit' me?!" Tamara had raised her voice to the roar of a young lioness. She not only captured the undivided attention of every gangsta in the room, but she crunked up their sense of loyalty and readiness to strike.

"Hell, yeah!" said Boo-bo and a couple of others.

"This our muthafuckin' city!"

"Ain't *nobody* standin' in the way of HBC family!"

Young Bread and Big Baby nodded, feeling the energy in the room. "All right, then, now where we at as far as our plan is concerned?"

"We got e'rthang set up," Cesar replied. He was ready to lay it all out.

Big Baby stepped forward with his hand up to silence Cesar. "We got locations on all but one, Winnie's right hand, Mo. He's missing, but he'll pop up and we'll get his ass. But check it out, though, T, you ain't gon' like this shit: we just found out tonight that Serene been fuckin' Mo."

"Who, Mo? You said his name is Mo?" Tamara asked for clarity.

"Yeah, Mo, Winnie's ace boone," Young Bread replied.

"That low-down, dirty tramp," Tamara said icily as she put two and two together. No wonder Serene had been so secretive about who she'd been fucking. She knew Tamara would have never approved of that relationship. When Tamara had asked Serene his name, she'd said "Reese." *Mo. Reese...Maurice.* Serene had tried to play mind games with Tamara and now Tamara wondered if Serene had been in on their scheme all along. Tamara truly felt as if she'd been stabbed in the back on a massive scale.

"You knew she was seein' somebody, huh?" Big Baby asked.

"The funky-cock hoe told me the nigga's name was 'Reese'." Tamara spat. "You think she was part of this from jump street?"

"We don't know," Big Baby answered. "But if she's with him when we catch him..."

"Yeah, merck her ass, too," Tamara finished.

"Hell, yeah," Young Bread agreed.

Tamara leaned her head down briefly to consider it all. This battle had become entirely too personal. Just when she thought she'd clearly understood her enemy.

Tamara looked up at her crew. "So, y'all ready to do this?" They all nodded in agreement.

"Well, what are we standing around for? Let's get into some gangsta shit!"

They had laid out their strategies. Everyone knew his role, and they dapped each other and began to depart. Tamara was to stay and hold down central at the Icon. She made her cousin Young Bread stay with her for protection and company. Even though he'd wanted to take part in the street executions and put in his work, he knew that Tamara couldn't and shouldn't be alone right now for several reasons. She herself had wanted to be in the streets puttin' in work, but Prince wouldn't have it, so therefore, Big Baby, Young Bread and the rest of the crew couldn't allow it, either. So everyone else left, and Young Bread stayed behind with Tamara, walkie-talkie in his hand, a long-range police scanner sitting on the table and a Glock .45 tucked in the waist of his Red Monkey jeans.

The events of this night would become street legend. It would be talked about in pool halls, clubs, in high schools, colleges, on the internet, on the street corners, by old gangstas and new ones comin' up. It would include gory details of shootouts and stabbings, dismemberments and decapitations, cats bein' caught slippin' with their pants down. They'd say, *"The boy caught a sniper shot to the side of the face while he was laid up in some pussy. Cold game."* Or, *"...caught him comin' out the motel room to check on his car alarm,"* or, *"Did you hear about the three dope spots that got kick-doored that same night? Cats got clipped racin' for their stash, but these wasn't no robberies. These was good ol' fashioned assassinations. Police found 'em with the dope, pills, money, all that shit intact. And get this: one of the cat's heads was 'missing'."* "What?" "Yeah." This bloody night of murder would forever be memorialized by the chain of events and media as *"Friday the Thirteen."*

Chapter Thirty-Two: PEGGY SUE

"Wuz goin' down, hood?" the lil' brown-skinned homie asked with more energy than anybody else in the holding tank that was built for thirty but was stuffed with over sixty men who, depending on his arrest and reason for being here, each had a look of concern on his face. Half of them were drunk, homeless or both. Some were passed out on the floor snoring like they were having the best sleep of their lives, dreaming they were still at the bar. Others were nodding off on the concrete benches that lined the right and left sides of the walls.

The inescapable stench that emanated from every direction made both Fatso and Prince not want to breathe; they could only take in small sips of air at a time. At first, Prince was breathing through his mouth to avoid the stank, but his mind told him that he didn't wanna taste that shit or take any of that shit in through his mouth, so he opted to breathe through his nose, instead, thinking that the hairs in his nose could act as a filter. He would just have to deal with the stank.

"Wuzzup, fool?" Prince responded, not nearly as hyped as the little brotha that Prince had gone to high school with. His name was Lil' Don and he was from Sunnyside, a neighborhood right across Cullen from South Park. Tamara and Young Bread were also from Sunnyside. Lil' Don extended his hand for a handshake, but Prince just put his fist out for a pound. This wasn't the time or the place for that touchy-feely shit. Fatso simply ignored the kid. There was too much going on.

"Say, mane, what you doin' up in heah, mane," Lil Don asked.

"Some bullshit. We'll be out of here in the next couple of hours," Prince replied, unwilling to reveal any particulars.

Lil' Don recognized Fatso as Prince's older brother. He didn't know Fatso as well as he knew Prince, but he did know that Fatso had gone to college as a Chemistry major and had a reputation for being the best dope-cooker on the Southside. "What's the deal, Fatso, you a'ight?"

Fatso nodded. "What's up, lil' homie? I'm chillin'," he answered grimly. His mind was somewhere else.

Reverting his attention back to Prince, Lil' Don says, "Say, lookout. This ain't you, dawg."

"Man, I ain't trippin' on these trumped-up ass charges. We'll be back in the streets in no time. Tonight, nigga! All these hoes want is some money. You know how it go."

"Oh, I know that ain't no problem. Buy the whole muthafuckin' case, huh?" Lil' Don said with a smile, fully aware of the Landaus' reputation for havin' that money bag.

"For real, tho, Prince, y'all niggas don't need to hit that tank up there. It's fucked up down here, mane. Harris County ain't no joke, daddy."

"I see. Shit, we ain't trippin', though. We finna be up. We ain't even gonna hit the floor."

"Well, it's a lot of the homies from the 'hood down here so if y'all do, man, y'all know you ain't gotta worry about shit. We got ya, baby. Ya feel me?"

Prince nodded. Fatso caught that part, too. Lil' Don was referring to the dorms and pods that made up the seven floors of the county jail. He was right, though: Harris County *ain't* no joke. The conditions and environment are fucked up. They had all heard the stories but Lil' Don had experienced it firsthand on several occasions. So, even though he didn't want to be there just like no one else wanted to be there, he was accustomed to the place. Even a few of the sheriffs and COs knew him by name.

"I ain't new to this shit, I'm *true* to this shit!" Lil' Don said with pride.

Fatso thought to himself, *How dumb is it that you are proud of your jailhouse experience?* But at the same time, Fatso understood that it was good to have soldiers on their team wherever he and his brother happened to be.

"I already know," Prince said.

"Hell, yeah! Either way, I hope y'all bounce up outta here soon, but you never know what these people gon' do. I done seen it all, mane, ya feel me? But either way, I'm down wit' you, hood."

Prince says, "We got Dick McLaren on it, so I ain't even much trippin'."

"Oh, y'all got Dick, huh? Yeah, y'all should be straight, then. Them judges and DAs can't stand that muh'fucka!" Lil' Don said. He laughed and shook his head.

A few guys looked up at Prince and Fatso talking to Lil' Don. Many were eavesdroppin', ear hustlin'; in jail and nosey as hell. They heard Dick McLaren's name and knew they were in the presence of some high rollers, and now they looked at these guys a little bit differently.

"Alll-ready, 'cause they know he gonna send a nigga home!" Prince said. "We going home, my nigga. So make sure you get me ya info, man. If you gon' be down for a minute, I'ma look out for you."

Lil' Don knew what *that* meant, and that was all he needed to hear. He knew that anybody who was affiliated with Prince's clique was paid. "Bet!"

Fatso looked to the right at the line of guys trying to use the two collect-call only payphones, men of all types with one common interest: getting outta jail. Fatso's mind had wandered back to a book he'd read while he was in college called The Secret. The book was about the law of attraction, how people could create anything they wanted in life by their thoughts and that any circumstances you were living with, you had brought upon yourself with your thoughts. Fatso looked at the dingy walls and the people surrounding him. The smell of despair filled his nostrils. The concrete bench was hurting his ass and his back. He wondered to himself, *Did I draw this situation onto myself? Is this a result of my thoughts?* Then, he thought of his grandmother. The fire. *Did I create or attract that to myself?*

He felt guilt building up in his gut, but he quickly rejected that feeling. He knew that what was done was done, that there was no going back. The book said, "Feel good and happy *now*, to fulfill your thoughts." He looked around at his environment. *How the fuck does a man 'be happy' in this situation?* A man was screaming in pain as he was being beaten down by several muscle-headed guards. It was a gurgled scream, as if they were choking him or torturing him.

Fatso thought of Winnie. He'd definitely gotten what he'd had comin' to him. *Winnie had attracted death to himself,* Fatso thought. *What am I feeling right now?* He thought of all the murders on the agenda for that night, how things would never be the same. Fatso refused to let himself feel guilty about it, and he forced himself to "feel good and be happy *now*". The secret. *Their secret.* The law of attraction. Fatso broke out in a big smile.

As Prince was carrying on his conversation with Lil' Don, he glanced at his brother and saw him smiling like Tyra Banks had just jumped out of his birthday cake.

"What's up with the smiley face, man?"

"Everythang is in order, P. Everythang is in order."

Prince was confused. "You think?"

"No doubt. *I feel it.*"

Prince laughed. "Well...whatever it is you smoking, mane, pass that shit!"

"Hell, yeah," Lil' Don agreed. They all laughed a little bit, and somehow, Fatso's vibe became infectious. Prince had been weighing a lot of risks in his head and he was worried, but he tried not to show it. There were so many things that he couldn't discuss with his brother in this setting. He felt a little better, for now, at least.

After eight hours had passed, they still hadn't been bailed out. After three holding tanks, they'd been forced to shower and swap out their designer clothes for some raggedy orange shirts and pants, their wrists had been tagged, and they were packed into an elevator like cattle and shipped to the third floor. They were each given a worn blue mat and a towel roll with a half sheet and some hygiene products: a thumb-sized toothbrush, a tube of generic toothpaste and a half-bar of blue soap with "TDC" stamped into it.

When they reached their pod, they realized that Prince and Lil' Don was to be placed in B-1 and Fatso was in B-4, which was right across the hall. Prince and Lil' Don were in a youngster tank, rock and roll, while Fatso was placed in the "old school" tank. Lil' Don explained that they try to separate family members, but they would still be able to communicate through the glass by hand signals and when they went out for recreation the next day. Fatso and Prince hadn't anticipated being separated, but they were too tired to complain; they both just wanted to lay down. Fatso's "feel good and be happy *now*" attitude had dissipated to a *"fuck this cockamamie bullshit!"* disposition. It was hard to hold on; he needed rest. Prince had spoken to their aunt Jewel by way of collect call from the last holding tank. Jewel said that Tamara was taking care of everything and to just be patient.

"Don't talk to anybody and don't trust anybody. Everything's gonna work out fine," she reassured them.

Prince had questions, but Jewel insisted on his patience. She reminded him that the calls are monitored, so he cut the call short. *She's right,* he thought. They'd just have to be patient. There was some real gangsta shit going on out there in the streets, and at least they were safe and accounted for. Prince couldn't help but to worry about his baby girl Tamara, but he knew she would be careful. Neither Big Baby nor Young Bread would allow her to do anything foolish, so he calmed down. When they stepped inside the pod, all the bunks were full, so Prince and Lil' Don laid their mats on the floor by the phones. There were several others sleeping on the floor. Lil' Don promised that in the morning, he'd make sure they each had a bunk. Fatso, on the other hand, got lucky and caught a bunk. A guy made bail and was catching out when he was coming in. Most of the pod was sleep. As hard as it was, the brothers laid down and finally got a little rest, both of them wondering what the hell had happened.

When the lights and televisions came on hours later, Prince woke up hungry as hell and dehydrated. He remembered that he'd refused to eat those bologna sandwiches the guards were handing out the night before, but he wished he had one now. Prince looks around and doesn't see Lil' Don. He jumps up and grabs the phone to call Dick. Once he's on the line, Dick informs Prince that there are some issues that he is trying to get sorted out with the DA before they can be released; specifically, the seventy-two hour hold. Prince's heart drops.

"What for?"

"Don't worry. I should be able to get it lifted and get you guys out by the end of the day. Just be patient. I just got into the office. Call back in a few hours," Dick recommends.

"I'll call back in *two* hours. Get us the fuck outta here, Dick!" Prince demands.

Prince hangs up angrily and goes to take a piss. Lil' Don had woken up about a half-hour earlier and had begun to assess the thirty-man tank to see who was who and what was what. There are a couple homeboys from South Park, a few more from Blue Ridge, Cloverland, the Tre, 5th Ward and the Southwest. Houston was definitely on deck. Lil' Don let them know who his homeboy was, and while only some of them recognized Prince's face, they *all* recognized the name. There were also a handful of cats from New Orleans, at least six, which was enough to start some shit. They also recognized the name.

When Prince was finished using the restroom, Lil' Don called him over to meet the homies and to get the bunks they took from a couple White boys. They didn't really put up a fuss; it was either their bunks or their commissary. White boys had the hardest time in the system.

"You hungry, hood?" one of the homies asked Prince.

"Hell, yeah. When they bringin' some food?" asked Prince as he sat down on his new bunk.

'They ain't bringin' that bullshit for another few hours, man, fuck 'dat, tho. Say! Y'all wanna put a lil' spread together for the homie?"

"Hell, yeah, what we need? I got jack mack, roast beef, whatever," another homeboy replied.

"Shit, what you like, P?" Lil' Don asked.

"Say, whatever y'all make, mane, I'm wit' it. I'm just trying to eat and drink sumthin'. I'm thirsty than a muthafucka," Prince said, and almost instantly, he had a soda in his hand.

Twenty minutes later, he was eating a jailhouse spread that tasted pretty good and was laughing and bullshittin' with some boys that would ride for him. The New Orleans cats were all huddled together, too. They were not at all in favor of how Prince was being catered to.

"Fuck that nigga think he is?"

"Nigga wasn't all 'dat when whodie 'nem merked his grandmamma."

"Hell, naw."

"I heard Winnie been missin' for like a week, tho."

"Oh, yeah?"

"Mm-hmm. I bet you 'dem niggas had somethin' to do wit' dat, too."

"You think?"

"Hell, yeah. Who else?"

"What about D-Boy Scat?"

"Nah, we make 'dem niggas too much money."

"It was that nigga right there."

"Hell, yeah, it makes sense. It had to been 'nem."

"Man, fuck 'dem niggas!"

******

Fatso had just hung up the phone. Dick had relayed the same information to him as it had been told to Prince minutes ago. He was able to think better after a few hours' rest; he was back on a positive note. Fatso also understood that the calls would probably be monitored, so he kept it all brief. He didn't even call Jewel for not wanting to draw any attention to her. In his tank, there was a cat in his thirties named Mario, who also happened to be Warren Lee's older cousin. He used to be a big-timer back in the day; he'd retired the game after he'd beat a murder case and opened his own trucking business. Life was good. Basic. He said he liked it that way. He was serving thirty days on a probation violation that he'd caught for being late for an appointment. He called it "the most bullshittiest bullshit in the history of bullshit," which made Fatso laugh. They sat down and ate a little something and talked a little bit.

"You know my cousin Warren. He's a muthafucka, boy," Mario said, shaking his head.

"Yeah, I hear he's runnin' a pretty tight ship over there, huh?" Fatso replied.

"Yeah, but when you get to a certain point in the game, you can't trust nobody. It's especially that way for a brotha. It seems like everybody is out to get you. Then Warren be watchin' them movies and shit. All the gangsta flicks from *Scarface* to *New Jack City* to *Paid in Full, Blow;* hell, even that independent shit, and he thinks that since he watches all that shit and thinks he's smart, he's gonna have a happy ending. I tell 'im all the time, 'Nigga, that shit is not real. There was a reason that none of them niggas had a happy ending."

Fatso laughed. He'd always enjoyed kickin' the bo-bo with old-school cats. They always had some wisdom or experience to drop, and Fatso didn't mind debating either.

"Yeah, but you know, we got so many original gangsta niggas runnin' 'round Houston that have retired from the game and now they chillin'. I mean, look at you. You might be on probation and shit, but if you got a trucking business rollin', you ain't doin' *that* bad."

"I spent over a hunnit' fifty thousand fightin' that murder case, and I got lucky. Most niggas didn't get that lucky. If I hadn't had that money to pay Dick's muthafuckin' ass, I'd probably be in El Paso somewhere right now, assed out."

"That's what I'm sayin', school. Boys is havin' so much money that they feelin' like whatever happens, they can pay for it. Like it's a matter of mathematics, really."

"Aw, shit, c'mon, youngsta! That's bullshit! Look at Noriega, Larry Hoover, Harry D. Them niggas had money, too...you think them niggas happy about how shit turned out? Hell, naw! You think Tookie was happy?

Fuck, no. These people got technology these days, and they slick wit' it. They package it like it's to your advantage to have these slick devices, then they use that shit against you to bust you at your own game, while you think you being slicker than a quart of Pennzoil," Mario laughed. "I'm tellin' you, it just ain't no win for a hustler these days, unless yo hustle is legit. But you young niggas is hardheaded, can't tell you shit. Like the game just started when you showed up wit' a prick and a pistol."

Fatso nodded his head. He was really processing some of the things that Mario was saying. It made a lot of sense, but Fatso still truly believed that you really just need to know your enemy. Hustlas spent a lot of time studying the streets and the game, and they need to devote just a much time studying their enemies' tactics. But of course, there was no point in arguing this point with Mario. He was an old-school cat who didn't think the drug game was viable anymore and was happy to be out.

"How well you know Warren, anyway?" Mario asked, breaking into Fatso's thoughts. Fatso thought of Warren's girl Kesha and how he'd had sex with her a couple of times since she'd been with Warren. She tried to keep something going between them, but he'd cut it off.

"We know each other well. We throw him a party every year for his birthday."

"At the M Bar?"

"Yeah, you been?"

"That's where I seen you at!"

"Al-ready," Fatso drawled, trying to remember if he'd seen Mario there. Suddenly he thought of his aunt. *"Don't trust nobody."* Fatso knew that sometimes the cops would put somebody in a tank with you to get close enough to you to talk about your case, then use those statements against you. The snitch would get a lesser sentence or would get off completely. Fatso became uncomfortable just that fast.

"Well, you already know, then, that Warren is non-negotiable. You seem like a smart dude, though, college education and all...what they really got on you?"

Fatso stared at Mario. *"Who is this dude?"* he wondered.

******

"Prince. Check it out, whodie. Let me holla at you right quick," the cat from New Orleans named Shortcut said as he approached the Houston boys that were sitting around the rear corner of the dorm. His crew was looking on from the TV area.

"What's up? You can talk to me right here, homie," Prince replied suspiciously.

Shortcut looked around at all the H-Town dudes sittin' around Prince like they thought he was some kind of king or something and this pissed him off even more.

"You know a cat named Winnie?"

Prince squinted his eyes, locking in on Shortcut's stare. *Is this a coincidence? Or is this nigga tryin' to be disrespectful?* Prince thought. Then he got his answer; Shortcut nodded his head and smirked as if to taunt Prince.

"Naw, I ain't neva heard of 'em." Prince lied, straight-faced and still staring into Shortcut's eyes. Shortcut is a short, stocky, dark-skinned dude with two gold teeth in his mouth, one in the left front and the other on the right side. Several of his other teeth were so rotten it looked like it hurt.

"Yeah? You sure you don't know 'em," Shortcut insisted.

Lil' Don sensed the tension. "Say, mane, nigga just said he don't know 'em. What da fuck wrong wit' you?"

"I ain't *talkin'* to *you*, nigga!" Shortcut spat vehemently, pointing his finger at Lil' Don.

Smack! Lil' Don stole the first lick, catching Shortcut on his left cheekbone. Then, all Hell broke loose in that tank. One of Shortcut's boys ran up, swinging four half-bars of soap in a sock and caught one of Prince's guys in the side of the face. He went down. Prince reached out and snatched the sock and threw two right jabs at the same time. Both connected. The New Orleans boys were outnumbered two-to-one, but they had heart. They fought all over that dorm. Before three minutes had passed, Shortcut was knocked out cold, two were in chokeholds, one was laid out acting like he was knocked out, and the other two had just given up. They were too tired and outnumbered. They just sat there and pleaded for the Houston boys to let their homeboys out of the chokeholds they were in before they died. They had been fighting so hard that Prince never heard the CO screaming over the mic.

"Stop fighting now, or we're gonna gas all you bitches!"

By the time those chokeholds started to cut off that circulation to the New Orleans boys' heads, a smoking canister shot through the chow hole in the heavy steel door.

"They gassin' us!" hollered an inmate who'd been watching the brawl from the safety of his bunk. Everyone started reaching for towels and blankets to cover their faces with, others were coughing uncontrollably.

Prince pulled his t-shirt up over his face but that was not working. His eyes began to burn like someone had thrown a cup full of bleach on his face. He dove for his bunk, keeping his face covered as he'd seen the others do.

"Just...cover your face...Prince, and...breathe. Breathe light!" Lil' Don yelled between gasps of air.

The chokeholds had been released as soon as the canisters had been thrown into the pod. Everyone was in panic mode, and right then, there was only one basic common necessity: breathing. Once Prince had gotten his breathing under control, he peeked up. His eyes were still burning like hot coals, but he could see, albeit blurrily. He saw White boys and Mexicans curled up in pain, crying and panicking. Houston and New Orleans were doing the same. A couple of guys were even standing over the aluminum sinks running water into their towels to breathe through. They had no idea that would only make it worse. In seconds, they were the loudest wailers. *Sometimes, the best pro-active attitude is to pro-sit-yo-ass-down and wait it out!* Prince thought. *This is fucked up. Why is this happening?* he wondered.

Prince looked down at Shortcut and two of his partners. Still covering his face, he squeezed his right hand around a fistful of blanket and felt that pain shoot through his wrist from those two deliveries he'd dropped off to ol' boys chin. Prince felt some pain in *his* chin, but he didn't recall being hit.

Lil' Don looked up from his bunk. "You all right, hood?"

Prince noticed that Lil' Don's eyes were almost bloodshot red. "I'm straight. Yo eyes is red as hell, fool. Are *you* all right?"

"Yo eyes red, too, nigga," Lil' Don observed. "That tear gas is a beast!"

"Man! We was just laughin' and bullshittin'. Now what?"

Just as he finished speaking those words, he heard a loud click. He got his answer through six lame sheriffs wearing light-weight masks and protective clothing. They were pissed.

"You bitches wanna fight? You muthafuckin' bitches wanna fight?! C'mon, let's fight!" taunted the biggest guard of them all.

"Which ones?" asked a slimmer version of the bigger one; he'd directed his question to the CO on duty who'd witnessed almost the entire fight. The CO began pointing out the people who were involved. Prince covered his face again, hoping the CO wouldn't remember him, but it didn't work. A few minutes later, Prince and fourteen other youngsters were being escorted to segregated lockup. They were stripped naked and pushed into a concrete cell with no mat to sleep on, no sheets, towels, nothing.

"Can I at least keep my socks on, man? Damn!" Prince asked.

"Take the fuckin' socks off 'fore we rip 'em off you!" the big one said sternly.

Prince knew he wasn't lying, either. He took them off and stepped into the cell, all alone in his birthday suit with a bright light and cold air that he couldn't escape blowin' from a vent in the ceiling. He stood there and looked around this foreign territory. He shivered and felt his skin tighten and goosebumps prickle up. He took a deep breath and smelled food in the air. It must be lunchtime. *At least I can breathe,* he thought. *What kinda shit is that? Where a man rationalizes the bare necessity of air as a luxury?*

"I'm getting outta this muthafucka. It ain't a prison been built that can hold me. I gotta get outta here," he said to himself over and over again, rocking back and forth on the cold concrete. Prince felt like he was in Hell.

******

Fatso had watched the whole thing go down. He couldn't see Prince, and that really made him nervous. He knew that Prince could hold his own, but from Fatso's perspective, he couldn't tell who was who and what was what. Prince was in the back corner with Lil' Don and several other Houston boys beating the shit out of their opponents who had started the mess in the first place.

"They 'bout to gas them youngstas. They keep some shit going over there. You better hope your brother ain't involved with that shit," Mario remarked. He, along with most of the tank, stood with Fatso and watched the mayhem take place.

"Where is he?" Fatso asked, scanning over his limited view. One thing was for sure, a few dudes that he could see were getting whipped badly. One young brotha with short dreadlocks was fighting two dudes, when, out of nowhere it seemed, somebody hit him over the head with something in a sock. He went down, and then that sock was hitting him over and over while the other two dudes stomped him out. Fatso was worried.

"I hope he's on the winning team," he mumbled. Fatso watched the hallway fill up with beefy COs and a tear gas can being thrown into the tank. He watched the tank fill with smoke that looked like death, then the guards banged on the glass on Fatso's side of the pod and told them to go to their bunks or else they'd be gassed, too. The inmates backed away from the glass,

but they didn't return to their bunks.

"These muthafuckas don't want no witnesses when they run up in

there clownin' them youngstas!" Mario yelled.

"They gon' beat the shit out them lil' niggas!" another guy added.

A voice came over the loudspeaker. "Everybody sit down at the

tables, face-down, NOW!" Again, the inmates ignored the command. They

knew the guards already had their hands full with the madness in one dorm.

Somebody yelled, "Fuck y'all!"

"They better not touch my lil' brother," Fatso said to Mario. Fatso

felt better when half the dorm, including Prince, got escorted into the

hallway. Other than his eyes being bloodshot red, Prince didn't look too bad.

They nodded at each other, and just like that, he was gone. Fatso jumped

back onto the phone and called Dick.

"You gotta get us outta here now, man!" Fatso yelled.

"I'm trying, Dwayne. Are you all right?"

"They just had a riot in Prince's cell. They gassed 'em and took him

to lockdown, so, fuck no we're not all right!"

"Those bastards! Listen, Dwayne. We've got a serious problem..."

"What now?"

"...but I've gotta tell you in person, so I'm gonna come visit you

shortly so we can—"

"Fuck that, Dick, tell me now!"

"It's not safe to—"

"I know all that shit. They might be listening. But I need to know

what's going on. Now!"

"Do not respond to what I'm about to say," Dick warned.

Fatso felt as if he were standing on the edge of a cliff. *"Tell me."*

"They filed more charges."

Fatso was leaning over the edge of the cliff, looking down.

"What...what kind of charges?"

Dick sighed and cleared his throat. "Murder one and conspiracy."

Falling. Fatso was falling. He closed his eyes, and his heart fell into his stomach. His knees became weak and he almost dropped the phone, but he caught it along with his composure and leaned against the white concrete wall.

"Naw...I..." Fatso groaned.

"Don't say anything. I'll be there...we'll talk then."

Fatso hung up. Twenty-five-to-life in the home of the death penalty. That's all he could think about as he leaned down against his arm which rested on top of the stainless steel phone casing.

"This is not going down," he mumbled to himself. "This is not happening."

******

Tamara stood in the visiting line on the first floor of the jail. There were seven lines of people waiting to see their loved ones, some lines longer than the others. Everybody was holding a small piece of paper with their inmates' information on it. When the elevators to the left opened and people walked out, the deputy ushered several others on. The brown-skinned, clean-shaven, middle-aged deputy whispered in the ear of a light-skinned girl with curly hair who wore a tight brown knockoff Chanel dress and see-through platform pumps that made her look like she'd just gotten off her shift at the Ice Cream Castles. She smiled flirtatiously at the officer and got on the elevator. The line moved forward as Tamara shook her head in disgust. She looked at her slip of paper that read, "Purnell Landau, 3-B-1".

She'd received the call from Dick that morning. The DA was pushing for murder. She knew there was a catch to the seventy-two hour hold. Her mind was racing a million miles a minute; she had so many questions, so many things to do. *Does Prince know?* she wondered. *What does he need? What does he want me to do? Who else knows?* She had to stop herself. She had to talk to him. *"I know what to do,"* she said to herself. *"But I have to tell him. I have to see him."*

When Tamara stepped onto the elevator, the deputy whispered in her ear, "Damn, you look good, baby. If you let me take you out, you'll never have to come to this place again."

"Pssst!" Tamara hissed. "You disgust me, five-dollar ass muthafucka!" The deputy laughed at Tamara as the elevator doors closed, but Tamara, along with the other women, knew that she had checked that sucka's pride.

"Good job, girl, I'da told him the same thing," said an older sister who was there with her two young boys. The boys giggled. They thought Tamara was fine, too.

When she arrived in the visitors' area, she sat down on a concrete stool in front of a thick Plexiglas divider and anxiously looked for Prince. She needed to see his handsome face, needed to hear him say that he's all right and tell her that everything is gonna be just fine. She waited fifteen minutes, twenty minutes. *What's taking so long?* she thought.

Then she saw him entering the hallway behind the guards' picket. He was too far away and there was too much Plexiglas between them for her to read him, but he was coming. When Prince walked around the corner, he was stone-faced, his eyes were bloodshot red and the left side of his jaw was slightly swollen. His shirt and pants were two different shades of orange, and his glow was gone. Tamara forced a smile from somewhere even as the tears welled up in her eyes. She knew at that moment that she would do absolutely anything to get her man out of this place.

"What's going on?" Prince asked as he sat down.

Tamara leaned into the steel grid to speak into it. The concrete walls made each and every sound echo, so she barely heard him. She made sure she didn't touch anything. She cleared the frog in her throat.

"What'd they do to you?" she asked.

"It was a big-ass fight..."

"What? I can't hear you. Talk louder," she yelled.

"They gassed us!" he hollered in reply. "What's up with Dick? When we getting out?"

Tamara took a deep breath and looked in Prince's eyes. "That's what I came to talk to you about."

He looked into her eyes and knew it was bad. "What happened?"

"They...baby, they filed murder and conspiracy charges." Prince was silent.

"Did you hear me?"

"Yeah, yeah," he replied blandly. "You remember everything, right?" he asked, referring to the plans they'd made a while back. Tamara nodded.

"Don't be scared."

"I'm not."

"Do it."

"Are you sure?" Prince nodded in reply.

"Okay," Tamara said. She had received the final confirmation she needed. "I love you, baby. I'm gonna take care of everything, all right? Just be strong. Stay hard in there."

Prince smirked. His woman tellin' *him* to stay hard cheered him up and and seemed amusing at a time like this. But she was right, and she was serious.

"Last night?" Prince asked.

Tamara ran her thumb across her neck from ear to ear. Prince nodded. He looked over Tamara's beautiful face and was reminded of why he felt the way he did about her. She's a stomp-down ass chick, down like four flats on a slab, but she had a gentle, sweet side to her that was as soft as the skin on her breasts. Prince was one of the only people who knew that side of her. Tamara saw that Prince was staring at her. She smiled and they shared a moment.

"Landau, time's up," the guard announced over the loudspeaker.

"I gotta go, baby. Any questions?"

"No questions. I love you."

"I love you, too, baby. Handle up."

Tamara put her palm against the glass, and Prince did the same; this was the closest they'd get to touching each other. Prince stood up as Tamara waved bye; she managed to maintain herself as he walked away. She had a job to do.

When Tamara jumps back into her SUV, she calls Jewel, Big Baby and Young Bread from the burnout cell phone she'd picked up a couple of days ago and told them to meet her at the Icon. Then she searched through her Evo for the phone number she'd been thinking about all morning. She typed "J-O-N-E-S" into the search field and there it was: *Mark Jones. Deputy Sheriff Mark Jones.*

Chapter Thirty-Three: THIRTEEN

"Tom Brody's office," Patrice, the secretary, said into the phone with a bit of an attitude. It had been a busy Monday, too busy. Her boss, Tom, had become excessively bossy and had been piling on the workload as the election loomed closer and closer. She'd considered just quitting on his ass right when he needed her most. *See how he likes that,* she thought. *And this damn phone won't stop ringing!*

"Chuck Yancey here. I need to speak to Tom immediately!" a voice blared into her ear from the the other end of the line. This was exactly the kind of stuff that annoyed her. There was no "Hello, Patrice," no "How are you, Patrice?" Nope, only demands. *Can a sister get a little recognition?* she thought. Patrice was half-Black with a White mother, a college degree, and two sons. She worked harder and carried herself better than two White women and a Mexican, but today was not her day. She hated Mondays and she had just wasted coffee on her blouse. Patrice knew exactly who Chuck Yancey was and he also knew her, yet he refused to acknowledge her. Tom Brody had been irritated all morning with the flood of calls coming in about the thirteen murders that had occurred over the weekend, but since he'd been such an asshole to her lately, she decided to return the favor. He'd asked her to take messages on all his calls until further notice.

"Hold, please." She put the Federal District Attorney on hold and transferred him through to her boss. She smirked to herself. She knew by the tone of Chuck's voice that he was not to be the bearer of good news.

"Yeah," Tom Brody said, wondering who and what the hell it was *now*, answered, annoyance apparent in his voice. He had a stack of files and a long list of emails to get through by the end of the day.

Chuck cut straight to the point. "Just how in the hell do you plan to explain thirteen homicides in one day?"

Recognizing Chuck's voice, Tom said sarcastically, "Well, howdy to you, too, Chuck!"

"Spare me," Chuck said dryly. "Please tell me they're all related."

"More than likely."

"Do you have any suspects?"

"We're working on it."

"You're 'working on it'? Do you know how close I am to taking this case? What exactly are you 'working on'?" Chuck asked mockingly.

Tom realized that being evasive with his old friend was not going to be effective right now, so he decided to tell him what he had.

"All right, here's the deal. Friday afternoon we picked up a couple of guys who we suspect to be the ringleaders of this Ball operation. According to a reliable CI, these guys, the Landau brothers, suspected some guys from New Orleans of murdering their grandmother in an arson that occurred almost six weeks ago. For what exactly, we're not sure. But I'm thinking it's got something to do with this Ball thing. Now, coincidentally, that same Friday morning we had received a dental records match for a fugitive the New Orleans Police had been looking for these past five years, a Black male named Winston Marshon. We found his remains in a similar arson. Lo and behold, our CI confirmed that he was the leader of the New Orleans gang, the

Landaus' rival. So, when it was confirmed that they were in custody, I charged them immediately with Marshon's murder. Now we are getting continued confirmations that the victims of the murders that occurred this past Friday were members of Marshon's gang. So yes, there is a very strong possibility that *all* these killings are related to the Landaus. We've got the investigation very much under control, Chuck."

"Hmm. Sounds like you do. Well, understand this. If one more murder charge is filed against these defendants, we're going to have to step in."

"I don't think that's gonna be necessary. I've got—"

Chuck cut him off. "That's the way it is, Tom. There is too much attention on this case, all right? Now, you asked for my assistance in the very beginning of this investigation, and now you expect me to stand on the sidelines while the media has a field day with this thing? No! It's not gonna happen. People are going to expect Federal action, so I'm going to be watching closely. I expect that you'll keep me posted."

So you can steal my spotlight? Yeah right, Tom thought, then replied, "No problem, Chuck. No problem at all."

Chuck smirked. "Very well, then, Tom. Goodbye." The line went dead.

"Fuck him," Tom said maliciously.

******

"Mommy, I wanna sleep with you and daddy," Lil' Warren whined as his mom, Kesha, pulled the Houston Texans comforter up around his neck.

"Not tonight, sweetie. Mommy doesn't feel good. Maybe tomorrow, okay?"

"You promise?"

"Yes, baby, I promise. Now go to sleep." Kesha said as she kissed her son on the cheek.

"Okay," he said defeated. Kesha began to leave.

As soon as she turned off the lamp next to Lil' Warren's bed, his night light turned on and he blurted out, "Mommy, can we go to the zoo tomorrow? I wanna see the monkeys."

"Mommy's gonna be busy, but I'll get Nanny to take you, okay?"

"Mmm, okay. 'Nite, mommy."

"'Nite-nite baby."

When Kesha walked out of her son's room, she felt worse than she had felt before she'd gone in. All day she'd been sad for her friend Tamara because of the situation her man was in. Kesha knew how the police worked; once they started digging, they wouldn't stop. Tamara and Kesha had been best friends since high school, and now Tamara wasn't calling as much. Kesha knew that her friend had to be extremely stressed out, which was having an effect on Kesha whether she liked it or not. She decided to retreat to the things that meant the most to her: her son, her man, her home, and her family, including Nanny, who was actually Warren's aunt and an absolute lifesaver because she kept the house and Lil' Warren in order.

"Is he sleep yet?" Warren asked as Kesha entered the bedroom. He was standing in front of the mirror, drying himself off after a hot shower.

"Nooo…he will be, though. He was tired. He wants to go to the zoo tomorrow," Kesha said in a sad little girl's voice, the voice she used when she wanted to let Warren know that she wanted to be babied.

He didn't respond right away because he was thinking about it. He knew he didn't have time for the zoo. "All right. We'll have Nanny take him."

"That's what I told him, but I changed my mind. I'm gonna take him."

"Good. He should like that."

Kesha was fluffing her pillows and pulling back the covers so she could climb into bed. She stopped and looked at Warren with those bedroom eyes that he had a hard time saying no to. He didn't look at her, but he could feel her stare.

"Will you come with us?" Kesha asked in the same baby girl voice.

He'd known *that* was coming. He kept his attention in the mirror and brushed his wavy fade.

"I got a lotta shit goin' on tomorrow, baby. I don't think I'ma have time."

"You *make* time for the things that matter to you the most, Warren," Kesha said firmly. The baby voice was long gone.

"I feel that," he said nonchalantly, still brushing.

"I mean, what's the point in having all those people working for you if you can't even make time for your family."

Still brushing, he simply nodded. He put down his brush and picked up his toothbrush and began to brush his teeth. He decided that it was still early and that he might go out and handle a few things that night.

Kesha changed her approach. She realized that she'd let her emotions get the best of her and men, especially *her* man, didn't respond well to nagging. She undid the bow on her red satin Donna Karan robe and threw it onto the bed. She had just recently taken a bath and rubbed herself down with strawberry mango shea butter. Her tall, curvaceous, naked body was glistening. She walked into the vanity area of the bathroom and wrapped her arms around Warren from behind. She laid her head against his back and squeezed her body against his.

"Daddy, I love you," she said in her baby girl voice.

In the mirror, Warren watched himself set his brush down. He paused, then placed his arms over Kesha's arms which were still wrapped around his abdomen and linked his fingers inside hers. She smelled lovely.

Kesha felt much better. "I need you now, baby," she whispered, kissing his back. Warren looked at the image in the mirror. His woman was calling out to him. He looked himself in the eyes and asked himself to stop being so hard. She was right about everything she'd just said. What *was* the point?

He turned around and hugged and kissed Kesha. He felt himself rising against her Brazilian-waxed slit. She reached down and grabbed his pole in her hand and lowered herself down to her knees. She licked around the head of his dick a few times before taking him inside her mouth. Warren ran his fingers through her Halle Berry as she made love to his piece, relaxing her throat and going down on him as far as she could, then wiggling her head from side to side to take in a little more, like she had an itch in her throat that needed to be scratched. Kesha's emotions were on high. She went from depression and sadness to anger, to compassion and sensitivity, and then finally to being horny as hell, which was all about to translate into some explosive love-making.

Warren knew that and had decided to give in to what his woman needed right then, emotionally and physically. Warren tilted his head to the ceiling and moaned, "Oh, shit, baby, I'm 'bout to come." Kesha stopped, stood up and wiped her mouth.

"What you doin'?" Warren asked indignantly, his dick bobbing up and down with every heartbeat.

"Baby? Are we going to the zoo tomorrow?"

Warren shook his head. That baby voice again. He peeped up at her and saw that she couldn't help but to grin as she awaited his answer. She was blushing and all. He found that to be so endearing.

"Yeah, girl, we're going to the zoo. Now c'mere." She agitated him but he couldn't help but to be amused by her demeanor...and her strategy.

"Unh-uh..." Kesha taunted, then turned and pranced over to the bed and crawled up onto it on all fours, arching her back invitingly and switching her round hips and ass until she reached the head of the bed. She turned around and beckoned to him with one pink-tipped finger.

"Mmm, you come here. I want you inside of me. I'm so wet, daddy," she moaned as she touched herself.

Warren laughed. "That's it, you're in trouble," he said as he made sure the bedroom door was locked.

"Oooh, come spank me," Kesha moaned teasingly, and he did. For the next three hours, Warren scratched every itch that Kesha needed scratched.

Warren picked up the remote and clicked the ceiling fan from the low setting to high. Kesha had her head laid on his sweaty chest, and all the covers and all but one pillow had escaped the war zone and found a peaceful place on the floor. No worries, they'll soon be replaced with a new set from the bathroom linen closet. He kissed Kesha on her forehead.

"That shit's really bothering you, huh?"

"Mmmm…what?" she replied sleepily. She was enjoying the moment, and she wasn't really sure whether he was referring to Lil' Warren, the Landaus, or his attitude.

"You know…the Landaus. I know it's fucking wit' Tamara that they got the money to make bail, but she still can't get them out."

"Yeah, it's a really tough time for her. I can only imagine, ya know. It's always easier being next to the person that's going through something than it is to *be* that person. It just makes me think…what would I do if it were *you*?" she said, then looked at Warren.

The situation had been on Warren's mind since he'd first learned of it from Kesha on Friday. At that time, he'd assumed that they'd be right out on those punk ass charges, but now that they were unable to get out, he was sure there was some extra shit going on, and that could only be one thing he could think of. He could have arranged a sit-down with or sent a messenger to see DA Tom Brody, but for what? It wasn't *his* problem. Only his crew, excluding Kesha, had direct knowledge of his relationship with the DA, and he intended to keep it that way. If anyone asked him anything that suggested otherwise, he would, of course, deny it to the end. Warren outwardly displayed sympathy for the Landau brothers, but he was actually comfortable with the way things were going. Prince and Fatso were from his 'hood, but the New Orleans boys, who were almost out the door anyway, were outsiders.

He could crush them with no conscience or consequence. Winnie was gone now, and he assumed that all the others would dissipate. Warren decided to sit back, watch and let things play out. He felt that in the end, everything would work to his benefit. He hugged Kesha closer under one of his arms and stroked her soft face with his other hand and lifted her chin up so her eyes would meet his.

"Don't worry 'bout that, Keesh. I'm smarter than that and my game's tighter, believe me. I'm straight. Me, you and Lil' Warren are always gon' be straight. A'ight?"

Kesha was practically in tears. "We can't ever let that happen...to us, baby...okay?"

"It ain't gon' happen."

"You promise?"

Warren hated to make promises because in the life he lived, there truly were no guarantees. In this situation, though, he knew Kesha needed that reassurance, that security.

"I promise you, boo. We straight," Warren Lee replied and kissed her. When Warren lifted his head, he saw that her eyes were closed and she was smiling as if she were in a fantasy that she didn't want to come out of. After a few moments, she finally opened her eyes and laid back down on Warren's chest.

"I just want you to support your friend right now," Warren said. "T is gonna need you now more than ever. No matter how many times she says she doesn't, she will need that support. I know; I've been through that kind of shit before, so just be patient with her, stay in touch with her. And keep me posted on everything that's going on so I can see how I can help, you know?"

Kesha raised her head and looked into his eyes. "Oh, baby, that's so sweet." She was genuinely touched by the suggestion he'd made. She kissed him on the lips again.

"Well, you know what they say."

"And what is that, boo?"

"That's what friends are for," Warren answered, smiling.

"Oh, God, that is so corny," Kesha laughed. "But you're right, though. I'm gonna call T first thing in the morning."

"That's what's up."

"I'm tired now, babe…could you grab those covers off the floor? That fan ain't playin'," Kesha said, pointing at the floor on Warren's side of the bed.

"For what? So they can get knocked off again?" Warren asked. Kesha blushed, then she responded with a playful attitude.

"I know you ain't sayin' what I think you sayin'."

"Hell yeah! You got me all night now. Round three. Let's go half," Warren said, rolling over on top of her.

"Half on what? We ain't goin' half on nuthin' but some birth control," she quipped. They laughed and began a new session, going round for round like they were brand new lovers.

******

"We don't have to leave, don't you see?"

"Fuck that! We're leavin'!"

"Baby, listen...listen to me!" Serene yelled, stopping Mo from pacing the hotel room floor. She had been laying on the bed when he'd walked in with the update. Now she was on her knees on the bed, dressed only in her lavender panties and bra.

Mo threw his hands up in sheer frustration. "What? What, Serene?"

"With Prince and Fatso in jail now, we can take over. They're not getting out! The DA is gonna hang them niggas. You gotta think clearly about this, baby!"

"Think about *what*? Almost all my niggas is dead, Serene! How the fuck we gon' take over and I ain't got my best soldiers no more? You think I wasn't on that list? 'Dem niggas was tryin' to merk me, too!"

"But they *didn't*, Mo! That's the point. *You're* still here; they're gone. Doesn't that tell you something?"

"Yeah, it tells me we should get the fuck outta here before *we* join the Dead Ballers Society, too!" Mo responded, flopping down into a chair.

He rubbed his temples. This situation was stressing him out. Serene knew he was scared. He had the right to be, considering the circumstances. But she didn't want to focus on that right now or even point it out. She didn't want to hurt his pride. She needed to wire him up to stay, to have some balls. Serene was beginning to have a different opinion of Mo. She was thinking, *These niggas just killed off your whole crew, you the only one left, and you wanna run? That's a damn shame.* She was feeling a little disgusted as if she were the one wearing the pants in this relationship. But, Serene had her own reasons for wanting Mo to stay. For one, Mo had the formula. She still hadn't figured out a way to get that. She didn't know where it was or what it looked like; she just knew that *he* had it. He'd told her that much, and she wanted it.

Bad. For that reason alone, she wouldn't let him leave her side. Wherever she had to go, when it came down to it, she'd go.

For two, Serene couldn't run off and leave her kids like that, and she hadn't thought of a good enough excuse to give her mom to keep them for who knows how long while she disappeared from the scene. She knew she'd be wrong as hell if she did that, but Serene already had it planted in her mind that if that's what she had to do, she would do it. She remembered hearing of mothers running off and leaving their kids to be with some nigga. She'd believed that was a crazy and despicable thing to do. Now she knew how they felt. She felt semi-justified in her thoughts, though, because she knew that in her case, there were much bigger things to consider than just some dick.

Serene sat down on the bed directly across from Mo. "Okay, look, baby. We can start a new crew. As long as we got the formula, it's plenty of workers out there. Everybody wants to make money, and we're sitting on a goldmine. Let's just give it a few more days to see what's going on and get our plan together. Nobody knows where we are. We're safe here, right here. Okay, baby? Just a few more days?" Serene pleaded.

Mo thought about what she was saying. *A few more days. Shit, she keep saying 'we' got the formula, but* she *ain't got shit.* He considered his initial strategy in pursuing a relationship with Serene. That whole plan was shot to hell now, but she was strong, beautiful. A good woman, and gutta, too. *Down for a nigga,* he thought. She had a point, though. He *was* the only one left. The last of the Mohicans with the keys to the fortress. But Mo was scared. He didn't want Serene to know that, but he was. He didn't have

Winnie no more to plot and plan with. Now, it was just himself and Serene. He decided that a few more days wouldn't hurt.

"All right, a few more days, but that's it! We'll just kick back and see who's who and what's what, but we gotta go after that, if it ain't lookin' good. We're just staying to regroup, ya dig? We gonna come back with a new strategy."

Serene nodded. A few more days. "Okay, it's gon' be straight. Now, come here so I can rub your back. You need to relax a little," she said seductively.

As Mo walked over to the bed and took off his shirt, he made himself another promise. He wouldn't allow Serene or anyone else get their hands on the formula or the book of *gris-gris*.

******

An older sister in her mid-forties steps off the Metro transit bus that runs up and down Old Spanish Trail. With her six-year-old son holding her right hand, she steps into the Whataburger on Old Spanish Trail and MacGregor and buys a $2.99 two-piece chicken finger platter which she has to share with her son because she doesn't have enough money to buy one for the both of them. Luckily, she's able to talk the server into putting an extra chicken finger in the box for her by holding up her Katrina evacuee pin. It had helped her in many a situation such as this one, but on some days, it was best for her to take it off and tuck it into her pocket in order to mingle amongst the natives and absorb some local benefits without being looked at like she was an unwanted refugee. She hated when people looked at her like that.

But today, her pin would serve its purpose. Once again, her status as a transplant from New Orleans was slapped in her face. This older lady, Ms. Jennifer Sykes, was here to participate in a protest meeting at the mosque across the street for the violent murders of the thirteen young men from New Orleans. Ms. Sykes wanted to talk to the speaker, a Mr. Darnell X, and his associate, Mr. Sheldon X, who was also her local representation on the matter since he was also a Katrina evacuee who advocated fair housing and equal employment opportunities for the New Orleans community. From what Ms. Sykes had heard, Sheldon X was a four-time felon back in New Orleans and Darnell X's reputation wasn't much better, but those things didn't bother Ms. Sykes. She knew everyone came from somewhere, and life is far from perfect where *she* came from. Besides, they seemed to be her only hope. Last Friday, Ms. Sykes had lost her oldest son and, consequently, her only source of income. Her son was Bernard Sykes, otherwise known as LuLu. As far as she was concerned, *someone* needed to pay for her tragic loss.

When she entered the sanctuary, the first thing she noticed was that it was far from peaceful. Loud voices echoed from inside the worship hall that sounded like a reflection of what she had been feeling these last two days: loss and frustration.

"We want action!" an older brother yelled toward the two brothers standing behind the podium. "You know who did it, the police know who did it, we *all* know!"

"I can assure you that the police are moving forward with this investigation," Darnell X stated firmly. "Murder charges have already been filed against the defendants in question."

"One count! One count! Do they know how many lives were taken last Friday, or have they lost count like they lose count of us any other time?" another man yelled.

"Oh, Lawd, somebody help us!" cried a grandmotherly woman who was rocking back and forth in a pew.

"I bet you they won't lose count if we storm up in that court building or the mayor's office!"

"Or River Oaks!" another woman added.

They were all just bouncing off each other now. It was really getting out of control, but they were all there to voice their concerns and frustrations.

"Give my baby justice or give me death!" Grandma yelled.

"Hell naw they wouldn't lose count!" another sister added. "That's what we oughta do!"

Ms. Sykes became excited as she took a seat towards the rear. These people were ready to take action. That's what she wanted to see. She was tired of her community being overlooked.

Sheldon X, the light-skinned brother with a hard military look, waved his hands and addressed the crowd. "Listen, now, please! Please, everyone, just calm down a bit and listen to what the brother has to say." The people obeyed.

"Brothas and sistas, I feel your pain. That's why we're all here today. The suspects are in custody and the investigation is ongoing, but you all have to take a moment and understand the judicial system. The DA's office is in a position where evidence has to be established to file more charges," Darnell X explained.

"Thirteen!" a tearful woman yelled. "Thirteen lifeless, beautiful young men! How much more evidence do those bastards need? I lost my baby! I have to find the money to pay for a funeral and I can hardly pay my rent!"

"Oh, Lawd Jesus, take me now!" Grandma yelled.

"Pardon me, but what are you gonna do for us, Mr. X?" asked a fairly well-dressed brotha. Ms. Sykes noticed that he seemed to be one of the only reasonable voices in the crowd. The man continued.

"You see that we're in an impossible situation. It's been one thing after another since Katrina brought us here, and now this. We're not all destitute and completely ignorant of the law, Mr. X, but this creates an impossible mental and financial situation for many of us. What are you proposing to do about that? What is the purpose of this meeting?" The room had quieted down a few notches. People were impressed with the man's tact. All heads turned towards Darnell X as they awaited his response.

"I called this meeting today...for exactly the purpose that it is serving, and that is for you all to come together and know that you have a voice, to know that you matter. I am going to do everything in my power to secure progress with the issues that were brought up here today. We'll raise funds, raise awareness, raise *Hell* if we have to. Whatever we have to do to make sure that your needs are addressed. The New Orleans and Houston communities must work together and understand that the same enemies that have been attacking our communities for generations are still attacking us today, only to make us think we are enemies when we are not. We are brothers and sisters, and we must all support one another in good times and in bad times. Because no matter where we come from, whether it be New Orleans, Houston, Dallas, Shreveport, Austin, Baton Rouge, wherever, one thing remains in common: we're all Black, all the time. FEMA wasn't designed to support us or anybody else. It was designed to police us in times of emergency. That's why they're so inefficient at it. We have to support each other. Otherwise, we will...self destruct," Darnell X concluded dramatically.

His words were felt among the people in the crowd; the mothers, uncles, brothers, sisters, aunties, fathers and cousins all believed those words and were beginning to feel that they had a voice to represent them.

Ms. Sykes stood up from her seat in the back row for the first time to address the concern that had jumped to the front of her mind. "Mr. X, are you gonna dig in your pocket to pay for some of these costs?"

Sheldon X looked to Darnell X just like everyone else. He knew that he'd been caught off guard with that one...or had he?

"Well...as I said...whatever I have to do within my power, I will do. So, yes, I would be willing to commit some of my personal funds if need be," Darnell X replied. He'd never admit it, but he felt a sense of regret as soon as the words left his mouth.

A woman jumped up instinctively. "I need your help!"

"I need help, too!" Ms. Sykes shouted. "That's why I asked the question."

"We need your assistance, sir!" cried out an uncle of one of the victims.

"Please help us," Grandma pleaded as if she were talking to God Himself.

Sheldon X knew that Darnell X had jammed himself up. He'd put his foot in his mouth big time. How was he gonna get out of this one? There was no way he was gonna help everyone—one or two, maybe. So, what would happen to the others? Were they just stuck out? How were they gonna bury their loved ones respectably? Sheldon's heart went out to his people; it filled up in his chest and became heavy. He felt the pressure overwhelming him. He was supposed to be their local representative, but he could hardly lead his own way out of a paper bag.

"Everybody calm down! We're doing the best we can!" Sheldon yelled. This time they were paying him no mind. The yelling became louder and they began to argue amongst themselves. The lady in the back who'd originally posed that loaded question was now threatening another lady with violence. It was getting completely out of hand. *What are we gonna do?* Sheldon wondered.

"Get your hands off my damn son! Bitch, don't make me hurt you up in here!" Ms. Sykes threatened. "I got nothin' to lose, bitch, *nothin'* to lose!"

All had already been lost.

Chapter Thirty-Four: KICK DOOR

"Dwayne Landau, pack your stuff. You're being moved," the loudspeaker crackled.

"What he say?" Fatso asked Mario over a game of chess.

"Pack your shit, young'n. You either made bail or you're being moved to another tank," Mario answered, smiling.

Fatso hopped up and looked towards the dorm across the hall. Prince came to the glass, nodding his head. He had been called to be moved, too. It was on.

Fatso shook Mario's hand along with that of a couple of others. He grabbed up his mat, blanket, sheet and towel and fumbled with them a little bit.

Mario laughed. "Let me show you how to do this, first timer." He tied the sheet in a knot around the center of the blue mat. "You beat this shit, get out there and do the right thang, young'n. Don't get caught up in this shit like Warren, a'ight?"

"All right, homie."

"And if you see my lil' cousin, tell him I said what's up," Mario said as Fatso grabbed up the ready-made bundle and headed towards the metal door.

Prince was going through the same ritual, except the homies that were left in his tank were all giving him their contact information in hopes that they could work for the HBC when they touched down. Prince didn't want to shatter their dreams, so he took the information he was given and told them he would get at them when he hit the streets. They were all looking forward to this commitment like they had just received a gift from God.

"Damn, the homeboy catchin' out?"

"Yeah, gotta make moves," Prince replied.

"I bet the DA gave you a bond, nigga. You goin' to the crib," Lil' Don said with a smile.

"I hope so, shit. I'm hopin' for the best, for real."

"You got my info, hood, don't forget about me out there. I'ma put in work for you."

"Already," Prince replied, shaking Lil' Don's hand and giving him a half-hug.

Within minutes, the two brothers are walking down the hall to drop off their mats and linens with a few other guys. When they line up at the elevator, Fatso and Prince catch each other's eyes. *This is it.*

One of the guys, a short Mexican with a Houston Astros star tattooed on the back of his bald-faded head, asked the CO, "Where we goin', boss?"

"Lil' Baker," the CO replied, referring to the jail at 1307 Baker Street, an old rehab facility that was turned into an additional jail for non-violent inmates. It was a short drive from the main jail at 701 San Jacinto.

"Al-ready!" the Mexican drawled. He was cool with that because Lil' Baker is a better, cleaner and more laid-back facility. Prince glanced at the CO's name tag, which read "Collins". *Nope, not him.*

When they get down to the holdover cell, they sat on opposite ends of the bench, not speaking. Prince had so many things running through his mind, and he really wanted to talk to his brother. *Fuck that, I ain't talkin' to that nigga,* he told himself, then glanced up to see another older brotha talking to Fatso. *Who is that nigga,* he thought suspiciously. He watched him intently.

Fatso was taking deep, controlled breaths as he reviewed a million things in his sharp mind.

"You ain't neva been to Baker?" inquired the older brotha.

"Nah," Fatso answered distractedly.

"It's way mo playa den dis shit ova heah. Real sinks, real, porcelain toilets with seats, and fresh cold-water drinking fountains. You gon' love it."

Fatso looked at the dude like he was the dumbest muthafucka on land and shook his head. "Yeah, a'ight," he said, then stood up and walked over to the steel door to peek out the window.

Prince giggled to himself as he observed the interaction. Thirty minutes later they're called to line up so they can be cuffed to each other in twos. Prince counts the line-up, 2, 4, 6....then he steps up in line behind his brother, which makes him number eight.

"Excuse me, man, let me get in here," Prince says to the Mexican with the star on his head. The Mexican gives Prince a crazy look but doesn't say anything.

"All right, let's move! Let's go!" yells the guard, a big and tall White guy. Prince glances at his name tag: "Lufkin". *Nope.*

The first shot consists of eight people and the rest are left behind for the second shot. The Mexican didn't like that. He eyeballed Prince as they walked out. "Bitch ass nigga," he grumbled to himself.

Prince and Fatso, now handcuffed together, are taken to a gated area outside. They both notice how good it feels to breathe some fresh nighttime air. Prince feels his pulse quicken as he realizes that they are one step closer to freedom. There is a white van waiting with its rear doors open like loving arms watiting to embrace their beloved property, and a yellow light shines inside the rear compartment of the vehicle.

A sheriff stands by, a Black guy. Prince could always tell the real sheriffs from the fake-ass COs: the sheriffs wore dark blue, and the COs wore white. The leading officer led them to the van.

"Load up," commanded the Black sheriff.

It was dark outside, but Prince was able to make out a slick S-curl type hairdo with a big part on the right side of the head of the buff, brown-skinned sheriff.

"We got another shot waiting on you after you drop them off," said Collins, the fat White sheriff, as the first shot began loading up onto the van. 2, 4, 6...

"Wait...you mean we have *more* inmates waiting? Oh, well, so much for job security," the Black one said sarcastically.

"No shit, Jones, we'll be in the welfare line before you know it," Collins quipped, laughing.

Prince's ears pricked up, and the hairs on the back of his neck stood on end. He focused in and inadvertently caught a glance at the nametag of the Black sheriff: *Jones*. Prince looked up at the sheriff to see him beaming back at him. Prince quickly looked away and wondered if Fatso had noticed that, and what the fuck was he so giddy about?

"Oh, no, not me. There's plenty of ways to make money," Jones chuckled as if it were an inside joke. "How many are left?"

"Seven, I believe."

"I'll see ya in a few ticks."

When Jones slammed the doors on the last two inmates, Fatso and Prince, he stuck his smiling face into the small view window on the back door.

"What's this guy, a fuckin' comedian or sumthin'?" asked one inmate.

Prince and Fatso nodded at each other. They noticed that the White sheriff who was driving the van looked back through the steel mesh divider and bulletproof Plexiglas to make sure everyone was in, waited a couple of minutes for his tail reinforcement cruiser to give him the go-ahead by flashing his headlights from outside the gate, and then he was off. He put the van in drive and pulled out of the powered gate, opened by way of a control center inside the building.

Prince and Fatso's only line of sight was directly in front of the vehicle through the Plexiglas viewer and directly behind them. The other six inmates were nonchalant, laughing and bullshitting about getting away from the 701 San Jacinto facility and how Baker was better, and how good it felt to be inside a moving vehicle. A couple of them knew how short the ride was, the exact route and all. Surprisingly, the Landaus did, too. Prince wondered if anyone could hear how fast his heart was beating right then; Fatso breathed deeply and slowly, thinking, *They'll be here, they'll be here.*

When the transport van came to a short bridge on Franklin which crossed over the railroad tracks, two black Suburbans sped off of a side street but seemingly out of nowhwere. One crossed directly in front of the driver and the other wedged itself between the reinforcement driver and the van.

"What the fuck is going on?" queried one inmate.

"Oh, shit, it's going down," another responded.

In a situation like this, the tail reinforcement was supposed to divert any hostile situation by any means necessary, but tonight, he was hesitant.

"Divert, divert; hostile situation, divert!" the van's driver yelled into his walkie-talkie. No response. He had no idea that his channel had been changed. Before he could try again, the rear doors to the Suburban that had pulled in front of the van flew open, and a figure in a black ski mask and an A-K opened fire on the van's windshield, aiming directly at the driver's head. The driver attempted to duck down and accelerate and swerve to the left, but it was too late. His bulletproof vest couldn't stop the entire hail of gunfire that came at him at almost point-blank range. Shots penetrated his vest and the side of his neck, and he'd be dead within minutes. Luckily, his crash into the back of the Suburban had the shooter shaken up enough to deter his line of fire towards the hood. The van came to a stop.

Prince directed the other inmates to stay calm, assuring them that they'd be getting out of there shortly. Another passenger from the front Suburban jumped out, Glock in hand, and opened the van's driver side door and snatched the keys from the driver. Two passengers from the rear Suburban grabbed Jones out of his cruiser. He was being cooperative, but that Chester-Cheese smile had been replaced with a nervous twitch.

"Stay still. Don't do nothing stupid!" one of the riders commanded Jones while taking his state-issued Glock from its holster.

"Just hurry up," pleaded Jones with his hands up. "I want my money tonight!"

The rider who'd grabbed the keys from the transport van driver opens the rear door and hustles Fatso and Prince into the rear of the front Suburban.

"Come on! Let's go, y'all!"

"Gimme the keys," Fatso demands. He takes them and unlocks his cuffs. The other inmates also hurry to get out, running in all directions.

"Give us a ride, take us with you," begs one guy who is paired up with another.

"Nah, man, you on your own," Prince says, slamming the door shut.

The guys run off, no time to waste. Big Baby hops out of the driver's seat of the rear Suburban and approaches Sheriff Mark Jones.

"We had a deal," Big Baby says.

Mark Jones, a little too confident for his position, smirks. "That's right. My people are waiting for that drop off tonight, so I suggest y'all make good on it immediately," he says. He is prepared for a long night of questioning.

"Fair enough," Big Baby replies. One of the two riders holding Jones, places Jones' state-issued Glock into Big Baby's gloved hand. Jones realizes his plan has gone all wrong.

"Nice doing business with you," Big Baby says, then fires two shots, *pop-pop*, into Mark Jones' face then drops the gun into the street.

"Let's go!" They all jump back into the rear Suburban, ready for a high-speed getaway.

Inside the transport van, the driver struggles with his last few breaths of life. The sound of gunshots brought him back to a conscious state like the alarm that woke him up that morning. He was down, slumped over the steering wheel and losing blood fast. He knew it'd been a setup. He knew he was a good guy and had to do something. He could still see the Suburban in front of him, about ten feet away. He reached for the gun on his hip; it was still there. He pulled it out. The Suburban began to pull away. The transport driver was running out of time; he had to do something now.

Being that he was in so much pain, he didn't know how he found the strength to cock the state-issued Smith & Wesson .9mm and fire three shots, *pop-pop-pop!* He heard glass shatter and someone yell. That confirmed to the lowly transport sheriff that he did everything he could in this hostile situation to ensure that justice prevailed. Now he could rest in peace. He feels the gun slip from his weak hand and blood seep into his air passage. He coughs and blood spatters onto the steering wheel. He coughs again. *Too much pain.* He stumbles into the dark. Lights out.

******

"All loaded up, Ms. McAaron. We're just waiting on our passengers," the pilot informed Tamara.

She'd just personally watched two cargo handlers load the items, three crates and two suitcases, from the back of her Benz truck into the cargo bay of the small Gulfstream. She'd been instructed not to leave the private aiport in Sugarland, or even sight of the plane until Prince arrived.

"Okay, thanks. Just keep the engines running. It should be any minute now," Tamara replied, trying to hide her nervousness by looking at her watch.

"You got it," the pilot said. Tamara rolled her window back up as he walked back towards the jet.

Where are they? This shit better go right! Tamara thought as she looked at the burnout phone again for the umpteenth time, then she checked her own personal phone. No calls. Earlier she'd received a call from Mark Jones on the burnout, giving her instructions where to drop off the rest of the money, another fifty grand. *Yeah, yeah, yeah, whatever,* Tamara had thought as she'd bullshitted her way through the conversation. She hated having to give the first fifty grand to a trifling ass dirty cop who was gonna die anyway. She thought about how he'd tried to flirt with her when she'd dropped the money off, even with Big Baby standing right there with her.

Tamara was infuriated. "Who does that muthafucka think he is?" she'd asked Big Baby when they got back into the truck.

"Training Day Syndrome," Big Baby answered simply, as if it were an everyday occurrence. "Dirty cops think they're untouchable because they've been doing this shit for so long. We gon' fix that shit up, though."

"Damn straight," Tamara confirmed. *Yeah. There was no way he could live after meeting me face to face and disrespectin' me like that. If he acted like that for something I want, I can imagine how he'd act for something he wanted. He definitely had to go. A muthafucka like that couldn't live to be a witness,* Tamara thought. *The tangled web we weave.*

Her thoughts were disrupted when the burnout rang.

"Hello."

"Get the doctor here right away. You remember the doctor?"

"Baby!...Um, yeah...the doctor. He's...he's on standby. What happened? Are you okay?" Tamara asked, mirroring the panic in the voice on the other end of the line. It was Prince.

"He got hit. My brother got hit."

"Oh, my God! Is it bad! Is he gonna be all right?"

"I don't know. Just go get the doctor! We're on our way."

"Okay, okay, he'll be here. I love you." The line went dead. The Benz truck was already in motion.

Chapter Thirty-Five: ILLEST MUTHAFUCKAS ALIVE

"Yeah...shit, that feel so damn good, baby," Mo moaned. "You got the best head in the world."

"Mmmmm," Serene moaned around a mouth full of hot pickle.

"You love that dick, baby?"

"Mmm-hmmm," she replied, unable to say much else. She stopped for a second, taking the dick out of her mouth to say, "Yes, baby, I love you and I love this dick," then went back to sucking.

Mo was sitting up, leaning back against the headboard of the king-sized hotel bed. All the lights were out except for the television, which was broadcasting the news. Both he and Serene were butt-naked. She was on her knees, and her head was in his lap. Her perfectly round, light-skinned lady lumps were hiked up in the air in front of him. He admired the arch in her back and how her small waist curved out around her perfect roundness; not too big, but perfect. He loved how it was firm, but soft, how it jiggled when he hit it from the back. Mo reached out and and rubbed her ass, then down the arch of her back and to her curly mane. Her head was bobbing up and down, and he was hard as steel in her mouth as he felt all the ridges of the roof of her mouth and the soft, wet warmth of her tongue and inner cheeks. Mo became flooded with emotion as he grabbed a handful of Serene's sandy brown curls.

"Goddamn, baby...I love you, too."

"Mmmm..." Serene moaned.

"Come here, baby. I want you to ride this dick. I wanna feel that pussy."

Serene stopped sucking and looked up at Mo mischeviously. "You want some of your pussy?"

"Yeah."

Just as Serene was climbing on top of Mo, one leg across his hip, one hand on top of the headboard, an announcement blared from the television.

"Breaking news! There has been an escape from the Harris County Jail, and two officers have been killed. I repeat..."

"What the fuck?!" Mo exclaimed, throwing Serene off him and onto the side of the bed.

"Oww! Damn, baby!"

Mo lost his erection instantly when eight faces of escaped inmates were flashed onto the screen, two of whom he recognized as Prince and Fatso.

"Oh, my God! That's...that's Prince and Fatso!" Serene gasped.

"Ain't *that* about a bitch!" Mo said slowly, as he watched the rest of the newsflash. Serene kept talking.

"They killed some cops?"

"They in a world of shit now!"

"Oooh! I bet you Tamara helped them!"

"Can you believe this shit?"

"Uh-uhhh!"

"Shut up, Serene! Just...shut up! I can't even fuckin' think with you runnin' your mouth!" Mo snapped. Serene stared at him with her jaw dropped open.

"Just pack your shit up. Fuck this, we're leavin'!" Mo commanded as he began to pace the floor. The news was now reporting something about a kidnapping in Friendswood. He puts on a pair of boxers.

"We *cannot* leave tonight! Do you know how hot the streets and freeways are gonna be? They're gonna be stopping everything moving!" Serene reasoned.

"Hmm," Mo mumbled. She was right, and he knew it.

She pushed her logic further. "For the next week, the city is gonna be on fire. We can't afford to get caught slippin' with all that work."

"You got me fucked up if you think I'm finna sit around here for a week!"

"It's the best thing to do, boo! Stay put. Stay still. Nobody is lookin' for us anymore but in the streets or even on the highway. We're targets."

Mo thought for a second. "I'll tell you what. You're right about tonight. It *is* too hot. But tomorrow, I'm gonna have some movers go pack up my crib. I'll hide all the dirt inside the furniture, and we'll follow the truck to Atlanta."

Serene considered Mo's suggestion. She really didn't want to do this.

"They're gonna stop that truck. If they stop and search that truck, we're fucked! That's too risky. Let's just be still."

"They won't. I'll make sure the drivers are White. A professional moving company, professional drivers. I'll pay whatever. It'll work out. That's the plan."

"Baby, think! We can just..."

"Look! That's the fuckin' plan, Serene! I'm not gonna argue wit' you. You either comin' with me or you're not, but that's what's goin' down. So, you tell me now." It was obvious that his mind was made up. Her debate was useless at that point.

"Baby, you *know* I'm rollin' wit' you, don't even say it like that," Serene said, defenseless.

"All right, then!" Mo said victoriously. He looked at the defeated look on his girl's face, and he softened. He sensed her conflict. "Look, when we get to Atlanta and get situated, you can come back and get your kids. We'll bring 'em out there with us until things calm down."

Serene looked up at Mo with a compassionate smile. Her chest became warm. She'd had Mo wrong in thinking he wouldn't accept her kids. "I don't want you to say that if that's not what you really want."

"What you mean? 'Dem is yo kids! I know that's part of what's holdin' you up, 'cause they a part of you. I respect 'dat. Whatever we was tryin' to do here, we can do there in Atlanta. It might take a lil' longer, but we'll be safe, and they'll be safe. But we gotta go; maybe not forever, but for a while. Let's get situated, and then we can come back and see what's up. A'ight?"

"All right, baby," Serene agreed.

"Bet."

"Baby?"

"What's up?"

"Thank you."

"Don't mention it, boo. It's me and you against the world," Mo said with a half grin. He was happy to be finally getting away and his girl was coming with him. Serene smiled back. She liked the sound of that.

******

"You gotta respect these fuckin' guys!" Warren Lee said to his crew, over his third drink.

The entire D-Boy clique is posted up at their regular Tuesday night spot, Live Sports Café on Main Street.

Scat agreed. "Say, lookout, that was some gangsta ass shit dem niggas put down, man!"

"Hell, yeah! Merked two cops, escaped from the county and got away like a muthafucka!" Nore added.

"Don't forget about Winnie and *his* whole crew. They dinosaured dem niggas," Duce reminded them.

"Where you think 'dem niggas at, Warren? I know *you* know." Scat quipped, grinning.

"Sheeit. The fuck if *I* know. Outta the country if they smart. And they still gon' have every agency in the world lookin' for 'em! They'll get caught sooner or later." Warren observed.

"Either way, dem niggas is gon' be legends out here. We need to do a movie about that shit!" Duce says.

"For real!" Scat agrees.

"And *we'll* be the good guys," Nore adds. They all bust out laughing.

"Say, check it out though: I *told* y'all this shit was gonna work out to our advantage," Warren reminds his crew.

"Yeah, true. Dem niggas is out da game! For how long remains to be seen, no doubt, but still..." Nore replied.

"You right. They are out...out of commission," Warren said, then continued, "I mean, don't get me wrong. Prince and Fatso, they whole crew, you could say they beat them people, got the whole sheriff's department on blast. It took balls to do that, big fuckin' rhino balls! Ha! But let's be real. They killed two sheriffs. If that woulda been two or twenty average niggas on the street, it wouldn't have made that much of a difference. You see, they've put *us* on blast, too. The streets is gon' be hot. Money 'bout to slow down. State and the Feds gon' be crackin' down because of this. It's election time, too. You see what I'm sayin'?"

They all agreed.

"Them niggas is gone in hiding some fuckin' where now, but *we* gotta deal with the aftermath," Warren said, shaking his head. "Ahhh...fuck it! H-Town niggas put that gangsta shit on they ass once again. It is what it is, and what's done is done. I wish them niggas the best, though, ya know? But honestly, I give 'em a week, maybe two at the most. But if they last more 'n a month..." he shrugs his shoulders and raises his eyebrows, then says, smirking, "Fuck it, we toast to them, anyway. Man, H-Town is the place. The streets is ours."

"Yeah."

"Al-ready."

"No doubt."

A feeling of brotherhood spread over them as they raised their glasses high and toasted to the streets and Prince and Fatso's great escape that had the entire city in an uproar.

******

"So, now what happens, huh?" Ms. Sykes asked Sheldon X. She was pissed. Her tone was aggressive, and the sound of cars in the background told Sheldon X that she was calling from a pay phone in an urban area. She was the fifth person to call Sheldon X today, bitching, moaning, and complaining. He was beginning to feel like all the New Orleans folks that were affected by Friday the Thirteen blamed *him* for the Landau brothers' escape from jail, and he was sick of it.

"I don't know, Ms. Sykes. I guess we wait until they get caught and let the DA press charges," Sheldon X replied dryly.

"Oh, *hell* no! So, you're telling me that I'm supposed to just sit around and wait while those murderers run around out here living like millionaires or whatever when I can't even afford to bury my son?!"

"The police are still investigating and...and, I don't know what else to tell you, Ms. Sykes. It's not my fault these guys got away."

"You need to tell me *something*, shit. It's yo' damn fault you stepped up to be the hero. So, what? You say you do this to help yo' people, so, here I go! Or did you think changing yo' last name to 'X' would be some kind of ego party?"

"Look, I don't have to put up with this, Ms. Sykes. I've tried to do everything I could do, and—"

"Well, it's not enough!" Ms. Sykes yelled into the phone. "It's not enough, all right? You and your friends wanna pop off at the mouth about the politics in the DA's office, but those goddamned bastards who murdered my son are free! If the DA would have filed all the damn charges at once, maybe they would have never been moved to have the chance to escape in the first damn place! Did you ever think about *that?!*" Ms. Sykes asked belligerently.

Sheldon X just shook his head in frustration. He knew that she really didn't fully understand what she was talking about, but he could relate to her pain, to her anger and desperation, and the fact that she was stuck between a rock and a hard place, two evils. Sheldon X felt that same desperation. He did want to help people, *his* people. Ms. Sykes was forcing him to look at his intentions versus his actual works. He felt so limited and almost helpless in the confines of his religion. Most brothas and sistas trapped in the everyday struggle to survive weren't interested in the message of the Koran or the Bible when they had immediate financial emergencies that needed action. *That* was the man that Sheldon X wanted to be, a man of action. He didn't want to sell his people dreams and religious concepts, he wanted to give them results, answers to their everyday practical issues, by any means necessary. *I'm tired of being the good guy that can't help anybody. Nobody gives a damn about that guy,* he thought.

At that moment, the conflict within the mind of Sheldon and Sheldon X reached its breaking point. Sheldon X wasn't working for Sheldon no more, he wasn't getting the job done. There were too many people in need for that kind of poor performance. There were too many resources and too much money out here in these streets for little kids to go to sleep starving at night, for mothers to not be able to respectably bury their children when death takes them far too early.

"You know what, Ms. Sykes? You're right. You're absolutely right. These people here, they messed up, and I'm sick of defendin' them. They really, really fucked up." Ms. Sykes was shocked as she listened to Sheldon X. She'd never before heard him curse. He continued.

"I'm not gonna lie to you, I don't know exactly what happened or what all is going on with this investigation. I only know what they tell me, which ain't much. But I'm tired of waitin', waitin' on the police for answers, our people waitin' on FEMA or welfare or housing or any other socialized program to give us validation, waitin' for them to make good on their promises. I'm tired of this shit! There's too much money in this city! So you know what, Ms. Sykes, between me and you, I'm gonna make sure your son LuLu gets a proper burial. I don't yet know how, but I'ma make it happen, all right?"

"A…all right. Well, I don't want you to get into any…" Ms. Sykes stumbled over her words, still in shock from Sheldon X's change of character and his outburst, but she liked this man more now, she liked his honesty. She cared about what happened to him.

"Just make the basic arrangements, Ms. Sykes. Don't worry about me; I haven't always worn this bowtie, ya know? It's time for action to be taken, because one thing I've learned for sure, hard times require hard decisions. You either do somethin' about the problems you facin' or *get* done. I'm tired of seeing my sistas get the short end of the stick, one disaster after another. When does it end? And when it all goes down, all you have is you. No one's obligated to help you. Some programs and people just *choose* to help you. I choose to help *you*, Ms. Sykes. I'm here, okay?"

"Thank you," Ms. Sykes said. She felt a huge burden being lifted from her shoulders.

"You're very welcome, sista."

"Oh, and Sheldon?"

"Yes, ma'am?"

"You can call me Jennifer," Ms. Sykes said with a blush that could be heard through the phone line.

Sheldon also smiled. "All right, Jennifer. We'll definitely be in contact."

Chapter Thirty-Six: JEWELS REMIX

"I am the master of the universe. All things that are in the universe are within me. I am the creator. *I am*," Jewel chanted into the complete silence of her luxury condo. The only thing that could be heard was the cracking of the wood burning inside the fireplace directly in front of her. The glowing flames danced off her brown face and closed eyelids. She sat Indian style on a red cushion in the center of her living room floor. *Inhale, exhale.*

"I am the master of the universe. All things that are in the universe are within me. I am the creator. *I am*."

So many thoughts had run through Jewel's mind since she'd gotten the news of her nephews' escape. She still had no idea how they were; she hadn't received any confirmation. She hoped for the best, and Jewel believed in her ability to speak the best circumstances into existence, so she spoke it. She'd thought well of their plan and the boys sense of well-being right now, but in her heart, she felt unsettled. She'd tried to quiet those negative feelings, but for some reason, it wasn't working, so she allowed those vises to run free and exhaust themselves by giving them no life. But some of her thoughts demanded her attention because of the circumstances surrounding them.

Inhale, exhale. Follow each breath. Dancing flames. She thought of the aggravated energy she'd assigned to Winnie back in New Orleans at the Superdome, long before he'd forever affected the lives of those in her family, how they were somehow connected, how the reality of that connection disrupted her peace and desire to control her life and the situations in it, how she allowed certain things to happen to fulfill that desire, how Winnie was an enigma, a force that had pushed circumstances out of her control, and how that frustrated her to no end. Jewel had cursed Winnie a thousand deaths which he diligently earned, came full circle to enter the gates of Hades right before her eyes. She'd put him in direct contact with his victims, made him feel their pain and hear their cries cheering him on into eternal flames. Full circle. Things had come to fruition. The law of the universe. She'd cursed Winnie, and he was dead now. But at what cost? *Did I cause all of this?*

Inhale, exhale. Follow your breath. The flames dance to a tune that cannot be recognized. *Fatso and Prince,* she thought, *they are good boys, men, rather. Full of beautiful energy, smart, handsome, ambitious. Both of them so full of passion, so full of life. What has become of them?* She missed them desperately. *Is what or who've they become good or bad? If there is such a thing as either? I've given them my ultimate blessing, and to what avail? What has become of them? Inhale, exhale. The universe is within me. I am. We all choose our own destinies. Their story is far from over, their purpose far from fulfillment. They've chosen the path of light and light is eternal. Inhale, exhale. Follow your breath. I am the creator. I am.*

What has become of me? What path have I chosen? The path of light, but yet, death and destruction follow me. Katrina followed me, surrounded us all with chaos, fed us hate and mistreatment, and then pushed us out of our cradle. Why? I'm the creator, not you! You have no control over me! Inhale, exhale. What has become of me? Can I repair some of the damages? Yes, but how?

Seeking reparation, a specimen of opportunity to bestow her good will, Jewel allowed her mind to roam free. Then, a beautiful face appeared behind her closed eyelids: *Tamara. Yes! I will guide her. I will introduce her to herself and the laws of the universe. I will balance the books. Inhale, exhale. I am the*

master of the universe. All things in the universe are within me. I am the

creator. I am.

******

"Aw, shit, T! The new crib is thowed, girl!" Kesha exclaimed as she walked around the boxes and through the new ocean-view condo in Galveston, Texas. Joint and lighter in one hand.

"Yeah, it should be straight once I get everything set up," Tamara said, looking around at the assortment of half unpacked and unopened boxes, artwork and pictures in bubble wrap. Her furniture was still wrapped in a thick plastic as if it were brand new.

"Damn, this is a lot of shit. I hate moving! Girl, I might just hire an interior decorator just to set all this shit up," Tamara said frustratedly as she dodged a few boxes on her way into the kitchen.

"What?! And give away all of *our* fun? Unh-uh! That's what *I'm* here for, girl, we got this. You just need to relax," Kesha said in encouragement to her stressed out friend as she lit the joint. She took three puffs and the sweet smell of blueberry hydro permeated the room. The portable stereo jammed Mary J. Blige.

"You ain't never lied. Shit, you want a glass of wine?" Tamara asked, already pouring a glass for herself. Kesha exhaled and tried to keep herself from coughing.

"What you think?" she choked out before she coughed repeatedly. Tamara brought Kesha a wine glass that was half full of White Zinfandel.

"Look at you. Don't die up in here, bitch. I just got here. That won't be a good look with the homeowners' association. Here." Tamara handed

Kesha the glass, and Kesha offered Tamara the joint, trading one intoxicant for the other.

Tamara declined to partake. "I'm straight."

"What's wrong, T?" Kesha asked incredulously. She was surprised at Tamara. They always smoked together.

"Nah, I just wanna get some of this stuff situated first, and then I'll relax a little bit," Tamara replied, then sniffed the air. "It smells good, too."

Kesha took a swallow of her wine while she inspected her friend over the globe of the wineglass. Tamara was stressed and bothered, but she was strong. She tried to play it off, but Kesha had long ago decided not to try to push Tamara. She knew they'd talk when the time was right.

"Well, I'll put it out 'til you're ready," Kesha said. The joint had already gone out. She looked around the living room area as if something would have changed since the last time she'd looked five minutes ago.

"Hmm...I think I liked the other spot better."

"Don't start that shit, Kesha," Tamara warned.

"All right, all right. You're right. I'm sorry. Besides, look at that view," Kesha said, referring to the floor-to-ceiling windows and patio that overlooked the Gulf of Mexico, the Seawall and Galveston Beach. "Now *that's* what's up! And since I'm the only one who knows where you live, I can come over and keep you company all the time."

"Mmm-hmm," Tamara mumbled in response. She'd walked over to the window and got lost in the ocean with Mary J. leading the way.

"So, where you wanna start? We should be able to knock this out kinda quick...Tamara!"

Tamara snapped out of her reverie. "Huh? What's up, girl? What's the deal?"

"You wanna do this, or do you wanna wait a while?"

"Wait for what, Kesha? I gotta get this shit done! If I wait anymore I'ma say fuck it and just hire one of those wannabe-Martha Stewart Extreme Makeover bitches to come in here and handle her business."

Kesha laughed, and Tamara smiled. "Shit, you laughin', I'm serious," Tamara quipped.

"I'm laughin' 'cause yo ass is crazy, but I should be insulted. I happened to like both those shows, so you better chill."

"This is me-eee, this is meee..." Mary J. sang.

"All right, let's do this." Tamara said, taking a swallow of her wine and setting the wineglass on the coffee table, which was one of the few things Tamara had already freed from the bubble wrap. "You take the kitchen and I'll take care of shit in here," she said, referring to the living room. "I gotta get this computer set up."

"Why I gotta do the kitchen? What if I misplace all your special wine glasses?"

"Oooh, you are getting on my nerves, girl...you cannot mess the kitchen up, Kesha, damn!"

"I'm just fuckin' wit' you, girl. Look at you getting all mad. I wonder if yo homeowners' association knows about that temper you got, 'cause if they don't, I'll sure tell them," Kesha said, then laughed as she walked into the kitchen.

Tamara couldn't do anything but shake her head. She had to admit that she was glad her friend was here. All Tamara could think about was

Prince, and Kesha was doing a good job of being a distraction. She could hear Kesha in the kitchen, busy cutting open boxes and unwrapping dishes. Mary was still singing her heart out, and the aroma of blueberry hydro still lingered in the air.

Tamara set her iMac computer on her glass-top desk. She stared at the 27" screen, which was blank like the hole in her heart. It reminded her of how her relationship with the man she loved with every fiber of her being was indefinitely altered, changed and mutated into something she was unsure that she could tame. She wanted to get the computer set up so that her relationship that once was could continue. Her love, encrypted, could live between thousands of miles on digital wings.

"Damn, baby," she whispered. *Thousands of miles,* she thought with a sigh. She took a deep breath; she could still smell the weed. Mary was still singing what Tamara was feeling. She looked up, and Kesha was out of sight, temporarily out of mind. Tamara felt a sense of being alone. *Alone.*

She stood up from the leather office chair, grabbed her glass of wine and walked over to the patio door. She slid it open and walked out into the cool salty-smelling breeze, taking a swallow of wine as the breeze blew her hair back away from her face. She looked down at Seawall Boulevard which stretched out to her left. It was lit up with cars and streetlights, stores, hotels and restaurants. The Hilton, the first hotel with a casino to open its doors in Galveston, was busy, as usual. A police car, flashing its cherries brightly, had somebody pulled over, and the officer was writing a ticket to the driver of a red pickup truck that had three people riding in the back like it's legal.

Tamara looked out past the beach to the ocean, the police cherries shimmering off the water. The police were the last people she needed a confrontation with. She looked out into the ocean, and there was water as far as the eye could see. A couple of lights twinkled out there; ships, probably, but they appeared to be thousands of miles away. *Thousands of miles.*

Tamara knew she could never tell anyone about what she had done, what she'd helped accomplish, what she knew. Kesha was her best friend, but Tamara had vowed to never discuss it, not with Kesha, not with the Feds, no matter what the consequences. She'd only discuss it with people that knew, only with the family. She thought of Jewel, her new mentor. She'd go see her tomorrow. She thought of Prince, and she looked up at the full moon that shined down on her and hoped and prayed that Prince was somewhere across that ocean looking up at it, too. *Damn, baby. Thousands of miles.*

******

Kesha had unwrapped a whole box of chinaware plates, saucers and bowls, set the entire set of silverware in a tray inside a drawer and had just opened another box that said, "THIS SIDE UP" on the side and top. She already knew what it was. She carefully cut the box open and peeled back the lid.

"*Why* do you need all these wine glasses, girl? You live by yourself." She got no response. Kesha poked her head from behind the huge refrigerator to look over the bar and saw that the patio door was slid all the way back and Tamara standing out on the patio. Kesha felt for her friend. This had to be impossible to deal with. She wasn't even sure if Tamara knew where Prince was. When she'd asked about it, Tamara had just shrugged her shoulders and shut down. Kesha wouldn't push the issue, she'd just be there for her best friend, and whatever Tamara wanted to tell her or talk about, she would. Looking at her out on that balcony, looking at the ocean, it was obvious she had a tremendous weight on her shoulders and a million and one dart-like thoughts piercing her conscience.

Kesha quietly walked over to the balcony and stepped out into the breeze. She didn't want to break Tamara's mood or derail her train of thought. The breeze felt good. Kesha didn't particularly care for the smell, and this is one of the reasons she rarely came to Galveston. In her opinion, it was a grimy, nasty little beach, and she much preferred the beaches of LA and Miami, or the beaches of Venice, Manhattan and Pompano. Those were the beaches she and Tamara would be frequenting soon, every chance she could get out. But, she figured she'd might as well get used to it, because this was the new spot.

The travertine floor on the balcony felt cool and kind of gritty to Kesha's bare feet. In preparation for the unpacking she'd planned to do, she'd kicked off the Fendi pumps she'd worn over to the new place. However, it didn't appear they'd be getting too much done that night. Kesha wondered if Tamara was ready to talk. She knew that Tamara knew *something*. She had to know. Her curiosity was getting the best of her. She stepped closer. Tamara's hair was blowing in the wind, the moon was full, and the water beyond was calm and broad. *Beautiful,* Kesha thought. She didn't want to disrupt the moment by speaking. She silently stepped to the rail next to Tamara and looked at her. Tamara's eyes were closed, and tears streamed down her face. The delicate reality of this moment took a grip on Kesha's heart as she realized two things about her best friend. One, she'd never, in all of the seven years they'd been best friends, seen Tamara cry, and two, after all that had

been set in motion, there was no turning back.

Chapter Thirty-Seven: TWO STEPS FROM HEAVEN

The two cargo Jeeps pulled up to the front of the beachfront villa, a nice four-bedroom, two-level villa that was fully furnished and spread with an incredible view. The owner hops out of the Jeep and runs up to the door and punches in a code on the realtors' lockbox hanging from the doorknob. He pulls the key out and unlocks and opens the double-entry doors on his new, not-so-humble abode.

He turned and said with a big grin, "We're in!"

"Do you want us to bring in your things, sir?" asked the sandy-brown skinned driver in a British accent.

"Oh, please believe it!" the owner said excitedly as he took a deep breath of the tropical air.

They'd made it. The private jet had landed on a private airstrip in Belize without a hitch. For Prince, it was a smooth flight; stressful, but smooth. For Fatso, however, it was excruciating, but he was alive. The doctor, who'd been there waiting for the jet to arrive, had literally been a life saver. He'd gone right to work. Fatso had lost a lot of blood, and he was weak. Prince and Young Bread had to carry him onto the plane.

As much as he'd kept repeating, "I'm gonna be all right, I'm gonna live," there was a little devil on his shoulder that tried to convince him otherwise. He'd started to believe that little devil when the doctor had stuck those tweezers into his shoulder to extract the bullet. The devil was winning; Fatso's positive thoughts were practically waving the white flag. Fatso yelled out in pain, "Auuggghhh!" He'd never felt pain like that before in his life.

Now he knew what brothas were talking about. He started getting dizzy, a sick, distant feeling. Consciousness was slipping away, and Fatso almost blacked out until Prince slapped him across the face.

"Stay wit' me, bro! Stay wit' me. Where you goin', baby, we gotta ball. Stay wit' me, ya heard?" Fatso nodded.

The next thing he knew, Doc had him wrapped up and rigged to an IV and an EKG. He drank cranberry juice until he fell asleep.

"He's stable. He'll be all right," Doc said to Prince. "We'll have to get him some private care immediately to nurse him back to health."

"Gotcha. I'll get it lined up first thing," Prince agreed. He thought of Nancy; she'd be useful right now.

Fatso woke up when the plane touched down, and he felt the pain shoot through his entire body. Prince helped him into the tiny bathroom and Fatso took a long piss. Taking a piss had never felt so good. He took a deep breath and knew that he was gonna be all right.

As sleepy as Fatso was, he stood on the front porch and watched Prince and the two drivers wheel all six crates and their luggage into the foyer, and he was content. He watched the drivers pull away and Prince helped him inside to sit down.

"We did it! We muthafuckin' free, Fatso! Ahhh!" Prince sighed and celebrated like a madman. Fatso smiled. He was out of it, but he enjoyed seeing his brother's antics. Fatso looked at the list of medicines and procedures Doc had listed on the sheet of paper for the new doctor and nurse they'd hire tomorrow. He glanced up at the six crates, which held $22.7

million dollars in cash. It made Fatso's insides tingle. Yeah, they did it. He really felt like they were gonna be all right.

"It's all you now, kid," Fatso said wearily to his little brother as if he were an old man on his last leg or something.

Prince had finished his mini celebration, and was now sitting down across from his brother. "I know. I got it," Prince replied, looking out at the ocean through his floor-to-ceiling windows, thinking, *Note to self: get some blinds put up.* He was confirming their plan. Prince would oversee Ball, with Tamara running the operation in LA that Prince had just successfully set up. Young Bread and Big Baby would hold down the business in Houston.

Once LA was consistent, they'd break New York, then Chicago, and then Miami. All the other major cities would fall in line. Prince would head all operations, communicating only with Tamara, while Fatso would concentrate his energy strictly on production and commodities. They had a contract on a 260-acre farm, where Fatso would spend most of his time running the new Magical Gardens....on steroids.

"It's kinda fucked up how things went haywire when it seemed to be so perfect. I kept thinking about that shit in jail...I wanted to talk to you about it, but I couldn't," Prince said.

"Say, bro, no regrets, remember? We movin' forward with our original plan...with just a few modifications. But I know what you're thinking: how does everybody, especially Tamara, carry on after all of this?" Fatso said.

"Yeah. Exactly. So many unresolved issues. I really gotta think about this shit, ya know? Just take some time and really plan and piece everything together. I gotta stay on note."

"Shit's different now, bro, so we might as well get used to the idea. We outlaws. *Ball* is outlawed. We international drug dealers now. Wanted. It is what it is. We made the best outta what we was given, huh?"

"Yep."

"Auntie Jewel and Tamara are set for life. They'll always be straight."

"No doubt. They straight."

"And *this* is *our* life," Prince said, looking around at his new crib. "Luxury livin', private jets, yachts and shit. All shimmery and shit!" He smiled.

"And a master plan," Fatso reminded him.

"And a throwed-ass master plan that won't fail!" Prince agreed, then cupped his hands to his mouth. "Houston...we have a-" He cut himself off, hopped up and headed towards the bar which he'd told the realtor to have fully stocked.

"Fuck it, bro, drinks on me! Let's have a Hurricane!"

The End........until Vol. 2 Stomp Down Chick.

I hope you enjoyed your visit to,

HardBall City
Vol. 1
Katrina's Baby
Novel and Mixtape Soundtrack

If you did not get your mixtape soundtrack with your purchase of this novel,

please go to: www.facebook.com/HardBallCity for the link to download your

copy today.

Come back and visit us soon.........Stay Hard!

Coming Soon from

<u>B-Mega Media Group/Black Minx Publishing</u>:

HardBall City Vol. 2: Stomp Down Chick

HardBall City Vol. 3: Death Becomes You...

HardBall City-The Movie and Mixtape Soundtrack

The Stand Up Kid: The Lajuan Moore Story

Novel, Movie and Mixtape Soundtrack

Mariposa: The Butterfly Connection

Novel, Movie and Mixtape Soundtrack

The Black Minx Trilogy Vol. 1:

My Ambitions as a Rider

Novel, Movie and Mixtape Soundtrack

Acknowledgements

Thank you God!! Its nothing like the feeling of success and completion!!...My greatest thanks is to my Lord and Savior Jesus Christ. Abundant Life Cathedral and my spiritual mentor, Dr. Ed and Sandra Montgomery for reassuring me the impossible and unthinkable is only one possibility away. Thank you to the power and energy of Life which has been my greatest teacher. Thank you to my Mother Queen Diane who, since I was a child, always believed I was great and would achieve my dreams. My eternally wise grandmother Mary. My old man Charles Dailey, who held it down for me and T-Lady my whole rodeo and then some. My kids, Kimani, Gabrielle, Aundre and their Mother Aunjelique for coming out on top in my absense. My lil Sister and Brother, Sara and Tommy. Kesha and Kequina. Anna and Tasha. All my lil cousins, I hope yall ready...

The whole Joyner Dynasty. My love is infinite!

(Tom, I need a interview Fam..Black America!!)

Chaundra Frank, thank you for helping me grow, and get this book done!.. RIP Charles Frank. Yung Loco, Dani Sax, for always being a friend and stomp down chick..Your coverwork is off the meatrack!!..danisaxdesignz.com. Lets geeeit it! Zandria Winn, my chief editor..Thanks so much..time for part 2 and 3!

My Brothers Lee, Chad, J.D., Splurge, Kev, Lush, Bigg Worm and Wrecka. My Uncle and big brother Derek for that Real Talk.

Mr. Robinson, my counselor from Hennepin county boys home, for being the first to recognize and nurture my talent...what up Kandi! ..My ALC family,

Charles and Cynthia Stamps, Monique, Nikeda Fowler, Toni and Ms. Sabrina, Word in Motion, Rick Marseilles and Earnest Walker, Mike Crockett, all my soldiers in formation....

I wanna thank the Harris County assistant DA, Kate Dolen, for hating me enough to light a fire under my ass to complete 12 projects, 250 songs, a degree and attain the true level of discipline needed to sustain balance in this crooked world and give birth to a Dynasty. Black Minx Family.

All my Texas partners, promoters and associates, H-Town..I love where we at and where we going. Twin Town..Duce, run that shit up there, bwah! Keep my name alive! Deshawn lets make this music. Big E, Dino, Down 4 Dirt, Fatso, Creep, Yon and Brae, what up. Wrecka, when ya T-Lady told me you was gone again, my heart broke! J. Isaac, Me-Ci, Paris and Ann Nesby, Love you. Ned, put something on it...I'm bout to take a look at Tyler in ATL in a minute...Real Talk!

New Orleans, I love you. May God bless us all and our kids rule the world. All my soldiers on the streets, in TDC and all the prisons across America..your time is right now! THE REVOLUTION IS NOW! Make a commitment right now that you are going to contribute to our world... even if you will never see the streets again, USE YOUR VOICE! USE YOUR VISION! you must remain CREATIVE and KEEP YOUR PEN PUSHIN!....1LOVE ETERNAL...

If its anybody I missed and you know your place with me...Its all Love... Stay Hard and catch me on Volume 2: Stomp Down Chick...... 100!

Please stay in contact with the Hardball City Team for upcoming releases, tour dates, news updates, FREE bonuses, contests and downloads....(REAL TALK: WE ARE GIVING AWAY REAL PRIZES, i.e. Vacations, scholarships, clothes...you know, stuff you'll be mad you didn't know about...So stay online with me and my team at:

www.facebook.com/HardBallCity

http://hardballcity.wordpress.com/

https://twitter.com/hardballcity

If you did not get your mixtape soundtrack with your purchase of this book, please go to: www.facebook.com/HardBallCity for the link to download your copy today.

If you would like to book a promotional date, i.e Book signing, concert date, radio interview, etc. please go to: www.facebook.com/HardBallCity

This book and associated products are available in all forms of digital distribution, including iPad, Kindle, the HardBall City mobile App and more at www.amazon.com.

©2012 by Troy Joyner

Black Minx Publishing

B-Mega Media Group, Inc

Printed in the United States of America

www.ingramcontent.com/pod-product-compliance
Lightning Source LLC
Chambersburg PA
CBHW031413240626
47154CB00001B/16